PENGUIN BOOKS

DRAGONLANCE® PRELUDES II

VOLUME ONE:
RIVERWIND THE PLAINSMAN

Paul B. Thompson remembers clearly the first real book he ever read, a prose translation of the *Iliad*. This was followed by *The Arabian Nights' Entertainment*, and his tastes were set for life. His first novel, *Sundipper*, was published in 1984. The next year Thompson began collaborating with Tonya Carter. Thompson and Carter have also written *Red Sands*, a novel in the TSR style, have contributed to the DRAGONLANCE® anthology *Love and War* and wrote *Darkness and Light*, the first volume of DRAGONLANCE® Preludes I. *Riverwind the Plainsman* is their third novel together.

Tonya R. Carter attended the University of North Carolina at Chapel Hill, where she met her husband, Greg, and her collaborator, Paul Thompson. After college she visited England and Ireland. There, in spite of her red hair and Irish ancestry, she was mistaken for an Australian several times. This prompted her to take up Gaelic studies on her return to the States. In addition to her collaborative work, she has written a number of fantasy, horror and science-fiction stories, including 'To Hear the Sea-Maid's Music'. When not writing, she enjoys shopping for books, travelling and skiing.

D1352352

FROM THE CREATORS OF
THE DRAGONLANCE® SAGA

LEAVES FROM THE INN OF THE LAST HOME
COMPILED BY TIKA AND CARAMON MAJERE, PROPRIETORS

THE ART OF THE DRAGONLANCE SAGA
EDITED BY MARY KIRCHOFF

THE ATLAS OF THE DRAGONLANCE SAGA
BY KAREN WYNN FONSTAD

DRAGONLANCE TALES:
THE MAGIC OF KRYNN
KENDER, GULLY DWARVES, AND GNOMES
LOVE AND WAR
EDITED BY
MARGARET WEIS AND TRACY HICKMAN

DRAGONLANCE HEROES
THE LEGEND OF HUMA
STORMBLADE
WEASEL'S LUCK

DRAGONLANCE PRELUDES
DARKNESS AND LIGHT
KENDERMORE
BROTHERS MAJERE

DragonLance Saga

PRELUDES II
VOLUME ONE

Riverwind
—the—
Plainsman

Paul B. Thompson and
Tonya R. Carter

Cover Art
CLYDE CALDWELL

Interior Illustrations
DOUGLAS CHAFFEE

PENGUIN BOOKS
in association with TSR, Inc.

For the SFWG, 1988-89
Mutatis mutandis
—PBT

For my parents
And, always, for Greg
—TRC

PENGUIN BOOKS

Published by the Penguin Group
Penguin Books Ltd, 27 Wrights Lane, London w8 5tz, England
Viking Penguin, a division of Penguin Books USA Inc.
375 Hudson Street, New York, New York 10014, USA
Penguin Books Australia Ltd, Ringwood, Victoria, Australia
Penguin Books Canada Ltd, 2801 John Street, Markham, Ontario, Canada l3r 1b4
Penguin Books (NZ) Ltd, 182–190 Wairau Road, Auckland 10, New Zealand

Penguin Books Ltd, Registered Offices: Harmondsworth, Middlesex, England

First published in the USA by TSR, Inc. 1990
Distributed to the book trade in the United States by Random House, Inc.
and in Canada by Random House of Canada Ltd
Distributed to the toy and hobby trade by regional distributors
First published in Great Britain by Penguin Books 1990
1 3 5 7 9 10 8 6 4 2

TSR, Inc.

Printed in England by Clays Ltd, St Ives plc

Part I
SLOW FALL

Chapter 1

Three Acorns

The men of Que-Shu gathered, drawn by the steady
toll of drums. A hundred men, straight-limbed and stoic,
formed two lines and filed into the Lodge of Brothers. They
left their herds in the care of sons who were too young to
witness the coming solemn ceremony. Fields and forges
stood idle for the duration of the rite. The women and children went about their business. It was not for them to be
curious.

No one could ignore the drums, however. Least of all
Goldmoon, first priestess of the tribe, daughter of Chief Arrowthorn. She stood just inside the door of the chief's house,
far enough in the shadows so as not to be seen. Perspiration
sheened her beautiful face, and she bit her lip nearly to
bleeding. The ceremony about to begin was the Anointing

of the Quester; the man to be tested was her beloved, River-wind.

Let him be safe, she prayed silently. You elder gods, keep Riverwind from harm!

Goldmoon did not voice her prayers aloud because she appealed not to the tribe's gods, but to deities worshiped in ages past, before the Cataclysm.

The Lodge of Brothers was nearly full. The windowless interior was stiflingly hot, lit as it was by stands of smoky torches. The men of Que-Shu filled the open space around a low central dais, their leather-shod feet scuffing loudly on the packed clay floor. On the dais, squatting with his face averted and his arms clasped around his knees, was River-wind. As the drums continued their rumble, he did not move. He might have been carved from oak for all the life he displayed. Yet within, Riverwind was aboil with thoughts and anxieties. He had demanded this rite, in preparation for his Courting Quest. Goldmoon and he had pledged them-selves to each other, but it remained for the laws of the tribe to recognize their joining. A man did not ask for the hand of the chieftain's daughter without proving himself worthy.

The doors of the lodge were closed. Massive wooden beams were lowered, barring them. Warriors with bare blades positioned themselves in front of the doors. The drums ceased their omnipresent beat.

Arrowthorn, robed in his most richly beaded deerskins, gazed at the men assembled. "Brothers!" he declaimed, "we are here to anoint one who would be chieftain after I am gone. One who claims the hand of my daughter, your priest-ess. But he that would be a god in the next life must prove himself worthy in this one." A deep murmur of agreement rose from the throats of the tribesmen.

"Riverwind, son of Wanderer, stand."

Riverwind rose smoothly to his feet. Though not quite twenty, at six and a half feet he was by far the tallest man in a tribe of tall men. Dark hair hung loosely to his shoulders. Riverwind wore nothing but a red breechcloth, and the lines of his rangy form had been daubed with red paint. He looked beyond Arrowthorn's right shoulder and saw a Que-Shu elder, Loreman, seated on a bench. Hatred seemed to glow from the old medicine man's face. His consuming ambition to put his own family in the chieftain's lodge had been thwarted by the death of his eldest son. Now Loreman could only wait, watch, and listen.

Riverwind knew that Loreman blamed him for his son's death. Not even the sworn word of Goldmoon, who had witnessed the fight, had lessened Loreman's hatred of Riverwind.

Arrowthorn was describing the way of the true warrior. Riverwind broke his gaze from Loreman in time to hear the chieftain say, "The path of a leader is often bitter. Are you prepared for the bitterness?"

Riverwind nodded. He was not yet allowed to speak.

Arrowthorn held out his hands. Far-runner, another tribal elder, gave him a thick clay cup, which Arrowthorn in turn offered to Riverwind. A viscous red liquid filled the cup to the brim. By the ruddy torchlight it looked very much like blood. Riverwind accepted the cup, raised it to his lips, and drank.

The brew was made from nepta berries, fruit so vile not even goblins would eat it. Riverwind's jaw locked, and his stomach threatened to rebel. Still, he swallowed the noxious juice and gave the empty vessel back to Arrowthorn. He kept his teeth firmly together and breathed quickly through his nose. Sickness gnawed at his empty belly, but Riverwind mastered it and kept the bitter brew down.

"A chieftain must be evenhanded and balanced in his judgment," Arrowthorn said gravely. "If necessary, he must suffer for his choice. Are you prepared to suffer for the sake of justice?"

Riverwind inclined his head curtly. It was a good thing he wasn't supposed to talk; he wasn't sure he could speak with the sour berry juice constricting his throat. An elder lifted the heavy cape from Arrowthorn's shoulders. Another man placed two pairs of baskets on the floor, one set for the chieftain, the other for Riverwind. They were deep reed baskets, the kind women used to gather eggs. Snowy white eggs filled them now. Arrowthorn took up his baskets and held them out at arm's length. Riverwind lifted his. He was surprised by their weight. Each basket held only ten eggs. Why were they so heavy?

Loreman was smiling. Riverwind wondered briefly at that sly, knowing smile, then concentrated on his test. He had to hold his baskets up just as long as Arrowthorn held his. If he weakened, if he lowered his arms or wavered enough to break an egg, his test was over. There would be no second chance.

Arrowthorn was thirty years older than Riverwind, but his shoulders were straight and his arms taut with good muscle. Time grew long in the lodge. The Que-Shu men, ever solemn, became restless. There were coughs and uncertain shiftings on the hard wooden benches. Arrowthorn's arms were as straight as iron and as unwavering as the smooth waters of Crystalmir Lake.

Riverwind held steady, too, though his shoulders ached and his joints burned. The nepta berry juice was still trying to come up. Sweat trickled down his chest. The baskets were so heavy! He didn't think he could hold out much longer—he knew he could not—

Riverwind inhaled loudly and deeply. Since standing with his feet rooted and his knees stiff was causing him to tire and sway, he began to stamp his feet. A rhythm came to him, much like the cadence played by the lodge drummers. Soon he was dancing in place, eyes fixed on Arrowthorn, hearing the music his heart played for him.

Arrowthorn was startled when Riverwind began to dance. No one had ever moved during the Weighing before. His own arms hurt, the stretched muscles quivering and tingling as if a thousand ants crawled across his skin. He kept control by sheer force of will. Blood pounded in his head, a throbbing only made worse by Riverwind's stamping feet. Too much. It was too much.

The chieftain's left arm wobbled as a shudder went through his body. An egg rolled off the pile in the basket and splattered on the floor.

"It is done!" cried Far-runner, most senior of the elders. Both men lowered their arms with groans of relief. Arrowthorn slipped his cape over his aching shoulders.

"You have earned your voice," he said, breathing heavily. "Speak, son of Wanderer."

"You are a strong man, Arrowthorn," Riverwind said, massaging his biceps.

Whispers behind the chief abruptly burst out into loud clamor. Loreman was remonstrating with Far-runner.

"The test is not valid," Loreman said. "Riverwind moved."

"He did not bend his arms, nor did he lose an egg," Far-runner replied. "There is nothing in tribal law that says a man cannot move his feet."

"Riverwind makes mock of the ceremony!"

Riverwind knelt down to examine his egg baskets. As he did, Far-runner said, "Ridiculous! He showed great perseverance and ingenuity."

Loreman was about to protest further when Riverwind wordlessly poured the contents of his baskets on the dais. There were only five eggs in each, and beneath them, five smooth, river-washed stones painted white. To demonstrate their hardness, Riverwind lifted one of the stones and let it drop. It landed with a loud, accusing thud. The Que-Shu men muttered angrily among themselves at the trick played on Riverwind. Soon all eyes turned to Loreman. Even Arrowthorn gave his elder a suspicious glance, but forestalled any accusations by saying, "One irregularity cancels out another. The test stands. Riverwind has won the right to continue." No one raised his voice after that.

The chieftain sat, flinging his cape back to free his arms. "There remains one final reckoning," he said. "He who would be chieftain must be free of fear. Will you take the final anointing, Riverwind?"

"I will."

Arrowthorn gestured to Stonebreaker, another elder. Stonebreaker had been famed in his youth for his strength. He'd gotten his manhood name because he could cleave stones in two with his sword. Now old and bent, Stonebreaker hobbled to the dais and placed a tall pot before Riverwind.

"This is the Oil of the Quester," Arrowthorn said. The lodge fell deathly quiet. "Take it, and rub it on your skin. But be warned: there is great magic in the oil, and dire phantoms will come to you once you have put it on."

"I am not afraid," Riverwind declared, though he was.

He lifted the pot lid. The oil was dark brown and odorless. Riverwind smeared the ointment across his chest and neck. It was warm, and after his hand passed away, his skin grew warmer still as the oil soaked in. The drummers began a slow cadence. Working down his legs, Riverwind rubbed his oily hands over his knees and calves.

The pulse of the drums reverberated in his head. Someone in the room was chanting. Riverwind straightened. His head swam. He staggered back a few steps, nearly tumbling off the dais. Men were chanting, but not the men in the lodge. Riverwind whirled, but no Que-Shu man present was making a sound.

He recognized the chant. It was the lament uttered at funerals. Who was dead? Riverwind looked down at himself. Rivulets of red ran down his chest and legs. It looked like blood.

"I am wounded!" Riverwind cried. He tried to stanch the flow of blood. The drumbeat thundered at him, keeping time with his thudding heart.

He felt weak. His knees sagged, and Riverwind folded down into a kneeling crouch. Blood pooled around him. His life, his strength, was flowing unchecked from his veins. He couldn't stop it.

"Goldmoon . . . Goldmoon . . ." Calling her name did not help. He heard laughter. Raising his head, Riverwind saw Hollow- sky standing by the lodge door. Hands planted on hips, Hollow-sky grinned arrogantly at him.

"Hollow-sky, you're dead," Riverwind protested.

"So are you!" the phantom retorted. "You're too weak, Unbeliever. How could a soft fool like you ever imagine he could lead the Que-Shu?" The dead man laughed again. "Or capture Goldmoon's heart?" Riverwind's own heart constricted in his chest. No one else seemed to notice the ghost. Loreman didn't cry out at the sight of his lost son.

"Lie down and die," Hollow-sky urged. "Stop fighting. It's easy being dead."

"No. You died. I did not."

"You cannot resist death, Unbeliever."

The drums—or was it his heart?—beat slower and slower. Riverwind's head bowed to the floor. He was weak and so very, very tired. All he had to do was lie down. His eyes fluttered closed. Sleep and rest were what he craved. So easy. Painless. The beautiful face of Goldmoon faded from his eyes.

"My son! Is this as a warrior should act?"

Riverwind's eyes opened. Beside the grinning Hollow-sky was another ghost, dimmer and smaller, but definitely there. It was Wanderer, Riverwind's long dead father.

"I can't stand," Riverwind said weakly, lifting his head an inch.

"It's only paint," Wanderer said. His figure grew more distinct. "Stand. Be a man."

"He's no Que-Shu," Hollow-sky said. "He's a worthless unbeliever, like his father."

"Rise, my son! She who awaits you commands it!" Bright light surrounded Wanderer.

"Goldmoon?" said Riverwind. He glanced down and saw that the widening pool of blood was in fact only a few drops of paint. Paint covered his hands, too.

"Stand, Riverwind!"

"Father," he said, shaking off the cold lethargy that had gripped him. Putting his hands on the floor, he pushed. He rose unsteadily to his feet. The image of Wanderer shone brightly in the dim lodge. The men around the brilliant figure paid no heed to the apparition.

"It's too late." Hollow-sky sneered. "You've failed!"

"Begone," said the spirit of Wanderer. "Go back to your unquiet grave." With a parting sneer, the phantom son of Loreman faded from sight.

"Father, how is it I can see and speak to you in this way?" asked Riverwind.

"The oil you bathed in contains roots and herbs that have the power of heightening the senses. For centuries our people used these magic herbs to communicate with the dead. After a time, the people confused these spirits with the true gods. The worship of ancestors, the making of our dead leaders into gods, came from this confusion."

Riverwind stepped to the edge of the dais. "Then the old gods truly live?"

"As they always have, my son."

"Why do they not make themselves known?"

The glowing form of Wanderer flickered. "I do not know the mind of the Most High," he said. His voice had dwindled to a whisper. "But their time is almost here again. You will have signs, my son . . ."

"What signs, Father? What signs?" But the interlude was over. Wanderer vanished.

The lodge was filled with smoke. The men of the tribe were gone. Doors, barred and guarded earlier, stood open. It was dusk. Riverwind felt a breeze blow through the dark house. It chilled his sweaty skin.

Suddenly, Arrowthorn and the elders were with him. Riverwind wiped his forehead and mouth with the back of one hand and stepped off the dais. He was exhausted.

"What has happened?" he asked his chieftain.

"You have passed your Anointing," Arrowthorn said.

"How long have I been here?"

"All day. The elders and I have been discussing your problem."

Riverwind wanted only a cool drink of water. His throat was puckered with the stale remnants of the berry juice. But he asked, "What problem?"

"You mastered your fear of death, but while you were conversing with the gods, our ancestors, you spoke many blasphemies."

Riverwind sat up and squared his shoulders. "What blasphemy?"

"You denied our gods, the forefathers who made us. I have long known that you share your father's heresy; sons cannot help but bear their fathers' notions, no matter how false. But I never thought to hear Wanderer's heresy spouted during a solemn rite," Arrowthorn said.

"The punishment for blasphemy is death," Loreman added. His hands were clenched into fists. He had heard Riverwind talk to his dead son. "The law says the guilty must be stoned at the Grieving Wall."

"You go too far," Far-runner said. "Riverwind was not of his own mind when he said what he did. His father's spirit influenced him, Loreman." Stonebreaker and the others echoed Far-runner's sentiments.

"What is to be done?" Riverwind asked.

All through the elders' wrangle, Arrowthorn had been silent, deep in thought. He had little liking for Riverwind as husband to his beloved daughter, but he had to admire the young man's performance this day. He couldn't dismiss Riverwind's right to quest for Goldmoon's hand, but perhaps he might teach him a salutary lesson.

"You shall have your Courting Quest," Arrowthorn said. "And, in the process, I hope to cure you of your heresy."

The disputing elders ringed their chieftain and Riverwind. Far-runner regarded Arrowthorn curiously. "How?" he asked.

"With no more than a single day's provision in his bag, Riverwind shall go forth to find proof that the old gods do exist."

Loreman smiled. "A wise decision," he said.

"How can he do it?" asked Stonebreaker. "You've set him an impossible task. The old gods are dead."

"He can always return and admit defeat," Loreman sneered.

"No honorable warrior—"

"Enough! As chieftain, I have spoken. We've seen that Riverwind has no shortage of courage and strength, but do you want an unbeliever as chieftain? Our gods will bring evil down upon us if we betray them. No, he must learn how great his errors are." Arrowthorn thrust a finger at Riverwind. "I charge you, upon your sacred oath, that you will take this quest or admit the falsity of your beliefs before all the Que-Shu people. What do you say?"

Riverwind folded his long arms across his chest. There was only one answer. "I will take the quest," he said.

*   *   *   *   *

Goldmoon was ecstatic when she learned Riverwind had passed his anointing. When she learned of the quest her father had given her beloved, her joy turned to consternation.

"Proof of the gods? What proof can there be? I felt the power of the old gods in the Hall of Sleeping Spirits, yet I cannot prove enough to satisfy the doubters!"

9

Riverwind stuffed strips of dried deermeat and lumps of pemmican into his shoulderpouch. "I could not refuse. If I had, we would be lost to each other."

She grasped his arm. His eyes met hers, and he saw her tears. They embraced.

"Don't weep, beautiful one. The quest isn't impossible. I'll come back, you'll see. Then no one can deny us—not your father, nor the elders, nor even the conniving Loreman."

Goldmoon choked back her tears. "Where will you go? What will you do?"

Riverwind drew back enough to study her face. Her brilliant blue eyes were gilded with tears. He brushed a drop of moisture from her cheek with his thumb. "I'll go where the sun and wind take me. The gods are not bound by mortal barriers. I will seek them in the quiet places—the mountains, deserts, the deep forests. I'll find them, then come back to you."

A smile lightened Goldmoon's face. Here, in Riverwind's arms, her doubts dwindled.

They kissed long enough for Arrowthorn to rap impatiently on the front pole of Riverwind's tent. Riverwind caressed Goldmoon's cheek and smoothed her radiant hair. "Time to go," he said.

Riverwind's tent was outside the wall of the village, by the road that led west to the land of the Que-Kiri. Arrowthorn and the elders waited for the young warrior. They made sure he carried only a scant day's rations. Riverwind was allowed to take his bow and his long-handled saber. In his old but well-oiled leather breastplate and his fringed deerskins, he was ready.

Goldmoon had dried her tears, but inside, her heart was breaking. In the three centuries since the Cataclysm had rent the land, the old gods had slept. They were so absent from the lives of the people of Krynn that most had forgotten them or had consigned them to the realm of dreams. How could one man, even her stalwart Riverwind, hope to succeed where generations had come to naught?

Riverwind made polite good-byes to the elders and cast a secret, loving look to Goldmoon. Then, he shouldered his pouch and strode off, his long legs covering the ground quickly.

"Riverwind!" Goldmoon called. He turned and waved, but never broke his stride. Arrowthorn glared at his daughter for her breach of behavior. Goldmoon missed the look. Her eyes were only for Riverwind as he followed the dirt road south and east until the curving village wall blocked him from sight. She put a hand to her throat and felt the amulet hidden under her tunic, the necklace Riverwind had given her during their journey to the Hall of Sleeping Spirits. It was wrought in steel, rare among the plainsmen, and was shaped like two teardrops touching tip to tip. The amulet had protected them from Hollow-sky's evil plan. She prayed now it would guide Riverwind to a speedy and successful end to his quest.

Arrowthorn's angry glare softened. He was moved by the sorrow in his only child's face, the face so like her mother's. But he was chieftain. The tribe's concerns must come before even his own child's happiness.

"Come, daughter," he said gruffly and stuck out an elbow. Gracefully, Goldmoon entwined her arm in her father's, and they preceded the elders back into the village.

*　*　*　*　*

Riverwind had no real plan. It was nearly midday, and the heat of late summer was upon the land. Once out of sight of Goldmoon and the Que-Shu elders, he slowed his pace and pondered what to do.

A rattling sound distracted him. Riverwind looked back at the village wall. Leaning against it was a dilapidated hut, little more than a lean-to, made of bark and mottled pieces of hide. Squatting on the ground in front of the lean-to was a shabby figure, an old man in rags of many colors. His hair was long, tangled, and wild. In a tribe of clean-shaven men, he had a long gray and yellow beard into which beads and tiny brass bells were woven.

"Catchflea," Riverwind hailed the strange figure.

The old man did not look up. His true name was Catchstar, because as a youth he'd hunted far and wide in the hills for bits of the stars that fell from heaven. When the time came for him to display more mature ambitions, Catchstar remained devoted to his odd pursuit. He did not take part in the affairs of the Que-Shu. Ostracized for his eccentricity, treated with open contempt, Catchstar grew more and more distracted. His unmanly habits and slovenly appearance earned him expulsion from the village—just as heretical religious beliefs had earned Riverwind's family the same fate. Small children christened the old man "Catchflea" as a cruel joke. In time, he would answer to no other name. Their similar standings had made the strange old man and the young warrior natural allies, and Riverwind often defended Catchflea from harassment.

"Going on a journey, yes?" asked Catchflea, absently shaking a dry gourd. Something rattled within. "A long, long journey?"

"Very long," admitted Riverwind. He wondered who would be the old man's champion once he was gone. "I may not come back for months, perhaps years." The thought gave him little pleasure.

"I'll miss you. No one else brings me rabbits." When Riverwind had a good hunt, he always shared his bounty with the old star chaser. In some ways, he was like Wanderer, Riverwind's father. Both men were dreamers in a tribe that did not esteem deep reflection.

"If you are going away, Catchflea has a gift, yes."

"What is it, my friend?"

Catchflea scratched his sharp nose. Beads and small bells tinkled in his matted beard. "Something to help you, yes." He moved the spotted yellow gourd in a wide circle. The top was cut out, and Riverwind could see small brown objects bouncing around inside. Catchflea crooned in a surprisingly tuneful voice:

> "All that comes and all that goes
> Moves in an endless circle.
> Count the days and count the stars
> Starting then and ending now."

Riverwind could make little sense of that. When he had finished singing this twice, Catchflea dumped the contents of the gourd out on the hard, dry earth. "Ha!" he exclaimed.

Three acorns lay in the dirt. They'd fallen in a rough triangle, with one point aimed directly at Riverwind.

"Here is your journey in a nutshell. Three nutshells!" The old man wheezed a brief laugh, accompanied by the faint tinkle of his beard bells. "This says you will go far away and be gone a long time," he said, pointing to the nut nearest Riverwind. "This means you will go amidst great darkness." He tapped a second acorn with one cracked and dirty nail.

"Evil?" asked Riverwind, sitting down in front of the old man.

"'Darkness,' I said, yes?" The last acorn Catchflea smiled at. "And out of the darkness shall come the seed of the new, which is like the old."

"What does that mean?"

"The new is the old? Natural, yes. That is all I can tell you." Catchflea scooped up the acorns and slipped them back in the gourd. Round and round went his wrinkled hand, shaking the gourd.

Riverwind had heard whispers that the old man conversed with spirits who told him the future, and he had a formidable record predicting whether Que-Shu mothers would have boy babies or girls. Riverwind couldn't dismiss Catchflea's remarks as idle talk.

He said, "Which way should I go?"

"Ha!" This time the nuts fell in a row. "East," said Catchflea. Riverwind scratched his head. The nuts weren't obviously pointing east.

"How do you know what they say?" he asked.

"How do you know how to breathe? How do you know when it's time to rise or time to sleep?"

Riverwind nodded. "I just know. I don't need to ponder it. The knowledge comes to me, and I know."

"That is it exactly, yes," said Catchflea.

Riverwind stood slowly, leaving the old man to gather his acorns again. East. Into the Forsaken Mountains. At least at this time of year the high passes would be free of snow—

The nuts clattered in the gourd. Catchflea dumped them out, crying for the third time, "Ha!"

Riverwind came out of his reverie. "What do you see, old man?"

Catchflea squinted up at the tall huntsman. "I am to go with you." The distracted lilt was gone from his voice.

Riverwind stiffened. "Perhaps you are reading them wrong," he suggested.

Catchflea shook his head. "There is only one meaning, yes. 'Follow and descend.' That is what it says."

"Descend?"

The jingle of bells accompanied Catchflea's bewildered headshaking. "I must do it. Auguries are not given to be ignored."

"You can't come with me," Riverwind said gently. "I'm going far. I have only enough food for myself for one day. You're much too old to make such a trek."

"I must, yes?" He heaved himself to his feet. Catchflea's knees and elbows cracked like kindling underfoot. "I won't be a burden to you, Riverwind. You need only tend to yourself, yes? I can fend for myself."

Riverwind grasped the old fellow by his shoulder. "You're not going."

Catchflea's dark eyes bored into Riverwind's. "It isn't only my destiny you tamper with. It is your own. The gods have ordained that we leave Que-Shu together. To flout their will is to invite disaster."

Riverwind dropped his hands. "What gods do you serve, my friend?" Catchflea did not answer, but stooped to trace a figure in the dirt. It looked like two teardrops touching tip to tip. Riverwind knew the sign of the goddess Mishakal. That same symbol, wrought in rare steel, he had given Goldmoon to wear secretly around her neck. He narrowed his eyes and stared at the old man.

"How do you know this sign?" he said suspiciously.

"Once it was known to all, yes. Now I see it only in the sky, traced in the jewels of the stars."

Riverwind wrestled with his dilemma. Catchflea was no ranger, not fit for forest or mountains. Still, his soothsaying was too accurate for Riverwind to discount. Perhaps he could take the old fellow along a short way, then leave him in some comfortable spot.

"I won't be a burden," Catchflea insisted.

"How long will it take you to prepare?" Riverwind said,

resigned.

The soothsayer bent over with a grunt and picked up his gourd and acorns. "I am ready," he said. "I have nothing else."

The lean-to contained only the mound of moss the old man slept on, some rags, and a rotting waterskin. Catchflea slipped his acorns into a fold of his much-patched shirt and tied the gourd to a loose strip of cloth. "No one in Que-Shu will mourn my leaving, yes?"

It was sadly true. Riverwind looked away to the mountains. Across the sunny plain, the eastern horizon beckoned, with the Forsaken Mountains only a blue-tinged smudge. Though not steep or especially cold this time of year, the mountains were dry and almost devoid of game. He'd have to hunt daily to ensure a steady supply of food. And now he was hunting for two, as he doubted Catchflea would be of much use in the wild.

The odds were certainly piled high against him. No horse, little food, and a vague old man to shepherd along—Arrowthorn's quest would test him severely. Still, he had his wits, his skills, and an unbending determination on his side. The old gods lived. For them, and for Goldmoon, Riverwind would defy any odds.

Chapter 2

Thunder Notch

Catchflea's aged limbs warmed in the afternoon sun, and he managed to keep up with Riverwind's long-legged stride. Because they needed food, they could not keep to the main road, the Sageway.

"There's a pocket of woods tucked into the shadow of the mountains," Riverwind said. "If we take that route, there might be deer, or a mountain sheep come down to forage." He reflected privately that had the old man not come, he could go a day or two on the dried meat and bread packed in his shoulder pouch. In that time he could be deep in the mountains, on his way to meet his destiny . . .

"—yield to your knowledge of huntcraft," Catchflea was saying. "Long are the years since I held a bow, much less a skinner's knife."

They strode across the plain, Catchflea jingling like a peddler's wagon on its way to market. Riverwind tried to ignore the annoying sound, but after a hundred score yards he halted abruptly and said, "When we get to the forest, you'll have to find a place and sit still. Those bells will warn away every animal in the country!"

Catchflea clutched his beard defensively. "I thought the sound pleasing."

"It's very musical, but game will take alarm from it."

"I will sit as silent as a stone, yes." They walked on, the old man holding his beard loosely with one hand to still the bells and beads.

Trees rose out of the grassy plain like a curtain; there was no gradual change from open land to dense forest. Before plunging into the woods, Riverwind paused long enough to string his bow. To secure his saber so it wouldn't rattle and frighten his prey, he wound a strip of soft deerhide around the brass hilt, binding it to the brass throat of his scabbard.

"Speak now, or hold your tongue until there's meat roasting on our fire," Riverwind said in a tense whisper.

"Good hunting," was all Catchflea had to say.

Riverwind nocked an arrow and slipped between the trees. With a good deal less stealth, Catchflea followed. Though he held his bells quiet, he was not accustomed to moving like a hunter. He blundered along, snapping twigs and almost running into Riverwind's back. Wordlessly, Riverwind pointed out where Catchflea should place his feet so as not to make as much noise. The old man did better after that, though he was still no match for Riverwind.

The forest was mostly pine and cedar, so thick that their progress was slow and winding. The forest floor was carpeted with pine needles and cedar berries, which were not edible. Deer, however, esteemed them, and Riverwind found signs where bucks had butted the trees in order to shake down more berries.

He spied a towering cedar with stout lower limbs and climbed up. Wild creatures were sharp-eyed and keen-nosed. With Catchflea along, the best thing to do was get above their level of sight and smell and wait for the prey to pass by. Riverwind boosted Catchflea up to the lowest branches, climbed past him, and hauled him up higher. With the old fellow safely settled in the main crotch of the tree, Riverwind inched out from the trunk on a stout limb and sat down, his feet dangling and his bow laid across his knees.

Wind washed through the evergreens, sounding like a far-off waterfall. The pleasant feel of the breeze and the quiet of the forest lulled the soothsayer to sleep. The branch swayed under Riverwind. His thoughts strayed to Goldmoon, as they always did, but still he kept watch for game. His vigil was interrupted, however, by high-pitched snores.

"Hsst!" he said to Catchflea. The old man never heard him, and went right on snoring. Annoyed, Riverwind plucked the resin bag from his belt. The little leather pouch held the resin and wax he needed to keep his bowstring taut. He threw this at Catchflea. The bag thumped off the old man's bowed head and landed in his lap. His snores still didn't waver.

Riverwind drew up his feet, ready to shake Catchflea awake. It was then he saw the ram. The magnificent beast was poised behind some pine saplings, its huge horns curling down to its wet black nose. Riverwind would have given much to be able to mount those horns over the door of his tent, but he could hardly afford to carry twenty pounds of ramshorn with him now. And a ram that old would be poor eating, too tough.

But where there's a ram, there's likely a ewe, Riverwind thought. He slipped the nock of the arrow over the bowstring. Catchflea let out a particularly loud snore. The ram responded, grunting low in his chest. He pushed aggressively through the saplings. Close on his heels came a sleek ewe, and behind her a pair of yearling sheep. Riverwind drew the bowstring swiftly and let fly at the yearling male. The animal gave a bleat as the arrow struck home. All four sheep bolted.

"Wake up, Catchflea!" the plainsman shouted. The old man awoke with a start and rolled off the tree. Riverwind snatched the front of his ragged coat in time to stop him from falling a dozen feet to the ground.

"I've got us a sheep!" Riverwind exclaimed.

"I hope you've got me!"

He dragged Catchflea to a stable sitting position and said, "Stay here. I've got to catch that yearling."

Riverwind slid down the trunk. In the young pines, he found traces of blood. The sheep was seriously wounded, but still might run for miles. There was nothing to do but follow. He drew the lacings of his moccasin boots tighter and set off at a fast lope.

Blood marked the animal's trail. From their tracks Riverwind could tell the old ram had gone one way, the ewe another. Both yearlings stayed with their mother.

His quarry was headed for the peak at the north end of the forest pocket, the forked mountain the Que-Shu called Thunder Notch. It was said that storms blowing in from the Newsea "broke" on the Forsaken Mountains, spilling thunder, lightning, and rain on the plains. Daylight was rapidly fading by the time Riverwind reached the first boulders at the foot of Thunder Notch. The young ram was remarkably strong, or else Riverwind's arrow was a poorer hit than he'd imagined.

Solinari, the silver moon, was waxing full. Its bright rays penetrated the clefts in the rock and allowed Riverwind to find the wounded sheep's trail of blood. The amount of blood was increasing. The end could not be far off.

Riverwind slung his bow over his shoulder to free his hands for climbing. He'd just reached the top of a house-sized boulder when he heard a chilling howl. Wolves!

He crouched atop the rock and saw a dozen gray forms hurtle past. The pack had caught wind of the dying animal and had come to claim it for their own. Riverwind swung the bow from his shoulder and whipped an arrow from the quiver. He crept along the top of the rock until he came to a small boxed-in ravine. The wolves had killed the wounded ram and were busy tearing it to pieces.

Instead of making a stealthy getaway, the angry Riverwind picked off one of the wolves by the carcass. The gray beast rolled away, dead, a hardwood shaft through its heart. The remaining wolves hardly noticed. Riverwind drew a bead on another animal and let fly. This time, the largest wolf present came over and sniffed its dead comrade.

The shaggy head raised slowly to the rock where Riverwind was perched. By the light of Solinari the wolf's eyes burned a deep crimson.

Riverwind had a third arrow nocked for the big wolf, but something in its manner stayed his hand. The pack leader threw back its broad head and howled, a cry both hideous and heartrending. The other wolves stopped gnawing the dead sheep and fell into a tight group on one side of the ravine.

The wolf leader trotted toward him. Riverwind realized the beast was probably big enough to leap up onto the table of rock with him. Riverwind drew and released an arrow in one swift motion.

The great beast dodged the missile! A twist, a roll, and the shaft buried itself in the stony earth. Riverwind pulled another from his dwindling stock. The wolf launched itself in a mighty jump. Riverwind backpedaled, fumbling the arrow away. Before he could reach for another, the wolf scrambled up the sloping face of the rock until it was on the plainsman's level.

"No—more—arrows!"

Three distinct words came from the animal's mouth. Riverwind recoiled, almost losing his grip on his bow. He thought for an instant to draw his saber—but no, he'd tied it into its scabbard.

"Beast, whatever you are," he said deliberately, laying an arrow against the bowstave carefully, "keep off, or I'll serve you the same as the others." He held tightly to the nock of the arrow, to keep his hand from shaking.

The huge wolf sat down on his haunches. In the uncertain light, Riverwind saw that the animal's feet were not clawed and furry, but ended in leathery-looking hands, human hands, with black nails. The creature's eyes glowed with some inner light, blood red. A long black tongue licked past wicked fangs. The beast had tall, pricked ears, but no tail.

The wolf-thing's jaw worked. "No more arrows."

Riverwind widened his draw. "Keep your distance then."

The weird human fingers flexed, gripping the boulder top. Riverwind understood how the animal had been able to climb up to him.

Raspingly the creature said, "You killed my kin." A snarl gurgled up deep from the furry gray chest. "One was my son!"

"I shot that sheep," Riverwind said. His sweating palms made it difficult to keep the bow drawn so tight. He eased off a bit. "Then the pack took it. I defend what is mine. Who are you, a wolf that speaks like a man?"

"I am Kyanor, first of the Nightrunners. We have come over the mountains to claim this forest as our own. No one may hunt here but us!"

"So you say. I have no wish to kill wolves, but the ram was mine."

Kyanor bared his teeth, growling savagely. "No one intrudes on our domain. We have been hounded and driven from place to place, but no longer. All who hunt in our forest will die."

The plainsman's arrow point centered on Kyanor's head. "I know nothing of your history, but you have the ram now, so take it and depart in peace," he said.

"What of my son? His blood stains your hands."

"Every hunter risks his life when he pits himself against nature."

"Empty human philosophy! The price of your crime shall be your life!"

Kyanor sprang on him. Riverwind released his arrow at half-draw. There was no time for another. The arrow hit Kyanor in the chest, but it didn't divert his howling pounce. He slammed into Riverwind, and together they rolled across the boulder top. The beast's fingers clawed at Riverwind, and in their thrashing, the plainsman lost his bow. Riverwind's large hands grasped the wolf's throat, choking him and keeping the snapping fangs away.

Kyanor was strong, and he pinned Riverwind on his back. The plainsman had to twist his head from side to side to avoid the beast's teeth. All through the fight, the rest of the pack stood in silent attention around the base of the boulder, their keen eyes following every move.

Black nails raked Riverwind's neck. Hot blood flowed. Riverwind dug his long fingers into Kyanor's throat. The wolf gasped and coughed, his tongue hanging out, dripping rancid saliva. Riverwind drove a knee into Kyanor's ribs. The wolf's strength slackened. Letting go with his left hand, Riverwind levered Kyanor off him. The strange wolf-creature rolled aside, choked nearly to death. While he was still helpless, Riverwind shoved him off the rock.

The wolves below broke into blood-chilling howls as their leader fell among them. Riverwind recovered his bow. The string had snapped, but otherwise it was intact. It mattered little; he hadn't enough arrows to deal with almost a dozen wild wolves. He would have to bluff them.

"Yah!" he yelled at them. Riverwind stood on the boulder, an arrow drawn back in the stringless bow. The yapping pack fell still. Kyanor rose unsteadily. Nine pairs of hungry eyes turned upward; their unwavering gaze was fixed on the plainsman.

"I don't know if you understand me or not, but the first one who makes a move at me will die." The wolves remained motionless, their ears laid back, black lips curled up to reveal knife-sharp teeth.

Riverwind climbed carefully down. He backed away from the pack. The wolves came forward in a body, a few noiseless steps at a time. Long shadows obscured their forms, making it hard for Riverwind to see them. Their gleaming eyes were the last things to disappear. Soon Riverwind saw nothing to threaten with his harmless bow.

A howl sounded on his right. An answering call drifted in from his left. The wolves were circling him. His back against a thick tree, Riverwind tore at the lacing binding his saber. While doing this, he shouted, "Kyanor! How many more of your brothers are you willing to sacrifice to get me? I have arrows and steel to deal with you all—is it worth it? Is it, Kyanor?" His saber was finally free and he drew it silently. Moonlight glinted on the long, polished blade.

An eerie screech in the darkness made the hairs on his neck bristle. He could imagine the hard, lithe bodies flitting among the cedars, seeing with precision in the night, though they were veiled from Riverwind's questing eyes.

Riverwind broke away from the tree and sprinted a few yards to another, flinging himself back-first against the fragrant, ragged cedar bark. Branches waved not far away;

was it the wind? The forest was as calm as a scene of death.

"Plainsman! Can you hear me?" Kyanor called.

"I hear you, Kyanor!"

"I'll remember you, plainsman! I'll know your scent should we cross paths again!"

"I'll save an arrow just for you," Riverwind said. Unseen, Kyanor howled a summons to his kin. They answered, a chorus of yips and barks individual to each animal. Then the forest was silent. Riverwind kept his back to the tree for a long time, listening.

Eventually, crickets began to whir in the undergrowth. That was a good sign. Riverwind sheathed his sword and let out a sigh of relief. If the wolves were still prowling nearby, the woods would be quiet with fear.

Riverwind ran, dodging through the pines and cedars. As he did, he was beset with a horrible thought: if the pack doubled back behind him, they could follow his trail to the place where he'd left Catchflea . . .

The great cedar bore no signs of violence. Indeed, the only sign of life Riverwind detected was a gentle snoring coming from above. He climbed to where the trunk split and found Catchflea there, sleeping peacefully.

Riverwind settled in the other side of the tree. He loosened his sword belt and passed it around a tree branch to hold him in the tree. His saber he jammed into a limb overhead. Riverwind tried to fall asleep, but every whisper of the wind, every nocturnal creature's cry, brought him to full wakefulness. It was a long night.

* * * * *

Sun filtered through the dark green fronds, the patterns of light and shadow weaving across Riverwind's face. The smell of resinous wood burning interrupted his slumber. The sudden remembrance of his fight the night before jolted him awake. Below, Catchflea was puttering around a small fire. Riverwind released his belt and swung down to the ground. His muscles ached from his fight and flight. The long scratches on his throat had dried with a coating of sticky black blood.

"Are you hungry?" asked Catchflea, his back to Riverwind. "There is food, yes."

"What food?" asked Riverwind. He was famished.

"Mushroom broth, greens, herb tea, and topa pods."

Riverwind approached and peered over Catchflea's shoulder in surprise. In the early hours of the morning the old man had risen and foraged for food. In Riverwind's copper pan he'd boiled wild mushrooms and dandelion greens. He'd brewed tea from sage and mint growing in a clearing not far away. And most surprisingly, he'd found a stand of topa bushes, whose green seed pods were delicious eaten raw.

Catchflea handed Riverwind a cup of tea with a mint sprig floating in it. The old man sat cross-legged by the pine twig fire, slurping mushroom broth and nibbling a seed pod. His eyes widened when he caught sight of the scratches on Riverwind's neck, but all he said was, "Eat, eat."

Riverwind sank down on his haunches. "You've been fooling me, old man."

"I?"

"Yes. You play at being the witless soothsayer, but you're really an old fox." Riverwind swallowed a mouthful of tea. It was good; the warmth spread down his throat and soothed his empty stomach.

"No one lives to my age by being a fool," Catchflea replied. "Careful, yes. Foolish, no. Especially when they have the ability to glimpse the future." He munched another topa pod. "What happened to your neck? Did you fall down?"

Riverwind told him about the wolves, Kyanor, and how he'd lost the sheep. Behind his beard, Catchflea paled.

"Wolves?" he murmured. "With fingers? You never said anything about wolves of any sort!"

"Anything can happen in the wilderness, my friend. There are worse things than wolves, with or without fingers." Riverwind drained the tea from his cup and dipped it in the soup. The brown forest mushrooms had a strong, woody flavor he found bracing. "What I want to know is: was Kyanor a beast that talked like a man, or a man confined to the body of a beast?"

"A man. He must be a man, yes?"

Riverwind chewed a stringy piece of mushroom. "Why so?"

"Only men can seek knowledge through magic," Catchflea said. "Men and like races. Animals do not have the wits to incant."

"So this Kyanor is a man who takes wolf form? Why would he do that?"

The old man shrugged. "Over the mountains is the lost domain of Istar, where magic ruled centuries ago. Many strange things came out of there when the Cataclysm claimed the land and sank it beneath the sea. This wolf-thing might be the offspring of an Istarian sorcerer." Catchflea dabbed his lips daintily on his sleeve, never mind that the sleeve was dirtier than his face. "Or Kyanor could be a man like us, but under a curse," he added.

"He did not complain of his place at the head of the pack," Riverwind said.

They went down to the spring Catchflea had found so Riverwind could wash his slight wounds. As they walked, Riverwind asked, "What happened to your bells? Your beard is silent."

The old man flushed. "I removed them," he replied. "I decided they didn't suit my new role as a woodsman, yes." Riverwind smiled.

The old soothsayer reclined on the pine needle-strewn bank and watched Riverwind clean the cuts on his neck.

"Do they hurt?"

Riverwind winced as he pressed a damp rag to the cuts. "No."

"They might fester," Catchflea mused. "I can make a poultice from blueroot."

"Not necessary. The cuts are clean now."

"Perhaps a salve to ease the pain? I believe I saw some numbweed nearby. Or I could use arrowgum, or perhaps—"

"Keep still, will you?" Riverwind said impatiently. Catchflea's face fell.

"I only want to help."

Riverwind didn't answer. He felt sheepish that, for all his admonishings about stealth and hunting, it had been Catchflea who'd fed them. His discomfort made him short with the old soothsayer.

Before night fell again, the two men set out to cross the Forsaken Mountains. Riverwind avoided the trail where he had encountered the Nightrunners, choosing instead to go up the stony face of Thunder Notch itself. Catchflea didn't balk at the task; in fact, he kept up with Riverwind much better on broken ground than he had on level terrain. Strong he was not, but very agile.

The twin caps of Thunder Notch loomed over them as they worked their way up the western slope. In most places they were able to walk upright, stepping carefully to avoid loose shale ledges and crumbly sandstone outcroppings. Sometimes, though, Riverwind and Catchflea were forced to go on all fours, clinging to the brittle face of the mountain with fingers and toes.

A little after midday they entered the Notch. All the plain of Abanasinia lay at their feet. Riverwind felt in good spirits.

"Farewell, Abanasinia!" he called to the wind.

"Farewell, Que-Shu!" Catchflea added.

Till we are together once more, Goldmoon, Riverwind thought. Broad white clouds raced over the Notch, a silent panoply hurrying west.

Catchflea fished the acorns from his clothing and put them in the gourd. He knelt on a flat table of rock and began to shake the gourd.

Riverwind leaned against the vertical spire of the north peak and said, "What are you looking for, old man?"

"Our new direction, yes." He droned the formula under his breath. "Ha!" he cried, spilling the nuts across the stone. For the life of him Riverwind could not see anything in the pattern of the acorns' fall. Catchflea scrutinized the humble oak seeds. In their pattern he saw the future.

"What is it?" asked Riverwind.

"You will go far, and be gone long years, face great darkness, and . . . the new is the old," Catchflea muttered.

"Just the same."

"Hmm, yes." Catchflea gathered the nuts and shook them again. The result was the same as at Que-Shu: "go east" and "descend."

Riverwind lost interest in what he could not understand. He went to the eastern edge of the Notch and gazed across the sea of peaks and valleys, all lower than where he stood. He picked up his quiver and shoulder bag. "Let's use the daylight we have," he said.

Catchflea put away his gourd. They crossed the Notch and entered one of the ravines leading off the peak. It was an easy trail, never too steep or too narrow. They kept to it the rest of the day. An hour before sundown, the trail opened out on a sloping, six-sided clearing that was rimmed by fallen boulders. Riverwind walked to a large rock at the high end of the clearing and dropped his gear.

"Might as well camp here," he said.

Catchflea surveyed the endless expanse of stone. "A very desolate spot, yes. This is why these are called the Forsaken Mountains." Riverwind agreed. "No fire tonight," the old man observed. There was no tinder.

"Cold camp for certain," Riverwind said. "I have some pemmican left."

They camped with their backs to a chalky limestone pinnacle, chewing lumps of salty pemmican and sipping water from Riverwind's goatskin bag. The clear sky darkened from lavender to deep purple. Stars appeared. The men said little. The air grew cold, and the old man's teeth rattled like the acorns in his gourd. Riverwind untied the horsehair blanket from the strap of his bag. The extra long blanket had been woven for his father by his mother. Though the zigzag designs had faded from red to warm orange and the edges were beginning to fray, Riverwind always used it on his forays into the wild.

He draped the blanket around Catchflea's shoulders. The old man looked grateful, but objected, "You will need this for yourself, yes?"

"My buckskins will keep me warm," Riverwind said.

Catchflea drew the blanket up over his head. His teeth stopped chattering. "Thank you, tall man."

They watched the stars, and Catchflea told what he knew of the lore of the sky. As he talked, a star fell flaming from the heavens. It traced a long, fiery path and vanished. The afterglow remained in Riverwind's eyes a long time.

"Tell me, old man: why did you hunt for fallen stars when you were young?"

Catchflea shifted on his narrow haunches. "I wanted to find proof of the gods, our ancestors. I thought, if the gods live in the sky, then anything that falls from there will bear evidence of their presence."

Riverwind was startled by the strange but logical premise. "What did you hope to find?"

"Anything. Some sign that beings greater than ourselves lived in the heavens." He sighed. "I found four fallen stars, and they were all the same. Lumps of burned stone, yes? It was then I decided the gods of our people were false, and the priestesses of the Que-Shu deluded."

"I believe in the old gods," Riverwind said simply.

Catchflea's eyes, shaded by the blanket, sought his companion's. "That's heresy, some say."

"Perhaps."

"Have the old gods ever spoken to you?"

"No, but I see the hand of Paladine, Majere, and Mishakal all around us. Where do you think your gift of prophesy comes from?"

"Do I know? I'm Catchflea the Daft, Catchflea the Fool." He grinned.

"You jest with me. I should call you Catchflea the Fox," Riverwind said. He leaned back, letting the field of stars fill his view. "When did you gain the power of augury?"

"In my twentieth year. I was returning from my fourth and last star-finding, which had taken me deep in the forest near Qualinost. I despaired of ever learning the truth. Our way, the way of the Que-Shu, was useless, yes? I felt my life was worthless, so I climbed to the top of a tremendous oak tree and prepared to throw myself off."

"What changed your mind?" asked Riverwind.

"The love of life was strong in me. I hung there with only my fingertips and my hesitation between me and death. I still longed to know the truth, and the god Majere appeared to me." Riverwind studiedopened wide. "Not in a human form," Catchflea said quickly. "I heard a great voice, and felt—a presence, yes? Majere told me not to despair, that the gods were not merely legends, and that my life had a purpose. 'What purpose?' I asked. 'We cannot speak plainly to mortals,' said Majere, his voice filling the whole sky around me. 'But we live. You must strive to regain what the mortal world has rejected. You must strive for truth. Truth is the final act in a long struggle between good and evil. The struggle is yet to come.'" Catchflea nodded to himself. "Forty years it has been, and I remember every word the god said to me."

Riverwind studied his companion. There was none of the daft, uncouth old man in Catchflea's story. He said, "You have been honored. No one I ever knew spoke with a true god."

"I climbed down from the tree—very carefully—and addressed the air: 'How shall I strive for truth, Great Majere?' Three acorns fell from the tree and landed at my feet. 'Take up these seeds and they will show you the way,' he said.

"By the time I got back to the village, I understood the future could be seen in the fall of the acorns. I also realized how deadly such a gift could be. The elders of our people would not suffer me to live if I proclaimed the truth to all."

"So you played the fool."

Catchflea nodded with vigor. "It was easy enough. Most already thought me a dreamer, yes? I let my hair grow wild and dressed in ridiculous rags. The children named me Catchflea, an insult I bore for the sake of truth."

"I call you that, too. I'm sorry." Riverwind laid a large hand on the old man's shoulder. He regretted many things at that moment, most especially his harsh words at the spring the previous day.

"Don't trouble yourself. I *am* Catchflea." He scratched to prove his point and laughed with his usual rusty wheeze. Then he asked, "And what of Goldmoon? Does she know she loves a heretic?"

"By rights, she is a heretic herself. Her own mother's spirit appeared to her in the Hall of the Sleeping Spirits and confessed the falsity of Que-Shu religion." Catchflea's face showed great surprise.

"The priestess of the people a heretic? Does the chieftain know this?" he sputtered.

"Arrowthorn hears and sees only what suits him. He listens to the poisonous mutterings of Loreman as often as he does his own daughter's good advice. His love for her at least allows him to tolerate my suit for her hand. Otherwise, I would have been stoned or cast out long ago," Riverwind said darkly.

"Cast out? You mean, like now?" Catchflea gently observed.

"The chieftain thinks he has bested me with an impossible quest. Yet I shall come through." Riverwind gripped the old man's hand. "You see, I believe it is the old gods' will that you follow me on my quest. You have heard Majere's voice and see into the future by his favor. Together, my friend, we will find proof." He released his hold. Catchflea massaged his hand gratefully.

"As for Goldmoon," Riverwind said quietly, "our love is not bound by tribal customs or village law. My life is pledged to Goldmoon, as hers is to me."

Chapter 3

Follow and Descend

Riverwind stood at the edge of a chasm. Below, hidden by billowing smoke, something deadly lingered. As he stood, he heard a sweet voice call his name.

"Goldmoon!"

On the opposite side of the chasm, Goldmoon waited, her fine, bright hair and white gown whipping about in the wind. She called to him plaintively. Riverwind felt helpless, desperate to reach her. There was no way across—no bridge, no rope, not even a vine to cling to.

Tall figures emerged behind Goldmoon. One was Loreman, the other, her father, Arrowthorn. They took her by the arms and pulled her back. She fought them, but they were too strong. Riverwind's heart raced. He must get across! He would go back and seek another route.

He turned abruptly, and there was Hollow-sky, grinning fiercely. He had a corpse's pallor, and his clothes were mottled with grave mold. Without a word, they grappled. Riverwind was bigger, but the dead man's strength was inexorable. Riverwind was pushed back. He dug in his toes, bent his knees, tried to get low on Hollow-sky's chest to get better advantage. It didn't help. His heels hung in the air. With one mighty shove, Hollow-sky hurled Riverwind into the chasm.

He hit bottom almost at once. Stunned, he could hardly move. Smoke filled his eyes and nose. The sound of movement filtered through his dazed mind. Riverwind's blood turned to ice water when a howl rent the thick haze.

The wolves! They were all around him. He tried to rise, got to his knees, but they were on him in one savage, silent rush. Riverwind broke their bones with his bare hands, but fangs tore into his arms and legs. The wolves knocked him onto his back and held him there. The largest wolf stalked up to his spread-eagled form. Kyanor. The beast's head lowered, his red eyes boring into Riverwind's. Razor-sharp fangs pierced the plainsman's throat . . .

Riverwind sat up so swiftly that he rapped his elbow against the limestone boulder behind him. A nightmare. His breath came hard and rough, leaving a plume of warm vapor in the mountain air. Not far away, Catchflea snored peacefully.

Be calm, he told himself. It wasn't real.

Or was it?

Somewhere on the dark escarpment, Riverwind heard a rustling noise, followed by a trickle of falling pebbles. The terror from his dream returned, but he mastered it. He'd been helpless in his nightmare. He was definitely not helpless in the waking world.

"Hsst, Catchflea!" he whispered, reaching for his saber. The old man missed a beat in his snoring, then resumed his usual ripsaw rhythm. "Wake up!" Riverwind repeated, punctuating his words with a prod. Catchflea snorted and his eyes batted open.

"Wha—? It's a dark morning, yes?"

"Ssh! There's someone out there!"

"Who could it be? Most travelers avoid the mountains."

"The Nightrunners," Riverwind said grimly.

"The wolves? What shall we do?"

"You do nothing. Stay here!" Riverwind drew his saber in one quick motion and rolled to a standing crouch. Though he listened with all his hunt-honed senses, he heard nothing. The night was still.

None of Krynn's moons shone at that hour, and the stars were feeble lanterns at best. Riverwind surveyed the gently sloping field of stone. It could have been a night-scavenging fox or bird. Or only his imagination, sparked by his terrible dream.

He'd almost convinced himself that there was nothing out there when he heard another sound: the distinct ringing of metal, like chain—or a sword hilt against armor?

The sound came from ahead, on his left. Riverwind pressed close to the perimeter of boulders and worked his way toward the noise.

Something scraped the rock behind him. He swung the saber in a backhand cut. The blade struck the boulder just an inch in front of Catchflea's nose.

"I told you to stay where you were!" Riverwind whispered fiercely.

"I saw something!" hissed the old man.

"What?"

"A blue light, like a will o' the wisp."

"Where?"

Catchflea extended his right arm. "Out there."

"I'll circle left. You stay here, unless you want me to trim that beard of yours the hard way."

Riverwind was a dozen yards away from Catchflea when he saw the eerie blue light. It was small and round, a feeble glow, about knee-high off the ground. It wobbled a bit back and forth, but didn't move away. Riverwind approached in a low crouch. Nearer, he saw a vague shape above the blue light. It was too lightly built to be Kyanor or one of his pack.

Abruptly, the silence of the chase ended when River-wind's quarry stumbled and fell with a loud jingle. He's wearing mail, the plainsman surmised. Gripping his saber tightly, he sprinted toward the light. The broken shale almost cost Riverwind his footing, though, and he skidded but kept his feet.

On the ground was a dimly glowing globe the size of Riverwind's head. Warily, he poked at it with his sword. There was a brass handle affixed. It was some sort of lamp. Riverwind picked it up. The globe was very lightweight. The blue radiance roiled and seethed within as he turned the strange object in his hands. A tingle passed through the handle to Riverwind's arm, so he hastily dropped the globe. This was no time to fool with magical devices.

A shadow darted across open ground a few yards away. Abandoning stealth, Riverwind followed the evasive intruder. The dim figure led him back toward his camp. The interloper paused just long enough to snatch Riverwind's deerskin bag and carry it off.

"Hold there!" the plainsman shouted. "Drop that!"

"He's over this way!" Catchflea cried.

"Get down, Catchflea!"

Riverwind picked up a hefty rock and threw it at the sound of fleeing feet. There was a soft thud and a faint gasp of pain. Riverwind gave a cry of triumph and charged after the intruder. He went only a few steps before bowling into Catchflea.

"Oof! Look out there!"

"Watch your feet—ow! Mind that sword—"

Riverwind untangled himself in time to see the silhouette of the thief as he righted himself and scrambled over a pile of boulders along the eastern rim of the clearing. The phantom had a familiar form: a head, two arms, two legs, but he couldn't tell if it were human, dwarf, or kender. The intruder paused briefly, then leaped over the rocks and was lost from sight.

"Come back with my pack!" Riverwind yelled. Almost all his meager possessions were in that bag.

He and Catchflea got to their feet. "Get the blanket and follow me," Riverwind said hastily. He sheathed his saber and made for the rocks where the thief had gone. The boulders were jagged and brittle, but Riverwind clawed his way to the top. He crouched on the crest and tried to pierce the deep gloom of the ravine below. It was like trying to see into a well of midnight.

A stone flew out of the dark and struck him stingingly on the chin. Losing his balance, Riverwind sat down hard and started to slide. He slowed his descent by digging in his heels, but decided this was as easy a way to get to the bottom of the slope as any.

The slope ended, but instead of the bottom of the hill, Riverwind's feet met empty air. As his legs sailed into space, he tried to grab ground on each side to stop his headlong plunge, but the ground was loose and rocky. Trailing a train of gravel, Riverwind slid off into a void and fell, and fell, and fell.

"Catchflea, look out!" was all he could shout. Agonizing, slow seconds passed as Riverwind fell feet-first into darkness. Any moment, the hard bottom would rush up and smash him, crush the life from his body.

Riverwind flailed his arms and legs, and still he fell, air flowing up, rippling the sleeves of his jerkin and making the tassels on his pants slap against his legs. Riverwind quickly realized something else: he was falling too slowly—far too slowly. His downward speed seemed no more than if he were running at a casual lope. Or was it that the air itself was thick, clinging to him like syrup, retarding his plunge? Something was slowing his fall. Something not natural. Magic.

That realization was frightening enough to make sweat break out on his face. As the fall continued, however, Riverwind overcame his fear. He looked up. He couldn't see the hole he'd fallen into. Around him were vague suggestions of wall moving past, but when he put out an arm to make contact, his balance shifted and he tumbled face over feet. After some frantic scrambling, Riverwind regained his poise. Thereafter he kept his hands at his sides.

He had no idea how long he'd been falling. He had no idea of time. Nothing but the wind and black walls surrounded the falling plainsman. "Where am I falling to?" he asked out loud.

"And how do we get back up?" replied a distant voice above him.

Riverwind called, "Catchflea, is that you?"

"It is me, yes."

"Where are you?"

"I should say thirty feet above you."

Riverwind tried to see him, but it was too dark. "Did you fall into the hole too?" he said loudly.

"No, I jumped after you."

"What!"

"Follow and descend, the acorns told me, yes?"

"Do you do everything those oak nuts tell you?" Riverwind asked.

"Everything, tall man."

Riverwind shook his head ruefully, but, somehow, he felt better knowing he was not completely alone in this bizarre plunge. Catchflea's thin voice drifted down: "How do we get back up?"

A blue glimmer appeared below. Gingerly, Riverwind bent at the waist to see it better. The light was the same color as the strange globe he'd found above. The glimmer grew closer. Then, it—or rather, he—swept past. It was another globe. Just like the first, except that this one was mounted on the wall of the shaft.

The fall went on so long that Riverwind became impatient. The blue globe vanished overhead, though he saw Catchflea outlined briefly in the feeble aura. When another azure dot appeared far below his feet, Riverwind decided to try to knock the globe loose. He wanted to take it with him to provide some illumination. He gauged his position. The sphere should just brush his outstretched fingertips.

His precarious equilibrium failed as he reached farther out. Riverwind crashed into the wall and bounced off. His hand rapped the globe smartly. There was no chance to grab it. The globe jostled free of whatever was holding it in place and, instead of falling with him, floated up and away. It narrowly missed the old man, still falling above Riverwind.

"What was that?" Catchflea cried in alarm. When Riverwind explained, the old man cried, "Don't meddle with them! You could disrupt the spell that cushions our fall."

The air, which had been crisp and cold as they went down, gradually got warmer and heavier. In quick succession, Riverwind passed through several rings of fiery hot stone, radiating dull red heat into the shaft. By this fleeting light he saw that the shaft at this point was about eight feet wide. The walls were smoothly polished.

He heard Catchflea exclaim as he dropped through the hot rings. After a word of encouragement to the old man, Riverwind decided to make one last effort to halt his descent. He drew his knife and attempted to drive it into the hard stone wall. The flame-hardened tip struck sparks, but didn't so much as scratch the dark rock. Riverwind lost his grip and the knife fell from his fingers. It fell far faster than he was going. A few seconds later he heard a clang from below. His knife had hit something. The bottom, perhaps?

All at once the shaft constricted to a narrow neck, as in a funnel. The strange force that restrained his fall brought Riverwind nearly to a halt in midair. Riverwind crossed his arms over his chest and slipped through the shaft's neck, banging his left hip and shoulder smartly before landing in the chamber below. Riverwind's legs folded under him, and stars swam in his eyes.

He lay stunned long enough for something soft to drape over him. By the smell he knew it was his horsehair blanket. Hard on its heels, Catchflea arrived at the funnel mouth. He hung for just a second by his fingers, then let go. The old soothsayer landed with a thud across Riverwind's chest.

"My apologies! You are not hurt, yes?" he gasped.

Riverwind coughed and lifted the skinny old man off him. "Nothing is broken," he replied. "Considering how far we've fallen, we can thank the gods for that." He tried to stand but became dizzy and collapsed again.

"My head is swinging like a dry gourd in the wind," he said, clasping his head between his hands.

"I'm quite giddy myself," Catchflea sputtered. He was lying flat on his back. Lifting an arm to point to the ceiling, he added, "There's the hole we passed through, yes. Do you think we could reach it from here?"

Riverwind rocked back on his haunches to see the aperture overhead. "That's twenty feet up," he said. "Even if you stood on my shoulders, you couldn't reach it." He suddenly realized how well they could see. The chamber was lit by blue globes. The lamps—each about the size of Riverwind's head—were spaced irregularly along the wall. Nearly a dozen were lit, but many others were dark.

The chamber was circular, forty feet across. The walls and floor were black basalt, dense and smooth, speckled with reflective mica. Beyond Catchflea was an open doorway, lit by a blue globe.

The floor had stopped heaving, and Riverwind's knees became solid again. He wobbled to his feet, gave Catchflea a hand, and hauled the old soothsayer up.

"What is this place?" Catchflea asked.

"I cannot tell you. Whatever it is, I don't like it."

"Oh? We are alive, yes?"

"Yes, but for how long? How will we get out of here?" Riverwind muttered. He limped to the wall and touched a glowing orb lightly with a fingertip. The stable light writhed within its sphere, arcing from side to side as if to avoid the spot Riverwind had touched.

"What are these things?" he wondered aloud. Catchflea was at one of the others. He lifted it off the cup-shaped base carved in the rock of the wall and held the globe at arm's length.

"At least we have light," the old man said. "Shall we go?"

Riverwind pulled his hand away from the seething luminescence and the light quieted. "Where?"

"To look for a way out, yes."

Catchflea picked up Riverwind's blanket, rolled it tightly, and tossed the resulting bundle over his shoulder. Riverwind drew his saber and started into the tunnel. "Don't you want a lamp?" asked Catchflea.

"No. There's something disquieting about those things."

Riverwind stepped into the passage. The tunnel stretched far ahead. At odd intervals a globe could be seen glowing. There were others that were dark. He scanned the ceiling and walls for some clue as to who could have made this place. What sort of strange creatures lived in this dismal underground place?

The floor sloped slightly downward. Riverwind raised a hand to his mouth to call out, but Catchflea prudently reminded him to keep quiet. "I've heard all manner of tales about evil creatures that dwell in the ground—miner goblins, kobolds, tommyknockers. Those who intrude on their domain seldom live to tell of it." Riverwind glanced back. The old man's face was pale and bloodless by the blue glow of the odd lamp. He wasn't jesting. Riverwind advanced more slowly, and kept his back to the cold, hard wall.

Aside from the strange lamps, there was little to see in the tunnel. The ceiling was arched, and whoever had cut the tunnel was evidently shorter than Riverwind. He had to crouch low to avoid the projecting globes. A light coat of dust covered the floor. Riverwind noticed his own footprints when he turned to speak to Catchflea.

"Put the light on the floor, old man," he said intently. "I want to see something."

They squatted in the center of the passage. "See, here are the marks of my moccasin boots," Riverwind said. His large, flat soles made broad smudges in the gray dust. "And these are yours." Catchflea's ragged footwear, laced up bits of leather and cloth, made distinctive prints.

"And there," Riverwind pointed, "is a third set." He spoke in a whisper.

Sure enough, a third set of feet had passed that way. The prints were quite normal-looking, though small and slim. A child, perhaps? The third one had preceded the two men, and had gone right down the center of the corridor. At a run, too; the toeprints were widely spaced and the heel print was almost nonexistent.

"The thief, yes?" whispered Catchflea. Riverwind nodded solemnly. The intruder had deliberately jumped into the hole, knowing the magic spell would lower him to this place. He and Catchflea were on the thief's own terrain now. Caution was paramount.

Riverwind hefted his saber, and they resumed the advance.

The tunnel bent sharply to the right. The globes here were dark, leaving Riverwind and Catchflea in blackness. Despite the mild temperature, the warrior sweated. It was oppressive, the close confines of the tunnel, especially when Riverwind considered all that rock over his head, heavy and impenetrable, pressing in, pressing down on him. Riverwind straightened his hunched posture slightly, and his head connected with the roof. Solid. Unyielding.

"Is the tunnel getting smaller?" he said tightly.

"Not that I can tell," Catchflea replied.

Riverwind moved uncomfortably. He could not stand straight in the tunnel. "Plainsmen were not meant to be moles," he muttered. He turned to Catchflea. "I want out of here. I want to see the sky, feel the wind on my face. I want to stand up straight!"

"How will you get there, tall man? Fly up the shaft, yes?" Riverwind had an angry retort ready, but the old man smiled disarmingly. "Your fear is not real, my friend. There is no present danger."

"I feel—closed in!"

"So you are, as am I. Pay no attention to it. I have mastered my fear. If I can do it, you can, yes."

Riverwind took several deep breaths. The old soothsayer was right. This tunnel was solid, in no danger of collapsing. There was no reason to be afraid. He said it aloud: "There is no reason to be afraid."

Light footfalls sounded ahead of them. Catchflea caught Riverwind's arm, eyes wide with alarm. Riverwind nodded. The thief was not far away. If he could navigate in this inky hole, so could the son of Wanderer.

"You, thief! Stand where you are!" Riverwind roared. The sound was deafening in the tunnel. The steps seemed to cease, then resumed rapidly. The odd metallic ringing was louder than before. "Follow," Riverwind said to Catchflea. He jogged down the passage with his saber in his hand. The floor sloped downward more steeply here. Riverwind slowed. He wasn't going to be tricked into another hole.

The tunnel bent back to the left. A misshapen shadow skittered crazily across the wall. When it vanished, so too did the thief's footsteps fade. Riverwind sidled around the corner and was dazzled by bright light. He threw up a hand to shade his eyes.

"What is it?" hissed Catchflea from around the corner.

"A room. The light is bright!" Gradually his eyes became accustomed to the illumination. Riverwind lowered his hand. "Come along, Catchflea, and be quiet."

They slipped into a very large, high-ceilinged chamber. The light came from a huge, disk-shaped lamp that hung from the ceiling by brass chains. Fire flickered within, flooding the room with light. Riverwind inched along the wall, his eyes going left and right.

The room was irregularly shaped. All around them were piles of goods of every description. Things seemed to be sorted according to what they were made of. There was a lot of wood: poles, tool handles, clapboards, shingles, beams of considerable thickness with the mortise holes still showing. Beyond the wooden goods were heaps of leather items: old shoes, boots gray with mildew, belts, gloves, leggings, arrow quivers, peaked caps such as foresters wore, thongs, lacings, a hodgepodge of hide products ranging in quality from the very decrepit to the pristine.

And there was more. Wicker baskets and glazed pottery. Jars of tar, beeswax, and soap. In all, the chamber resembled a merchant's warehouse.

Riverwind and Catchflea wandered among the piles of stuff, pondering the wisdom of thieves who stole old shoes instead of gold. While Riverwind headed to the right, the old man went left down a narrow aisle. There, discarded carelessly with three rolls of homespun linen, was Riverwind's bag. The lacing was still drawn tight, the contents untouched.

"Over here! I found it!" Catchflea called hoarsely.

With his height, Riverwind was able to see over most of the piles. He found Catchflea and gratefully slipped the bag's strap over his shoulder.

"There's wood aplenty here. Maybe we could build some sort of ladder?" Catchflea said. He reached under the hem of his tattered shirt for the gourd and acorns.

"What are you doing?"

Catchflea knelt on the stone floor. "Trying to find out what we should do," he said. He began the invocation over the acorns. Another sound—droning voices—drifted to them.

"Someone's coming," Riverwind whispered. "No time for that now." Out came the saber.

The welter of voices, echoing through the tunnel, grew

louder. The speakers seemed unconcerned about being heard, for they were talking in loud, harsh voices.

Riverwind motioned to Catchflea to stay put, then tip-toed around a pile of sawn planks and climbed up the side. Lying prone on the top planks, Riverwind peered over the end. Six figures poured into the next aisle. Five wore bright steel armor on their chests and legs. Their helmets were curious, shaped like tall, divided cones. The sixth person was smaller and wore a loose shirt and kilt made of some shimmering black fabric. The neck of the shirt rose up in a cowl that covered his face in shadows. He was held firmly in the grip of one of the larger figures. He spoke in tremulous tones.

Riverwind did not understand their speech. These folk spoke like no one he'd ever heard before.

The loudest soldier, who had to be the leader, stood gazing around the room. He made a sharp demand of the little one in black. When an answer was not forthcoming, the leader rapped him with a short metal baton. Riverwind frowned. He didn't like cruelty, whatever its logic.

The little fellow spoke slowly, gesturing at the array of goods around him. With rapid, angry words, the leader pointed in the direction Riverwind and Catchflea had come, and then to the way they themselves had entered. The small one made plaintive sounds. The leader seized him by the shirt and flung him into the arms of the other soldiers. They dragged the protesting fellow away.

Riverwind climbed down and got Catchflea from his hiding place under the homespun. Come with me, he signed to the old man. Say nothing.

They skulked along an aisle parallel to the soldiers and their cringing captive, always keeping bales of booty between them. In the heart of the chamber was an open space. There, two soldiers forced the captive to his knees. The leader approached from the side with his sword raised.

Riverwind acted. He knew a pending execution when he saw one.

"Ha!" he cried, springing into the clear. The soldiers started back. They were considerably shorter than the plainsman, whose height seemed to intimidate them. They drew stubby swords and closed together, armored shoulders clanking as they fell into line. Their helmets were closed with hammered metal visors resembling very stylized faces, with embossed grimaces and chiseled eyebrows. The condemned fellow, whose features were still hidden by the drooping cowl, pointed excitedly at Riverwind and chattered volubly. Riverwind didn't need an interpreter to understand a triumphant "I told you so!"

The soldiers' leader stood forward. He raised his short, heavy-bladed weapon.

"Well, now, bully," Riverwind said. "You're fine with unarmed boys. Let's see how you do with me."

He was easily two feet taller than they, and his saber twice as long as their short swords. Still, there were five of them. The leader barked an order at his men. They fanned out behind Riverwind and presented the blunt points of their swords.

"My friend," said Riverwind to the reprieved victim. "I've saved your neck, but it may cost me my own." The little fellow, still on his knees, regarded the warrior with a quizzical tilt of his head. "I hope you're a good person. I'd hate to die saving a scoundrel."

The leader attacked, slashing overhand at Riverwind's chest. Riverwind parried and gave ground. The other soldiers joined in halfheartedly. Riverwind scowled and shouted at them, and they flinched, never closing to a threatening distance.

He traded cuts with the leader, at one point scraping his saber on the bizarre leering helmet. The leader staggered back, shaking his head. Riverwind pressed home, shouting a Que-Shu war cry that made the chamber ring.

Then, two quick surprises changed the odds of the battle. The small, unarmed stranger got off his knees and leaped quickly out of the way as the fighting threatened to overwhelm him. As he flung himself out of harm's way, the cowl that had heretofore covered his face fell back. Riverwind glanced at him and halted in surprise. "He" was a she! A crop of short, spiky hair ruffled out of the black cowl and stood straight up on her head. Her skin was pale ivory, and her eyes enormous and black. Her pointed ears stood out

43

from her close-cut hair. Riverwind had never seen an elf before, but he'd heard enough about them to know he was looking at a girl of elvish blood.

At that precise moment, Catchflea appeared, a knout of wood in his hand. He'd heard Riverwind's war cry and was rallying to help. "I'm with you, tall man!" he shouted gamely.

Unfortunately for Catchflea, the four timid soldiers were between him and Riverwind. They obviously decided the daft-looking old man couldn't be very dangerous, so they swarmed him. The firewood was struck from his hand, and down he went.

Riverwind had stared too long at the elf girl. The soldiers' leader struck him from behind with the baton. Riverwind fell against a stack of clay pots and sent them clattering to the stone floor. Before he could regain his feet in the potsherds, the leader advanced and struck the plainsman again on the head. The burning lantern flared wildly in Riverwind's eyes, then all was dark.

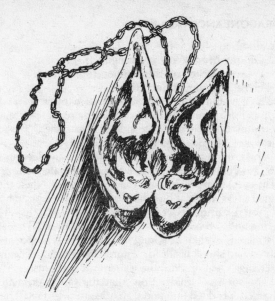

Chapter 4

Di An

The soldiers dragged Catchflea and Riverwind out of the chamber, to a wide corridor, and dumped them against the wall. The black-eyed elf girl knelt by Riverwind and put the neck of a copper bottle to his lips. He coughed and opened his eyes.

"By the gods!" he sputtered. "Is that water or brine?" The girl kept the bottle at his mouth even when he tried to turn his face away. His hands were chained tightly to his sides.

"Enough!" he said and shoved the bottle with his head. The girl took the bottle away. She tugged Catchflea to a sitting position and gave him some salty water, too. The old soothsayer choked and shook his head.

"Are you trying to poison me?" he said groggily.

"It's all right, Catchflea," Riverwind said. "She means to

be kind."

"Oh, my head. What happened?"

"We were bested by these underground elves."

"Elves!" exclaimed Catchflea.

"So it would seem. Did you not notice the girl's features?"

Catchflea squinted at the spiky-haired creature, now withdrawn to the opposite side of the tunnel. "Branchala bless me," he said. "You're right, tall man."

The gruff leader appeared. He flipped the leering visor up. His countenance was like the girl's—pale skin, prominent eyes, sharp chin, and long, thin nose. When the girl piped a few words at him, he raised his baton as if to hit her.

"You're a brute," Riverwind said matter-of-factly. "A blustering bully who beats on defenseless children." The leader, distracted, rattled off a long interrogative sentence at him. Riverwind shook his head. "I don't understand." The useless exchange went on until the leader quit in disgust.

The soldiers, bolder now that the tall plainsman was chained, prodded him and Catchflea to their feet. The tunnel ceiling here was even lower than the one before. Riverwind's head bumped the black stone. He had a momentary rush of claustrophobia, but it receded quickly. He didn't want to show any weakness in front of his captors.

The girl and the leader led them down the passage. Riverwind stumbled along, back bent and arms tied. Catchflea was likewise chained. Blue globes lit the way, but there were as many that did not shine. Riverwind wondered what fueled the strange spheres, and why so many were dark.

"Where do you think they're taking us?" asked the old man.

"To the surface, I hope," Riverwind replied.

"In Silvanesti, yes?"

"That I can't even guess at."

One of the soldiers trailing Catchflea decided to trip him. The old soothsayer sprawled hard on the floor, bashing his nose. Blood flowed from one nostril to his tangled beard.

Riverwind turned around. The four elves had their visors open, and one had a smirk on his face. Riverwind lashed out with one long leg and caught the smirker in the chest. Propelled by the powerful kick, the elf sailed back into the darkness and landed with a jingle of falling metal. His comrades laughed, and even the leader smiled.

"At least they've some idea of fair play," Riverwind said. Catchflea got to his feet shakily.

"And a rough sense of humor, yes," he said sourly.

The girl dropped back from the leader's heels and walked slightly ahead of Riverwind. He said, "I wonder why a child like this is off prowling dark tunnels?"

"She may not be a child. Elves are longer lived than us."

"Oh?"

Catchflea coughed. "This child might be a hundred or more years old," he said.

As the two men spoke, the girl studied them both unblinkingly. Most of her attention was for Riverwind. He kept his voice as calm and unthreatening as he could.

"Thank you for the water," he said. "If water it was. It wasn't as bad as Arrowthorn's nepta berries, at any rate."

The girl rubbed the tip of her nose. He wished she hadn't; it made his itch, and he couldn't scratch.

"What's your name?" asked Riverwind. "I am Riverwind, son of Wanderer. This is Catchstar—"

"Catchflea," corrected the old man.

"We are Que-Shu. Who are you?" finished Riverwind.

She yawned, displaying small white teeth and a carrot-colored tongue.

"I'm wasting my breath, aren't I?"

"You are, yes," Catchflea said.

"At least my head's still on my shoulders." Riverwind gave the girl a slight smile. "And yours too."

The tunnel zigged and zagged through the bowels of Krynn. So far did they travel that Riverwind had a fleeting thought that he might end up returning to Que-Shu, only miles underground. Of course, he had no idea which direction they were traveling, or how far underground they actually were, or where Que-Shu was, for that matter.

The trail was so narrow in some parts that the party had to go single file. This was awkward for Catchflea, but awkward in the extreme for Riverwind, being as tall as he was and not having the use of his arms. Both men bumped their heads and barked their knees on sharp outcroppings. The girl doubled back at one point and took hold of Riverwind's chain. She steered him gently through the obstacles, never saying a word. When the tunnel finally broadened again, she left Riverwind with the leader and went back to bring Catchflea along. She was not so careful with him, and he protested loudly.

"We see who her favorite is, yes?" the old man said grumpily. His nose had stopped bleeding, but he had fresh gouges on his shins.

"Maybe it's your beard," Riverwind said. "These elves don't seem to favor facial hair."

"Barbarians," the old man muttered.

The dead air of the corridor freshened. A definite breeze, warm and scented with a smoky tang, washed Riverwind's face. The blue globes were more numerous, and the men could see that they had descended below the strata of basalt into a more mixed realm. Crystals glinted in the walls, and streaks of red and purple stone showed in the worn floor. There were signs of water, too; ruts eroded along the right side of the passage emitted a moldy odor.

After one more sharp turn to the right, the tunnel ended. The gloom of the close passage gave way to brighter air. Riverwind straightened his back and stopped walking. The girl tugged vainly on his chain. He would not budge. He was taking in a sight of great wonder.

"Catchflea" was all he could say. The old man stood by Riverwind's shoulder, mouth agape.

They had arrived in a vast cavern, several miles long and at least a mile wide. It was a true cave, with mighty stalactites twenty feet long hanging from the roof, four hundred feet overhead. On the distant right side of the cave was a rough opening to another cavern, also filled with light.

The cave's floor was broad and flat, forested with garishly hued stalagmites. Yellow, blue-white, and orange concretions sprouted from the floor. Even more remarkable was the truly enormous number of blue globes that clustered on the conical towers of stone. Riverwind couldn't begin to count them. Many were dark, but enough were lit with their unnatural, moving light to make the cavern as bright as the Que-Shu village at twilight.

The elf leader unsnapped a catch on the neck of his helmet and removed the headgear. He had broad shoulders for his height, and these rose and fell when he sighed. The leader's hair was long and shining white, though his face gave no clue as to his age. In a conversational tone, he spoke at length to the two men. He gestured at the great cavern and sighed once more.

A path had been cut through the stalagmites. Once away from the tunnel mouth, the girl bolted free of the soldiers and ran. Two of the trailing soldiers started after her, but the leader called them back.

"I'm sorry to see her go," Riverwind said. "Hers was the only spark of kindness I've seen in these people."

"I hope she runs far, yes. Then they cannot hurt her," Catchflea observed.

The breeze was stronger in the upper end of the cave. Tinkling chimes of bronze and copper hung from thin chains between the peaks of the stalagmites. Catchflea was enchanted by the sound. He wandered unconsciously toward the chimes, until the soldiers steered him back. They were less brutal this time. The cave seemed to inspire a mood Riverwind could only think of as reverence.

The acrid smell was more pronounced in the cavern. A yellowish haze hung in the air near the roof, swirling around the hanging spires. The odor reminded Riverwind of a blacksmith's forge—burning coal and hot metal.

The path broadened near the arched opening into the next cavern. The leader pointed into the new cave and said one word: "Vartoom."

"What does he mean?" asked Riverwind.

"Vartoom," the leader repeated. "Vartoom."

"Sounds like a name, yes," Catchflea said. Raising his voice, he said, "I understand; your home is Vartoom, yes?"

"Vartoom," said the leader, then resumed his march.

Where the first cave ended and the second began there was a deep chasm, too deep to estimate. Across this gulf was a narrow bridge of stone. The leader walked quickly onto the span, though it was no wider than his own foot. He urged Riverwind to follow. *"Moyun!"*

The plainsman balked.

"I can't balance on a narrow track like that!" Riverwind said. "Not with my arms bound!" The leader waved and repeated the word "*moyun*" to him.

Catchflea looked over the edge and blanched. "Mercy!" he gasped. "We can't do it!"

"They don't understand that we'll get dizzy and fall," Riverwind said. The soldier behind him gave him a little push. "No," he said, planting his feet. "I'll fall." The elf pushed harder. Riverwind snapped his head around and scowled at him. "NO!" he said more loudly. The soldier fell back to his fellows, muttering nervously. The leader kept repeating "*moyun*," with less and less patience.

"Take off our chains and we'll follow. You needn't bind us. There's no place for us to escape to," Riverwind said, twisting to present his chains to the leader. The gist of his meaning seemed to penetrate the language barrier. The leader crossed back briskly and untwisted the length of wire that secured the ends of the chain. Riverwind shrugged off his bonds and rubbed some feeling back into his chafed arms. On a word from their leader, the elf soldiers drew swords while the leader freed Catchflea.

"I don't think they trust us," the old man said.

"*Moyun*," said the leader.

The ramp was not only narrow, it was also glass-smooth. The soles of Riverwind's deerskin boots slipped on the treacherous surface. Catchflea essayed a few steps on the dizzy bridge, then backed off. A soldier poked him in the stomach with his sword point. Catchflea yelped and bounded away.

"Let me have my shoes off, yes?" he screeched, pointing at his feet. The elves watched impassively as he unwound the rags that held his cobbled-up bits of leather on his feet. On the bridge he proceeded more surely, gripping the cold stone with his bare toes. The soldiers, shod in metal-studded sandals, came nonchalantly after him.

Despite a few scary slips, Riverwind made it across. The leader, hands planted on hips, frowned at his awkward progress. He said something that sounded sarcastic. Riverwind was glad he didn't understand the words. The tone was insulting enough.

The ground on the other side of the bridge was carefully terraced in a series of broad, low steps. The stalagmites had been hammered off at elven shoulder height—Riverwind's waist level—and the flat stump tops decorated with delicate metal sculptures. Catchflea was intrigued, especially by the abstract ones. Coils of brass wire, silver bells, and rods of green-patinated copper, all balanced on pinpoint bases, moved gently in the wind. Catchflea put out one thin hand to touch the airy treasures.

A soldier smote him across the shoulders with the flat of his blade. Outraged, Riverwind whirled and grabbed the offender by his polished backplate and hauled him off his feet. Armor and all, the elf probably weight one hundred and fifty pounds. Riverwind hoisted him over his head and held him there. The elf howled in fear and anger. The leader brandished his sword and spoke imperious commands.

"You want him down?" Riverwind puffed. "Have him then!" He heaved the squirming bully at the remaining two soldiers. The elf landed with a crash, though his comrades were timely in their dodge.

Breathing hard from the exertion, Riverwind said to the leader, "If you want to abuse us, at least give us swords, so we can fight like men!" The head elf yelled right back at him. The debate was still raging when the elven girl returned.

All fell silent. The girl was not alone. Beside her was a rather tall elf, dressed in an ankle-length skirt of shimmering copper thread. His hair, like that of the soldiers' leader, was white. His thin, pale chest was bare, and he wore a necklace of copper tubes strung radially around his neck.

The leader of the soldiers snapped something angry at the newcomer. The skirted elf replied in soothing fashion and gestured at the girl. She shrank away from the soldier, speaking in pleading tones. Riverwind was fascinated by the interplay, even though he couldn't fathom the tongue.

Catchflea had recovered from his blow. Coughing, he joined Riverwind. "Why did he do that? I only meant to touch the bells, yes?"

"Who knows? Perhaps touching them is taboo." He pointed to the skirted elf. "This one looks like a priest."

"He sounds kindly," Catchflea said. Riverwind agreed,

though for all he knew, the two elves could be arguing over who'd get to execute them.

The soft-spoken "priest" elf reached into a hidden pocket in his skirt and brought out two bits of jewelry. The girl bowed her head with great deference and took both pieces. She approached Riverwind and held one up for him to see: it was an amulet, wrought in gold, which fit neatly in her small hand. At first Riverwind thought it was made to represent a butterfly, but upon closer inspection he saw it was actually a likeness of two elfin ears joined in the center.

"You want me to wear this? A gift?" he asked. Riverwind had to bend far down to get within the small girl's reach. She dropped the chain over his head. He straightened, and the heavy amulet swung against his chest.

"Thank you," he said.

"You are welcome," she replied.

"I understand you!"

"As you should. You wear the Sign of True Hearing, which makes our words known to you." The girl's eyes were bright on his face. "My name is Di An."

"I am Riverwind, son of Wanderer, of the Que-Shu."

Catchflea tugged impatiently on his sleeve. "What is it?" Riverwind asked.

"*Gug murga lokil la,*" said Catchflea. Riverwind stared. He couldn't make out a thing his companion said. "*Grom sust idi wock!*"

"Let me give him a Sign also," Di An said. She hung an identical amulet around Catchflea's neck.

"—supposed to get by with no one to talk to? I'll go mad, yes?"

"Ho there, old one; can you understand me now?" Riverwind said.

Catchflea blinked rapidly. "By my ancestors! So I can."

"This is not proper," the elf leader said darkly. "The intruders would have been easier to control if they didn't know what we were saying."

"If you cannot persuade, you cannot control," said the skirted elf. He faced the Que-Shu men and smiled. "I am Vvelz. I greet you in the name of the Hall of Light." The head soldier harumphed. "And this impatient person is Karn, lieutenant of the Host."

"Who are you people?" Riverwind said.

"We are the people of Hest," Vvelz said.

"What is this place?" asked Catchflea.

"We are near the city of Vartoom. We shall all be going there soon."

More questions formed on Riverwind's lips, but Karn said, My mistress awaits our return." To Vvelz he muttered, "I shall tell Her Highness of your meddling."

Vvelz dismissed him with a wave. "Do what you will. It is I who sits at Li El's right hand, not you." Karn snorted and pushed Riverwind and Catchflea into motion.

A few yards down the terrace steps a horseless wagon stood on level ground. Karn, his soldiers, and the two humans mounted the open back. Vvelz stood by the empty trace poles. After a nod from Karn, he raised thin white arms over his head. Though his lips never moved, Vvelz's voice rang inside Riverwind's head, commanding: *Come hither, diggers, and take up your burden.* Riverwind's head reeled as the command was repeated. He felt as if he'd been struck a blow. To Catchflea he said, "Did you feel that?"

"Not only us," the old man replied. "Look!"

One by one, small elven figures clad in black appeared. Di An joined them. They approached Vvelz like sleepwalkers, their eyes glazed, their arms limp at their sides. At additional commands from Vvelz, the elves arranged themselves at the handles attached to the twin trace poles. Ten black-clad elves, male and female, filled the spaces at the handles. Vvelz climbed in the wagon with the others.

"Where to, Karn?" he said cheerily.

Karn gave him a sour glare.

Vvelz shrugged and lifted his hands. *To the palace, and be quick!* The elves bent their backs, and the wagon lurched forward. Riverwind had a strong urge to leap over the side and join them, for Vvelz's words resonated in his mind with awful persistence. Only as miles passed beneath the wagon's wheels did the strange compulsion fade.

Catchflea was likewise gripping the side rail tightly, looking dazed. Karn studied their reactions closely. Riverwind mastered himself, and focused his mind on the black-garbed elves hauling the wagon along.

"Are these people slaves?" he asked. "I loathe slavery; it is a wicked institution."

"They are diggers," Karn said laconically.

Catchflea said to Vvelz, "You are a sorcerer, yes?"

Vvelz inclined his head. "I am a fellow of the Hall of Light, just as Karn is a fellow of the Hall of Arms. Those who do not qualify for either house remain diggers."

Riverwind was outraged. Turning his gaze from the straining backs of the diggers to Vvelz, he said, "Who speaks for the diggers? Who protects them and champions their needs?"

Karn laughed. "They get what they need," he quipped.

"We look after them," Vvelz said calmly. "They are very important to us."

"As a farmer tends his beasts?"

"More like a father tending his children." Vvelz glanced at the diggers. "Every Hestite has the chance to enter the Hall of Light or the Hall of Arms, once they reach adult age. Those with strength and agility take up the sword; those with wit and magical talent apprentice as sorcerers. Those with none of these traits work as diggers."

Riverwind was not mollified. Before he did serious harm by insulting their captors, Catchflea interrupted.

"Am I correct in thinking you are elves?" he asked.

Vvelz recoiled so sharply that his flowing silver hair lashed across his shoulders. "You must not speak that word!"

"It is forbidden!" added Karn. His hand moved toward his sword.

Riverwind and Catchflea exchanged a glance. "You will forgive me, yes?" the soothsayer said. "I did not know."

Riverwind noticed that while Vvelz was agitated, the diggers pushed the wagon faster. Somehow his will acted like a spur to drive them on. Some of the diggers stumbled trying to keep up. The plainsman saw Di An, the smallest elf present, slip from her handhold as larger diggers outstripped her effort. She grabbed futilely at the handle as it tore away. She fell. The diggers behind her trod mindlessly over her.

Riverwind vaulted over the side and ran ahead of the iron-shod wheels. He shoved his way through the diggers and snatched up Di An mere seconds before the front right wheel would have cut her in two.

Vvelz halted the wagon. "Is she hurt?" he inquired.

Riverwind brushed grit from the girl's face. She was featherlight in his arms. "Bruises only. I will put her in back."

"No," Karn said sternly. "Diggers do not ride with warriors."

"Then I shall carry her."

And he did. The diggers reformed and fell to heaving the wagon again. Riverwind strode alongside with Di An cradled in his arms. Shamed to ride, Catchflea stepped down and shuffled ahead to keep pace with his companion.

"If you walk, tall man, I walk," he said.

Di An groaned and stirred. She came to, and when she saw where she was, she thrashed wildly.

"Please! Put me down!" she cried.

"It's all right," Riverwind said gently. "I have you."

"No! I must pull with my brothers!" She squirmed out of his grasp.

"You were hurt, child. Take your ease a while, yes?" Catchflea said.

"I cannot! The High Ones command us serve, and I must—" Tears streaked her face. "You're hurting me."

Riverwind opened his arms, and Di An dropped to the ground. Before the astonished men could say anything, the elf girl was back in her place, hunched over the trace pole of the heavy wagon.

"You see," called Karn from the wagon, "Hestites know their place."

Catchflea grabbed Riverwind's arm. The plainsman was taut with barely suppressed anger. "Be prudent, tall man," he hissed. "We are strangers in a very strange country. Let's listen twice before we answer once, yes?"

Riverwind nodded curtly. "You're pretty wise for a fool who talks to acorns," he muttered. Riverwind put a hand on Catchflea's shoulder and, together, they walked on toward the underground city of Vartoom.

Chapter 5

City of Smoke and Fire

They rolled across a spacious plain, wider than the previous cavern and with a much higher ceiling. Clouds actually formed in the upper reaches, muting the light from the enormous brazen sphere that blazed at the peak of the cavern's vaulted roof. The plain was carpeted with floury gray soil and, most remarkably, grass and flowers. They were not like any plants the Que-Shu men had ever seen before. Their stems and leaves were a listless gray-green, and the flower petals were brilliant shades of orange, pink, and yellow. After receiving a nod from Vvelz, Catchflea plucked a gaudy pink blossom and put it to his nose.

"No smell," he said.

"It doesn't look real," Riverwind remarked. He rubbed the petals with his thumb. "I'd swear it's painted!"

The way was carefully laid out by fitted blocks of gray granite, so old and worn that the wagon's wheels fit neatly into ruts in the stone made by countless wheels before. The smoky smell was much stronger on the plain. It was enough to make Riverwind's nostrils burn.

"What is that odor?" he asked over his shoulder.

"Is there an odor?" Vvelz replied lightly.

"The giant smells our foundries," Karn said contemptuously. "They displease his delicate nose."

"Do you have many foundries?"

"Indeed, yes. We make everything we need of metal or minerals," the sorcerer said.

The grassland ended. On each side of the road, dwarfing wagon, elves, and men alike, were great conical piles of broken rock and cinders. These were mine tailings, Vvelz explained. This was the unusable residue that remained after the ores were fired to give up their metal.

"So much of it," Catchflea marveled. The tailings rose one hundred feet and more, and were over twice as wide at the base. Hundreds of piles crowded alongside the road, sometimes spilling over onto the granite pavement. The diggers tramped on, even when the glassy cinders cut through their flimsy copper mesh sandals. Riverwind saw the bloody footprints and said nothing. He ached to up-end the wagon and its haughty occupants. His hands clenched into fists. But no, Catchflea was right. Prudence demanded he keep his temper in check.

The tailings went on for miles. Hour after hour they traveled, and Riverwind felt oppressed by the dismal scene. It was so poisoned, so lifeless. While the soldiers and Vvelz sipped from silver bottles, the diggers' feet churned up a cloud of thick gray dust. It powdered their black garments. Where sweat ran down their skin, dust collected, streaking their arms and faces with noxious, gritty paste. Legs aching, Riverwind longed for the clear blue sky and fresh breezes of the upper world.

Around a bend they came upon a gang of diggers adding to the mine rubbish. A slab-sided hopper on iron wheels was being tipped forward by a dozen elves equipped with long metal rods. They braced their rods against the top lip of the hopper and pushed. The car swung up, axles screeching. A shower of blackened clinker poured out on the side of a mound, which was already fifty feet tall. Other diggers swarmed over the half-emptied hopper. Riverwind and Catchflea stared at the filthy laborers as they walked past. The diggers returned the gaze with blank, humorless faces. To his dismay, Riverwind noted that there were at least twelve more hoppers brimming with dirt and ash lined up behind the first one. The diggers had many hours of sweaty, back-breaking labor ahead of them.

The region of tailings abruptly ended with a high stone wall. There was no gate to block the road, only a wide opening in the wall. The wall itself was easily sixty feet high, and ten feet thick at the base. All sorts of stones had been used in its construction.

"A strange rampart," Riverwind said. "What does it defend?"

"Nothing," Karn said. "The Hall of Arms protects Hest with sword, not with stone walls."

Vvelz cleared his throat. "The giant asks a legitimate question. Tell him what the wall is for."

"I see no reason to tell our business to any overgrown foreigner who asks," Karn snapped.

"It isn't a state secret," Vvelz said dryly.

"It's to hold back the dirt, yes?" said Catchflea. "The remains of your mining?"

Vvelz nodded. "Precisely. In times past, the tailings crept too close to the city. Our springs were poisoned and our crops endangered. Then the wise master of the Hall of Light, the venerated Kosti, decreed that a wall be built to hold back the debris."

"And when was this?" asked Riverwind, looking back to survey the piles of tailings.

"One thousand, six hundred and forty-two years ago."

Catchflea tripped in the wheel rut, he was so astonished. Riverwind steadied the old soothsayer. "I had no idea this place was so long settled," he said.

"Ah, we are a very ancient people," Vvelz said. Karn folded his arms and made growling noises.

Inside the wall, the scenery was brighter. They were almost directly under the great bronze lantern that lighted the entire cavern. Another wall loomed ahead, lower and thinner. This wall was dotted with nasty spikes along the top. As the wagon drew abreast of the gap in the second wall, Vvelz halted the diggers. They shuffled to a stop and lay over the wagon handles, gasping for breath.

"Vartoom," said Vvelz, lifting his hand in a graceful gesture.

The city merged with the cavern wall to the left, but the panorama Riverwind and Catchflea beheld was astonishing. The rising ground was sculpted into broad terraces, and on these level platforms the dwellings of the Hestites were built. The lowest terrace was a crowded warren of rough limestone and basalt, with small, round windows and smudgy, smoking chimneys. The intermediate levels—of which Riverwind counted seven—were more orderly arrangements of white-veined granite. These houses were carved on the outside with graceful fluting, whorls, and bas-reliefs. The doors were of brightly burnished copper.

But it was the topmost terraces that caused the Que-Shu men to gape in awe. Two hundred feet above the basest dwellings rose spires of translucent alabaster and marble. The spires joined together in complexly carved facades, designed to look like knotted cords or the roots of a gigantic tree. The massive columns climbed upwards many hundred feet to the roof of the cavern, there growing into the ancient, vibrant stalactites.

"Amazing," said Catchflea at last.

"There is no other city that can rival it," Vvelz said proudly. "As diamonds and precious metals are found underground, so the crown jewel of Krynn is found in this cavern."

He turned back to the panting diggers and once more called to them in his telepathic voice: *Attend and be quick! Push!* Though Riverwind heard Vvelz's command, it seemed less intense than before. Perhaps he was getting used to it. The wagon creaked along with Riverwind and Catchflea in its wake.

Ramps led from the cavern floor up to the first terrace level. The tired diggers faltered on the slope. None of the soldiers stepped out to lighten the load.

"Can't you do better?" Karn said impatiently to Vvelz. "Spur them on." The sorcerer clenched his upraised fists.

Push! Ignore the strain—sweet rest awaits you in the city. Push! Push! He lashed at them psychically. The diggers buried their cut and bleeding feet in the dry cinders of the roadbed. They churned and writhed at the handles, but the grade was too much for them. Finally, Vvelz relented and summoned other diggers to assist.

> *Listen who can*
> *Come hither and bend*
> *Your backs to our task.*
> *The vassals of Her Highness*
> *Are needed with haste.*

Thirty elves, all clad in digger black, filed down the ramp. Some got behind the wagon to push, others packed in around the crowded trace poles to help pull.

Riverwind dug an elbow in Catchflea's side. "I'm going to help," he said. The old man unhesitatingly followed the tall warrior. They leaned over the backs of the shorter diggers and planted their hands against the rear of the wagon. The diggers paid them no mind, but the soldiers snickered and made rude comments.

"Ugh—pay them no mind," Catchflea said. "Oof!"

Riverwind narrowed his eyes at the soldiers. "No proper warrior despises hard labor," he grunted. "No man is better than the work he does with his own hands."

The slope eventually vanished, and the wagon rolled forward in a rush. Vvelz dispersed the diggers and stepped down from his place. Karn and the soldiers followed.

"Why have we stopped?" Karn asked.

"I thought it would be instructive for the giants to see the city in a more leisurely fashion," Vvelz replied smoothly. "We can always get more drudges if we need them."

The broad street that fronted the terrace was thick with diggers. They paid little attention to Riverwind and Catchflea, but moved about their tasks with heads downcast and shoulders drooping. Catchflea watched them intently, his wizened face a mix of pity and thoughtful speculation.

"They have no wills of their own," Riverwind said. To Vvelz, he added, "Is it magic that keeps them docile?"

"Certainly not! The common folk of Hest are diligent and loyal to their masters. No magic compunction is necessary. Oh, we do use the Call and the Summons on them, but only to give them direction and purpose. The diggers are docile because they are content."

Riverwind could not believe it. He recalled Di An's frantic scramble to resume her place pulling the wagon. Fear made people act that way, not loyalty.

"Enough idle wagging," Karn said. He raised his sword an inch out of its scabbard and slammed it back down. "Her Highness awaits!"

The soldiers formed around the Que-Shu men, two behind and one on each side. Vvelz and Karn led the way. They had not gone half a dozen steps before one of the trailing soldiers called out to Karn.

"What about this one, sir?"

Riverwind and Catchflea looked back. Di An still lingered by the wagon. She leaned over the trace pole, panting in exhaustion, but her eyes were bright upon them.

"Come here, girl," said Karn. Di An moved quickly to him, but stopped just out of his reach. "Since you're responsible for bringing these outlanders here, you must face Her Highness's judgment."

Di An paled. "It was a mistake, noble warrior! I—I did not bring them here! They chased me—"

"Don't talk back, digger. Get over there." He gestured to Riverwind. "And don't lag!" Karn barked.

Karn and Vvelz moved away. The soldiers prodded the plainsmen and Di An into motion.

Riverwind touched the elf girl's shoulder. She was trembling violently. "Who is this 'Highness'?" he said in a low voice.

She raised large, terror-filled eyes to him. "Li El, First Light of Hest. A terrible mistress! She will have my head!"

"Not with us here," Catchflea said soothingly. "After all, Riverwind is experienced at saving your head."

Di An lowered her eyes. "Thank you, giant."

He lifted her pointed chin until their eyes met once more. "Riverwind is my name."

"Why was Karn trying to shorten you?" asked Catchflea. "What was your crime?"

"Warriors do not need a crime to slay diggers," she said grimly. "But what I did was disobey the oldest law in Hest, not to go to the Empty World above."

Riverwind asked, "Why did you?"

Di An glanced at Karn and Vvelz. They were involved in their own conversation ahead. The soldiers lagged behind several paces. Softly, she said, "It is what I do. I am a barren child, so my life is of no value. I am sent up the slow passage to the Empty World to find things we do not have in Hest."

The light of recognition dawned on Riverwind. "I see. So all the ordinary goods in that chamber—wood, leather, cloth—you collected because you don't have such things underground?"

"I did not collect them all. There are other barren children."

"If it is forbidden to go above, then who sent you?" Catchflea asked.

Before she could reply, Vvelz spoke. "See, giants, the foundries and workshops that produce all the marvels you see in Vartoom," he said proudly.

The left side of the avenue was lined with low, oval doors and round windows, the sills of which were stained with soot. Inside, sparks danced and fire flared as diggers toiled over crucibles of molten metal. Vvelz gave leave for the humans to have a closer look. Riverwind and Catchflea hunched down and peered in an open window.

It was stiflingly hot inside. Against a background of flickering flames and acrid smoke, dim figures moved with the stiff motions of clockwork puppets. A bar of red-hot metal was drawn from a furnace by two elves with tongs. A gang of four diggers fell to beating it with hammers. Fire splashed around the cramped room like errant raindrops.

Catchflea backed away quickly. His face was red and sweat had trickled into his beard. "By the gods, I'm baked!" he exclaimed.

Riverwind blotted his face with his leather wristbands. "Not even the dwarf smiths of Thorbardin live and work in such an inferno."

Vvelz entwined his fingers and regarded them beneficently. "Here in Hest we wrest the finest metals from the ground. We make everything we require in these foundries."

Ramps and stairs of stone led from the Avenue of Foundries, as Vvelz called it, to the next, higher terrace, the Avenue of Artificers. The diggers were just as numerous here, but instead of smoke and fire, the street resounded with hammer strikes and the clatter of machinery. Again, the sorcerer bade the Que-Shu men look in any window. They saw elves making chain, drawing wire, and hammering bronze and copper into thin plates.

"Do you notice," Catchflea said in the barest whisper, "there are few children about?"

"There's Di An."

"She's no child, whatever she says. I mean little ones."

Riverwind knew the old soothsayer was right. He asked Vvelz about the lack of children.

"There have not been many children born these past years," the sorcerer said thoughtfully. "I believe it's due to—"

"Mind your tongue," Karn said, tersely. "Her Highness will tell the outlanders what she wants them to know."

The third terrace was the Avenue of Weavers. There, fine wire was woven into copper or tin "cloth." By brushing on certain chemicals, the metal cloth could be colored. Riverwind saw mounds of black-dyed copper, the universal wear of the diggers.

Soldiers became more numerous as they ascended the city levels. The common soldiers showed great deference to the officers. Karn was evidently a high personage, as ranks parted for him and armed elves stood at attention while he passed.

The sixth terrace was called the Place of Swords. Here there were no diggers at all, only soldiers in bright steel or burnished brass. Vvelz explained that the differences they saw in armor and helmets was due to the different regiments in the army, or Host.

"I don't like this," Riverwind muttered. "All these swords, and us with only our bare hands."

"Be easy, tall man. There's no obvious threat yet," said Catchflea.

"Tell that to Di An."

The girl was trembling so badly now that Riverwind had to brace her with his arm. Vvelz and Karn led the little band to the center of the street of the sixth terrace. There, guards with drawn swords stood on each side of a monumental gate, its supporting columns made from naturally formed, gigantic quartz crystals. They raised their short-bladed swords in salute as Karn approached.

"Inform Her Highness that I have returned, with prisoners," Karn announced.

"Guests," Vvelz corrected.

Karn glared. "We shall see."

One guard departed with Karn's message. He returned a few minutes later with a single-word answer: "Come."

"I am afraid!" Di An declared, trying to pull back.

Catchflea ruffled her short, stiff hair with one hand. "The gods are merciful," he said, looking down into her frightened eyes.

"So men say," Riverwind said. "I hope it's true."

Through the gate was a long colonnade of quartz crystals, open to the air. Honor guards lined the way, their closed visors embossed to resemble the faces of lions. The elves' metal shoes clanked loudly on the brilliant mosaic floor, which was made up of millions of tiny garnets, peridots, and amethysts. A second gate, twenty feet tall and made of riveted iron plates, swung inward as they came near.

Within, the palace was dim, as a heavy vaulted stone ceiling blotted out the brazen "sun." Statues of Hestite warriors filled the entry hall, all larger than life and wearing complete suits of armor. Each statue bore the name of a dead warrior: Ro Drest, Teln the Great, Karz the Terrible, Ro Welx. All looked stern and soldierly. None looked sympathetic.

The entry hall ended with a vaulted passage that led into the next hall. A blazing hearth, ten feet in diameter, dominated the far end of the room. More curious were the scores of blue globes mounted on carved stone pedestals on each side of the walkway. The tallest pedestals were nearer the walls, the shortest close to the center path. The display was solemn and arresting.

"What are these things?" Riverwind said. "I thought they were lamps."

"Perhaps they are, and this is some kind of shrine," Catchflea said. Di An was too frightened to say anything.

"What are you mumbling about there?" Karn asked.

"These globes, they are lamps, yes?"

Karn laughed unpleasantly. "This is just a collection of old relics," he said. He laughed scornfully.

Vvelz frowned. "They are lights indeed," he remarked, not looking at Karn. "Very old, some of them."

"Why are some dark?" asked the plainsman.

The sorcerer's gaze slanted at him. "In time, all lights go out," was all he said.

At the hearth Riverwind noticed that, while the fire blazed as high as his chest, it did not crackle, spark, or hiss like all the fires he'd ever seen. Moving closer still, he discovered it gave off no heat. In the midst of the flames were bright, glowing piles of coals.

"What sort of fire burns without heat or smoke?" Riverwind queried.

"This is the Hall of Light," Vvelz said. "The sorcerers of Hest created this magic fire centuries ago. In all that time it has not diminished."

"What does it burn?" Catchflea wondered aloud.

"I do not know," Vvelz confessed. "The parchments upon which the secret was written decayed long ago. Only the fire remains, silent and cold." An expression like sadness or pain passed quickly over his face, vanishing when Karn called after them.

"Come along," the soldier said impatiently. "Her Highness awaits."

They circled the hearth, and behind it was another huge door. Lion-faced guards opened the door for them. The room beyond was circular, thirty paces wide, and the ceiling was domed. The surface of the dome was a vast mosaic, showing a heroic figure leading a haggard group of elves from a shattered town to a hole in the ground.

"Karn? Is that you? Come forward." It was a light voice, female, that came from no certain direction, yet filled the domed room. Karn replied with great courtesy, and preceded the others into the room.

They entered to the sound of chimes and splashing water. Neither chimes nor water was visible. A delicate aroma drifted in the air, not like flowers exactly, more like the freshness that sunlight imparted to morning air. The center of the room was screened from view by a circular wall of golden drapes, hanging from linked brass posts. Riverwind could just see over the top of the curtains. Something glittering and golden moved inside the screened area.

Karn drew aside a drape. Vvelz, Riverwind, Catchflea, and Di An entered. The elf girl immediately threw herself on the polished floor, face pressed against the cold mosaic. Riverwind looked straight at the figure before them, but it took him a few seconds to realize what he was seeing.

Seated on a sculpted stone couch was a beautiful elven woman. Her milk-white face was framed by a golden hood that fell to her shoulders, covering her hair. The hood was cut out to reveal her ears, which were high and tapering. Gold beads of decreasing size studded the shell of each ear. Her lips were painted deep red. The rest of her figure was lost in the elaborate folds of her golden garment, a loose clerical robe woven of hair-thin gold wire.

Karn dropped to one knee. "Gracious Highness," he said with verve, "I have brought you these prisoners, whom I captured deep in the southern caves."

"Lost foreigners," Vvelz said smoothly. "Innocent travelers, who perchance fell into your realm, Li El."

Absolutely emotionless eyes passed over the Que-Shu men. "Which is it, then? Intruders or victims?" Karn opened his mouth to give an opinion, but Li El transfixed him with a single upraised finger. Her eyes fastened on Riverwind. "Speak, giant. You alone."

Riverwind swallowed and found it unexpectedly difficult to make a sound. Was it fear, or was it the beauty of that unwavering gaze?

"Your Highness," he began, "I am Riverwind, son of Wanderer, and this is my friend, Catchflea. It is entirely a trick of fate that we are here now."

Li El leaned back on her couch. The smell of a sunlit morning intensified. She said, "Who tricked you then?"

"We were camping in the mountains when we were robbed in the night. Hearing a thief, we gave chase, then fell down a deep shaft. Some unseen hand supported us, and we arrived in your domain, unharmed by the fall."

Li El slowly clenched a hand into a fist. "Karn, did you locate this shaft?" she said with icy precision.

"No, my lady—"

"Why not?"

The warrior's face paled inside his helmet. "I—we—caught this thief—" He indicated the cringing Di An with his foot. "—and shortly thereafter captured these outland giants. I thought it best to return to you at once."

The queen of Hest stood abruptly. All the pleasant sensations in the dome were gone: the chimes and splashing water were silent. "The shaft, foolish Karn, is more important than a digger girl or a pair of giant barbarians. All the old slow passages were supposed to have been closed a half-century ago. How is it this one escaped our notice?" She never raised her voice above a conversational level, but Karn winced under Li El's questioning like a slave under a lash.

"I will return at once, Highness! With twenty warriors, I will find this cursed shaft, and—"

"You will do nothing until I give you leave," Li El declared. The short hairs on the back of Riverwind's neck prickled, and a new aroma reached his nose—incense, sharp and spicy. The sounds and smells, he deduced, must be controlled by Li El's magic.

To Vvelz, the queen said, "What do you know of this affair, brother?"

Vvelz waved a hand carelessly. "Not very much. I was waiting for the return of Karn's troops, as you ordered, when I snagged this digger running out of the tunnel. She babbled some wild tale about giants. When Karn entered the upper cavern, I met him and put the amulets on the outlanders so they could converse and understand us."

"Very convenient, that," Karn muttered.

"As for the shaft, as you said, dear sister, all of them were closed by your edict fifty years ago."

Li El sat down in a crush of crinkling gold cloth. "Were they? I wonder."

"No one could create a new one," Vvelz remarked. "No one but you."

Karn couldn't stand it any longer. "Your Highness, what is to be done with the outlanders?"

"Done? Why should anything be done? This barren child did not act of her own will; someone commands her. Exactly who, we will discover." Di An's breath caught in an audible gasp. "She led these humans here. Do you propose I execute them for trying to recover their property, or for stumbling in the dark?"

"No, Highness; that is, yes—"

"Hold your tongue. Karn, you are a brave and steadfast captain, but a poor leader. For not seeing your task clearly, I consign you to the High Spires for three days, where you may meditate on your lack of clarity."

"That isn't fair! Your Highness knows how hard I strive for her—"

Li El's glare stopped him cold. "Are you disputing my order?"

Karn got very red in the face, but he replied stiffly, "Your Highness's will shall be done." He turned on one heel and marched away. The soldier shoved his way through the golden curtains, muttering. His footsteps faded rapidly.

Li El rose from her seat. The pleasant, soothing sounds returned to the chamber. Water splashed softly and chimes tinkled. The smell of bitter incense was replaced by the clean tang of rain-washed air. "Come closer, strangers," Li El said. "I would know more about you."

Without really meaning to comply, both plainsmen took a step forward. When they did, they revealed Di An, still crumpled on the floor. She huddled behind Riverwind's leg, trying to avoid the queen's eye. She didn't succeed.

Li El swept a hand through the empty air. A distinct bell-like sound rang out, and two soldiers appeared. "Remove the digger," she said.

The guards closed in. Riverwind stood in their way. "She

is no danger to anyone," he said.

Li El regarded the match of the tall plainsman and two Hestite warriors with evident interest. "She must tell what she knows," she said. "Give no more thought to the digger, giant. After all, she is a thief."

The guards moved hesitantly to seize Di An. Riverwind tensed. Catchflea tugged on the back of the tall man's shirt, warning him to be calm.

"Sister, if it will prevent bloodshed, I will take the girl myself and question her," Vvelz said placidly. Riverwind and the Hestite soldiers looked to the queen for her answer.

"You are too soft-hearted," Li El said after a long pause. "Are you sure you can get at the truth?"

"If I fail, I will send for your experts," Vvelz promised. Li El relented, and her silver-haired brother gathered the girl up from the floor. He hustled Di An from the room, and the guards stood back, awaiting new orders.

Riverwind's large hands were closed into fists as he watched Vvelz take Di An away. Gently, Catchflea said, "She will be all right. I know it."

Riverwind cast a skeptical look at the old man. "Do your acorns tell you so?"

"No," Catchflea said, entirely serious. "But I believe that Vvelz will not harm her."

"Come, come," the queen said. Bells chimed. "I would know more about your world and ways. Tell me, old giant, of your country and its people."

Catchflea launched into a discourse on Que-Shu, its people and its customs. While he was engaged, Riverwind found he could not take his eyes off Li El—though she never once returned his gaze. Sweat broke out on his brow as he tried to divert his eyes to the golden curtains, the ceiling, anything. He succeeded only in lowering his gaze to her hands. Li El's right hand was at rest, but the fingers of her left moved in slow, intricate patterns against the armrest of her couch. The movement ceased abruptly.

"And that, Highness, is how we came to be here," Catchflea finished with a flourish. "May I ask how it is that your people come to be living so deep underground?"

Li El's arched brows flexed over her jet-colored eyes.

"What? Has the Empty World so soon forgotten the Great Hest and his people?"

"We are a different race," Catchflea said diplomatically. "Not well schooled in history."

Li El swept down from the couch. Once she was off the platform, it was easier to see how small she was. The top of her head scarcely reached Riverwind's chest. But neither man could take his eyes off her, so compelling was her presence.

"Two thousand, five hundred years ago, the inhabitants of Silvanesti and the humans of Ergoth fell into war. For fifty years and two they fought and ambushed and massacred, until the plains and forest fringes of Silvan were desolate, lifeless regions. The warlord Kith-Kanan kept the hordes of Ergoth at bay by skillful strategy, but dissension in the capital prevented him from taking the war to the humans and gaining the final victory. So the Kinslayer War sputtered on without resolution.

"Our great ancestor, Hest, or in the old tongue, Hestantafalas, was a general in the Host of Silvanesti. He wanted to carry the fighting to the human city of Caergoth itself, to extinguish the barbarian masses of humankind from the western plains—" Here she paused, aware once more to whom she was speaking. "The passions of the ancient past live with us still. Do not be offended."

"We understand," said Riverwind. The wall of gold drapery suddenly seemed more threatening than before. He couldn't see any exits from the domed room, or even where the door they entered by was located. There were no guards, and that made him nervous as well.

"—a serious clash at court," Li El was saying. "Great Hest refused to endorse the truce. King Sithas's guards seized him and threw him in prison.

"When the king's brother, Kith-Kanan, heard what had happened to his lieutenant, he returned to Silvanost to win freedom for Hest. King Sithas refused. Hest was too dangerous, he said. His actions were treason, and he had to perish for his insolence.

"A scaffold was built, but Hest's head never rolled into Sithas's basket. Nine soldiers broke into the dungeon and freed the hero. Together they fought their way out of the city. What a struggle it was!" Li El raised a phantom sword. The room filled with shouts and the clang of blade on blade. Her voice echoed through the domed room. "The ten of them slew sixty-three of the king's bodyguards. Sixty-three! Hest went to his fortress town of Bordon-Hest and prepared for a siege. Sure enough, Sithas sent his most loyal general, the dreaded Kencathedrus, to capture and destroy Hest and all his people."

Li El lowered her arm. The sounds of combat faded slowly. Catchflea trembled, and Riverwind looked uneasily over each shoulder. He could smell blood freshly shed. The room was as clean and empty as it ever had been.

Li El hugged herself as if she were chilled, and returned to her couch. Eyes averted, she sank onto the seat.

"The situation grew desperate. Hest was not equipped for a long siege by trained warriors. There were hundreds of women and children in Bordon-Hest, and only four hundred fighters. A terrible slaughter seemed only days away."

She lifted her head. A thin, wide smile shone from Li El's face. Her eyes were fierce with triumph. "In his most critical hour, Hest approached his chief sorcerer, the great Vedvedsica. 'There is a way to escape, my lord,' he told Hest. The great lord asked how, since neither he nor his people had wings with which to fly away from the host of Kencathedrus. 'It is not wings that are needed, great master, but lamps.' Why lamps? Hest wanted to know. 'Because it is very dark in the world below,' Vedvedsica replied.

"The wizard explained his plan, and Hest approved. All the people in Bordon-Hest were cautioned, and Vedvedsica made his preparations. On the twenty-fourth day of the siege, in the year two thousand, one hundred and forty, a mighty earthquake struck Silvanesti. The disturbance centered at Bordon-Hest, and the town's ruination was complete. The walls and buildings fell in upon themselves, burying everyone in the rubble. Or so it seemed. What Vedvedsica had done was open a crack in the ground through which all the people of Hest, from the highest born to lowest, escaped. Then Vedvedsica's magic brought the city down, filling the hole and preventing anyone from dis-

covering what became of the great lord and his followers."
Li El rested her sharp chin on the back of her right hand.
"Until now."

The vast rotunda was silent for several heartbeats. Riverwind tried to gauge how best to answer Li El. The tale of the
impudent lord who wanted so badly to exterminate humans
won little sympathy in his heart. He could not say as much
to the Hestites' queen.

Hesitantly, he said, "Much has happened since your ancestors went underground. Krynn is not as it was twenty-
five hundred years ago."

"Do the green halls of Silvanost still stand?"

"It is said they do."

"And do the sons of Sithas still reign there?"

"I don't know—"

"We are all under sentence of death for treason, every
generation born since Hest brought us here. When the great
lord himself died a thousand years ago, his last words were:
'Beware the Empty World above.' Hest's dying command
has become our most sacred law," said Li El.

"Others have gone to the surface, yes? Like the girl we followed?" asked Catchflea.

The proud serenity on Li El's face vanished. Anger replaced it, anger so tangible it struck the men like a blow.

"There are fools who try! I have been lenient with them
too long. Now I see that I shall have to root them out, once
and for all. When I catch them, they will die." Again she gestured, and a gong they could not see was sounded. More
soldiers appeared. "Muster a full cohort of the Host," Li El
said. "Have Karn's escort show them where the digger girl
and the giants were found. I want the location of the slow
passage, and all contraband brought down from the surface."

"What of us?" Riverwind asked.

"You? You shall remain in the High Spires until I decide
what is to be done with you," she declared. Half a dozen
Hestite warriors closed in on the two men. Riverwind
turned suddenly to them, and they stopped, awed by his
commanding height. Catchflea instinctively drew closer to
the plainsman.

Instead of admonishing Riverwind to go quietly, Li El simply reclined on her couch and said nothing. A small smile quirked her lips.

The guards mustered their resolve and moved in. "You've no right to keep us prisoners!" Riverwind shouted. An elf slammed his shield against Riverwind's back. The plainsman's outrage, so long held in check, boiled over. He seized the edges of the warrior's shield and thrust him away. The lightweight Hestite sprawled on the gem-filled mosaic floor.

"What are you waiting for?" Li El asked mildly. "Take them away."

"We are peaceful men," Catchflea pleaded. "Innocent, yes!" He got bashed in the head with a bronze shield for his words. Riverwind grabbed the two nearest elves each by the neck and dashed their heads together. The guards menacing Catchflea turned away from him and drew their swords. Riverwind yanked a sword from the belt of one of the unconscious Hestites.

"Get behind me, old man!" Riverwind cried.

Two elves attacked. Riverwind parried their short blades and forced them back with quick jabs at their unprotected faces. How he wished he had his saber! These Hestite weapons were too small for him. It was like fighting with a boy's practice sword.

His long reach enabled Riverwind to meet both elves even when they spread apart. One's sword jarred hard against the crossguard of Riverwind's stolen blade. The thick brass held, so he turned his wrist out, driving the elf's point away and his own point in. The blunt sword skidded off the warrior's shield. Riverwind slashed hard to his left to ward off the other soldier. The elf backed into one of his fallen comrades and tripped.

Catchflea scrambled out of the way of the fight. Li El swept her arm and sounded her magic bell once more. Soldiers flooded the throne room.

"Twenty more at your back!" Catchflea warned.

"Well?" Riverwind said hastily. "Are you only a herald of bad tidings? Do something!"

The old soothsayer was no fighter. With a sword in his hand, he was more likely to cut himself than any foe he

73

faced. The only other thing he possessed was his gourd and three dried acorns.

Acorns!

He dug the gourd and nuts out of his ragged clothing and brandished them over his head. "Stop where you are!" he shouted. "In these small seeds I have confined the power of a thunderbolt! Stay back, yes, and hinder us not, or I shall hurl them at you!"

The soldiers froze. Riverwind's opponent paused to listen to Catchflea's tirade, and the plainsman whacked him smartly on the head with the flat of his blade. Down he went. Riverwind whirled to the old man.

"This is inspired," he whispered.

"I am gifted with terrible powers," Catchflea intoned. "One toss, and you will all be reduced to ashes!"

Li El alone was not impressed. Leaning back on one elbow, she said, "What are you waiting for? Subdue them." The guards showed a distinct lack of enthusiasm for the task.

"You cannot escape," Li El said, reasonably. "Not the palace, much less Vartoom."

Riverwind believed her, but he wouldn't admit it. "We'll go back the way we came," he said, putting on a bold front. "No one had better interfere."

Li El sighed. A trilling note sounded. The ranks of sword-armed elves parted. Four soldiers, dressed in light mail, came forward whirling strange-looking devices over their heads—three metal balls joined by a length of chain. Catchflea menaced them with his harmless gourd, but the elves were not bluffed. They flung the bolos at the old man. Two wrapped up his arms and legs. The gourd hit the mosaic floor. The guards flinched. When nothing else happened, they gave a concerted cry of anger and swarmed over the plainsmen. The sword was snatched from Riverwind, and both men were carried bodily from the room.

Li El stepped lightly down from her throne. She picked up Catchflea's gourd. The acorns rattled within. She turned the gourd over, and one by one shook the acorns out into her hand. No emotion at all showed on her beautiful, still face.

Chapter 6

The High Spires

Shouting all the while, the soldiers bore Riverwind and Catchflea roughly along a winding passage that ascended through the solid stone of the cave wall. Up and up they went, banging against projecting rocks and the low ceiling. The yelling elves ran faster as the path constricted into a tighter and tighter spiral. Ten elves carried Riverwind and six had Catchflea. A swarm of others followed, all shouting ferociously.

The spiral passage suddenly ended on an open platform dug out of the cave wall. Riverwind's heart climbed to his throat when he saw where they were: three hundred feet or more above the city, nearly to the roof of the great cavern! For a moment he had the horrible thought that the Hestites were going to hurl him and Catchflea off. They didn't. Butt-

75

ing against the lip of the platform was a span of milk-colored limestone. This dizziest of bridges rose in a gentle arch and disappeared a dozen yards out in the drifting smoke and haze.

The soldiers set them on their feet. One cried, "To the Spires! To the Spires!" and the rest took up the frenzied cry. They waved their swords and poked the men in the back with the sharp tips to spur them on.

"Well, old man, what do you think?" Riverwind asked. "We can die fighting, or we can go out on that span and fall."

"Those are not the only choices, yes?" Catchflea said desperately. "Ouch!" An elf pricked him on the calf of his leg. "We could go out and not fall off."

Riverwind inhaled deeply and bellowed, "Stand back!" His size still impressed the Hestites, and they did stand away. The plainsman walked to the edge of the platform.

Light from the brazen sun threw weird shadows from the forest of stalactites. Foundry smoke drifted around the hanging spires. Riverwind coughed as sulfurous fumes swept over him. Through watering eyes he could dimly see a dark mass far off in the smoke, at the other end of the bridge.

"Come along, Catchflea," he said. "Let's show these cave-folk how Que-Shu men face danger."

"On my hands and knees," the old man muttered, closing in behind Riverwind.

The bridge was only six inches wide, and rounded. A fine film of soot coated the upper surface; just enough, River-wind mused, to make it slick. He slid his feet onto the glassy surface. It seemed sturdy enough. He brought his trailing foot up slowly. That was the way to do it. Inch along. No hurry, no sudden stops.

Catchflea imitated him. Only once did the old man look down. Instantly he regretted it. Vertigo punched him in the stomach; his head spun. So did the concentric streets of Var-toom, far below. Catchflea flailed his arms—

"Tall man!" he gasped. "Help me!"

Riverwind turned in time to see Catchflea topple. The drop beneath him was over a hundred feet. Riverwind threw himself at Catchflea. He hit the bridge chest-first. The impact drove the air from his lungs, but he reached out and grasped Catchflea's arms. The old man slid steadily over the rounded rim of the bridge. Riverwind wrapped his long legs around the limestone span and dug his fingers in Catchflea's rags. The old cloth frayed and ripped, sending up puffs of dust.

The Hestites, who up till now had been jeering, fell silent. One shouted, "Get a leg up, old giant!" The rest joined in, calling out advice.

Catchflea tried three times to get his right leg over the bridge, but his heel could find no purchase and skidded off. Tears streaked his dirty face. "I cannot do it," he groaned.

Riverwind said, "Try again! This time I'll pull you just as you swing your leg up!"

Catchflea was old, but wiry. He threw his leg up again. Riverwind's arm muscles knotted, drawing the old man toward him. Catchflea's heel caught. The elves cheered. With much effort, the old man worked his leg over until he was straddling the bridge. He and Riverwind lay nose to nose, panting for breath.

"Are you set?" asked Riverwind.

"I think so, yes."

Riverwind sat up and swung himself around. He and Catchflea proceeded, sliding along astride the bridge. The soldiers and the cave wall submerged in the smoke and were lost from sight.

Gradually their destination took shape. A number of especially stout stalactites had been used to support an airy platform. Iron bands circled the spires, securing a floor made of square iron rails. Riverwind grasped a rail and hauled himself onto the platform.

A dark figure appeared in the smoke. "Who's there?" When neither man replied, the figure came forward. It was Karn. "So, the outlanders were sent to the Spires, too. How fitting."

Riverwind dragged Catchflea off the bridge. The old man clung to the floor like a sailor to a barmaid.

"This is like no dungeon I ever heard of," he wheezed.

"It wasn't built to be a prison," Karn said. His pointed features twisted into a sneer. "Once this was the private aerie of

77

the King of Hest. Now, it's where Her Highness sends those who displease her."

"There's no gate, no barred door," Riverwind noted.

"None are needed, giant. Two guards stand at the end of the bridge, ready to dispatch any who try to leave." Karn growled low in his throat. "I, who serve Her Highness like a slave, sent here with two barbarians!" He glared at the men. "I should have slain you in the tunnel. And that digger girl, too."

"Bitterness is no answer, yes," Catchflea said.

"We share a common prison," Riverwind added. "Couldn't we work together to gain our freedom?"

Karn sneered. "I don't expect you overgrown barbarians to understand a warrior or his code of honor," he said. "My life belongs to the queen. Her will is mine."

"But she sent you here," said Riverwind.

Karn folded his arms. "I won't be here long. Her Highness needs me. I am her right arm."

"From what I've seen, there are many arms in Hest, yes? Perhaps you are not as valuable as you think," Catchflea remarked.

The elf warrior flushed and took a step toward where Catchflea and Riverwind still sat on the floor. He glared hatefully down at the old man. "You know nothing about us!" Karn rasped, breathing heavily. "I may have to take such insults from Vvelz because he is the queen's brother, but I won't take them from you!"

He stepped back from Catchflea, and the old man breathed a sigh of relief. "Vvelz is a weakling and a meddler," Karn continued. "He is tolerated by the Host only because of the loyalty we bear Her Highness."

"He seems witful enough," Catchflea ventured carefully.

"Master Vvelz is infamous for his wit. And for using it to aid the diggers. He will subvert the natural order of Hest! Favoring diggers over his own kind—" The flow of words trailed away. After a second of head-shaking, Karn said, "Kinthalas take his eyes!"

The Que-Shu men exchanged a long and meaningful glance. "Why would Vvelz favor the diggers?" asked Riverwind softly.

Karn waved the question aside. He dropped on his haunches and scrubbed through his pale hair with his fingers. "Politics, pah! Don't ask me to fathom such things. It's not a fitting subject for a warrior to discuss."

Karn stared morosely across the chasm, lost in self-pity. Riverwind drew Catchflea away from the sullen warrior.

"There are many things afoot here," Riverwind said in a low voice. "Did you hear the queen blame Di An's thievery on someone else? She said the girl was commanded to go to the surface."

Catchflea scratched his bearded cheek. "You think it's Vvelz, yes?"

"Could be."

"What are you two muttering about over there?" Karn asked loudly.

"I was wondering if there is anything to eat?" Catchflea inquired politely.

"How do I know? Am I servant? Look around." He grinned nastily. "But beware the floor's edge; there is no rail to keep you from walking right off into the chasm. Still hungry, giants?"

"What I am is tired," Riverwind replied truthfully. He scanned the smoky expanse of iron flooring and sighed. "The air here is very bad. Maybe it's fresher farther away."

"It doesn't get any better," Karn said.

"I would find out for myself." To Catchflea, he murmured, "Let's go where we can speak without Karn hearing."

"And find food, yes?"

They wandered away. A short distance into the haze they found a brass urn three feet tall. It was full of stale, brackish water, which they drank anyway. Riverwind soaked a kerchief and tied it over his nose and mouth. Catchflea plucked a rag from his shirt and did likewise.

"What are you thinking, tall man?" he asked as they walked slowly through the High Spires, watching for sudden drop-offs.

"I am thinking of Goldmoon," Riverwind said simply.

"Ah."

"Catchflea, you're old enough to recall the time when Arrowthorn became chief, aren't you?"

The old soothsayer nodded. His rag mask made him look like an elderly bandit. "There was a feud between the followers of Arrowthorn and the men who wanted Oakheart as chieftain. It was a bad time."

"My father told me of those days. There was fighting in the streets, theft, burning of houses and crops, even murder."

"Oakheart's murderer was never found," Catchflea said. "It was only because Arrowthorn was with many people when it happened that he wasn't accused of the crime."

"So he married Tearsong and became chief."

"And a strong chief he has been, yes. But what does this have to do with your thoughts of Goldmoon or our situation here?"

"Such a bad time may come again to our people if I am opposed as chieftain," Riverwind replied. "Goldmoon already faced death when Hollow-sky tried to kill me. I don't want her to be a target in a feud." He looked around at the shifting smoke. "And this place—if brother and sister are plotting to bring each other down, then you and I are in the worst possible position."

Catchflea stopped his ambling. "The first to die, yes?"

"As foreigners, we'll be blamed for everything."

"What can we do?"

Riverwind brushed tears from his smoke-stung eyes and coughed. "Let's try to get some rest, then see what comes when we waken," Riverwind said.

"An excellent idea. I am wrung out."

They tried to make their way back to the brass urn, but the smoke and lack of landmarks confused them. The Que-Shu men wandered aimlessly a short distance until Riverwind called a halt.

"A strange dungeon, but an effective one," he said. "Not knowing how big this place is, we could wander in circles and never find the boundaries."

Catchflea sat down where he was. "Then all places are the same." Soon he was asleep and snoring, even as the noxious smoke poured over him.

Riverwind lay down and closed his eyes. How strange it was that only a short while ago he had set out on his courting quest and now found himself in an underground world embroiled in a political struggle. But the ways of the gods were not easily fathomed by humans. Perhaps these elves were important in his quest. Perhaps they would end up helping him.

A sigh escaped his lips. He fervently hoped there was some point to all this. His quest was of paramount importance. His quest and his future marriage to Goldmoon. He relaxed and allowed sleep to overtake him. Though he had hoped to dream of his beloved, Riverwind's sleep was silent and deep and dreamless.

* * * * *

Riverwind felt a touch on his face. Lightly, fingers traced the line of his jaw. He stirred and brushed at the disturbance. A small thumb and forefinger tweaked his nose gently. He snorted, almost awake, then settled back into slumber. A finger tickled his ear until the itching sensation was too strong to ignore. Riverwind snapped to a sitting position. The kerchief he'd tied over his nose and mouth was up around his eyes. He snatched it off and saw Di An.

She signaled for him to remain quiet.

"What are you doing here?" he whispered.

"No noise. We leave," she said.

"But how—?"

Di An put a small finger to his lips. "You want to go, don't you?"

He roused Catchflea. The soothsayer coughed and cleared his throat. "Argh," he grumbled. "Now I know how a smoked ham feels."

They drank greedily from a flask Di An offered them. Being in a cave so far from the sun, Riverwind didn't know if it was night or day. The bronze sun burned on, a dull orange orb far out in the smoke.

"Why are we being so quiet?" Catchflea hissed. "Who can hear us?"

"Ro Karn," said Di An.

"Did you bring us weapons?" Riverwind asked. "A sword would improve my spirits greatly."

"Follow and make no noise," Di An said. She crouched low and sprinted away, her bare feet tapping lightly on the iron floor. Riverwind and Catchflea trailed her at a circumspect pace. They couldn't see more than ten feet ahead, and chasing Di An was not the safest thing in the world to do, as they well knew.

They caught up with her as she knelt by a copper chest. "This was sent for you," she said. The men crouched beside her. She raised the lid. Inside were brightly colored fruits and vegetables: apples, pears, plums, radishes, carrots. Two tin bottles held more water, and in the bottom of the box were two stubby Hestite swords. Riverwind slipped one of the weapons through his belt. Catchflea declined the other.

"I'm no warrior," he objected. Riverwind didn't press him to take it.

They fell upon the food. "I can't remember the last time we ate," the plainsman said.

"It's been too long ago, yes," Catchflea mumbled through a bite of pear. "Even this sorry stuff is welcome."

It was sorry food indeed. For all their brilliant colors, the apples and pears lacked any sweetness, and the vegetables were bitter and metallic-tasting. The men's frantic chewing and swallowing slowed and stopped. Catchflea paled.

"I'm going to be ill, yes."

"I am too," Riverwind muttered. "Is this stuff poisoned?"

Catchflea grasped his stomach. "I pray it is—at least we won't suffer long!"

Di An gawked at them. "What's wrong? This is warrior food. It's very good."

"It's tainted," Riverwind gasped.

The elf girl shook her head in wonder and helped herself to an apple. She sank her teeth into it and munched away with every evidence of satisfaction. "Come," she said. "They are waiting." With that, she darted off, still devouring the fruit.

"'They'?" Riverwind repeated. Catchflea, who had been sipping water to clear the taste of bitter radish from his mouth, looked alarmed. Riverwind said, "If enemies wanted to trap and kill us, they wouldn't put swords in our hands, would they?"

"No," the old man said. "They'd probably poison us."

Riverwind, gripping the sword tightly, set off after Di An. Catchflea lingered by the chest, still holding his stomach. Riverwind went no more than twenty yards and found the girl waiting by a gigantic stalactite a dozen feet wide. Where the massive spire thrust through the floor, several iron rails had been bent back, creating enough of a gap for Riverwind and Catchflea to squeeze through. Di An waved for him to come on.

"Where are we going?" he insisted again.

"Just come!" Di An pushed herself forward and slipped into the hole. Riverwind ran to the opening and looked down. Di An was floating slowly down, hands held tightly against her sides. The slow-falling spell again.

A commotion arose in the smoke behind him. He turned and saw two figures struggling. Catchflea cried, "Tall man, help!"

Riverwind dashed back. He found the old man fighting a losing battle with Karn for possession of the second sword Di An had brought. Riverwind shouted a challenge. The elf warrior punched Catchflea in the belly and seized the sword.

"I knew you were up to something," Karn said triumphantly. "Surrender, giant!"

"You'll have to fight, bully," Riverwind replied.

Karn whirled his sword around his head and cut hard at Riverwind. The plainsman easily turned the attack and countered with fast slashes at Karn's face and neck. He knew from experience that fighters used to armor would retreat if these vulnerable areas were threatened. Karn backed up.

"Get moving, old man!" Riverwind snapped. Catchflea crawled weakly behind him. "That way." Riverwind tossed his head. Catchflea tottered to his feet, clutched his stomach, and shuffled toward the stalactite.

"You can't escape!" Karn yelled.

Riverwind sidled away, always keeping his sword toward Karn. He found the old soothsayer leaning on the stone spire, breathing hard.

"What are you waiting for?" Riverwind said. "Jump!"

"Down there?" Catchflea gasped. "Are you mad?"

"The slow-fall spell, remember?"

Understanding gleamed in the old man's eye. "So? Be of stout heart, Catchflea!" he admonished himself. "Here I go, yes!"

Catchflea eased himself into the space between the stalactite and the floor. Eyes screwed shut, he let go the stone spire and plunged a few feet before an invisible net slowed and caught him in its folds. The spell felt different than that in the long shaft that had brought them to Hest—weird tickling sensations crawled over his skin, like the strands of an enormous spider web. The spell was different in another way, too, for Catchflea could feel himself fall faster, slow down, fall, slow, and so on as he descended. He prayed aloud to Majere to strengthen the hand of whomever was performing the spell.

Riverwind saw his friend disappear. In the next instant, Karn was on him, slashing madly, first from one side, then the other. Riverwind retreated before the elf's wild assault until he felt the great spire at his back. He couldn't lower his guard long enough to get through the opening in the floor. If he could just distract Karn for a moment . . .

Riverwind reversed his grip on the Hestite sword and hurled it at Karn. He turned to jump. Something hard hit him square on the back of the head. He pitched forward, crashing into the stalactite and falling to the floor, still in the High Spires.

Riverwind shook off the blow, but as he started to rise, he felt a cold steel edge against his neck. "Give me a reason to strike," Karn said. Riverwind saw, not ten inches from his outstretched hand, Karn's sword. The fighter had caught him by throwing his own sword at Riverwind, retrieving the plainsman's weapon, and pinning him as he lay stunned.

"Stay your hand or die," Karn rasped. "I want Her Highness to prescribe your fate." His dark eyes gleamed.

Riverwind drew in his arm.

*　　*　　*　　*　　*

The panorama of the great cavern spun around Catch-flea's feet. This giddy swirl, combined with the lingering taste of the Hestite food, made him sick to his stomach. He vomited all he had eaten, but felt better for it.

Catchflea couldn't see where he was falling to. He appeared to be moving laterally as well as vertically. Above him, the High Spires seemed very far away. The smoke thickened and closed in, and even that landmark vanished. He was lost in the smoky void.

Then his feet struck solid ground. Catchflea's knees folded from the shock. A cluster of figures surrounded him.

"I'm so glad to be down!" he declared. "Thank—"

Before he could finish, a heavy drape of copper mesh was flung over his head. Catchflea was lifted onto the shoulders of a dozen silent Hestites. He protested loudly, but the mesh muffled his cries. He tried to kick, but he was held by too many hands and the mesh weighed him down. Catchflea was spirited away without even knowing that Riverwind hadn't followed him out of the Spires.

Chapter 7

Tears of Blood

Karn marched Riverwind at sword point back to the High Spires' bridge.

"What do you intend to do with me?" asked Riverwind.

"I must tell Her Highness what has happened. The elder giant won't get far."

"Catchflea is more clever than he appears." Riverwind hoped the old soothsayer was safe, wherever Di An had taken him.

"My mistress will glean him out no matter where he goes," Karn boasted. The limestone bridge emerged from the smoke. Riverwind did not understand how Karn and Di An were able to find their way in the murk. Perhaps elves had keener eyesight than humans.

"Ho-la!" Karn shouted to the guards on the other side.

"It is me, Karn!"

After a second's delay, a faint voice replied. "We're not to converse with you, my captain!"

Karn's eyes scanned the shifting smoke ahead of them. "Nalx, is that you? Listen to me: go to Her Highness and tell her the giants tried to escape. One got away, but I caught the younger one. Tell her, Nalx. She will reward us both."

"A hard tale to believe, my captain!" said the guard. "Where could the giants escape to?"

"How should I know? There's magic afoot, fool, and if you don't tell Her Highness, what do you think her reaction will be?"

There was a longer delay. Finally, Nalx's voice said, "I will do it, Ro Karn. What a feat, to capture a giant *twice*—"

"Yes, yes. Go quickly, Nalx!"

After several minutes, Karn stiffened. "An entire company of soldiers!" he exclaimed to Riverwind.

The plainsman squinted into the gloom, but saw absolutely nothing but smoke and noxious vapors. However, he trusted the elf's eyesight.

Nalx called, "You are to cross with the prisoner, Ro Karn!"

"We come!"

The plainsman straddled the bridge as before and inched across. Karn sauntered behind him, his narrow feet comfortably centered on the slick stone path.

A score of pikes was leveled at Riverwind as he gained the platform. Karn had been right about the number of soldiers. An officer raised his arm in salute. "Ro Karn, Her Highness bids you come to her at once."

With a jaunty, triumphant air, Karn slammed the sword Di An had brought to High Spires home into his scabbard. Another elf stepped forward and handed Karn his helmet. "I kept it for you, sir," he said.

The warrior seated the iron helmet on his head and sighed with satisfaction. "My thanks, Sard." He looked up at Riverwind. "You see, giant, how quickly fortune changes."

Riverwind regarded him disdainfully. "Yes, and it may change again, and not to your liking."

Karn laughed. He ordered the soldiers into formation and

took his place at their head. They marched in lockstep down the spiral tunnel to Li El's throne room.

The escort halted outside the golden curtains. The domed room was suffused with the spicy scent of incense, and the formerly bright lighting had been dimmed to twilight level. Karn and Riverwind entered through a flap in the curtains.

Inside the gilded circle, the room had changed. The couch was gone, replaced by an elaborate carpet woven of silver and copper. Li El sat on the floor in the center of the circle of red and silver. Her golden hood was thrown back, revealing a cascade of rich, red-brown hair. She was the first denizen of Hest that Riverwind had seen with such beautiful dark hair.

A shallow basin rested on the floor before her, warmed by the fitful flame of a tiny brazier. Her head was bent to the basin as she peered into its depths. As Riverwind watched, the queen of Hest dropped blue powder across the liquid in the basin. It hissed loudly, and coils of vapor poured over the sides of the bowl. The pale blue vapor was the source of the strange incense.

Karn cleared his throat. "My queen, I bring you tidings of—"

"I know," Li El said softly, without looking up. "I know all."

Karn paused, taken aback, then continued, "The elder giant escaped before I could stop him. Someone helped him with a chain or a ladder."

"The girl helped him," Li El said in a flat, emotionless voice. Her hand disappeared into her robe and came out with a lumpy piece of red crystal. This she carefully dropped into the basin. "The same digger girl you caught in the tunnel," she said.

"But—but how, Highness? The digger was taken away for questioning—"

"By my brother." Karn looked at Riverwind rather help-lessly. "Do you not see, stupid Karn?" The soldier flinched, but Li El went on relentlessly, "My brother is the one who has been casting the spells, making passages to the surface, and helping those diggers who flee Vartoom!"

Blood suffused Karn's sharp features. "Traitor! I knew it!"

"You did not," she said, and her voice was barely audible. "Even I did not."

"Your Highness," Karn said quickly, "give the word and Vvelz will die today!"

"Vvelz has gone beyond the reach of your sword." Li El gently blew the accumulated mist away from the surface of the liquid. A red glow emanated from the basin. The sorceress-queen was silent for a long time. Karn fidgeted, then cleared his throat.

"Speak," said Li El.

"What shall I do with this giant?" he asked.

Li El lifted her face to them. Both the Hestite warrior and the Que-Shu plainsman recoiled. The queen's dark eyes had turned solidly red, and tears the color of blood trickled from their corners. Thin tracks of red inched down her smooth cheeks.

"Long have I striven to rule Hest firmly, to make it rich and great. I deposed the last decadent son of Hest and made myself queen in order to save the diggers from the tyrant's heavy hand. And what gratitude do I get but desertion, treachery, and sabotage?" The flow of blood-tears increased. Riverwind felt a coldness grip his heart. Li El's voice was icy and calm. Somehow he knew that she did not weep from sadness, but from deep and violent rage.

She stood and walked toward the transfixed elf and man. The tears trickled down onto her golden robe.

"What do you say, giant called Riverwind? Shall I be merciful to those who would bring the kingdom to ruin? To my own flesh and blood who has betrayed me?" She turned to face Karn but continued to address Riverwind. "Or shall they bleed until their transgressions are washed away. Until all treachery is gone. What do you say, giant?"

Riverwind couldn't say anything. A tightness had coiled itself around his throat. Li El's anger filled the room like a vile perfume, rooting him to the floor and rendering him powerless to utter a sound. Karn seemed to be similarly stifled. Over the queen's shoulder Riverwind could see that the basin she'd been performing her spell in was boiling. Large bubbles burst in the liquid, spattering more blood-colored drops on the floor.

"How dare they plot against me!" Li El said, her voice rising. "I, who make the fruit ripen and the light burn in the cavern. My people need never know hunger or darkness, and all I require is obedience and hard work. But even these small things they cannot give me. So I *shall* scourge them, the entire Blue Sky cult, root and branch." She looked at Karn once more. The warrior was trembling slightly, but his face was resolute.

"You are too dull a tool for this job," Li El said to Karn. "Loyal and brave, but far too dull to catch that pack of jackals my brother serves." She turned to Riverwind. The malevolent aura the queen exuded pierced his heart and soul. He felt a tremor start in his hands and, with great effort, he clenched them into fists. His training as a Que-Shu warrior helped him to keep his face stoic as he looked down at the queen's blood-streaked face.

"Ah, giant, you are a fighter indeed. With the proper arms and motivation, you could wipe out my enemies practically on your own."

Karn's calm expression had changed to one of shock. His lips worked but no sound came out. Oblivious to the soldier's distress, Riverwind fought his own inner battle and managed to voice a single word. "No," he whispered.

Li El smiled slightly. "No? Do not be hasty, my fine giant. I have not yet told you what my terms will be. You may reconsider." His eyes told her plainly what his tongue could not say. "You still think not? I see I shall have to persuade you."

Riverwind wanted to run, or fight, do anything to break this dreadful numbing hold Li El had on him. Karn was in no condition to stop him, but the plainsman could scarcely get his legs to move. He slowly shuffled his feet around, and made a convulsive effort to take a step. Li El didn't even hurry. She followed him with patronizing languor, like some horrible bloody wraith pursuing a guilt-ridden man.

Riverwind stumbled and pitched forward. He rolled over and tried to get up. Li El loomed over him.

"Why struggle so, my friend? In the end, all will be the same," she said soothingly. Li El pressed her fingers to her cheeks, staining the tips red with tears. She bent slowly and reached for Riverwind's face. Just as her blood-stained fingers lightly touched his cheeks, Riverwind screamed.

"Goldmoon!"

Karn's face was a picture of his inner torment. His arms and legs twitched with his efforts to move. When his queen touched the giant barbarian, both vanished in a soundless burst of white light. The magical lethargy that had held him paralyzed ended just as suddenly. Karn leaped to the spot where they had been.

"No!" he shouted, drawing his sword. "I was to be your chosen one. I, Karn! You can't take that outlander instead of me!" Karn cut the air furiously with his blade, hurting nothing. "Me! It is me! By blood and test, I am the one!"

He turned on the queen's magic basin. The liquid within was now clear and as smooth as glass. In his fury, Karn stormed over and kicked the basin. Hardly had the iron toe of his sandal touched the brass rim of the dish when the basin dissolved into a wisp of white vapor.

Karn cursed and screamed and stamped his feet in impotent rage.

*　*　*　*　*

The silent Hestites carried Catchflea a long way. He couldn't tell how far, but it was some time before they set him on his feet again. They'd gone a distance on level ground, then up a steep incline. It was ridiculous to the old man, being carried when he certainly could walk.

He lost the fear he had felt when the elves first grabbed him. Catchflea was astute enough to realize that his best chance to stay whole and healthy was to not resist. After going to all the risk of breaking him out of the High Spires, they couldn't harm him—could they? Di An wouldn't lead him into a trap—would she?

The elves lowered him to the ground, and the heavy mesh cover was whisked away. It was cool and dark wherever they'd brought him. Catchflea rubbed his eyes and sat up.

He was in some sort of old building. Gracefully carved columns spiraled up into the darkness. Some were cracked, others fallen. The floor consisted of worn squares of white stone, thickly covered with dust. A stirring in the recesses behind Catchflea warned him that he wasn't alone. As his eyes adjusted to the lack of light, he saw that the room was full of Hestites, all looking at him.

Catchflea stood up. Whispers flitted around the columns like fireflies on a summer night. He heard light footsteps. Di An appeared. That cheered him; here, at least, was a familiar face.

"What's going on?" he asked her. "What is this place?"

"Not much of a giant," a deep voice said, ringing hollowly.

"Who's that?" Catchflea quickly scanned the sea of faces.

"The other one is much taller," Di An said.

Catchflea turned to her once more. "Riverwind. Where is he?"

"He never jumped," she replied faintly. She shifted her feet nervously, looking to the shadows behind her.

"Then Li El has him," said the bass voice.

Catchflea started toward Di An. "You must help him! Karn will have his head!" he exclaimed. He reached out to the elf girl. "Can't we go back for him?"

"Ro Karn is the least of your friend's worries," boomed the voice. "No, we cannot save him."

"*Who are you?*"

Di An took Catchflea's hand and led him into the shadows. Hundreds of small elven feet scuffed in the darkness, following them. The old plainsman nervously watched over his shoulders as the nearly invisible crowd crept along behind him.

Ahead was an open space between close-set ranks of columns. There, over twenty blue globes had been set. Their strange light threw weird shadows on the thing Di An was taking him to see.

It was a thick section of stone blocks, standing free of walls or columns. The surface facing Catchflea was carved in deep relief with the face of an elf. The eyes were nearly squinted shut, the mouth an enormous open hole, black and empty. The entire relief was nearly as tall as Catchflea. In the eerie light, the old man couldn't tell if the expression on the stone face was joyous, outraged, or agonized.

"You are not much of a giant," boomed the stone face.

"That is a label your people gave us. Among my people, I am counted a small man, yes," Catchflea said. He wasn't terribly impressed with this idol, whatever it was. He well knew some mortal Hestite was behind it.

"Then the human may have value," said another voice, higher and more cultured. The old man recognized this second voice as Vvelz's.

Catchflea decided to be bold. He said, "I'm pleased you think so, brother of Li El." The steady whispering of the Hestites behind him ceased. The stone mouth was silent.

A flame erupted near a pair of columns. It illuminated the figure of Vvelz, who approached Catchflea and Di An. In the palm of his right hand a small flame danced. He carried no torch; the fire sprang directly from his hand.

"Mors is right," Vvelz said. "You cannot help Riverwind. Better to stay with us and join our cause."

"But what is your cause?"

"We are the Blue Sky People," said the deep voice, which Vvelz had called Mors. "It is our sacred purpose to leave these dark caverns and dwell again under sun and sky, to live as free people, subject to no tyrants. We will cast off our chains and rise into the light, and no one will force us back into the ground."

"Very admirable, yes?" Catchflea said dryly. "But who are you?"

"Yes, come out," Vvelz said. He held his burning palm up high and clapped his other hand into the flame. Small spurts of fire flew from his fingers to all parts of the room, where they ignited stands of torches. These strange devices resembled young trees, skillfully wrought in iron. At the tips of their metal branches, a small blue flame appeared. As more and more were lit, their soft hissing filled the air.

The room was vast, and a large crowd of diggers lined the walls. Far off on Catchflea's left was an arched doorway and a set of broken steps leading out and down.

Catchflea heard a tapping, like metal on stone. A slim golden rod appeared from behind the stone face. It groped around, tapping against the wall behind the face and on the floor. An elf appeared, holding the end of the rod. Vvelz gave Catchflea a nod. The old man stepped forward.

Up close, he saw the Blue Sky leader was typically short in stature, but broad of shoulder and well-muscled. The most arresting thing about this Hestite were his eyes. Both were sealed behind layers of white scar tissue. Now Catchflea understood the tapping—a questing rod: the Blue Sky leader was blind.

"You stare at my eyes," the elf said harshly. "They are a gift from Her Highness. When I was expelled from Vartoom, she had my eyes put out as a warning to other would-be heretics."

"Who are you?" Catchflea asked quietly.

"My name is Mors, once Ro Mors, captain of the Host. You are the one An Di calls Catchflea?"

"An Di?" asked Catchflea, confused.

"I forget," said Mors. "Being a barbarian, you don't know the nuances of our tongue." He held out an arm, and Di An hurried to him. She nestled against his side. "Di An, An Di; it is a token of affection to call her so."

Catchflea smiled at the girl. "Thank you for helping us," he said.

She looked downcast. "Riverwind did not escape."

Catchflea touched a gnarled, dirty hand to her cheek. "He doesn't submit easily. We will see him again."

The old plainsman saw that more and more Hestites had emerged and filled the empty floor space. He was amazed; there had to be at least six or seven hundred elves huddled in the ruins. He asked Vvelz who they were.

"All the diggers who have run away," the sorcerer explained. "They threw down their picks and plows and joined the Blue Sky People. They come to us because they are tired and hungry, and because they can't bear Li El's tyrannical yoke any longer. Someday soon Mors will lead them out of the caverns into the light."

"So many!" Catchflea marveled. "Why don't you just depart? Surely Li El can't stop such a crowd."

Di An led Mors to where the old man and the sorcerer were talking. "She can," Mors said. His voice was deep and rough. "Running from her is not the answer. We must take the fight to Vartoom itself, seize the tyrant and lead *all* the people of Hest to the sky at once!"

Some of the diggers set up a cheer when they heard that. Mors scowled fiercely at them. "Be quiet, you fools!"

"Li El can't hear them," Vvelz said with a sly, reassuring grin.

"Why not?" asked Catchflea.

"Long ago, this was a temple to one of the gods, now forgotten," Vvelz said. "In ages past, the people of Vartoom came here to worship. The priests would inhale fumes from sacred incense and utter prophecies through the image of the god's face. Now, they wouldn't dare come near this place."

"No one worships here now?"

"Even the god's name has been lost."

"If there are gods, it is they who have forgotten Hest," Mors said bitterly. "We do not need them. We shall take destiny into our own hands."

"The temple is known to be a haunted place," Vvelz continued. "In the reign of Great Hest's third son, Drev the Mad, the priests were massacred and the sacred hearth extinguished by the king's order. It is said the dying priests cursed the line of Hest and that their ghosts walk the temple, seeking vengeance."

Catchflea's eyes were wide. "Do they?"

Vvelz looked left and right. "I have heard things—seen glimmers in the deeper sanctuaries." He shrugged.

*   *   *   *   *

Once the Blue Sky People had adjusted to Catchflea's presence, they went about their routine business as if he weren't there. Food was passed around, ragged copper mesh clothing was patched, and teams of elves distributed items stolen from the surface. It was both amusing and touching to Catchflea to see the Hestites tugging on old leather shoes and felt hats as if they were silk and satin, and eating with worn wooden spoons and plates as though they were finest porcelain.

With Di An as his guide, Mors went to the stump of a broken column and sat down. Bread was brought to him, and a wooden cup, carved from a single piece of oak, was placed in his hand. Catchflea was given the same plain victuals, but his cup was Hestite tin.

"Master Mors," he said, chewing the tasteless, dry bread, "what convinced you to lead this band up from the caverns? After all, it was by going underground that the Hestites managed to survive."

Mors rumbled, "It was the willfulness of Hestantafalas that condemned us to live like vermin in the dark. Had he obeyed his sovereign and kept peace, none of this suffering would have come to pass."

"You were not a digger, yes? How did you come to have such sympathy for them?"

"Let me tell him," Vvelz interjected. Mors took a drink of mineral water and grunted his agreement.

"I shall have to go back quite a ways," Vvelz said. He cleared his throat. "When the Great Hest and his chief magician, Vedvedsica, died, their children naturally inherited their fathers' places. The first son of Hest became king and the children of Vedvedsica his magic counsel. Before long there was rivalry between the royal house and the sorcerers. To augment themselves, each faction recruited talented ones from the common people. Those who served the royal family formed the Hall of Arms, a warriors' guild, and those who followed the Vedvedsicans were known as the Hall of Light. A system was established whereby children were tested at a very early age to determine if they were fit for either house. Those who were fit for neither, as you know, worked as diggers. A balance was reached, and for centuries the people of Hest flourished.

"Then, in the reign of Great Hest's second son, Jaen the Builder, things began to go wrong. Crops failed repeatedly, and the diggers went hungry. Several of the mines collapsed, killing many. Most strangely, fewer and fewer children were born. Many that were born were barren, and did not grow to adulthood." Catchflea looked over at Di An. The elf girl sat at Mors's feet, her knees drawn up to her chin. She stared unblinkingly ahead, and her gaze did not waver when Vvelz spoke of the barren children.

"The Hall of Light blamed the warriors' greed for the failures," Vvelz continued. "Too much time was spent digging for iron and gold, and not enough care was paid to growing crops, they said. The Hall of Arms blamed the sorcerers. They claimed the magicians weren't providing enough light in the cavern, making the crops sickly and thin."

"Who was right?" asked Catchflea.

"Both," Mors said suddenly. When he offered nothing more, Vvelz went on.

"Jaen died in a fit of apoplexy, and his younger brother, Drev, became king. Drev spoke darkly of magical plots against his brother's life. When he was sure of the warriors' loyalty, he tried to crush the Hall of Light. The temples were closed and priests were killed. Many of the elder sorcerers were imprisoned and executed, including Vedvedsica's daughter Ri Om. I was but an apprentice then, and my sister a journeyman."

"Are you descendants of Vedvedsica?"

"He was my great-uncle," Vvelz said with pride. "The conflict seemed over, and the warriors triumphant, but they did not reckon on the ambition of Li El. Her powers, even as an unlearned girl, were extraordinary. She accomplished the great levitation at ten and could forcibly read minds at fourteen—" Mors cleared his throat and rapped his rod on the floor. Vvelz said in a low voice. "Mors does not want the diggers to hear how powerful my sister really is. He says it undermines their morale."

"Mine too, yes," said Catchflea shakily.

"Li El advanced rapidly through the depleted ranks of the Hall of Light," said Vvelz. "Usually it takes a century or more for a journeyman sorcerer to reach the first rank, but she did it in thirty years. Only much later did I discover how she accomplished this; Li El would secretly challenge higher ranking magicians to contests, duels of magic." He shook his head. His voice was tight. "She was an astonishingly beautiful girl. Most of the other magicians were male, and very, very foolish. She bested them all and confined their souls in crystal spheres."

"The blue globes!" Catchflea exclaimed. Vvelz nodded. Catchflea recalled Karn's laugh when he had asked if the globes were lamps. What a fine jest Li El must think it was, to light the corners of her realm with the captive souls of her rival sorcerers!

"By the time my sister became First Light of the Hall, there were barely a dozen sorcerers left. They were all elderly and ineffectual," Vvelz said.

"And you suspected nothing during her rise?" the old soothsayer asked, incredulous.

Mors let out a loud laugh. "He knew, old giant! For a long time our Master Vvelz thought his sister's ambitions would further his own. Only later did he realize she would not spare him either if she perceived him as a threat to her plans. To save his neck, he acted lazy and weak. Li El did not consider him a threat—which, indeed, he was not—so she spared him."

Anger replaced sadness on Vvelz's face. Catchflea quickly spoke up and explained his own position among the Que-Shu, and how he had adopted a similar policy. Vvelz warmed noticeably to him after hearing the tale. "You see, Mors," he said. "Wisdom is the same in the Empty World as it is in Hest." Mors snorted derisively.

The old man sensed a certain chilliness between Vvelz and Mors, so he quickly returned to Vvelz's narrative. "So Li El conquered her fellow magicians. How did she overcome Drev and the Host?"

Vvelz glanced at Mors, but the blind elf turned his gaze down toward Di An. His expression was unreadable. With a shrug, Vvelz resumed. "There my sister relied on more ancient methods. She convinced the captain of the palace guard that she loved him, and won him to her cause. He in turn found disgruntled warriors in the ranks to join the conspiracy. It wasn't difficult. Having suppressed the Hall of Light, Drev thought his throne was secure. He paid his soldiers poorly, and put many to work in the mines alongside the diggers. He had an insatiable lust for gold.

"The day came when Li El and her captain seized the palace. Very little blood was shed. One or two confused guards resisted the plotters and were slain. Drev fled to the upper floors, pursued by Li El and a hundred warriors. They trapped him at the audience window, where the rulers of Hest were wont to throw coins or gems to the diggers on feast days. Poor, insane Drev screamed at Li El and called for his guards to save him. He pleaded with her to spare his life." Vvelz's lips tightened. "That gave Li El a great deal of pleasure. Rather than face the swords or Li El's spells, Drev finally threw himself from the window and died on the steps far below."

The old temple was quiet, save for the sounds of the Blue Sky People moving in the background. Di An rose to fetch Mors another cup of water. While she was gone, the blind elf said, "Tell the giant all, Vvelz." The sorcerer looked uncomfortable and said nothing. "Tell him!" he barked. "Please, don't spare me my full measure of guilt."

"I think I know," Catchflea said softly. "You were the captain who helped Li El, yes? You loved her."

"So true," Mors replied bitterly. Di An returned with his refreshment. "I betrayed my king and my position for her love. I succeeded only in bringing greater hardship to my people. And in the end, I, too, suffered a bitter betrayal."

Catchflea's brow wrinkled in thought. "Karn is her right hand now. Was it he?" At Vvelz's nod, Catchflea added, "Why was that so terrible?"

Mors shook with fury. He crushed the clay cup in his fist. "Ro Karn," he said, "is my son. Li El is his mother."

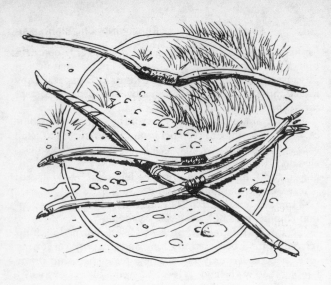

Chapter 8

The Golden Fields

Riverwind walked with Goldmoon across a sunlit field. Brilliant white clouds scudded from horizon to horizon. All around them was the sound of chimes tinkling in the wind.

"Are you happy?" asked Goldmoon, her smile as bright as the day.

"Very happy," Riverwind replied. He saw his beloved, the field of green grass, and the blue sky. He did not see the truth.

Small, dark-haired Li El looked up at the plainsman. "It made me glad to have you back," she said, appearing to him as Goldmoon. "I thought you would never return."

Riverwind halted and passed a hand before his eyes. "I don't—I don't remember how I got back. Or why I returned." He turned suddenly to the image of Goldmoon. "I only know that I love you."

"There has been trouble," Li El said calmly. Her small hand was lost in Riverwind's grasp, but she squeezed his hand reassuringly. "Plotters have tried to overthrow me."

Riverwind tensed. "Loreman," he growled.

"Yes, that's the one." Li El seized on every bit of information the plainsman offered. "He wants to kill me, my love."

Riverwind pulled the sorceress to him. "No one shall harm you, not while I live." Li El smiled, her cheek pressed against his chest. The sound of his pounding heart was loud in her ear. She asked him to say it again. "No one shall harm you while I live," he said fervently.

They resumed their walk. The Que-Shu village came into view as they topped the hill. It was only a dim outline, for Li El had not sharpened the details of her illusion yet. She needed more of Riverwind's memories in order to make her spell strong and believable.

"Should we go back?" she asked.

His hand went to his empty scabbard. "I've lost my saber."

Li El touched his hand. "I have a sword for you," she said. "There's much to be done."

The scene dissolved, and Riverwind found himself in a dim building. He thought it might be the Lodge of Brothers—and as the image of the lodge grew in his mind, so did Li El's illusion. He did not question how they had suddenly come to be there. Riverwind was like a sleeper, to whom all the strange occurrences of a dream are logical.

Goldmoon offered him a long, heavy sword, pommel first. Riverwind accepted the weapon.

"This isn't my saber," he said vaguely.

"No, brave Riverwind, but it's the finest sword I could find." This was the first true thing Li El had said. The sword, in fact, had belonged to the great Hest, twenty centuries ago. In his time, Hestantafalas had been counted a giant among his elven brothers, so his sword was nearly the proper size for Riverwind.

Lights flared in the lodge. Riverwind was confronted with three attackers, all of whom looked like his old foe, Hollowsky. He raised his new sword.

"This cannot be!" he declared. "You are dead—all three of you!"

"They are evil!" Li El said urgently. "You must save me!"

The three images of Hollow-sky attacked. Riverwind met the center one, parried, and slashed right and left to ward off the others. The center Hollow-sky twisted his face in a grimace of pure hatred. He thrust his short, straight blade at the plainsman's chest. Riverwind fended off the attack, grasped the hilt of Hest's sword with both hands, and brought the blade up in an underhand swipe. The keen point caught this Hollow-sky in the chest. The scowling attacker gave a shriek and lost his sword. He reeled away, and Riverwind thrust through him.

The foe to his left attacked next, though he seemed shrunken and shorter than the Hollow-sky Riverwind remembered. There was no time for reflection, as this enemy scored a cut across Riverwind's cheek. Blood flowed, and sweat stung the plainsman's eyes. This Hollow-sky shrank further, and his ears grew points. Riverwind was confused. This was not his dead foe from Que-Shu. But still he fought; a terrible compulsion drove him to charge the smaller man and bowl him over. Riverwind raised his point high. The fallen warrior lifted his empty hands in a plea for mercy. Riverwind held his blade back.

"Kill him!" Goldmoon cried. "He would kill me if he had the chance!"

Riverwind stared at her. Though strong-willed, Goldmoon knew the quality of mercy well and cherished it. His beloved would never say such a thing. Riverwind stepped back. For an instant, Goldmoon, too, seemed to be shorter than he remembered. Then, she was her beautiful self again. A golden aura surrounded her and it reached out and touched him. His qualms were washed away. Goldmoon would never ask him to do anything that wasn't right. He must kill to save her.

With the second Hollow-sky dead, the third showed considerable reluctance to fight. His blade met Riverwind's only twice before he dropped it and fled. Riverwind, panting heavily, asked Goldmoon if he should pursue the fleeing Hollow-sky and slay him.

"No," she said coolly. "He will do no harm." She surveyed the bloody lodge hall. "You have done well. You are an excellent champion."

"What?"

"Never mind," Li El said. "Go and rest now. Later, we will find the plotters and wipe them out. You must be strong, my brave Riverwind. Only then will I be safe."

He came to her and tried to take her hand. His fingers were stained with blood, and she avoided his touch. Riverwind's face was troubled as he looked at his hands. "I'm sorry," he said. He didn't wish to stain her white skin.

"Don't worry," Li El replied, though she regarded his still outstretched hand with distaste. "I'll come to you later. Go now and rest."

Still holding the sword of Hest, Riverwind wandered off in a daze. He passed through some golden curtains and spied a low stone couch. There were no such curtains or couches in the Lodge of Brothers, but still he did not question the illusion. The sword dropped from his hand, and he lay down on the couch, exhausted.

Li El surveyed the scene in the hearth room of the palace with satisfaction. Riverwind had fought and beaten three of her best guards. Her illusions needed some minor improvement, but by the time he went against the rabble led by Mors, Riverwind ought to cut quite a swath.

"He fights well, doesn't he?"

Li El broke out of her reverie and saw Karn lurking among the statues of Hest's dead heroes. "Why are you skulking there? Come out!" He did.

"The giant is just the tool you need to crush Mors," Karn said bitterly. "I wasn't good enough."

She looked toward the golden curtains. "Yes," she said softly. "He will be perfect."

Karn went to the first dead warrior. "Rjen," he said. "A good swordsman. Did you have to let the giant kill them?"

"This is not a game, Karn."

He stood over the second slain elf. "Mesk. He and I trained together."

Li El rubbed her slim white hands together. "Stop being such a child," she said tersely. "I had to test the strength of the illusion I've cast on Riverwind. And so I did."

Karn's shoulders sagged. "So what is next, Highness?"

"When the barbarian wakes, I want you to muster two cohorts of the Host. You will take them out and scour the cavern for Mors." Li El adjusted the folds of her golden robe and slipped her hood up over her dark hair. "Oh, and find the soldier who ran away just now. What is his name?"

"Prem. His name is Prem."

"Yes. Find Prem and put him under arrest. I won't have cowards serving me. Is that clear?"

"Yes, Highness."

Li El swept from the room. Karn watched her go. His anger at Riverwind's usurping of his place was gone. He had buried it as he had buried countless other hurts inflicted on him by the ambitious, unstoppable queen of Hest. Li El was merely using the outlander to reach their goal. Once they had attained that goal, the barbarian would be of no further use and he would be discarded. He was merely a tool. Karn was still lieutenant of the Host. He was still the son of Li El. Her chosen champion.

* * * * *

Vvelz received Mors's permission to show Catchflea the Blue Sky People's collection of objects brought down from the surface. Vvelz believed there might be useful things amid all the junk, things to use against Li El. He hoped that Catchflea could sort through the debris and identify the artifacts of the Empty World.

Catchflea and Vvelz picked their way up an ancient staircase littered with loose stones.

They came to a cleft in the rock wall of the cavern. It wasn't an obvious opening; projecting rocks had been chipped in such a way as to cast shadows over the hole. Vvelz slipped through, beckoning Catchflea to follow.

A squarish chamber had been cut out of the rock. Blue globes were distributed along the wall in cut niches. Catchflea let his hand rest gingerly on the nearest one. The blue light within quivered and roiled around. Sadness gripped the old man. This feeble light had once been a living, breathing Hestite. He wondered if it had been male or female, good, kind, lazy, homely. Did it still live inside the sphere? Did it yearn for freedom or the release of death?

"Come along," Vvelz urged. Catchflea took his hand away.

Stacked at the rear of the room were all sorts of things. Catchflea saw a stand of longbows, with only frayed bits of bowstring clinging to them.

"Those could be very useful," he said, pointing to the bows. "If you had strings—and arrows to shoot."

"What are arrows?" Vvelz asked. Catchflea blinked. He told Vvelz, with many hand gestures, the parts and practice of archery. The sorcerer was amazed.

"In the old chronicles, it was written that warriors could slay enemies at two hundred paces, but I always thought they threw spikes or daggers at each other!" He picked up a longbow of seasoned yew. "How could we make strings for them?" he asked.

"Well, I'm no bowyer, but I've seen men weave strong twine into bowstrings, then seal them with beeswax."

"Twine? Beeswax?"

Catchflea mopped his brow. This wasn't going to be easy.

"Twine is string, combed out of fibers like cotton or flax." Vvelz had no idea what he meant. Catchflea kicked about in the assorted goods and found a hank of rope. He showed this to the sorcerer. "Twine is thin, tough rope."

"Can you make this twine from rope?" the elf asked.

"I might, yes, though I'm no craftsman."

Farther along they found a few quivers full of arrows, though the feather fletching had rotted off most of them. Catchflea gave the quivers to Vvelz to hold, and they continued to poke among the piles of surface world goods.

Most of it was trash: leather shoes and belts so old they'd dried out and curled up into tight rolls, an assortment of rusty woodworking tools the Hestites had taken for exotic weapons.

"What is this?" Vvelz held up a nasty-looking device.

"A brace and bit. It bores holes, yes."

"Pah, that's ghastly!"

"In wood, Master Vvelz, only in wood," Catchflea

assured him.

Then they came to a great selection of jars and pots. Catchflea squatted down and lifted one lid after another. Spices. Moldy nuts. Wooden buttons.

"Your scouts must have waylaid every traveler in Ansalon to gather this assortment," Catchflea muttered.

"They had strict orders," Vvelz said. "Never to take large items or those things that are highly valued above. There's enough gold and gems in Hest already."

The old man found a jar full of chestnuts. They had dried, splitting their skins. He peeled one and ate it. It was so good, he grabbed a handful and nibbled them as he crept from pot to jar to pot.

"Tell me, Master Vvelz, who is Di An? She seems very close to Mors."

"Just a digger girl, a barren child. She's quite adept at prowling tunnels and stealing small items. As for Mors's affection, I believe they have known each other a long time. There's a rumor that it was Di An who first found Mors after he was blinded and driven out of Vartoom. She took care of him until he was strong again."

Catchflea spat out a chestnut shell. "And you, when did you join Mors?"

Vvelz dipped a finger in a pot of cracked pepper. He tasted the black powder and coughed violently. "Poison!" he gasped.

"No. Pepper." Catchflea put a pinch in his mouth. It burned, but not very much. "We use to flavor food."

Vvelz's eyes were watering. "You Empty Worlders must have iron stomachs!"

Catchflea chewed and swallowed the last of his chestnuts. "Master Vvelz, would you tell me how it came to be that you chose to work against your sister?"

"Ha-ha-*shoo!*" Vvelz sneezed and rubbed his nose. "Does it matter?" he sniffed. "Is it not enough that I risk my life to help Mors's cause?"

"It matters, yes. It occurs to me that if Li El wanted a spy close to Mors, you would be an excellent choice." He folded his arms across his chest. "A spy, or even an assassin."

Vvelz turned his left hand palm up. His eyes widened,

and he uttered a short, archaic spell. Catchflea quickly stepped back from him. A spark glowed in the sorcerer's up-turned palm. The spark grew into a small flame.

"You want to know, do you? Can you understand if I tell you? I have spent my entire life under the thumb of my heartless, ambitious sibling, who always considered me more servant than kinsman." Vvelz spoke slowly and softly. "She crushed good and wise sorcerers, whose only fault was not realizing the power of their opponent. She took the love of a brave warrior, bore his son, and then raised that son to hate his father. Her crowning achievement was using Karn to betray Mors. She gave the diggers an entire half-day of rest so that they could attend the ceremony she had pre-pared for Mors's blinding. That day was—that ceremony was . . ."

Words failed Vvelz, and he squeezed the flame tightly in his fist. Sparks and droplets of fire splashed to the floor. "I am ashamed she calls me brother. I will see the end of Li El, no matter who I have to side with."

Both men were silent. Vvelz was lost in dark thoughts of his sister, and Catchflea, discomfited by the tragic tale, looked beyond the elf's shoulder at the pots. There were so many. Pots and pots of—

"Pepper!" cried Catchflea.

"What?" said Vvelz. "Are you stricken?"

The old soothsayer rushed by Vvelz. "No! No, pepper is the answer!"

Catchflea swept an arm around in a half-circle. "There must be fifty pounds of pepper here," he said. "If all Hestites are as sensitive to it as you are—"

Vvelz's expression had brightened. "I begin to see! You mean to put this pepper in the warriors' food?"

"No, better! Throw it in their faces! They'll be so smitten with sneezing and weeping, your Blue Sky People will be able to disarm them easily. Riverwind can be rescued that way, too."

"Why won't our people be sneezing?" Vvelz asked.

The old man froze, his enthusiastic expression giving way to consternation. Then, his face brightened once more. "Why, give them kerchiefs to wear!" he exclaimed. "It will work! Let's tell Mors right away!"

But Mors was not impressed. "I'd rather see you repair these bow-things you found," he said with annoyance. "I would rather strike the Host from long range than close in with unskilled fighters and toss dust in their faces."

"Master Mors, even if I could fix all the bows, you would not have enough to make a difference against the entire Host. And archery is not a skill easily learned; it takes much practice, yes."

"How much practice?" Mors said.

"In Que-Shu, boys are taught archery not long after they learn to walk. A lifetime's practice makes them peerless archers."

"My people have only to hit close ranks of warriors," Mors insisted.

Vvelz intervened. "Perhaps we could adopt both plans. The bows will cause great harm to the warriors' spirits, and the pepper will send them to defeat."

"I don't like it," Mors grumbled. "True warriors do not fight by throwing dirt in their enemy's eyes. It's not honorable."

"Is it honorable to blind their captain and chase him from the city like a worthless beggar?" Vvelz said, knocking Mors's rod from his hand. The blind elf leaped to his feet.

"You gutless hand-waver! I may be blind, but I can break your neck with one hand—"

Di An, who had been listening quietly to all this, grasped Mors's leg and said, "Good Mors, don't hurt him. Master Vvelz seeks only to counsel you." She retrieved Mors's staff and placed it in his hands. The blind warrior's rough hand gripped her small one.

Mors relaxed. "What is your point?"

Di An looked at Vvelz. The latter said, "You do not owe Li El honorable combat. She is the one you are fighting. The Host is merely her instrument."

The scarred eyes turned to the sound of Vvelz's voice. "And Karn? What do I owe him? Stinging powder? Darts flung from two hundred paces?"

"You could forgive him," Catchflea said softly. "He has served Li El all these years, and that should be punishment enough."

"It was his choice," Mors said, sitting back down. "Bring the bows and the pepper from the hiding place. We will scourge Li El with flowers if that's what it takes. As for my son, if he will follow us to the world of blue sky and sunlight, I will try to forgive him."

"And if he won't?" asked Vvelz.

"Then he can lie in the tomb next to his mother."

* * * * *

Two cohorts, almost a thousand warriors, tramped in ragged lines across the floor of the great cavern. Karn had divided them into four units called Diamond, Ruby, Emerald, and Garnet. He commanded the Ruby Division, and Riverwind was with him, under one of Li El's illusions. He thought he was tracking Loreman and Hollow-sky after their attempt to kill Goldmoon.

"I've not been in these mountains before," Riverwind said. The wheat field they were crossing was tall and sparse. Wind was uncommon in Hest, but a slight, swirling breeze stirred the weak stands of grain.

"The wretches have hidden from us for years," Karn said, eyeing the plainsman uncertainly. Talking to the bewitched giant was like talking to a sleepwalker. Karn wasn't sure what the outlander saw or heard in his present state. Shame burned deep in his heart at having to employ this overgrown lout. Karn believed that he was good enough to crush the rebels; he didn't need a befuddled giant to assist him.

Riverwind felt the circling wind and smelled the ever-present smoke in the air. Yet he saw the plain of his homeland under a golden yellow sun. His heart beat fast. Goldmoon was safe only if he could catch and slay the evil men who wanted her dead. His long legs covered the ground in great strides, and his escort was strung out in a long line, trying to keep up.

"Slow down," Karn said irritably. "Infernal giant," he added under his breath.

Riverwind did more than slow, he stopped. His keen eyes caught a glint of steel on the slope of the mountain ahead.

"There," he said, pointing.

"What?" said Karn, shading his eyes from the brazen sun.

"Someone is up there. Carrying a sword. It must be them," Riverwind said. His pulse quickened in his chest.

Karn saw, not the illusion of mountains, but the abandoned temple where his ancestors had once worshiped. "You're wrong. We checked there already. The diggers must be dispersed in small bands throughout the caverns."

"They are there," Riverwind insisted. He started off at a fast lope.

"Wait! Halt! I command here!" Karn shouted. Riverwind slowed. Goldmoon had told him to obey this short fellow. Karn hustled up. "Remember, you do as I say!" he said hoarsely. "That, ah, mountain is infested with evil spirits. Our quarry would not be hiding up there."

"Why not? If I wanted to hide, I'd go where evil spirits were rumored to live. Ghosts would keep visitors away."

The other soldiers had caught up and were listening with evident interest. The giant's words made sense to them.

"Goldmoon said to search the tunnels in the south wall— I mean, mountain range. An army of rebels could hide there." Those were Li El's orders. Besides, Karn reasoned, nobody would dare hide in the ancient temple.

Riverwind did not advance toward the temple, nor did he turn. The rest of Ruby Division slouched to a halt behind the plainsman. "The enemy is there." He raised a long arm and pointed again at the distant temple.

Karn had had enough of the outlander's arrogance. "Form a line of march!" Karn raged. He cursed at the Hestite soldiers until they formed two parallel lines. "Now stand there until I order you to move!" To Riverwind, he said, "You will obey my orders without question, understand? Her Highness—Goldmoon—expects you to do as I say."

Riverwind looked down at the man. "Yes, Captain."

The Ruby Division made off for the south wall. Riverwind walked slowly alongside the column, his gaze still fixed on the abandoned temple, which he saw as a mountain. He had seen the glint of steel there. He really had.

Chapter 9

Lost Diamonds

Karn, Riverwind, and the Ruby Division reached the south wall many hours later. As Karn had said, the cave wall was honeycombed with holes and tunnels, many of which had been carved out of the limestone by early Hestites and used as homes. The soldiers went in by twos and threes, rooting through the rubbish collected at the mouth of the caves, searching for signs of recent habitation. They found none.

"They could be deeper in the wall," Karn mused. One of his subordinates said timidly that it did not seem likely. "Oh? Why so?" Karn asked.

The filthy, mud-coated Hestite replied, "Water has trickled down through the walls, my captain. In most of the caves a foot of water has collected at the back. There's nothing else in them but mud and broken pottery."

Karn sat on a round boulder and said, "Well, keep looking. The scum are likely to be in the last place you think to search." The weary soldier saluted and returned to the hunt.

"Shall I go, too?" Riverwind asked.

"No, I don't want you to get wedged in some tight spot," Karn answered absently. "Those holes weren't made by giants."

All through the day Karn had been receiving messages from Li El in the city. Messages from the other divisions of the Host also arrived, brought by runners. While his troops ransacked the south wall caves, runners from Emerald Division and Garnet Division arrived from the mining district, with news that no Blue Sky rebels had been found. Karn scratched his hollow cheek and pondered what to do next. The queen's grand design was bearing little fruit so far.

"If the Diamonds find no sign of the enemy in the orchards, we'll go back to Vartoom," Karn said. "Her Highness will have to employ her Art once more to find signs of them."

They waited for a runner from the Diamonds to arrive. None did. Riverwind stood off to one side, his mind wrapped in visions the queen conjured for him. Li El exploited all of his emotions: his love for Goldmoon, his fear and distrust of Loreman and Arrowthorn, his guilty exultation over the death of Hollow-sky. His mind was aboil as he relived these events over and over. Outwardly he looked calm, even somnolent. Li El had insisted on fitting him with what bits of Hestite armor would fit him. Greaves and vambraces were laced to his arms and legs. A gorget protected his neck, and an open helmet covered his head. It was Hest's own helmet, though on Riverwind it fit like a skullcap.

The plainsman longed to be back with Goldmoon. Danger was all around them. Loreman and his followers would come armed, not with sabers or bows, but with common rocks. Heretics were stoned. Heretics such as Riverwind and his beloved.

Karn idly chewed a dry biscuit. His troops were slowly filtering back to the plain, having examined every dirty hole in the wall. Soon some two hundred and fifty warriors were sprawled among the mossy stones.

Vartoom was a pale blue shadow in the floating veil of smoke. Karn squinted at the outline of the city. Should he give the order to return? Should he present himself to Li El empty-handed? She would not be pleased. Perhaps he could blame it on the giant . . .

A commotion drew Karn out of his musings and roused Riverwind, too. Two Hestites were carrying a limp body over to a soft patch of moss. Karn leaped to his feet. Riverwind followed him.

"What is it?" the plainsman asked dully.

"Stand back, you're blocking the light," Karn snapped. He loosened the strap on the warrior's helmet and pulled it off. The wounded Hestite's face was red and swollen, particularly his eyes and nose. Karn knew him by the marking on his breastplate. He was with the Diamond Division.

"What happened?" Karn demanded of the Diamond.

"Ambush," the soldier said through inflamed lips. "Our captain—killed. A choking fog spread over the company. We couldn't see. The warriors—suffocated, sneezing. The division was—wiped out," he gasped.

Karn sank back on his haunches. "Wiped out? Wiped out?" He grasped the wounded man by the arms and hauled him to his feet. "*Wiped out*?" he shouted in the elf's face.

"My captain, look!" said another Hestite. He pointed to the wounded Diamond's back. The light plate armor had a hole in it. The wounded man bled copiously. The jagged stump of whatever had made the hole protruded.

"By our lady," Karn breathed. "What in Hest's name is that?"

"Arrow," Riverwind said. "Broken off."

The warriors looked at him without comprehension. "What is 'arrow'?" Karn asked desperately.

Riverwind regarded him in puzzlement, but went on to explain what an arrow was, and how it was shot.

"Do the rebels have such weapons?" asked one of Karn's soldiers. Others took up the question and its implications. Karn let the wounded warrior go and jumped to his feet.

"I cannot fight an enemy who hurls darts at us from far away! Her Highness must be told of this at once!

DRAGONLANCE Preludes

Trumpeter—where's that damned trumpeter? Sound the muster call. Call Garnet and Emerald back to us."

A slender young elf climbed atop a large boulder and put a brass cornet to his lips. The shrill notes echoed and re-echoed across the vast cavern. A few moments later, horns from the other two divisions responded.

Riverwind knelt by the forgotten, wounded soldier. He was dead. The plainsman closed the elf's eyes and his fingers came away stained with black powder. He touched his tongue to the stain to clean it away. His tongue burned. Pepper. His dark brows drew together in a frown. That did not make sense.

"You!" Karn said, poking Riverwind's shoulder from behind. "Pick him up and carry him." Riverwind scooped up the dead warrior easily in his arms. The Rubies milled around, worried and uncertain. Karn bullied them into formation, and they set out directly for Vartoom. They hadn't gone two miles before the Emerald Division appeared, coming toward them through a grove of stunted apple trees. The warriors staggered as they ran. Some had lost their weapons. Many clutched their faces in their hands and sobbed loudly.

Karn halted his soldiers. A corporal from the Emeralds lurched up to him and sagged to the ground at Karn's feet.

"My captain," the elf gasped. "I beg to report the Emerald Division routed!"

Blood suffused Karn's face. "Routed by whom?" he screamed.

"Sir—Captain—they wore the arms of our Diamond Division!"

"That's impossible. The Diamonds were attacked and defeated a few hours ago," Karn said.

"There were hundreds and hundreds," the elf cried. "Some were just diggers. Others wore warrior's plate and carried swords. And—there was a wagon—"

"Wagon? What wagon?"

"Yes, sir. It was pushed by diggers with masks over their faces. Smoke came out of a pipe on the wagon, smoke that blinded us and made us weep and sneeze."

Karn drew his sword and scanned the orchard. "How long ago was this?"

"Not long, my captain. Perhaps an hour or less."

Riverwind laid the slain Diamond warrior down and came to Karn's side. He'd heard what the elves had said.

"Shall we pursue these agents of Loreman?" he asked.

"Pursue?" Karn was quickly losing what little composure he had. "We'd better prepare to defend ourselves!"

"They won't attack us. Not here," the plainsman said.

"How do you know?" Karn's body quivered with rage and his face was nearly purple.

"They ambushed two bands of warriors. They'll not attack a fully warned group in the open," he said. "Loreman would more likely sneak around us and head for the village." This idea hit him with belated force. "Goldmoon! She will need us!"

"What are you raving about? Vartoom is still defended by the Host." Karn took several deep breaths. The tremors in his limbs stilled and his color began to return to normal. "I have decided what we will do. The Emerald warriors can join us. We'll skirt the orchard and try to make contact with the Garnet Division."

"And then?" asked the Emerald corporal, still sniffling.

"Then—then I will consider what to do next," Karn said stiffly.

About a hundred soldiers of the Emerald Division filled in the ranks of Karn's troops. The Hestites marched on, keeping the orchard on their left and the city on their right. Fear was infecting the rank and file, fear made worse as the surviving Emeralds told their story to their brothers in Ruby.

"The choking clouds!"

"Javelins raining from the air—"

"Hundreds of armed diggers, and they weren't afraid of us!" And that, more than anything, terrified the warriors.

*   *   *   *   *

Catchflea surveyed the mass of prisoners taken by the Blue Sky People in their first two attacks. Almost three hundred warriors knelt in a close circle, stripped of arms and armor, guarded by grinning diggers. The pepper fog had been successful far beyond the old soothsayer's dreams. Two diggers, one a former miller, the other an expert forge-maker, contrived a bellowslike device that sprayed the pepper at the enemy. Mounted on a wagon, the pepper fog machine had ensured their amazing early victories.

The bows, however, were less successful. True, the Blue Sky's first apprentice archers had hit several of the Diamond warriors in the first attack, but before the fight was over, all but one of the bows was broken. In their excitement, the diggers used their valuable bows as clubs, splintering them against the warriors' armor.

Mors was in a buoyant mood. Di An led him to the place where the warriors were being held. Vvelz followed silently behind the blind elf.

"How do they look?" Mors asked.

"They weep," Catchflea replied. "For shame and the pepper in their eyes, yes."

"You proved your worth, old giant," Mors said. He clapped Catchflea on the back. "Just think what we'll accomplish together in the future." Catchflea didn't like the sound of that. Seeing the red-faced, weeping warriors made him sad. And the dead from both sides haunted him. He had been with the Blue Sky People only five days. What indeed would be the result if he continued to aid Mors? He thought of Riverwind and wondered where the tall man was.

Vvelz was unhappy, too. Formerly Mors's most important advisor, he now found himself shunted in favor of Catchflea. Mors had begun to ask the old man's advice on matters other than those concerning the surface world—like how to govern Vartoom once Li El was deposed. Catchflea tried to shy away from the subject, since Li El was far from finished, but Mors insisted, asking about the Que-Shu political system. Catchflea outlined his people's method of electing a chief.

"A strange doctrine," said Mors. "I can understand the part about choosing a brave and resourceful warrior to lead you, but what is that about marrying the previous chieftain's daughter? What has that to do with finding a strong ruler?"

"We believe it important to have a chief who is close to the gods," Catchflea said. "Our chieftain's daughter is the spiritual leader of our people—our priestess."

"Are your priestesses skilled in magic?" asked Vvelz.

"Almost never."

The sorcerer's light-colored eyes widened. "No?"

"The Que-Shu have little to do with the magical arts, other than healing and communing with the spirits of our ancestors."

Vvelz assumed a look of deep concentration. "By your ways, then, the best thing Mors could do, once we defeat the Host, is marry Li El and rule with her."

The blind warrior moved with remarkable speed. He jabbed the end of his staff into Vvelz's stomach. The slender sorcerer doubled over in pain and shock.

"Why—strike me?" Vvelz groaned.

"You should not make such remarks," Mors said stiffly. "And thank your destiny I didn't have a sword in my hands."

Vvelz backed away, shooting venomous looks at Mors. He slowly straightened, rubbing his bruised stomach. Catchflea offered to help him, but the sorcerer coolly declined the old man's hand. The air was thick with tension. Catchflea wondered what would happen next.

A digger ran headlong into the scene, tripping on a stone and sprawling at Mors's feet. Catchflea grasped the digger by the back of her black copper shirt and hauled her up. It was Di An.

"The warriors are coming!" she gasped.

Mors jumped up. "Where and how many?"

"Very many—more than we have faced before," the elf girl said. She flung an arm out, pointing. "That way."

Mors didn't see her gesture, but he scowled. Standing well out of the reach of the blind warrior's staff, Vvelz said, "Karn did not do as you expected. He did not retreat to the city."

"No, someone has stiffened his spine," Mors said darkly.

"The other giant is with Karn," Di An reported.

"Riverwind is with him?" Catchflea asked. Di An looked to the old man and nodded once. "He would not help Li El willingly," the old man insisted. "He must be under a spell."

"It matters not why he is with them," Mors replied. "If he

fights for Li El, he must die as surely as any other warrior of the Host."

"No!"

"I've no time to argue; there's a battle brewing."

"If you want my help, you'd better grant me this favor," Catchflea said. "Riverwind is my friend, and he must not be harmed."

"Are you holding me up?" Mors planted his fists on his narrow hips.

Catchflea measured the distance between them, hoping that Mors could not strike him. Quietly he said, "That's the price of my assistance."

Mors thrust out his chin. "You have been valuable to our cause," he said. "I will tell my people to take the giant alive if they can." Then Mors was off, shouting at his followers. Tired diggers appeared from the orchard and surrounding fields, their shirts stuffed with stolen fruit. Over a thousand diggers had been armed with everything from swords taken from dead Hestite soldiers to farm tools and mining equipment. The wagon with the pepper spraying device creaked out of the trees toward Mors. A few minutes after Di An had brought the news, the rebel army, such as it was, had assembled around its blind general.

"People of the Blue Sky," Mors announced. "The tyrant Li El has not yet learned her lesson. As I stand here speaking to you, a large number of warriors is crossing the valley floor beyond the orchard. We must fight again today." A loud murmur went through the crowd. "I know!" Mors said. "You are tired, but the task is too great to be done leisurely. We must smash the warriors wherever and whenever we find them, and only then will we gain our victory."

Vvelz sidled up to Catchflea and Di An. "Do you believe in final victory, old man?" he said, barely above a whisper.

"More than I did before, yes," said Catchflea. "We've beaten Li El's troops twice already."

"Small bands, greatly outnumbered," Vvelz countered. "Ambushed and frightened by weapons they've never seen before. Those out there now know what to expect. And your friend is with them. What do you think our chances are now?"

The old man put his arm around Di An's shoulders and looked Vvelz square in the eye. "Our chances are as the gods decide, yes. Just as it always was."

Vvelz pursed his lips and turned away. He walked off among the scattered boulders and soon was lost from sight.

"What is his problem?" Catchflea wondered aloud.

"He is afraid," Di An said. "Her Highness will do terrible things to him if she catches him."

Catchflea ruffled his hand through Di An's short, sparse hair. "Are you afraid?" he asked gently.

"Yes." She shivered. "But not really for myself."

"Oh? You fear for Mors, yes?"

The Blue Sky army broke up as Mors finished his speech. The weary diggers filed into formations, ready to meet the enemy as they rounded the orchard. Di An ducked out from under the old man's arm and said, "Not only for Mors."

Chapter 10

Blood and Gold

Once, when he was a boy, Riverwind witnessed the passing of a company of mercenaries through the forest south of Que-Shu. His father had warned him from the earliest age to beware of such marauders, so when the boy heard the menacing, unmistakable clatter of steel in the woods, he climbed a tall maple and hid among the dense leaves. The soldiers passed directly beneath him.

First came the horsemen. Fifty pairs of men on big animals, they wore rusty, dented breastplates and carried long lances. He could not see their faces, but coarse, dark hair hung down from beneath their helmets. The horsemen rode slowly and silently, eyes always scanning the trees for signs of movement.

On the riders' heels came a marching contingent of foot

soldiers. Riverwind saw them better because they had doffed their helmets and went bareheaded. They were great, burly fellows with yellow or red hair plaited in long braids. Fearsome, broad-bladed axes rested on their shoulders. They paid little attention to the woods on each side, instead laughing and talking among themselves in a language the boy did not understand.

After the hundred or so axemen there came a band of archers. They wore leather armor only, and their step was light and springy. Their longbows were fastened on their backs, and each man carried a spike-headed maul. They spoke in quiet, clipped sentences, a fashion Riverwind well knew. It was the way of the huntsman, who spoke only enough to communicate with his fellows and not enough to scare off game.

As these wondrous and frightening sights moved below him, Riverwind felt his grasp on a slender branch give way. The twig snapped. He saved himself from falling, but the twig fluttered down to the road. An archer saw it fall and re-trieved it. Riverwind held his breath, but the man merely walked along, twirling the leafy stick between his fingers. Just before the archer had passed out of sight, and just as Riverwind had begun to sigh with relief, the man swiftly drew an arrow from his quiver, nocked, pulled, and re-leased it in one smooth motion. The iron-tipped shaft struck the tree just beside Riverwind's head. The shock and vibra-tion shivered through the tree.

The boy nearly fainted with fright. The archer called out in clear Que-Shu: "Mind yourself, friend; a twig can kill as surely as an arrow." And with that, the archer walked on. No one else had seen.

Strange that this old recollection should come to him now. Or not so strange; Riverwind's mind was lost, wander-ing through deep corridors of memory. He encountered many phantoms there: childhood friends and foes, his fa-ther, his lost brother, Windwalker, as well as Loreman, Hollow-sky, Arrowthorn . . . but not Goldmoon. Where she should have been in his memory, bright and beautiful, he saw only shadows, heard only muffled voices. Where was Goldmoon?

"What are you muttering about?" asked Karn.

"Where is Goldmoon?" Riverwind said.

"You know very well she's in the city. She's waiting for us to root out and destroy these rebels." Karn was weary of this stupid charade. He and his warriors had marched almost forty miles back and forth across the cavern.

"What city is that?" Riverwind said. The shadows in his mind were spreading, obscuring even the most recent parts of his memory.

"Vartoom," Karn snapped. "Stupid barbarian."

Vartoom. Riverwind sorted his motley recollections. "The underground city?"

The elf warrior did not bother to reply. The end of the orchard was in sight. There was a rocky gully to cross and, on the other side, the pit and workings of a deep gold mine. From where he was, Karn could see that the mine was empty. No diggers bustled about, pushing carts of gold ore to the smelter. The whole excavation was vacant. That was not right. Li El had ordered the gold mines to be worked continuously.

"Halt," Karn said, raising his hand. Behind him, four hundred soldiers slowed and stopped in a long, straggling column. Riverwind swayed a little on his feet. He was so terribly confused. Around him were the fields of his homeland, green grass undulating in the breeze. But ahead, in the midst of the green, was a gaping hole. A rock-filled gaping hole. There seemed to be mine carts around it. He shook his head. Li El's distance from the plainsman and her increasing preoccupation with the myriad problems caused by the spreading digger revolt were weakening her hold on Riverwind. Each small, conflicting bit of reality that managed to penetrate his befuddled mind only served to undermine her spells further.

"I don't like this," Karn muttered. "Where are the workers?"

Just then, a lone figure appeared on the other side of the gully. A warrior, wearing the armor of the Garnet Division. The figure raised a hand high in greeting.

"Ho-la!" Karn shouted, grinning. "It's a scout from the Garnets!"

"A twig can kill as surely as an arrow," Riverwind murmured.

"Overgrown idiot," Karn rasped. "Her Highness has saddled me with an idiot." He waved vigorously at the Hestite across the gully. Cupping his hands to his mouth, Karn called, "How far away is the rest of your company?"

"Half a mile," said the distant warrior.

"Go back and tell them to stop where they are and be on watch for the rebels," Karn shouted. "We will cross and join you."

The figure waved a hand.

"That's not a good idea," Riverwind said.

"Shut up." Karn turned to his tired troops and told them they would soon be joining the last of their comrades in safety on the other side of the ravine. The Hestites raised a cheer.

Riverwind clamped a strong hand on Karn's shoulder. "It's a trap," he insisted.

"Get your dirty hands off me!" Karn snarled. When Riverwind was slow to comply, he broke the plainsman's grip and stepped back. "I think Her Highness miscalculated. You've been as useful on this march as an ore cart. When I tell the queen how worthless you are, maybe then she'll get rid of you once and for all."

"Goldmoon will not listen to you," Riverwind said. A trace of true emotion crept into his voice. "You're being tricked into dividing your force. The rebels are near, and they will attack."

"How do you know this? How? Do you have magical sight? What is the source of this penetrating wisdom?" Karn said sarcastically. "Eh, giant? What do you say?"

"The one you hailed was not a flesh and blood person, but a shadow. I could see through him," Riverwind said. "I could see—I saw through him."

Karn snorted. "I'll not waste any chance to crush the rebels. If they are near, it is my duty to give them the sword." He waved his soldiers forward. The warriors made four single-file lines and started into the gully.

The elves scrambled down the loose gravel slope, skidding on their heels, sprawling in the trickle of water that flowed down the center of the gully's bottom. Smeared with black mud, their armor dented by stones, the warriors reached the other face and started up. When about fifty warriors had gained the far side, Karn went down himself. Red boulders rose out of the mud like berries in a bowl of gruel.

Karn slipped and slid like his troops, but he climbed to the far side and yelled back, "Come on, giant! Or are you watching for people who aren't there again?"

Riverwind dropped heavily down the slope. The rocks were rolling under his feet; he lost his footing and fell back. The polished helmet came off and clattered to the ground.

"Ha-ha-ha! The great warrior!" Karn sneered. "I've seen old crones who could walk better than you, ha-ha!" He was still laughing when the arrow hit him in the back.

Karn stumbled forward a step or two. He could feel the shaft in his back, feel the heat of his blood flowing out, but he could not accept what had happened. The giant's shocked gaze was on him, then it slid past his shoulder to stare at something behind him. Karn tried to turn around, to see what was there, but a red haze filmed his eyes and he suddenly felt the rocky ground bang the back of his head. The brazen sun filled his eyes.

The Blue Sky People set up a concerted cry of fierce joy and fell upon the divided bands of warriors. True to their heritage and training, the Hestite soldiers formed ranks as best they could and presented shields and swords to the rebels. Several hundred Blue Sky People swarmed out of the rocks surrounding the gold mine. Those not armed with stolen weapons threw stones. The seventy-odd warriors on Karn's side of the gully locked their shields together and hacked down any digger brave enough to close within sword's reach. The warriors on the opposite bank shouted encouragement to their comrades and crowded forward to enter the gully, eager to join the fight.

Riverwind stood amid a shower of fist-sized rocks. The gully was full of milling Hestites, yelling and waving swords. The soldiers packed in tightly, trying to scale the slope exactly behind the small circle of their brothers on the far bank. Bodies began to roll down the slope, knocking down other warriors who were trying to reach the battle.

Amid all this chaos, the plainsman strode head and shoulders above the rest. He fended off rocks with his shield. He shoved aside the turmoil and confusion in his mind. The enemy had shown himself. Now was the time to end the threat to Goldmoon once and forever.

"Form ranks—don't crowd!" he cried. The Hestite soldiers paid him no heed. The whole of Karn's force was now either in the gully or on the far bank. Senseless, wounded, and dead warriors were piling up at the foot of the slope.

A deep, rushing sound filled Riverwind's ears. It was like the wind. The soldiers around the plainsman began to scream and claw at their faces. Riverwind couldn't tell where the rushing sound came from. It was a steady *whoosh-whoosh*, not really like the wind, more like a great beast breathing.

Black smoke rolled through the air. It settled more quickly than smoke usually did, enveloping the warriors. Coughing erupted from three hundred throats. The smoke was actually dust. Riverwind's eyes flooded with tears. He blinked them away and drew his sword.

The elves were more affected by the dust than Riverwind was. As he climbed the stony slope, warriors collapsed around him, gasping for breath. Their ranks thinned, and Riverwind was able to make it to the top.

The scene he found was like a dream of the Abyss. Hundreds of black-clad figures surrounded the warriors, all screaming at the top of their lungs. Rocks flew, swords flashed, and blood flowed. Riverwind saw these black-garbed figures and knew they were agents of Loreman.

In the center of the swarm of diggers was a wagon on which a bellowslike contraption puffed gouts of black dust at the Hestite warriors. Diggers pumped away, making the engine spew the noxious stuff from its flared bronze nozzle.

Riverwind shouldered to the line of shields and broke through. The Blue Sky People gave way as the plainsman advanced. A few brave ones thrust swords at him, which he easily parried. A shower of rocks fell on him. They hurt, but they weren't going to stop him.

Black dust flew directly into his face. Riverwind sneezed

repeatedly and his eyes watered, but he kept coming. Diggers only half his height tried to stop him with swords they'd picked up only a few hours earlier. The sword of Hest cleaved through them one after another, yet always there was another hate-filled face to replace the one he'd just slashed at.

The plainsman leaped onto the wagon and cut down the diggers manning the bellows. The keen elven steel of Hest's blade split the soft copper and bronze of the bellows, spilling the pepper on the diggers nearest the wagon. They wheezed loudly in spite of their masks and fell over themselves trying to get away from the choking dust.

"Rally to me, men of Que-Shu!" Riverwind roared over the din of battle. But the Hestite soldiers could not hold, much less rally. The last part of Mors's trap had been sprung when two hundred Blue Sky diggers rushed the soldiers in the gully. They'd been hiding around the bend, lying low in the mud. Their black clothes camouflaged them, and when they rose up, it was as if the ground itself were coming to life. Without Karn to keep them in order, the warriors broke. Some fell on their knees and begged for mercy. Others dropped their weapons and ran.

Riverwind raged at them to stand and fight. Then a particularly well-aimed rock hit him above the ear, stunning him. By the time he shook it off, he saw a Que-Shu man standing above the mob of black-clad figures.

"Loreman!" he bellowed. Riverwind waded through the sea of diggers toward the author of all his misery. Loreman, the crafty, plotting serpent . . . if Riverwind died in the next minute, he knew he would be satisfied if only he could bury his sword in Loreman's heart.

The Que-Shu elder did not attempt to get away. He watched Riverwind cut his way toward him, but he didn't move. Brave old fox, the plainsman grudgingly thought.

The diggers ceased trying to fight Riverwind and merely evaded his slashing blade. A lane opened in the mob, direct from Riverwind to his intended target. The old man waited calmly.

"Loreman, it's time for you to die!" Riverwind declared.

"I'm not Loreman," the elder said.

"I can see who you are! You can't lie your way out of your fate now!"

"Look again, tall man! You can see who I really am, yes?"

Riverwind raised his sword high. He focused all his rage on the gray-haired figure before him. Nothing would stop him. Nothing. The world could explode in flames, and he would still kill Loreman. And yet—his arm refused to strike. *Thrust home! Use the sword!* a voice screamed in his head. *Here is your enemy helpless—kill him! I demand it!*

Goldmoon's face loomed in his mind's eye. Her blue eyes were clouded with hate, her smooth white face contorted by rage. *Kill my enemies!* her voice shrieked. *Kill them all!*

Beloved! his heart cried out. Goldmoon would never, could never, say such a thing to him! She had never looked at anyone, not even Loreman, with such ugly, bald hate. Her face began to change, its soft, rounded smoothness becoming thinner, more angular.

Kill them all! the woman's voice screamed again, and Riverwind dropped the sword as his hands clutched his head. He fell to the ground. The distorted, ugly face of Goldmoon ranted and shrieked at him. Her face changed further. The gold hair darkened and thickened. Soon it was a rich red-brown shade. This was not the face of Goldmoon. It was the queen of Hest—Li El!

"Riverwind?" the old man said.

Riverwind lay face-down on the ground, sharp rocks nicking his face. Finally, the soft voice of the old man penetrated his throbbing temples. He moved with great care and looked up. "Catchflea," he said hoarsely.

The old soothsayer smiled. The eyes that looked up at him in exhaustion were his friend's eyes once more. Catchflea had felt his knees turn to sand when he'd first seen Riverwind striding toward him, murder in his eyes. He extended a hand to the large warrior.

Riverwind got to his feet and looked around him like a man seeing home again for the first time. He and Catchflea were in the center of a vast crowd of diggers, standing silently, watching them. The edge of the circle of diggers opened and Di An appeared, leading a blind elf by the hand.

"Is he himself?" asked Mors.

"He is, yes," said Catchflea.

"Riverwind," Di An said breathlessly.

He smiled at her, then followed her gaze, looking down at himself. Li El's gift of Hestite armor looked incongruous on his tall, rangy form. He tore the lacings and flung the undersized breastplate away. The diggers seized the engraved armor and began to stomp on it, obliterating the heraldic crest of the great Hest.

Di An led Mors to Riverwind. Catchflea introduced the leader of the Blue Sky People. Conscious of his position, of what he'd done, the plainsman sank down to his knees. "I place myself at your mercy," he said. "I know I have fought against those I should have helped. Many are dead because of me."

The elf girl regarded Mors expectantly. Catchflea went to Riverwind's side. He said, "He's not responsible for what he did, Master Mors. You know Li El's power."

The blind elf cocked his head to one side. "Am I to do nothing to him then? What do you say, Vvelz?"

"Vvelz isn't here," Di An said.

"No, not when there's fighting, I'm sure. Find Master Vvelz for me." Mors's command rippled outward through the crowd.

"The warriors are done," Catchflea said. He surveyed the now quiet battlefield. "Though I fear a good number got away to warn Li El."

Mors said, "You, giant: I will spare you, as the old barbarian wishes it. He has been of great service to me, so I owe him a boon."

Riverwind thanked Mors wearily.

Gradually the Blue Sky People returned from chasing the scattered warriors. The dead and injured were separated, and those still living were treated. Catchflea noticed that even as the rebels sorted themselves out, more diggers appeared, joining the ranks. They were fresh runaways, still bearing their tools and still coated with the soot from the foundries. With the newcomers came the word that all of Vartoom was in turmoil. Soldiers ran in the streets, bawling the news. Karn was dead, the Host defeated, and Mors was coming. Li El was making no attempt to calm her people.

She did not appear among them, nor did she use her considerable presence to bolster her flagging troops.

"We have won?" asked Di An.

"Not so easily. She's gathering her strength," Mors said, "though her witcheries against Riverwind must have drained her considerably. Where is Vvelz? I want to know what she's plotting."

"We've found him—" Diggers bore their victorious leader along. Catchflea, Riverwind, and Di An followed in Mors's wake. Near the lip of the gully, the crowd parted, revealing Vvelz on his knees in the bloody mud. Beside him was Ro Karn. Vvelz was working a healing spell on him.

"Will he live?" Mors asked once the situation was explained to him.

"Only as long as you wish him to," Vvelz replied tersely. He tossed the broken arrow into the gully. His hands were covered in blood. "I thought you would want me to aid him, Mors."

"He knew what he was doing."

Vvelz glared up at him. "This is your son!"

"He's Li El's creature."

Catchflea coughed. "Mors, how much does the queen value Karn? Perhaps he would be useful as a hostage, yes?"

Mors hung his head a moment, then replied. "Put him in a wagon under guard. If he causes trouble, kill him. Otherwise, bring Ro Karn with us to Vartoom." Mors cast a hand about, trying to find Di An. The barren child was usually right at his side. "Where are you, Di An?" he called. Mors could not see that she was with Riverwind some ten yards distant. The exhausted plainsman had finally collapsed and was sitting quietly while the elf girl gently washed the cuts on his face. Catchflea hurried over to them.

The blind elf put out his hands slowly, reluctant to blunder about on his own. He feared he was all alone till he felt another hand grasp his. Mors gripped the hand, though it was sticky and damp.

"I'll lead you," Vvelz said. The blind elf said nothing, but closed his fingers tightly around Vvelz's hand, smearing himself with Karn's blood.

Chapter 11

The Last Choice

The Blue Sky People advanced on Vartoom in a quiet mass, without formation or order. Everywhere they passed, diggers threw down their tools and joined them. A sense that something vitally important was happening possessed the Hestites. The warriors captured with Karn were abandoned. Riverwind was surprised to see many of them fall in with the crowd and walk peacefully beside the same diggers they had tried to slay only hours earlier.

"Why are you surprised, tall man?" Catchflea said. "The cause they fought for now must seem totally lost. And Li El is not loved by any of them."

Riverwind looked at the chains around his wrists. Mors had insisted the young plainsman be bound, so that if Li El reasserted her power over his mind, he could do little real damage to the digger army. "Her cause is not lost yet. Li El is very powerful on her own."

The old man put a hand on the young man's back. "She is, yes, but she cannot hope to defeat so many. Mors will drown her in rebellious diggers if she resists."

"She will resist."

In the center of the moving mass of Hestites strode Mors and Vvelz. Those ahead broke down walls and fences so the blind elf could go forth unimpeded. He maintained a tight grip on Vvelz's hand. The sorcerer did not complain.

Behind Mors, four diggers carried the unconscious form of Ro Karn. Vvelz had stopped his bleeding and closed his wound with the healing spell, but the shock and damage of the arrow was still there. Riverwind and Catchflea followed behind the elves carrying Karn, and trotting at the tall plainsman's side was Di An.

The crowd stopped only once. A canal was cut in the stone floor of the cavern, watering the wheat fields at the base of the city terraces. There were two broad stone bridges across the canal, and these were blocked by hastily assembled contingents of the Host. The Blue Sky People milled about, uncertain whether to charge the bridges. Mors, Vvelz, the plainsmen, and Di An gradually worked their way to the front of the crowd.

"Who is that?" Mors called.

A soldier with a golden sun riveted to the front of his helmet replied, "Hail, Ro Mors!"

"Quarl? Is that you?"

"It is, Ro Mors."

"Stand aside, Quarl. You cannot stop us."

"I have my orders," the warrior called back.

Mors turned away from the bridge. "Take the bridges," he said loudly. Armed diggers closed in, swords and spears flashing by the brazen sun's light.

Quarl advanced his thirty warriors to the center of the bridge. Along the banks of the canal, diggers began slipping into the sluggish water and wading across. Smoke obscured the second bridge, but the clatter of arms reached his ears, telling Riverwind the battle there was joined.

The Blue Sky diggers moved cautiously. It was one thing

to ambush warriors in open country, hampering them with pepper and flying rocks. But to meet them face to face in the confines of a bridge, sword to sword—they went forward slowly indeed. The warriors behind Quarl grew impatient and shouted taunts.

A blast of hard wind swept over the bridge, swirling smoke in the diggers' eyes. Vvelz snatched his hand from Mors's grasp. "Lie down and cover your heads!" he shouted.

"What are you babbling about?" Mors demanded.

"Li El—!"

The dull boom of thunder rolled down the cavern. Ripple patterns appeared on the canal's surface. The wading diggers cried out as the water surged forward, rising in a wave twice their height. A smoke whirlwind formed over Vartoom. The Blue Sky People screamed and fell to their knees, covering their heads with their hands. Soon, out of a crowd of thousands, only Mors and Riverwind were left standing.

"Rage on, Li El!" Mors roared. "See if you can blow me away!"

Hardly had he spoken when the ground beneath his feet started to shake. On the bridge, warriors and diggers alike forgot their fight and stampeded to safety. The whirlwind engulfed the warriors on the far side of the bridge. They were lifted shrieking into the air. Li El was savaging her own troops.

The diggers on the bridge almost made it to safety. When they were only a few steps from solid ground, the bridge pavement between them and the shore cracked and collapsed into the canal. The diggers wavered on the edge of the drop until the whirlwind rolled up behind them. Panicking, they leaped into the churning water and were carried away.

Riverwind tried to shield his face with his arms, but smoke and flying grit stung his eyes. He fought his way through the cowering Hestites to Vvelz and dragged the sorcerer to his feet. "Do something!" Riverwind shouted. "Stop her, or we'll all be finished!"

"I can't," Vvelz wailed. "She's too strong!"

Riverwind shook the terrified elf and bellowed, "Try, damn you!"

He set Vvelz on his feet. Silver hair flying in the wind, the sorcerer shakily extended his hands. He cried, "Attend what you hear!" His words echoed in the plainsman's head, even over the thunder of the whirlwind.

Vvelz incanted: "Storms and shakings of the ground, begone! Smoke and vile vapors, depart! All is order, all is calm! Attend what you hear!"

The funnel cloud actually retreated, and the maelstrom in the canal subsided. Riverwind shouted encouragement to the sorcerer. Sweat popped out on Vvelz's face. Tremors racked his body. He clenched his thin fingers into fists.

"Obey the balance of nature! Disperse, you creations of an evil mind! You cannot exist any longer. Begone! Begone! Begone!"

The whirlwind shrank to a narrow, writhing column of dense black smoke. The canal lost its wild fury and lapped slowly around the fallen stones of the bridge—and the bodies of drowned diggers.

Vvelz turned to Riverwind and Mors. His eyes were huge in his face. Astonishment shone from his face. "She is beaten!" he whispered. His face flushed with joy. "I have defeated my sister at last!"

Even as he spoke, the black coil of smoke swooped down like a monstrous tentacle and seized Vvelz. It wrapped around him three times and hoisted him kicking and crying into the air. Instinctively Riverwind leaped at the smoky coil, trying to save the sorcerer. His bound hands passed through it and were stained black with soot. He seized a sword dropped by a digger and chopped awkwardly at the inky tentacle; his cuts had no effect. Vvelz screamed for help, for mercy. His arms and legs were pinned to his sides, rendering him unable to cast a spell.

The coil of smoke withdrew rapidly across the canal. Vvelz's desperate cries grew fainter with distance. Riverwind stood at the break of the old bridge, gasping for air and watching Li El's magic carry her brother away. The black tentacle diminished to a smudge. Then, it was drawn into the palace and disappeared. Silence enveloped the old bridge.

It took some hours to get all the Blue Sky People across

the canal. Most simply waded over. On the far side, a ruined wheat field greeted them. The whirlwind had plucked every grain off the stalks, leaving an eerie scene of brown straw and twisted stems. Vartoom was only a mile away. It looked deserted.

Soon they reached the ramps leading up to the city. The crowd—hardly an army—flowed up the angled streets. Curious Vartoom diggers came out and mixed with the Blue Sky folk. Many joyous reunions began in the street, as those who'd run away to join up with Mors met friends and relatives who'd stayed behind.

A small band of soldiers appeared when Mors and his people reached the Avenue of Weavers. One look at the mob was all they could handle. They fled.

"They've no stomach left," Mors said, when told. "It was not so in the days of the Great Hest. Every warrior would have given up his life to defend the great lord."

"Li El does not inspire—nor deserve—such devotion," Riverwind said grimly. "And the sight of a thousand armed diggers would take the fight out of almost anyone."

The way was uncontested to the very doors of the palace. The massive metal portals stood apart, beckoning them to enter.

"We have to go in, yes," said Catchflea. He made no move to be the first.

"It's my place to lead," Mors said. He gently pried Di An's fingers loose from his hand. "But not you, Di An."

"I go where you go," she whispered.

"Not this time, An Di." Mors flipped back his black mesh coat and drew a slender, elegantly worked sword from a hidden scabbard. "This will be my staff," he said.

He went forward, waving the sword back and forth before him. Halfway to the doors, flames erupted in the entry. The diggers shrank back. Di An cried a warning to Mors.

"I feel no heat," he said, matter-of-factly. He kept walking.

"What do you think, old man?" Riverwind asked.

"I feel heat, yes."

Mors walked right into the flames. The shocked cries of hundreds of diggers changed to relieved sighs as he stood in the fire without any sign of pain. "There is no fire here," he said.

"An illusion!" Catchflea exclaimed.

"Undone by the one she blinded," Riverwind said.

Knowing that the fire was not real, the others walked hesitantly through it. Riverwind felt nothing more than a slight prickling of his skin.

The interior of the palace was a shambles. Stone furniture was smashed, woven wire tapestries were shredded. Soot stained some rooms, and here and there dead warriors were found. In the hearth room, the statues of Hest's heroes were despoiled. Bronze heads and limbs littered the floor. The blue globes were gone from their stands. None were to be seen anywhere.

The great hearth blazed as it had for centuries. Mors tapped his sword against the circular hearth and swung around it. He could not see the wreckage of the palace. And he could not see what had suddenly caused the others to stop in their tracks.

"Mors," said Riverwind tightly.

"What is it?" The blind elf paused.

"Unchain my hands, Mors."

"When I choose." Mors turned toward the throne room.

"Unchain him, please," Di An said. Mors paused, hearing something in her strained voice.

"What is it?" he asked.

"We've found Vvelz," Catchflea said.

In the center of the hearth fire the giant statue of Hest had been set. Chained to it was Vvelz. His mouth was open and his eyes stared out at them in an expression of pure horror, but he made no movements, made no sound. The weird, silent flames bathed him. Catchflea described the awful tableau to Mors.

"Li El's work," he said simply.

"Can we help him?" Di An whispered.

"He's dead," Riverwind said, turning away.

"I misjudged him," Mors said. He stood, his face turned toward the cold fire. "We would not be here now if Vvelz hadn't fought off Li El's magic."

Diggers filed into the room in awed silence. For generations, the palace had been as unattainable to them as the stars. Since the destruction of their temples and the massacre of their priests, the diggers had looked upon the palace as home to their gods. Now their bare, dirty feet trod the mosaic floor where Hest himself had once walked.

"Come, all of you," Mors said when he heard their hushed whispers. "We have taken destiny into our hands."

He found the door to the throne room closed. Mors lifted one metal-shod foot and kicked the double doors open. He strode in, sword in hand, and said, "Come out, Li El. Don't make me hunt for you."

High, feminine laughter filtered through the golden curtains surrounding the throne. Mors grimaced and thrust out his sword. It snagged in the curtains. He slashed hard left and right, bringing down a long section of the drapes.

Seated on her golden couch was the queen—erect, hood in place, every fold of her gown arranged just so. Her hands rested, one atop the other, in her lap; the delicate fingernails had been gilded. She looked like a statue of gold and ivory.

"You always were melodramatic," Li El said. Riverwind and the others came to the gap Mors had cut. Li El's gaze flicked briefly to them, then returned to Mors. "Not to mention crude and predictable. What do you intend to do now? Kill me?"

"There's fear in your voice, El Li. I can hear it," Mors replied sharply.

"Don't call me that!"

"Why not? There was a time you enjoyed me calling you that."

"Never," she snapped. The queen stood, the wrinkles in her robe falling in a crinkle of gold. "You can't assume any affection from me, Mors."

Mors gestured, snapping his fingers, and the quartet of diggers hurried forward with Karn. They laid him carefully on the floor at Mors's feet.

Li El's haughty expression wavered. "They told me he was dead."

"Do you care?"

"He is my son!"

Mors shrugged. "Mine as well."

"Son!" Riverwind exclaimed. Catchflea murmured an affirmative, and the tall plainsman said, "You treated him like a foolish servant. You never had a kind word for Karn."

Li El flinched and raised her hand. Sparks crackled in the air. "He is a warrior. I had to make him strong. There is no place for kindness between a sovereign and her servant!"

Mors lowered the tip of his sword to Karn's throat. "Come here, Li El," he said. She didn't move. "Come, or I'll kill him."

She stared down at her son's motionless body. "You couldn't."

"Couldn't I? What do you think?"

Li El stepped down from the dais and approached Mors. Her golden hem swished over the mosaic floor. Riverwind had a sudden pang of fear for Mors. If she should touch him, would Mors fall under her spell as he had?

But the blind elf knew what he was doing. He presented the point of his sword to Li El. She deliberately let the sharp steel dig into the gold of her robe.

"Now," she said very softly. "Kill me, Mors. Run me through. It's what you want to do, isn't it?" The throne room rang with tension. Mors stood with his head turned slightly away from the queen, listening for movement. When he did not immediately strike, a tiny smile lifted Li El's lips.

"You can't do it," she whispered. "You can't hurt me."

"I cannot," Mors said, whipping the sword away. A small, involuntary gasp was drawn from Li El as the sword point flicked across her stomach. "Because it is not my place to take personal revenge. It is for them to say what happens to you." He waved over his shoulder to the mass of awed diggers.

Li El laughed. Sweet aromas wafted through the room and far-off chimes tinkled. "Them?" she said. "How can they possibly judge me?"

"A trial," Catchflea interjected.

"Yes, a trial," Riverwind added. "Let the new masters of Hest judge the old."

The queen's laughter died. A frown darkened her face, and she raised her hand to point at the Que-Shu men. Riverwind braced himself for a spell, but Mors heard her moving and brought his sword tip up to her neck, just below her right ear.

"If you so much as breathe, I'll have your head off right now. And you know I will do it." Li El lowered her hand. Mors smiled, tight-lipped and sardonic. "I like this notion of a trial. We can seat a panel of diggers as judges, and I will act as their advocate."

"No," she hissed. "You would let a band of dirty, ignorant diggers decide my fate?"

"Who better?" Riverwind said. "They know your cruelty and indifference better than anyone."

"*Never!*"

Mors's smile evaporated. "It will be done."

So intent was everyone on the exchange between Mors and his queen, no one noticed as Karn opened his eyes. He took in the scene, heard his mother and father trade hateful words. When Mors resolved to have Li El tried and executed, Karn heaved himself to his feet. The plight of his mother and queen had steeled his weakened body to action. Pale, stooping, his face white with pain and a lifetime of anger, he attacked.

"Mors! Watch out for Karn!" But the blind elf didn't know where Karn was. He swung his sword in a fast circle to ward off his son. Karn waited until the blade had passed and leaped on his father. Riverwind and Catchflea moved to help Mors. The diggers began to shout, and Li El lifted her hands . . .

She uttered a single word in an ancient tongue, and a veil of impenetrable darkness fell upon the room. Over all the tumult Mors's voice roared, "Block all the doors! Use your own bodies if you must—but don't let them escape!"

Riverwind felt several small bodies bounce off him and go reeling away in the darkness. A door clanged against stone, and a shaft of reddish light intruded on the queen's spell. A door to the hearth room had swung open as diggers pressed to get out. The eternal flame, cold and unchanging, still burned on the hearth, though its light was muted. And even more weirdly, the statue of Great Hest and the body of Vvelz glowed like beacons. Black shadows flitted to and fro between Riverwind and the light of the hearth.

A scream. Riverwind knew a death cry when he heard it. "Catchflea! Are you all right?!" he shouted.

"I'm alive, tall man."

With equal suddenness, the darkness ended. He spied Catchflea across the room, bent over, examining something on the floor. Riverwind pushed through the crowd and found the old soothsayer standing over the bleeding body of Karn.

"He grappled with Mors and lost," Catchflea said sadly.

Riverwind asked, "Is there anything you can do?"

"Not for a wound like that. If Vvelz were here . . ." Catchflea covered his face with his hands. "It's all too much, tall man. Just too much."

"I know." He laid a hand on Catchflea's shoulder. "Where are Mors and Li El?"

Catchflea raised his head. "I don't know. I didn't see them."

The diggers tore down the wall of golden curtains and discovered a secret door. It was ajar. Riverwind appropriated a sword from a Blue Sky fighter and kicked the door fully open. He found himself at the bottom of a stairway leading up. He charged up the steps, the old plainsman and a hundred diggers on his heels. The stairs bent right and continued up. They ended on a long, straight corridor. Riverwind charged into the corridor.

And was rudely shoved back. There seemed to be nothing in his way, so he tried again. Once more an invisible barrier threw him back.

"Li El has blocked this way!" he said.

Di An wormed her way to the front of the crowd. "We can try the promenade," she panted. "Out there!"

The front facade of the palace featured a long balcony, which ran along its second story. The whole group reversed direction and ran downstairs. Di An led the Que-Shu men to a concealed set of steps on the outside of the building that reached the promenade.

"How did you know this was here?" asked Catchflea.

"Master Vvelz took me this way before," the girl replied.

The diggers were inflamed now, outraged that Li El might

have escaped and might have hurt their leader Mors, too. They tore the ornamental metal shutters off the windows and climbed in. Some returned to unlatch the heavy doors off the promenade so the Que-Shu men could enter. The mob ransacked luxurious sleeping rooms and found great stores of food, which the hungriest fell upon ravenously. The whole affair was degenerating into a riot of plunder when the cry went up that Mors had been found.

Riverwind ran, covering long stretches of polished metal tile with his long legs. Di An puffed along in his wake. He skidded to a stop when he saw the floor ahead had fallen in. Mors stood on a narrow fragment of stone, surrounded on all sides by a deep drop. He and the stone he stood on floated in midair.

"What holds up your feet?" Catchflea said.

"Li El's joke," Mors replied from his perch. He was calm, but deeply angry. "The floor collapsed around me, as you see. I cannot move. If I even lift one foot, the spell supporting this stone will instantly end."

"We need a rope," Riverwind said.

Di An arrived and saw his predicament. "Mors!" she cried.

"Be still, Di An. I'm not dead yet."

Di An grabbed the digger nearest her and yelled in his face, "We'll do a mine pick-up! Understand?" The digger agreed enthusiastically.

Riverwind moved out of the way as fifteen diggers threw themselves face-down on the floor. Twelve sat on top of their fellows, linking their arms around the legs of the digger behind. Ten more climbed over them, leaning farther and farther out over the hole. Eight more piled on top of this, then six on top of that, making a lopsided pyramid of living bodies. The two diggers who clambered far out to the end were just an arm's length from Mors.

Di An scaled the living mound as the last link. She crept forward on all fours, deftly finding holds in the sea of bent backs and entwined limbs. She reached Mors and wrapped her thin arms around his neck.

"An Di, what are you doing?" he asked in shock.

"Saving you," she replied. "Climb on."

The digger pyramid swayed and groaned under the added strain of Mors's weight, but it held. He climbed to safety, then Di An returned. All the others, from the farthest back, climbed home. As she held Mors's hand tightly, Di An explained to an astonished Riverwind that the technique was one the diggers used to rescue comrades in mine disasters.

"Never mind that now. Li El must be found!" cried Mors.

It didn't take long. The diggers were ranging all over the palace, and a group that was looting the upper floors found Li El hiding in an alcove. She sent them shrieking down the corridor.

Mors and Catchflea entered the end of the hall just as Riverwind and a swarm of armed diggers filled the opposite end. Li El ran toward them, meaning to scatter them like chaff, until they presented a hedge of unwavering sword points. She turned back toward Mors.

Her golden hood was down, and her dark hair was in disarray. She lifted her arms as if to cast some dread spell, but her arms shook so violently that she dropped them quickly to her sides. Desperation gleamed on her sweat-sheened face.

Mors approached her slowly, waving his bloody sword.

"You never understood, you stiff-necked, stone-brained fool of a warrior. I had to be hard! The people of Hest have no place in the Empty World. Up there we would be just another small city-state. Here, in the caverns, we are citizens of an empire."

"An empire of darkness and silence," Riverwind said. "Let the Hestites find the sunlight again!"

"Your world is dying, yes," Catchflea put in. "Your air is full of smoke and your crops will not grow on magic much longer. If the Hestites stay in these caves, they'll all eventually die. Your race will disappear."

"Lies!" Li El stamped her foot and a dull boom echoed through the palace. She was weak with fatigue. "Humans only want to exploit we of the elder race. If you lead the diggers to the surface, Mors, they will end up as the barbarians' slaves."

Her crazed eyes roamed the crowd and saw only angry, bitter diggers, the slaves she'd mistreated for decades. She stared at the bloody sword as Mors drew closer and closer. Suddenly her back straightened and one shaking hand lifted the golden hood back over her hair. Li El turned toward one of the windows in the corridor.

"No!" cried Catchflea. "Stop her, Mors!" Li El opened the chiseled iron shutters. They were four floors above the Avenue of the Heroes. Without another word or a single backward glance, Li El stepped through the window.

Riverwind threw himself at her, too late. He saw a brief flutter of gold, then the queen of Hest disappeared from his view.

He turned to Mors. The Blue Sky People's leader rested his hands on the pommel of his sword. His face bore an expression of complete satisfaction.

"Why didn't you stop her?" Riverwind asked.

"A last favor to a beaten foe." Mors's mouth hardened to a thin line. "And to a lost love." When the plainsman didn't say anything, he went on. "Don't you realize? This is the same window from which the last son of Hest leaped, so many years ago."

Chapter 12

Embassy to the Sky

A NUMB SILENCE SETTLED OVER VARTOOM AFTER THE
death of Li El. Slowly, gradually, the people of Hest began to
realize what had happened. Acting on advice from Catchflea, Mors ordered all the mines and foundries to be closed
for two days. Spontaneous celebrations broke out in the
streets, and the Blue Sky People circulated freely, spreading
their message of hope.

Mors did not occupy the palace. Instead, he set up a plain
iron chair in the Hall of Arms and governed from there. The
warriors of Hest came to him and pledged their fealty. Most
he gruffly dismissed.

"Your loyalty is like a bar of pig iron," he told them.
"Heavy to bear and mostly useless!"

The old soothsayer urged him to moderate his tone. "It's

strange for you to despise them for failing to protect Li El, yes. Why not make them your brothers again? Give them reason to want to protect you?" he said.

Mors fidgeted a while and replied, "There is something in what you say." He turned his unseeing eyes to Catchflea and added, "You are wise for an overgrown barbarian."

"Is size a measure of wisdom?" Riverwind asked.

"Not in your case," the elf leader snapped.

Later, when the Que-Shu men were alone, Riverwind complained about his position, now that the queen was overthrown. "Mors still thinks of me as a threat," he said. "And I'm not! All I want is to leave Vartoom and resume my quest." Each day he remained in the underground world seemed like an eternity to the tall plainsman. His thoughts were filled with Goldmoon. How long it had been since he'd last seen her!

Riverwind looked out from the palace balcony over the city. Diggers were dancing in the streets. Fruit wine was flowing, and the sharp smell of it filled the air, replacing the usual drifting smoke. Over the last few days the air had cleared quite a bit, but once the furnaces were stoked up again, the choking pall would return.

Just then, Di An came running. "Ho, giants!" she said. "Mors wishes to see you right away."

"How is his temper?" asked Riverwind.

The elf girl shrugged and said, "He has something to tell you."

The Que-Shu men exchanged probing looks, then followed Di An back to the Hall of Arms. A fair number of warriors was present, swords at their sides. Riverwind's fast walk slowed when he saw that.

"We are here," Di An announced.

"Come here, An Di." The girl went and stood by the blind elf's side. Mors said, "I would have some words with you, giants."

"We're listening," Riverwind asked.

"These warriors," Mors waved a hand at the body of armed Hestites, "have agreed to serve the order of Hest."

"Will you take the crown?" Catchflea asked, surprised.

"No, I'm too old and too blunt to rule. I want there to be a new kind of rulership in Hest, where no one person has power over all the others. Something like a guild, or a warriors' council."

"Very interesting, but what has it to do with us?" Riverwind said.

"The end of our path has always been a return to the surface world," said Mors. "We cannot simply migrate the whole population at once. I want to know what conditions are like on the surface. I want to know if the sons of Sithas still bear ill will to the people of Hest. Therefore," Mors drew himself up straight in his iron chair, "I want you, Riverwind, to go back to the Empty World as an emissary of Hest."

The plainsman was speechless. He had not expected to be given such an easy path that led exactly where he wanted to go. He suspected a trick. "How can I?" he said unevenly. "I'm no diplomat."

"I do not expect you to be. I will send one of the Blue Sky People with you to speak on my behalf. You will be their guide and protector in the upper world."

"Perhaps I could speak for you, yes?" Catchflea suggested.

"No."

"No?"

"You will not be going," Mors replied firmly. "You, old giant, will remain in Hest to advise me on the creation of a new state of Hest." Riverwind and Di An stared at Mors in surprise. Catchflea simply looked down at the worn stone floor, a frown gathering on his face.

"Suppose he doesn't want to stay?" Riverwind said.

"He must," said the elf leader. The implication of the armed warriors was now clear. Riverwind was about to make a more belligerent demand for Catchflea's freedom when the old soothsayer caught his arm.

Riverwind asked softly, "Do you want to stay?"

"I am tempted."

"But why?" exclaimed the tall plainsman, turning to stare at Catchflea. "These are not your people."

"It is a good thing to be needed, tall man. No one in Que-Shu ever needed Catchflea the Fool for anything, save the butt of a joke. If Mors wants me to be his counselor, it is a tempting thing."

Riverwind regarded his friend a long moment, trying to decide if he were serious or not. "What about the augury, old man? You're supposed to go with me wherever I go, remember?"

"I remember," Catchflea said tiredly. "I think—"

"How is Riverwind to get back to the surface?" asked Di An. "With both Vvelz and Li El gone, there is no magic to send him. He will have to climb all the way."

"I will find him a guide," Mors answered simply.

"I will do it!" Di An said eagerly.

The blind elf shook his head. "No, An Di. You are my eyes. I can't spare you. There are many among the Blue Sky People who have been to the surface. One of them will guide him."

Sullenly Riverwind said, "When do I go?"

"As soon as provisions can be gathered for you. Tomorrow at this hour." Mors stood abruptly. The warriors snapped their metal-shod heels together in attention. Mors held out his hand and Di An took it. As she led him away, the elf girl turned and regarded the frustrated Que-Shu men. Her look was troubled.

* * * * * *

"I have decided to go with you," Catchflea whispered.

"Are you sure?" Riverwind said, similarly hushed. They were in the barracks of the Hall of Arms. Hestite warriors were all around them.

The old soothsayer said, "Being compelled to stay is not good, yes. And, as you said, the augury of the acorns cannot be dismissed." He gripped Riverwind's arm. "My place is with you, tall man."

"Good!" Even more softly, Riverwind said, "How will we escape?"

"I don't know . . . if we run, we would be lost in the tunnels. And I would not care to trust Mors's mercy if we run and are caught again."

"He has a hard heart," Riverwind agreed. "If I leave you

here, he will never let you go, I believe. So we must escape."

"But how? The Hestites know these caves far better than we do, yes."

They went back and forth in low tones until a warrior and a Blue Sky digger came to take Catchflea. Mors wanted to arrange the distribution of stored grain, and he needed the old man's advice.

"I will see you again," Riverwind said significantly.

"I am sure of it, tall man." The old soothsayer cut a strange figure in his ragged clothes, flanked on one side by a warrior in lion-embossed armor and a male digger in black copper mesh on the other. Riverwind watched them go with many misgivings.

*　*　*　*　*

Riverwind walked the empty corridors of the palace. They were filled with wreckage left by the Blue Sky People after they despoiled the place. The plainsman stepped over bits of furniture, wall hangings, and other things he could not recognize. The Blue Sky People had a great deal of rage. Li El had been a manipulative tyrant, but Riverwind found he could not hate her. Mors, on the other hand, was an iron-fisted dreamer, and Riverwind disliked him completely. As he walked the halls, the plainsman tried to sort out why he felt that way. Some residual effect of Li El's impersonation of Goldmoon, perhaps?

He stopped suddenly as a dim figure popped out of a side corridor. The stranger stepped into a slim band of light from an open skylight.

"Hello, Di An," said Riverwind.

"Did I startle you, giant?"

"A bit. You're not sleeping now?"

"I couldn't." She came closer. "I have bad dreams."

He smiled at the girl. "I have them, too, sometimes. When that happens, I go out of the village into the forest and sleep under the stars."

Di An wrinkled her forehead in thought. "I have seen stars. Those are the little coals that glow in the dark sky?"

He nodded. It was easy to forget that Di An had been to

the surface.

Di An had been to the surface!

Riverwind knelt and grasped the elf girl by the shoulders. She stiffened. "Are we friends?" he asked. "Do you trust Catchflea and me?"

In the low light, her eyes had an almost reddish cast. "I do. You saved me from Karn, back in the tunnel."

"Catchflea and I need your help. We want to go home."

"Mors wants the old giant to stay."

"He wants you to stay, too. If the three of us went, we'd all get what we want."

"Mors would be very angry," she said. "Who would be his ambassador?"

Riverwind shook his head. "I don't have to be the one. You could do it, Di An. Your people have enough gold and gems to buy anything they need from the upper world. Catchflea and I have our own lives to lead."

She moved out of his grasp and considered what he had said. Finally, she asked, "Is there a giant woman for you?"

He had to chuckle. Goldmoon, a giant! "Well, yes. I want to get back to Goldmoon."

Di An looked away, a mask of frustration coming across her small, sharp face. "Our fight against Li El is finally over, and more and more I wish to have a say in what happens. No one here listens to me. I'm only a barren child. Mors doesn't really need me; any child could lead him. He doesn't listen to me either."

Riverwind phrased his next sentence carefully. "Di An, there are many wise people in the upper world," he said. "One of them might be able to help you."

"Do you think so?" Her voice was loud with excitement.

"Shh. I would not say it if I didn't think so."

Di An glanced furtively left and right. "I do know ways to the surface that no one else knows. It could be done." Her countenance darkened. "Mors would never forgive me if I left."

Riverwind stood. "I won't ask you to do anything you don't wish to do. But you can help yourself and your people. Time is short. I'm being sent tomorrow."

Di An chewed her lower lip as she considered. "The old

giant sleeps in the Hall of Arms. We can fetch him," she said. Riverwind felt relief wash over him. She turned and dashed off along the dark corridor.

"Di An, wait!" he hissed. Riverwind followed, banging his shins on table legs and chairs that crouched broken in the shadows. "Wait for me!" he called hoarsely.

They met again on the short causeway leading from the palace to the Hall of Arms. Vartoom was eerily calm. The furnaces and forges were still idle, and the streets barren of elves. Hand in hand, the tall plainsman and the elf girl stole down the sloping bridge.

The Hall of Arms was filled with snores and snorts. Warriors slept in every available spot. Di An moved lightly around the recumbent forms. Riverwind had to walk with great care. More than once he nudged a sleeping soldier, but the Hestite merely grumbled and rolled away from Riverwind's feet.

Catchflea lay with his back against a curving buttress, hands folded across his stomach. Di An and Riverwind stood over him. The elf girl looked to Riverwind. He nodded. She bent over to prod the old man awake, but before she touched him, Catchflea's eyes opened.

"Greetings," he whispered. Di An was so surprised, she lost her balance and sat down hard. Her copper clothing made a loud *clink* against the stone floor.

"Shh," came a voice from the darkened hall. "Tryin' t'sleep . . . "

Riverwind hauled Catchflea to his feet. Clumsily the three of them crept out of the hall.

"What's this about?" Catchflea said when they were on the causeway.

Riverwind ruffled Di An's short hair. "I've made a pact with Di An. She is going to guide us up and out."

Catchflea blinked and looked toward the girl. "Oh? And what do you get out of this pact?"

"I'm to grow up," the elf girl said importantly. Catchflea opened his mouth to say something further, but Riverwind forestalled him.

"Time is short," the tall warrior said. "We must gather supplies and get away before Mors notices our absence."

"Wait," Catchflea said. "I want to consult the acorns." Di An was baffled, so Riverwind explained what the acorns could do.

Catchflea knelt at the mouth of the cave and silently intoned the magical words. He then overturned the gourd.

"Well?" asked Riverwind.

"It's not good. Are you certain you want to hear it?"

"Go ahead."

"The oracle says, 'One will die, one will go mad, and one will find glory.' " No one spoke for a long time.

Finally, Riverwind cleared his throat. "You know, old man, you haven't handled those acorns in quite some time. Maybe you've forgotten how to read them."

Catchflea scooped up the nuts. "Whatever our destiny is, we have to go meet it; it won't come to us."

The strange trio hurried down the causeway, Di An in the lead. Before they left Vartoom behind them, Di An gathered climbing gear and food for them to carry. The food was mostly thick, heavy wheat bread filled with nuts, dried fruits, and a little meat. It was much like the pemmican Riverwind had begun this journey with. The elf girl also recovered Catchflea's acorns and gourd and Riverwind's saber. She found their possessions in a cabinet in Li El's private chambers. The old soothsayer hugged the gourd to him like a long-lost love.

Part II
ASCENT

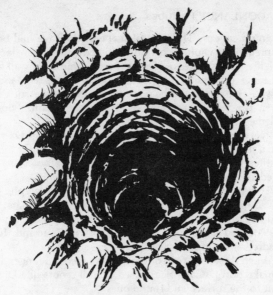

Chapter 13

The Well of Wind

Di An led them out of Vartoom, turning toward the far end of the great cavern, where the plainsmen had never been before. Here the floors and walls converged in a rocky funnel shape, with only a round black opening leading out.

There was no soil to grow things here, only rock and mineral concretions. They climbed over the jutting stones toward the hole ahead. Riverwind observed that the opening seemed too smooth and round to be natural.

"It was only a crack many centuries ago," Di An said. "The sons of Hest had it widened."

"Why?" asked Catchflea.

"For the tombs of the great," the elf girl said. "Here are the resting places of Hest and all his sons."

The temperature dropped suddenly when they entered

the tomb cavern. The natural shape of the cave had been adapted into a vaulted corridor. Along the walls were larger than life-sized statues of Hestites in full armor. They all had the same expression, something between a sneer and a frown. The actual tombs were niches cut in the rock between the legs of the statues. Hammered bronze doors sealed each grave.

Riverwind halted before a statue of a Hestite. The warrior held a short bow in the crook of his arm. He knew the living Hestites had forgotten how to make or use bows, so he asked Di An how old the grave was.

"This is Lord Trand," she said, reading the glyphs engraved on the tomb doors. "Victor of twenty combats. He died eighty years after Hest led the people into the caves." She counted quietly on her fingers. "Two thousand, four hundred and eighteen years ago."

"When the wood rotted, the Hestites were no longer able to make bows," Catchflea mused. "Until scouts like Di An went to the surface and found ones."

"Two thousand years ago," Riverwind said. "Di An, how old are you?"

She scampered ahead among some tumbled rocks. "Two hundred and sixty-four," she said.

Catchflea bumped into Riverwind's back. "Pardon! What's the matter?" he asked. Riverwind told him Di An's remarkable age. "The barren children do grow older. They just never grow up, yes?"

"Come this way!" Di An's voice wafted back. The orange glow of her mineral oil lamp rose and fell as she waved to them. Riverwind reminded himself not to treat her like a child. After all, she was more than ten times as old as he.

Di An was waiting for them in a seeming dead end. The lamp threw odd highlights on her sharp features.

"What now?" asked Riverwind.

"We must go through there." Di An pointed down. At knee height there was an opening in the wall. It was as black as the Abyss and promised to be a tight fit for the humans.

"Go through that?" said Catchflea. "There is a better way, yes?" Di An solemnly shook her head. "Surely you didn't use this tunnel every time you went to the surface."

"No, I mostly used the shaft you fell down," she said. "This way should put us out on the surface near where you fell down the shaft."

"Should?" Riverwind asked.

"I haven't gone this way in a long time." Di An squatted and slipped into the hole easily. Riverwind motioned for Catchflea to go second.

Catchflea got down on his belly and wriggled into the hole. "Ow!" he cried, his feet still scrambling in Riverwind's sight. "Low ceiling!"

"I'll keep that in mind," Riverwind said dryly. When the old man's feet finally disappeared, he dropped down and peered into the cramped tunnel. The old feeling of being trapped by the massive weight of stone, returned— Riverwind took a deep breath and thought of Goldmoon.

The tunnel was just barely wider than his shoulders. He had to inch along, rocking his shoulders from side to side and pushing with his toes. The only light was the bobbing lamp Di An pushed ahead of her. By common consent they had agreed to use only one lamp at a time, to conserve oil.

It was warmer in the tunnel. Catchflea's mutterings ahead were sometimes punctuated by Di An's higher-pitched voice. Sharp stones dug into Riverwind's elbows and chest, and brushing the tunnel roof invited a scalp cut. How much longer? Would they have to go all the way to the surface in this rat hole? He would go mad, suffocate, scream, and tear at the rocks. The hard, unyielding rocks . . .

"Stand up, Riverwind." He opened his eyes and saw Catchflea's much-patched moccasins in front of his face. The tunnel had opened onto a ledge in a wide vertical shaft, whose upper limit was lost in velvet darkness.

Di An sat on a boulder, munching a hunk of hard gray bread. The lamp sat between her feet, flickering. Riverwind noticed the steady breeze flowing upward in the shaft.

"Where are we?"

"The Well of Wind," said Di An. She gnawed off a healthy piece of bread and mumbled through it, saying, "At times the wind moves so strongly here it nearly carries you off your feet."

"How do we get out of here?" Catchflea queried.

Another big bite. "Climb," she said.

The walls were rugged, with many jutting rocks and crevices to use for handholds. Di An dusted the bread crumbs off her lap and showed the plainsmen how to use the hooks and chains they had taken from the city. "Reach up with the hook," she said, "catch hold of the wall and pull yourself up by the chain." Catchflea was doubtful he could manage but in the end had little choice.

Di An scaled the wall with practiced agility. Riverwind followed, so that he could help pull Catchflea up. "How long have you been exploring these caverns?" Riverwind asked the elf girl.

"Many years," she replied. "Before Mors enlisted me, I was a food fetcher in a tin mine. My job was to run up and down the mine tunnels, bringing food to the diggers. Before that, I worked for Rhed the mason, stamping out tiles and feeding them to the baking kiln."

"That sounds like hard work for a girl," Riverwind said.

Clink. Di An wedged a hook into some rocks and hauled herself hand over hand up the chain. "I began my job with Rhed when I was one hundred and forty-seven."

A sharp downdraft flattened the climbers against the wall. Then, like a giant exhaling a breath, the wind rushed back up the shaft, whipping Riverwind's hair into his face.

"Will that continue?" yelled Catchflea, ten feet below Riverwind.

"Could get worse," Di An replied.

"What?"

"Could get worse!" Riverwind shouted.

"Will there be any warning?" the old man asked.

"You can hear the hard blows coming down the shaft, but it's the updrafts that are most dangerous," said Di An. Poor Catchflea couldn't hear her. Di An leaned out on one arm and shouted, "You can hear the hard blows—"

Her hook broke off the rock she was anchored to. Di An fell backward. Riverwind braced himself and snatched the trailing length of her chain. The impact the elf girl made when she reached the end of her chain almost jerked Riverwind from the wall, but he slowly raised his arm, bringing Di An back to the rock wall very near Catchflea.

"You are well, yes?" he asked.

Riverwind pulled her up to him. The chain was fastened to a copper belt that encircled her waist. He asked if she'd hurt anything in the fall. "Nothing," she assured him. "Let's go." He smiled at her bravery. She climbed on, using Riverwind's shoulder and the top of his head as stepping stones. She reeled in her dangling hook and started all over again.

They climbed for more than an hour, ascending two hundred feet. In one way the darkness was an asset to the inexperienced Que-Shu men. If they'd been able to see how high they'd gone, vertigo might have paralyzed them both.

A broad ledge greeted them and all three gratefully rolled onto level rock. At their backs was a smooth-walled tunnel, slanting off into the darkness. Di An indicated that their route was on the other side of the shaft, a much smaller tunnel they would reach by inching around the ledge.

"What's wrong with this way?" Riverwind said, jerking a thumb at the wide, round passage.

"I saw three barren children die trying to go that way. They went in, chained together, and in less than a hundred heartbeats came tumbling out, blown by the wind like dust." She glanced down the vertical shaft. "It is a long drop."

Her lamp was burning low. The wick sputtered and wavered, unable to draw any fuel from the copper reservoir. Riverwind got out his lamp and lit it from Di An's, which he then blew out.

Riverwind took the lead, as he was the strongest, on the narrow ledge that ran around the shaft to the tunnel Di An had indicated. The wall bulged outward over the ledge, making it devilishly hard to keep a grip. More than a few times Riverwind's hook slipped off the dark, gritty stone. Di An inched along behind him. A chain was hooked to the copper belts all three wore. Catchflea waited until the chain from Di An to him grew taut.

"Come on," she said.

"I can't do it," he said weakly.

"Why not?"

"My arms are not strong enough to hold me up."

"You climbed well enough to get here," said the elf girl.

"Using my feet and legs, yes." Catchflea pushed his ragged

sleeves up, displaying his bony arms. "See? I'll not make it."

"You've got to try," Riverwind called from his advanced position. "We'll help." So saying, he doubled back on his arduous trail, pushing Di An back to the original ledge. They switched their chain linking around so that Catchflea was in the middle. "We'll keep the chain short and tight for you," Riverwind said. "That will hold you to the wall. Then hold on as best you can."

The old man wasn't happy, but he could hardly stay where he was. Di An took charge of the lamp so Riverwind could use both hands in climbing. The tall plainsman led off again with Catchflea in close tow.

The passage they wanted was nearly halfway around the shaft, about twenty yards along the slippery ledge. They were making fair progress when Riverwind's right hand slipped. He waved frantically to recover his balance, digging in with the hook in his left hand. The taut chain snapped at the soothsayer, whose grip was never good, and Catchflea dropped off the ledge. Di An promptly drove her grappling hook through the links of her chain into the wall and braced herself. Catchflea hit the bottom of his chain. This time Riverwind wasn't braced to keep his place. He fell backward off the ledge, leaving little Di An to anchor.

The chain snapped out straight, crushing the copper belt against Riverwind's ribs. His breath was driven out, and the grappling hook shot from his fingers. It vanished in the black shaft. It fell so far he never heard it hit bottom.

Di An was in a terrible position. She couldn't pull either man to safety, much less both. She couldn't even move for fear of losing her grip; and her belt was being hauled low on her thin hips. Catchflea dangled in midair five feet below her, and Riverwind five feet lower.

"What can I do?" she said, terror and the strain tightening her voice to a squeak.

"The wall looks rough here," Riverwind said. "I'm going to try and get a grip on it." He shifted his weight to make himself and Catchflea swing. On his third try, he slammed into the wall. He heard Catchflea hit the rock.

"You all right, old man?"

"No! But get on with what you're doing, yes?" Riverwind

found niches for his fingers and toes. He climbed sideways, rising and crabbing to his right. He drew even with Catchflea's feet, pressed against a smooth spot on the wall.

"Is the rest of the rock around as smooth as this?" Riverwind grunted.

"Yes—I've nothing to grip at all," the old man said.

Riverwind called to Di An and explained he couldn't go higher from where he was. "I'll have to go back to the ledge," he said.

"Hurry," was all she managed to say.

He clung to the wall like a fly, moving when a good toehold caught his eye. He thanked the gods Di An had taken over as lamp bearer. Scaling this deadly surface encumbered by the light would have been impossible for him.

"Riverwind!" Di An said sharply. "How far are you from the ledge?"

"It's just out of reach."

"Then reach it quickly! The links in my chain are opening!"

The weight of two men on the iron ring was too much, and the pinched link was spreading. Di An could only watch helplessly as the gap grew wider and wider. "Hurry, giant! Hurry!"

Riverwind had no place to put his right foot. His left foot was firmly planted in a dished-out spot, but his right was unsupported. He stretched his right arm, digging at the gray rock with blunt fingernails, trying to scratch out a hold. Finally, the plainsman bent back on his left knee and sprang for the ledge. Just as his hand clamped on the rim, the link gave way. Catchflea fell, yelling and crying. In the half-second he had to spare, Riverwind hoisted himself onto the ledge and grasped the chain in both hands. He was nearly jerked over by Catchflea's weight, but he dug in his heels and hauled the old soothsayer to safety.

Catchflea kissed the level stone of the ledge and wept with relief at his salvation. "Thank you, merciful gods," he said.

They were safe, but now Di An was marooned. Without a safety chain, she moved nimbly back along the rim, hopping the last two feet into Riverwind's arms.

"I've got to rest," Catchflea said. "My insides are still

swimming like salmon in a rocky stream."

"Mine, too," Riverwind admitted.

Without his hook, and with the chain broken, there was no question of proceeding Di An's way. The only option open was the wide, smooth tunnel, the same one that had cost the lives of three of Di An's comrades.

After a short rest, they continued. The passage was a good eight feet in diameter, so Riverwind had no trouble with headroom. The floor sloped gently upward, and progress was easy. Di An drifted to the rear, always keeping behind Catchflea. The windblast tunnel frightened her. To help take her mind off this danger, the old man began teaching her the Common language. This would help her survive in the upper world. Catchflea found she was an apt pupil.

"I wonder how the walls got to be so smooth," Riverwind said. The lamp picked up thousands of grains of mica, making the tunnel glitter like a wall of diamonds. "There's no sign of water. The rock is dry."

"Wind can wear down stone, yes?" the old man replied. "Sand can smooth out the roughest path if propelled by a strong enough breeze."

"Where does the wind come from, Di An?" She didn't answer, so Riverwind repeated his question.

"The surface." She peeked around Catchflea's narrow waist. "I hear there are great winds on the surface, where the sky is not fettered by stone walls."

"True enough." Riverwind smiled at her description. "There must be a considerable opening in the ground for all that wind to come in."

"A cave?" suggested Catchflea.

"At least. I was thinking of something much larger, like a crater or some sort of sunken pit. Wind can swirl around a hole like that and be swallowed."

The angle of the slope increased, and it became harder to keep footing on the smooth floor. Banged knees and skinned palms became common. Finally, a small plateau leveled out the tunnel, and the three travelers stopped to rest.

"Maybe it runs all the way to the surface," Riverwind observed. He squinted ahead into the gloom.

"That would be good," Catchflea mumbled. He was

almost asleep.

Riverwind downed a swallow of bitter Hestite water and said, "I'm going to scout ahead. Stay with the old fellow."

"Don't go far," Di An warned. "It is death to become lost here."

"Not to worry." He left his shoulder pouch and went on with only the oil lamp. The ruddy sphere of light diminished as Riverwind climbed the sloping tunnel.

Di An watched until even the glow of the lamp was gone, then she sighed. She laid her head against Catchflea's shoulder. The soothsayer said in a drowsy voice, "An admirable fellow, yes?"

She started. "Yes."

"Riverwind is pledged heart and soul to another; you should keep that in mind."

Di An shrugged. She lowered her head to Catchflea's tattered shirt again.

Riverwind found that the wind passage suddenly forked into three directions, only a few hundred yards from where Di An and Catchflea rested. One branch continued almost straight up; another dived sharply down from Riverwind's feet. The third slanted up at a more gradual angle. Ease of travel alone was reason enough to take that route.

The old man and the elf girl were sound asleep when the young plainsman returned. He woke them. With clumsy movements and sleepy eyes, Di An and Catchflea rose and followed Riverwind. They obediently trailed him into the left branch of the tunnel. Then a sound filled the passage, a sound like the distant call of a ram's horn.

Di An's sleepiness vanished. "The wind!" she cried. "May the gods help us!"

"What'll we do?" exclaimed Catchflea.

"Grab hold—take hold of each other! It's our only chance!" Riverwind shouted.

The booming sound grew louder. A puff of dust swirled around the trio, now huddled in a heap on the tunnel floor. A wall of wind, invisible and roaring, hit them like a hammer. Despite their combined weight, the wind got under them and pushed them down the tunnel.

Over and over they went, bump, bang, slam—screaming

and praying and shouting warnings to each other as they tumbled. Once they were lifted completely off the floor and flew a few feet. Then they were back at the branching of the tunnels. They rolled into the open mouth of the downward slanting shaft.

This tunnel was short, and Riverwind's stomach lurched as their bouncing ride through the tunnel gave way to a drop through open air. The force of their plunge tore their grips apart, and Riverwind found himself alone, falling through a depthless void.

Chapter 14

Topaz Falls

After a timeless drop through the air, they hit water. Riverwind sank a long way before he could kick back to the surface. He broke the top of the water. By the dim illumination in the cave he saw Di An floundering. He swam to her in a few powerful strokes and seized her by the collar of her copper mesh blouse. She spat and snorted ferociously, flailing her arms to keep herself afloat. All she succeeded in doing was hitting Riverwind in the eye.

"Be still!" he said. "I have you!"

"Halloo!" Catchflea called. Riverwind spied his friend on a rocky little island a score of yards away. He kick-paddled toward him, holding Di An up with his right arm. He deposited the wretched elf girl on the island and crawled out himself. Di An coughed and sneezed the water from her lungs.

Catchflea patted her back consolingly.

"That's odd." Catchflea said. "We can see."

Riverwind shook his head, flinging droplets from his sodden hair. "Yes," the plainsman said. "But where's the light?"

"Ah, over here." Catchflea leaned back and rubbed his hand against the pinnacle of rock that jutted up from the center of the island. What resembled green moss came off on his hand and glowed faintly. The cave they had fallen into was coated with luminous green moss.

"Curious, yes, how this could grow so far from the sun, yet make its own light," Catchflea said. He gave a tentative lick at the smear of green on his fingers and immediately spat. "Ock! Oh well, I had hoped it might taste good."

As their hearts resumed normal rhythm, they sat with their backs to the pinnacle and surveyed the watery grotto. It was a big, irregular cavern, full of razor-sharp stalactites. The water was an odd golden color. Somewhere off to Di An's left, a muted roar told of falling water.

Catchflea stood and stretched. When he did, there was a brittle snapping sound and his clothing broke in several places. "Merciful gods!" he said. "What is this?"

Riverwind carefully bent his right elbow. His usually supple deerskins felt stiff and brittle. He bent his arm farther, and the elbow of his shirt split open with a glassy cracking sound.

Di An flexed her legs and a shower of bright crystalline powder fell around her feet. She stooped to examine it.

"Topaz," she said, showing the crystals to the men. "The water leaves behind topaz when it dries."

"Our clothing has been turned to stone!" Catchflea said wonderingly. His beard had gotten doused, too. He touched his beard experimentally. Sure enough, it was stiff with newly formed crystals.

"What shall I do? If I nod my head, my beard will break off!" he said.

Riverwind touched his own glassy hair. "Then disagree with everything," he said. "And only *shake* your head."

Most of their possessions had absorbed the topaz water and were slowly hardening. Both men's moccasins cracked. Every bend sent a shower of powder to the ground.

"If this continues, we shall soon be naked," Riverwind said. His boiled leather armor, being waterproof, was not affected, nor was the short mail skirt he wore beneath his buckskins.

It was obvious they couldn't remain on the little island forever. In some places the water lapped at the sheer cave wall; in other locations a strip of moss-covered "beach" could be seen. Riverwind suggested they make for the beach across the lake, toward the sound of the falls.

Di An shrank from the notion. "I cannot swim," she said faintly.

"I'll carry you on my back," Riverwind offered.

He swam slowly away from the island, doing a gentle breast stroke. Di An hung on tensely, straining to keep her face as high above the water as she could. Catchflea showed surprising ability as a swimmer, kicking ahead and making the beach ahead of Riverwind and his passenger.

The rumble of the falls was louder. A thin crack in the wall proved the way out. It was a tight fit, but the walls were so thickly coated with moss, they were able to slide through. Upon emerging in the next cavern, all three of them were smeared with faintly glowing green paste.

"You look like a ghost!" Catchflea said to Riverwind.

"And you look like a wilted fern, old man." Riverwind grinned and flung drops of moss sap from his fingers.

Di An pushed past them and headed for the sound of the falls. The cave was cluttered with boulders and rounded mineral deposits that suggested melted blocks of ice or softened lumps of butter. Still gooey and glowing, Riverwind and Catchflea followed her.

Around a bend they came face to face with the falls. They all halted, stunned by the majestic beauty.

The falls were in a high conical cavern, five hundred feet from floor to ceiling. They issued from the apex of the cone and plummeted with feathers of wild spray two hundred feet to a ledge that jutted into their path. The water flowed horizontally for some five feet, then plunged off the edge of the ledge another three hundred feet to the floor. At the bottom of the falls, where the three travelers stood, was a pool of churning froth, colored golden brown. Where centuries of crystal-laden water had splashed on the walls, thick brown deposits of topaz, probably dozens of feet thick, now hung. The walls were studded with faceted gems.

"There! Do you see?" Di An pointed her long finger high in the air. By the ledge three hundred feet above them was a dark, circular opening.

"What is it?" asked Catchflea.

"The tunnel we tried to take in the Well of Wind would've brought us there," Di An said. "That's our way out."

The cavern wall seemed to present no great obstacle. The rugged face had plenty of hand- and footholds. It was decided that Di An would scale the wall and, once she reached the tunnel entrance, she would let down a chain for the heavier, less agile men to climb.

Riverwind and Di An sorted through their climbing gear. Catchflea, bored, wandered off along the edge of the pool. Mist and spray drifted over the mossy shore, muting the green light. The steady roar of the falls drowned out the voices of his comrades. Catchflea wanted a sample of the topaz so abundant here. Gems often had magical and healing properties, and these subterranean topazes were likely to be especially pure.

Every surface above the level of the moss was covered with topaz. Catchflea examined and rejected a number of large crystals as flawed. He wanted a perfect stone to take back to Que-Shu.

He walked around an outcropping and was confronted with yet another wonder: a forest of topaz crystals growing at various angles from the rock floor. Some of the crystals were a foot tall and only a few inches in diameter, but some were as tall as he and more than a foot thick. He stared open-mouthed at the spectacular forest and then, with a gleeful yelp, headed in. Though he would have dearly loved to take one of the magnificent pillars of topaz home, he realized it might be more prudent to try to dislodge one of the smaller ones. Picking his way over the sharp, crystal-covered ground, he searched for a specimen of good carrying size. He was trying to pry one loose when he noticed the toe of a soldier's boot.

Catchflea recoiled, sprawling backward in the topaz forest. He looked up and saw an elven warrior, sword up-raised, standing several feet away from him.

"I am a friend!" Catchflea declared. "And unarmed, yes!" The warrior did not move. Catchflea repeated his friendly assertion while getting to his feet. His moccasins were almost gone, and he didn't relish the idea of running over the sharp topazes to escape a Hestite soldier.

The warrior still hadn't moved, so Catchflea approached him. He almost laughed aloud when he came within a few feet. The warrior was a statue!

"Halloo!" he called when he saw Riverwind and Di An again.

"Where have you been? It's dangerous to go off by yourself," Riverwind said sternly.

"Yes, yes, but I've made a wonderful discovery," the old man said. "Come see!"

He led them along the shoreline to the forest of crystals, where the stone soldier stood. Behind the first was ranged an entire company of statues. Di An counted eight rows of four and reported that there could be more, but in the dim light it was hard to tell. Some had their swords upraised and others stared toward the ceiling. Little detail of armor or facial features was visible. Only the smooth, golden topaz.

"You see?" Catchflea said. "Isn't it amazing? Why would anyone set up so many statues in this lonely place? Do you know, Di An?"

She scratched her head. "I cannot say. They are not Hestites, though, I am certain of that."

Riverwind frowned. "Who else could be down here?"

She didn't reply but stepped over the jagged gemstones to get a closer look. Standing on tip-toe, Di An peered into the face of the first warrior. With a loud gasp, she stumbled backward. The grappling hook she'd been holding fell from her hands and she fled to Riverwind.

"That's no statue!" she said. "It's a real warrior, encased in stone!"

Riverwind and Catchflea exchanged incredulous looks and hurried to the first figure. Sure enough, on closer examination, the translucent citrine stone showed the planar features of an elven male. Eyebrows, eyelashes, and tiny facial wrinkles could be seen inside the cold gemstone shell.

"What calamity could do this to an entire company of fighters?" Catchflea breathed.

Di An shivered. "Only Vedvedsica had that kind of power."

Riverwind stood nose to nose with the elf warrior. There was something odd about his face. He studied the fellow closely and finally said, "He's alive. His eyes follow me."

Catchflea and Di An fell back a pace. The old soothsayer looked down the silent ranks of frozen soldiers. "Alive?" he whispered. "All of them?"

"I want to know who they are," Riverwind said, stepping back from his inspection of the warrior.

"Warriors of Sithas," Di An said quietly. She had moved even farther away.

Riverwind drew his saber—itself coated with a thin veneer of gemstone—and said, "I cannot walk away from these imprisoned wretches, knowing they are alive inside tombs of stone." He raised his saber and tapped the pommel experimentally against the elf warrior's breastplate. The topaz rang and the warrior remained unmoved. With more force, Riverwind smote the same spot twice more, and the crystalline coating cracked and fell away in large chunks.

He broke the topaz away from the elf's chest, arms, and neck. The warrior's sword arm, when freed, fell to his side. The coating on the warrior's face was now seamed by hundreds of cracks. The plainsman was able to pull it away. When his face was clear, the warrior exhaled with a dry wheezing.

"Free!" he croaked. He inhaled and exhaled deeply several times. Suddenly, he seemed to recollect his surroundings. He looked wildly around the grotto. "Where is the vile sorcerer? Where is Vedvedsica?"

"Not here, that is for certain," said Riverwind. "Who are you?"

"I am Kirinthastarus, captain to His Highness, King Sithas of Silvanesti," said the warrior. "Who are you, human?"

Riverwind introduced himself and Catchflea. Kirinthastarus said, "And the renegade?"

The elf girl hid behind Riverwind, until the latter pulled her into the open. "This is our friend, Di An, no renegade. It is because of her we found you."

Kirinthastarus's eyes narrowed. "Did she turn against Hest?" he asked. "Does she know where Vedvedsica and the rebels have gone?" As he spoke, he bent to free his own feet, using his sword.

Riverwind was about to answer these odd questions when Catchflea interrupted. "Captain," he said, "do you know how long you were imprisoned in the topaz?"

The captain straightened and answered at once. "A day or two perhaps." Catchflea and Riverwind exchanged astonished looks.

"What?" said Kirinthastarus. "Have you news of Hest? You must tell me. My warriors and I must complete the task given us by our great king."

"Ah, what task is that?" asked Catchflea.

"To locate the hiding place of the rebels led by Hestantafalas and bring them to King Sithas's justice."

Di An uttered a cry and tried to flee. Riverwind caught her around the waist and lifted her off her feet.

"Let me go! Let me go!" she said, running in midair. "These warriors will kill my people!"

"Be at peace, little one." To Kirinthastarus, Riverwind said, "I don't know an easy way to tell you this, Captain. You have been entombed in that crystal shell for two and a half millennia. The monarch you serve has long since gone to his rest, as has Hest himself. Di An's people are only the children and grandchildren of the people who followed him into the cavern."

For an instant, shock registered on the warrior's face. His jaw hung slack and his eyes widened. He stared at the three of them, his gaze finally coming to rest on Di An. Staring at her, he said firmly, "Lies. You are agents of Vedvedsica. I should have known it. Did you free me from the topaz in order to kill me?"

Riverwind shook his head. "No, Captain. We tell you the truth. King Sithas sent you out over twenty-five hundred years ago. Your mission is pointless."

The elf warrior removed his helmet and emptied it of

topaz dust. He shook more dust from his dark hair. "I have no orders from anyone to forget my task. If we had not been magicked by Vedvedsica, the rebellion of Hestantafalas would have been crushed." Kirinthastarus replaced his helmet. "I will complete my task."

He presented sword and shield to them. The sword point wavered a bit. Riverwind saw nothing to be gained by fighting, but he kept his saber up until he, Catchflea, and Di An could safely retreat.

"He will free his comrades," Di An said.

"We'll be long gone before that happens," Riverwind said.

"But what of Hest? They might sack Vartoom!"

"If they can find it. There are no signposts down here."

They hurried to the foot of the overhanging ledge. Di An slung the heavy loops of chain over her shoulder and started up the wall. Catchflea kept glancing over his shoulder in the direction the warriors would come.

Di An climbed badly, slipping and losing easy handholds. "Slow down!" Riverwind called. "You'll hurt yourself!"

If she heard him, she paid his advice little heed. Di An scrambled to the midway point and looked down. From her high perch she could see what Riverwind could not. "Warriors coming!" she cried.

"Get behind me, old man," Riverwind said. Catchflea flattened himself to the base of the overhang.

Kirinthastarus appeared with two soldiers. He'd not taken the time to free all of his company. Like the warriors of Hest, the elves were greatly overmatched by Riverwind's superior height and length of reach, but three of them could get around the plainsman and take him if they were at all skilled. And history recorded that Sithas's warriors were skilled indeed.

They moved in halting fashion, and Riverwind thought they must be stiff from their magical imprisonment. As they drew nearer, he saw that a dramatic change had visited the elves. Kirinthastarus's hair and eyebrows had whitened, his skin grayed, and his limbs had become shrunken and palsied. The other elves were in similar straits.

"Look, Catchflea," he said. "Time has not forgotten them after all!"

"Surrender!" Kirinthastarus croaked. He could barely walk now, and his short sword's tip dragged on the ground. "For-ward for the glor-y of Sith-as," the captain hissed.

One of his fighters collapsed and didn't get up. Kirinthastarus closed to within a sword's reach of Riverwind. By then he was a horror to see: eye sockets hollow, lips curled back, teeth exposed. The proud warrior was a walking corpse.

The short sword thrust weakly at Riverwind. The plainsman parried with no difficulty. It was Kirinthastarus's last gesture. He sagged to the gem-covered ground. His followers were already bleached bones and scattered armor.

"I don't believe it," Catchflea said, awed.

"They aged two thousand years in the few minutes of freedom they had," Riverwind said. He looked away to where the thundering falls hid the rest of the warrior band. "We shouldn't tamper with the others."

"Yes," Di An said with great relief. "Let's leave here. Quickly."

As Riverwind began the ascent, Catchflea turned over an elven shield with his toe and said, "I wonder who is better off: Kirinthastarus, or his still captive company?"

Chapter 15

Creeping Death

It was warm in the passage at the top of the ledge.
Mold and dirty gray fungus hung in sticky strips from the
ceiling. Damp collected on the walls and ran down to a pool
on the tunnel floor.

Catchflea sneezed. "This is an unhealthy place," he said.

"Courage, old man," said Riverwind. "We won't be here
long." But the tall warrior found himself shivering in spite of
the warmth.

Di An crouched on the wet floor and fiddled with the only
oil lamp they'd saved after their fall into the mineral lake.
She struck her flint and steel expertly and soon had the lamp
producing a feeble, flickering light.

She moved ahead, weaving from one side of the tunnel to
the other. Riverwind followed cautiously down the center

of the tunnel, eyeing the lower quarter of the walls and floor. Catchflea zigzagged behind him. The passage ran as straight and level as an arrow for miles. There was nothing much in it but stinking mold and stagnant water.

Something crunched under Riverwind's foot. His moccasin boot was little more than a thick sole held on by straps, but when he raised his foot he saw a gleam of white embedded in the leather. He called Di An, and she wove her way back to him.

"Throw some light this way," he said. She pushed the lantern down.

Bones. Riverwind had trodden on the skeleton of some small animal. He picked the bones out with his fingers and examined the fragments by lamplight. "Rat," he declared. "A large one."

"This deep underground?"

"Rats aren't noted for their sense of direction," Riverwind said, dropping the fragments.

"How did it die?" asked Di An, staring at the small bones.

"Who can say?" Riverwind remarked. "It might have starved. There is little for it to eat down here."

The elf girl continued to gaze at the shattered skeleton. "It was killed. Devoured. Nothing left but hard bones." She held the light in front of her and stared down the dark passage. "In these regions, be careful where you step," she said gravely. "There are things in the ooze that do not take kindly to being trod upon."

Before either man could raise a question, Di An strode quickly away.

"What did she mean, 'things'?" asked Catchflea, hushed.

"You ask me? Be careful where you step," Riverwind said.

Di An moved so rapidly that she was leaving them behind. "Di An!" Riverwind called. "Slow down! Wait for us!" He shook his head and muttered, "What's gotten into her?"

"If she is so afraid, then I am also, tall man."

They jogged after Di An, splattering black water with each step. The lamp was all they could see, about one hundred feet ahead. Once more, Riverwind called out to Di An to stop. All of a sudden, the back-and-forth motion of the light ceased, and they heard Di An give a short, sharp cry.

Riverwind broke into a run. The older Catchflea could not keep pace with him and dropped back, complaining. Riverwind ran on, the motionless lamp his goal. As he got closer, however, he could tell the lamp was lying on the tunnel floor, unattended. Of Di An there was no sign.

He drew his saber. "Di An!" he shouted. "Can you hear me?"

Catchflea wheezed to a halt beside him. "Where is she?" he panted.

"I don't know. Something took her." He probed the walls with his sword. Solid rock. He could see ahead for a hundred feet or more and there was no indication that Di An was still in the tunnel. In fact, the lamp showed that her footprints ended just about where Riverwind stood.

He tried to sort it out. A drop of water splashed on his toe. Two more drops hit Riverwind's face. They ran down his cheek to the corner of his mouth. Salty. Why should dew be salty? Dew was fresh, sea water was salty.

He looked up. There, flattened against the ceiling of rock and staring down at him was Di An. Her mouth was covered by a strand of a thick black substance, and her wrists, ankles, and waist were similarly banded. Her tears were the moisture Riverwind had felt. The entire ceiling was thick with tarry black stuff that writhed like a living thing.

Catchflea saw it, too. "Merciful gods!"

Horror rooted the two men in place.

Part of the creeping death released its grip on the ceiling and collapsed over the plainsmen, landing on them like a heavy, wet sheet. It was sticky and drew them in tight. Riverwind felt gluey tendrils cover his eyes, nose, and mouth. All was darkness and silence as the wet, warm mass filled his ears. The black blanket of goo clung to him and squeezed, trying to force all the air out of his lungs.

He slashed with his saber, awkwardly. The ooze parted easily, but just as easily closed the cuts again. The monster had no blood to spill, no head to lop off. How could he fight it? Fear knotted his stomach and squeezed his heart even as the creeping death crushed his body.

The amorphous creature knocked Catchflea down and enveloped him up to his waist. He pounded it with his fists, but it was no use. He might as well have punched pudding. The monster wrapped around his legs and squeezed. Catchflea cried out in shock and pain.

Di An kicked and struggled. She watched the thing envelop Riverwind. Black tar crept over his face and covered his entire body. The elf girl shrieked, and the sound reverberated through the tunnel.

Riverwind heard the blood scream in his ears. He had to have air! His head felt as though it would burst any second.

The thing slowly drew Catchflea into it. The old soothsayer clawed at the slimy floor but found no grip. He had no weapon, either.

"Old man!" Di An gasped.

"I hear you!" he replied.

"Get the lamp. Burn—burn the thing—!" Black goo slid over her mouth once more.

But he understood. With his right arm Catchflea was able to grasp the lamp. He fumbled the wick holder out and sloshed oil on the black killer. The burning wick hit the iridescent pool of oil, and the pool burst into flame.

The creeping death went wild. It flopped and rippled as the burning oil boiled its tarry flesh. Bubbles formed and burst in it, making a horrible stench. The creature's clinging, sucking grip on Catchflea slackened, and he scrambled free of the flames. Di An was suddenly released and she fell, landing painfully on the tunnel floor. She rolled away. The two of them stared at the hump of tarry ooze that covered Riverwind. He was not struggling.

Thunder rolled across a red sky. Riverwind stood in a forest clearing, clad in his ceremonial beaded deerskin trousers. The air was very, very cold. He saw a gleaming light on the other side of the clearing, like a star brought down to the ground. He felt warmth on his face and bare chest, radiating from the star. He walked slowly toward it.

"Riverwind!" He looked over his shoulder at Goldmoon. His heart beat faster in his chest. Her hair was like silver fire in the light from the star. "Don't go, Riverwind. Come back to me!" she pleaded.

"Son." The voice of Wanderer came from the star. "Come to me. Enter the light, and we will be together forever."

Riverwind's steps slowed. He was pulled both ways. Goldmoon's eyes were brilliant and shining. He glanced at the star and then back at her. He was so very cold! He held out his hand to Goldmoon.

"Take my hand," he said. "Take my hand, beloved . . ."

Warm air filled his lungs. Riverwind coughed violently. That hurt; his ribs were bruised. He raised a hand to his face and encountered someone else's. The smooth, sharp chin had to belong to Di An.

She was bent over him. Catchflea was on the other side. "He breathes!" Di An said.

"We thought you were dead," Catchflea said. "Di An breathed life back into you."

Riverwind's chest ached and his arms felt like lead as he forced himself to sit up. An unmerciful throbbing pounded his temples, but he embraced Di An. "Thank you," he said hoarsely. Her slender arms went around his neck.

The creeping death still smoldered several yards away. In a last attempt to save itself from the fire, the creature had let go of Riverwind and had oozed down the tunnel toward the distant waterfall. It had only managed to get ten paces before the fire consumed it. Once the creature was destroyed, the fire had quickly died in the wet, moldy tunnel.

"Was this the danger you tried to warn us about?" Riverwind asked. Di An cast her eyes down.

"I didn't truly know what it was. Many of my comrades entered the wet tunnels and never came out again. We used to find only their bare bones near the entrance."

"Why did you run away from us?"

"I—" She wiped her sweaty face. "I was too afraid to think clearly. I'm sorry." Changing the subject quickly, she said, "You've lost your Amulet of True Hearing."

Riverwind felt for the necklace. It was gone.

"Mine is lost also," Catchflea said. "It's a good thing you learned Common so quickly, yes."

Riverwind tried to stand, and they supported him to his feet. "I'm all right," he said.

From the wet tunnel they passed into a series of caves that spiraled steadily upward. They moved in darkness now, with only Di An's acute vision to guide them. Once they found patches of the luminous moss, which Catchflea scraped off and spread on his clothes to provide some light. But when the crushed moss dried, the greenish light dissipated, and they were again in darkness.

Time lost its meaning in the silent night world of the caves. Riverwind and Catchflea stumbled along, steering by touch. Food ran short, then ran out. The caves were dry and devoid of life.

"The awful fruit of Hest would be delicious now," Catchflea finally said. "Even the bitter water would be good."

"Is there water soon, Di An?" Riverwind asked.

"Not so long now," she replied. They continued on a short way, and without a word, Di An passed back her copper bottle to Riverwind. He knew she was offering him her last drops, and he couldn't drink it. He held the bottle for a while and passed it back to her. If she'd noticed he hadn't taken any, she didn't say.

Strata came and went, some steaming hot and others bone-chillingly cold. At one point they skirted a zone of incandescent magma flowing in a trench, and not an hour later they crossed a subterranean glacier. There was a harrowing moment when Catchflea tried to lick a chunk of ice he broke off the glacier's edge. The old man's tongue stuck fast. Only with judicious applications of their last remaining water were they able to loosen the ice from Catchflea's tongue.

"You never took the dare, I see," Riverwind remarked.

"What dare?"

"To kiss the river. When I was very young, the boys of Que-Shu used to go to the river in winter and take dares to see who could kiss the frozen surface the longest."

"That's silly," said Di An.

"The point was, the longer a boy held his lips to the ice, the harder it was to remove them."

"I did not play much with the other boys when I was young," Catchflea said wistfully. "I always regretted that, yes. Until now."

On the twentieth day after leaving Vartoom, the trio was resting in a rock niche, hungry and thirsty, when they heard voices and the unmistakable sound of digging. This so galvanized them that Catchflea leaped up and banged his head on an overhanging rock. Riverwind tripped over his friend, and Di An got stepped on.

The old man and the elf girl complained loudly until Riverwind shushed them. "Quiet!" he hissed. "Who knows who these people might be?"

They lay silent for a time. Lights showed in the distance. Bobbling, weaving lanterns appeared on the other side of their cavern. The voices grew louder and more distinct.

"—to find rocks," said one squeaky voice. "What look like?"

"You big 'spert! You 'sposed to know!" added another.

A raspier voice put in, "Mine like stew. Many things in it."

"Gully dwarves!" Catchflea whispered. "We must be near the surface!"

"They think they're in a mine?" Di An muttered. "They're very stupid."

"Aghar aren't known as philosophers," Riverwind said, using the formal name for the gully dwarf race. "But they'll know a quick way out." He leaned forward on his hands.

"What are you going to do?"

Riverwind smiled in the dark. "Introduce myself," he said.

On hands and knees, he crossed the cave diagonally to get in front of the gully dwarves. Riverwind's battered moccasins skidded on some loose stones. The four lanterns stopped swaying.

"You hear?"

"I hear. Got club?"

"Uh-huh. Got knife?"

"Uh-huh."

That wasn't reassuring to the plainsman. Gully dwarves were not much respected as fighters, but a club and knife indicated trouble. They might attack first and flee later.

A shaft of light flashed over his feet. The lantern carrier gave a hoot and swung the lantern back.

"Big feet here," he reported. The feeble light flickered over Riverwind's crouching form.

All four lanterns were brought to bear on the plainsman, outlining him in orange highlights. Riverwind raised a hand to shield his eyes from the glare and stood up.

Four lanterns hit the cave floor simultaneously as the gully dwarves gave a concerted shriek. Four pairs of bare feet slapped the ground in headlong retreat. Riverwind never got to say a word.

He retrieved a lantern that still burned, then fetched Di An and Catchflea. At the site where the gully dwarves had panicked, they found tools and a small leather bag. Catchflea turned the bag upside down, hoping it held food. All that fell out was a lumpy red rock. Di An picked it up.

"Cinnabar," she said.

"What is cinnabar?" asked Catchflea.

"The ore of quicksilver," said Di An. "A difficult and dangerous mineral to mine."

"Dangerous? How?"

"The dust is poisonous," she said. "It invades the body. Insanity and death follow quickly." The elf girl sniffed. "But they'll find no cinnabar here. This is a limestone cave."

Catchflea righted another burning lantern and opened the tin hood so that light leaped out across the cave.

"That's where they went!" he called. A dark hole five feet high showed in the near wall. Closer examination showed it was not a natural opening.

Riverwind shone his light through the hole. The dwarves were fast on their feet, bare or not; they were long gone from the cave. "I say we follow them," he said. "Wisdom is not their strongest virtue, but gully dwarves always know the quickest way to safety."

The path was clearly marked with gully dwarf jetsam— rags, worn tools, and, most tantalizing, apple peelings, melon rinds, and gnawed chicken leg bones. Catchflea dawdled over the last as though they were diamonds in the rough.

"Roast chicken," he mused. "I'd shave my beard for a whole roast chicken."

"Be careful of oaths you make, old man," Riverwind said. "You may have to keep them." Di An said something he didn't quite hear. He asked her to repeat herself.

"Water," she said. "I smell water."

Chapter 16

The Cursed City

They hurried toward the smell of fresh water.
Around them the walls, spires, and spikes of cave architecture glistened with dew. The water sparkled like gems in the light of the torches on the walls.

There were holes in the ceiling farther along. Crude ladders with closely spaced rungs reached down through the holes to the cavern floor. Gully dwarf ladders. Their rungs looked as if they had been broken and patched together; all the rungs sagged noticeably. The three companions stood beneath one of the round holes, peering up.

Riverwind felt disappointment settle like lead in his empty stomach. "We are still underground," he said dully.

They seemed to be at the bottom of another vast cavern, for they could see walls rising hundreds of feet all around.

The hole they peered through was thirty feet above them and too small for them to make out details of the upper level. But it was definitely still underground.

"I hear water," Catchflea said. "At least there is that."

Mingled with the blessed thunder of falling water was another very familiar sound.

"Forge hammers," Di An said, tilting her head to hear better. "There is metalworking here."

"Where is *here*?" Riverwind groaned. For all he knew, they could have passed through the center of Krynn and emerged on the far side.

A light patter of feet sounded, and the stumpy figure of a gully dwarf ran past the hole. The three stepped away from the opening. Four more Aghar scurried by.

Di An wanted to know what gully dwarves were. Catchflea tried to explain.

"First there were humans, who worshiped the god Reorx, many, many years ago. They grew wise in the making of things and soon decided they were too wise to follow Reorx on the Path of Neutrality. They made war on their neighbors, made slaves of their captives, and generally acted base and greedy.

"For this Reorx punished them. He humbled their pride by taking away their human stature, making them little people." Here Catchflea blushed a bit, aware of Di An's own diminutiveness. "Thus was the race of gnomes created. But the gnomes lost none of their creative talent, only the willful greed. Gnomes are tireless experimenters, and they brought down the Graygem of Gargath, a source of great magic. The Graygem altered some of the gnomes again, beginning the races of the kender and dwarves. Dwarves and gnomes sometimes married, and from their unions the Aghar, or gully dwarves, sprang."

"These gullies are poor folk?" Di An asked.

"They usually live in squalor and are despised for it," Catchflea said with sympathy. "A paradox of prejudice, yes? To confine a people to living in garbage heaps and ruins, and then hate them for being dirty and stupid."

"We should be very careful entering that cavern," Riverwind said, staring up through the hole thoughtfully.

Di An asked, "Are the gullies so dangerous? They ran from the sight of you before."

"They were surprised. But, no, they aren't so dangerous. What I'm worried about is what else we'll find once we leave the shelter of the cave. Aghar seldom work for themselves; more often, they are the slaves of a more powerful race."

Di An frowned at that.

"A race that is hoarding cinnabar," Catchflea added thoughtfully.

"So it seems," Riverwind replied.

Riverwind was first on the ladder. Its rungs creaked suspiciously under his weight. He was twice the size of any gully dwarf, who weren't famous for the quality of their carpentry anyway. Riverwind took the rungs three at a time and hoped they wouldn't snap. The ladder bowed and wobbled, but he managed to reach the top. He braced himself with his arms and peered out.

They were indeed at the bottom of another huge cavern. Riverwind was in the middle of what looked like a city street—but what a strange city! The fine stone buildings were tumbled-down ruins. The walls of the cavern were dotted with odd sights. Ledges and ridges held the remains of ancient dwellings. Here and there, light filtered out of the crumbled buildings, proof that someone occupied them.

Di An tapped his leg. "You going out?" she said.

Riverwind levered himself up and popped out of the hole. The ground around the hole was paved with worn stone blocks. This had been a busy street once, long ago. There was something familiar about this place; he tried to remember. What was the name of the city that fell into the ground during the Cataclysm? His father had told him a tale about it.

Di An, moving like a wraith, slipped out of the hole and crouched beside Riverwind. Catchflea came out at last, wheezing. Both the plainsman and the elf girl said, "Shh!"

They had come out at the intersection of three roads, all lined with burning torches, near the ruin of a large, round tower. The tower was a broken shell now, but it afforded the three a good place to take cover.

Riverwind, Catchflea, and Di An peeked through holes in

the tower wall. On their right, water gushed down the walls of the cavern, pooling and flowing down the center of the road. On the other side of the street stood a large, low building, obviously constructed out of the remains of earlier houses. Smoke drifted out of crude chimneys in the roof. The door and window openings were empty.

The stream of water flowed down the center road and into a small pond. Rising behind the pond was an elegant, decayed facade with columns and a peaked roof. It was probably a palace. More solid buildings bulked beyond.

To their left was another long, low building. This one had torches on brackets along the outside.

"What do you make of it?" Riverwind asked.

"Very cozy, yes. But who lives in a ruined city besides gully dwarves? And where is everyone?" Catchflea queried. When Riverwind didn't reply, the old man said, "I want water and food. And I can see where the water is, yes?"

He strode out of the ruined tower before Riverwind or Di An could stop him. Catchflea peered furtively down the street, then walked to the stream. He knelt and buried his face in the bubbling water.

Riverwind licked his cracked lips. So far, so good. "Seems safe enough," he murmured. He stepped over the low, crumbling wall. "Are you coming?"

"No," Di An replied. Where there were slaves, there had to be masters. The idea made her very nervous.

"Very well. I'll fill a bottle for you." Riverwind took out his copper canteen and unscrewed the stopper.

Catchflea was splashing water on his face and neck when Riverwind joined him. "It's glorious, yes!" he said. "Finer than the finest vintage."

Riverwind agreed by burying his head in the cool, sweet water. He and the old man drank deeply and sluiced the liquid over their sweaty bodies.

Back in her hiding place at the ruined tower, Di An could bear it no longer. The lure of the water was too strong. She stood to leap over the rubble of the tower.

And just as quickly dropped back down again. There were five horrible-looking creatures moving stealthily up on Riverwind and Catchflea! The creatures were taller than the gully dwarves and heavily built. They wore leather armor and carried short swords. The elf girl chewed her lip in desperation. If she called out, she might alert other creatures. If she didn't call out . . .

One of the creatures swung his sword and knocked Riverwind into the stream. The young plainsman came out sputtering in surprise. He found himself facing five goblins. Though more than a head shorter than the tall plainsman, the goblins were armed and he was not.

"Don't move," growled the goblin. "Drop weapon."

Catchflea was staring at the soldiers. He made as if to sidle away, but two of the creatures advanced on him, swords drawn. He stopped moving, a nervous smile on his face.

"Drop weapon in river, now," said the leader more loudly.

Riverwind drew his saber out with his left hand, but instead of dropping it into the river, he tossed it in the air and caught it with his right hand. The creatures all moved back a pace, grumbling and muttering.

"You drop!" the leader shrieked poking his own weapon at the plainsman. "You drop or I call big boss!"

Riverwind considered his ability to make a run for it around these fellows. Five armed and angry goblins were more than he could handle, what with the added handicap of Catchflea. He sent his gaze toward the old man. Catchflea gave a tiny shrug. He would be of no use in battle.

"He don't drop, Grevil," rasped one of the goblins.

The leader growled, and one of his followers whacked the speaker smartly on the head with the flat of his blade. The unfortunate fellow dropped like a stone and lay silent.

One down, Riverwind thought.

"Grevil!" a voice boomed out. All the goblins jumped as if they'd been struck. Grevil—the leader—yelled, "Big boss coming! Now you drop!"

Riverwind glanced to his right, and his body stiffened in shock. It was not another goblin that approached. A creature fully his own height, broad, brawny, and covered in green scales strode rapidly toward them. Yellow eyes with vertical pupils glittered in the torchlight, and a toothless beak of a mouth finished off the fearsome face. The tops of short, leathery wings rose over his head, and Riverwind was astonished to see a long, spiked tail lashing behind him. The creature wore plate armor on his chest, arms, and the fronts of his legs. Only twenty yards separated the scaled, reptilian warrior from Riverwind.

Catchflea gasped. "What in the name of Majere is that?" he hissed.

Suddenly, a rock whizzed from the tower wall and struck Grevil in the head. He whirled, and a veritable rain of stones pelted the goblins. Riverwind knew who threw stones like that. Di An.

He caught a glimpse of her short, stiff hair outlined against the white stone walls of the old tower. The goblins were yelling and slashing at the rocks with their swords. Riverwind leaped and ran, yanking Catchflea to his feet.

"Come on, Di An!" he shouted. She hopped over a low stone pile and ran like a rabbit.

"Down the hole, both of you," Riverwind snapped. Di An reached it first. She clasped the ladder rails and gripped with her feet, sliding down the long, flimsy length in two blinks of an eye. Catchflea arrived puffing, and he was unceremoniously stuffed down after the elf girl. Riverwind had to wait his turn, but now the goblins were upon him. Behind them came the scaled warrior.

Catchflea was halfway down the ladder. Riverwind traded cuts with the goblins, who gave way as the scaled warrior arrived. He wielded a mighty cleaver of a sword. The blade of Riverwind's saber whipped back and forth as the far heavier sword chipped deep notches in it.

More goblins were arriving all the time. Riverwind glanced into the dark hole. He couldn't see Catchflea, but the ladder was still shaking. Any moment now . . .

His foe caught him with a stunning blow to the side of his head with the flat of the blade. The impact made Riverwind's ears ring and his vision go red. A hot, itching line of blood ran down his face. Riverwind stepped back and thrust his sword point straight at the creature. It skidded off the warrior's bowed breastplate. The creature brought its wedge-shaped blade down on Riverwind's hilt. The plainsman's weapon snapped cleanly, the curved portion of the saber falling to the ground.

Riverwind threw the useless hilt at the lizard man and dropped through the hole. He meant to grab a rung on his way down. His left hand missed, his right caught, and he jerked painfully to a stop ten feet below the opening. A burning torch whizzed by him, and a crossbow bolt flickered into the darkness. Riverwind scrambled to get his feet on a rung to relieve the pain and pressure on his right arm. As he got one foot in place, the crude ladder finally gave way, then crumpled, taking Riverwind with it.

* * * * *

Cool water trickled on his face. Riverwind saw Catchflea and Di An. The girl poured water in her palm and applied it to his face. He tried to sit up, and pain raced through his chest and shoulder. He fell back.

"Lie still," Catchflea said. "You had quite a fall."

Riverwind looked around. They were back in the lower cave, among the milky limestone concretions.

"The goblins have been looking for us," Catchflea said. "They dropped torches through the hole and shot arrows at random, but they haven't put down their own ladder yet."

"They can't know how many of us are down here," Riverwind said. "But they'll come eventually."

"What was that scaly thing?" asked Di An. Her thin, angular face was scratched. So were her hands.

"I don't know, but he's not friendly. Have you ever heard or seen his like, old man?"

"No, never."

Di An let a few droplets fall from her palm to Riverwind's lips. "Shall we go back?" she asked.

"Where? To Hest? I think not."

Catchflea thought for a moment and said, "The gully dwarves, they come down here. Perhaps we could parley with them, yes? They would certainly have food and water. If we approach them the right way, they might help us get around the goblins."

"They are stupid and ugly and smell bad," Di An said. "It is foolish."

"They're basically good folk," Riverwind countered. "I've dealt with them before. They are simple, but Aghar have been derided for so long that they understand what it means to starve and suffer. I think they'll help us."

Di An was silent. Finally, her gaze came to rest on Riverwind. "This is a mistake," she said. "But I agree to try it your way." She stood and walked away, into the shadows.

Riverwind sighed and lay back on the ground. "Old man, do you think this is the right thing to do?"

Catchflea didn't answer. He was staring after the elf girl. Riverwind repeated his question.

"What? Yes, tall man," Catchflea replied. "I agree that it is our only choice." He paused. "But I think perhaps you should speak to her."

"And say what? I'm as frightened as she is." Riverwind rubbed his abused ribs. "I only want to get back to my quest. It seems like years since I parted from Goldmoon."

"Something more than fear is troubling her, my friend." The old soothsayer hesitated a long moment. "I believe she is in love with you."

"That's ridiculous! She's a child."

"A child ten times your age," Catchflea said gently. "Speak with her. I'll stand guard." The old man walked slowly back to the hole in the cave ceiling.

Riverwind lay still for a few minutes. Di An in love with him? It couldn't be true. She had been acting strangely lately—rude, nay-saying. There was some other answer. She must be homesick. The gods knew *he* was.

Goldmoon, my beloved, he thought, how far away you seem now.

* * * * *

Di An was crouched in an especially dark corner of the cave, away from the torchlight. She was miserable and she didn't know why.

The trek from Hest had been arduous. She and Catchflea and Riverwind had faced many dangers. The warriors of the dreaded King Sithas. Hunger and thirst. The creeping death. She shuddered. She had watched Riverwind die. She had seen his face go white and still. It was worse than when he had been under Li El's enchantment. He had truly died. When he had at last taken air back into his lungs, Di An had felt a great rushing of joy. It was more than a gladness felt for a friend—she'd had many friends before among the scouts of Hest. This was something more.

"Di An?" Riverwind's voice carried through the cave. "Where are you?"

The elf girl heard the concern in his voice. She made herself stand and call out to him.

"I was getting worried," he said. "I thought something might've happened to you."

"Something has," she blurted.

He took her hand in his own and the warmth of his body made her shiver. "You're freezing," he said. "Let's move toward the light." He led her to a rock by one of the torches and sat down, bringing their eyes more on a level.

"Tell me what is bothering you, little one."

Di An jerked her hand from his. "I'm not a child, Riverwind!" she exploded.

He was taken aback. "I know that, Di An. I'm sorry." He looked closely at her. "You've been crying. What's wrong?"

Her struggle to hide her feelings was plain on her face. It was a battle she lost. "We have suffered through so much together," she said, "yet you cannot wait to be rid of me! I see it in your face, tall man. You want nothing so much as to be on the surface again, free to return to your—*people*." She turned away from him to hide her angry face.

Riverwind realized then that Catchflea was right. "Di An," he began, "it's no secret that I ache to get on with my quest. I have to fulfill it if I am to have the hand of the woman I love." She stiffened when he said that. His voice softened. "You have been a fine companion and a friend. That need not end, ever."

Her thin shoulders rose and fell with a musical clink from her copper mesh dress. "It is difficult," she said, "never to fit in. Who am I? In Hest, I was a barren child. In Vartoom, I was Mors's eyes. Here in the tunnels and caves, I am Di An, the same as the old man and you. One of three."

"You're still one of three," Riverwind said gently.

"But soon to be left behind. What am I to do on the surface? Where shall I go?"

Riverwind had wondered about those same questions himself.

"I'll be honest with you," he said slowly. "It won't be easy for you. But you can become anything you can make of yourself. No one on the surface cares if you're a barren child or a digger. Be a traveler, a trader, anything you want. Be free, Di An. Free." He said the word in her language. "*Varin*."

He reached out and gathered her into his arms. She buried her head against his chest and wept a bit. Riverwind sorrowed that she was so unhappy because of him. He knew that her future would not be an easy one.

Chapter 17

Brud Stonesifter

They took turns watching the hole, but nothing hap-pened for many hours. Riverwind was sitting wedged between two limestone boulders, sipping water from his canteen, when he heard voices from above. Seconds later, a stumpy figure appeared in the hole. It was a gully dwarf. A rope was tied around his thick waist, and someone was lowering him through the hole.

"Make slow!" the Aghar said. He promptly dropped almost six feet. "Slow, dungheads! Slow! Turn rope!" The rope twisted, rotating the little fellow in a circle. He had mouse-colored hair, liberally coated with soot. His stubby fingers were blackened, too. "Make lower," he said, and he was lowered to the cave floor.

"Torch!" A flaming brand almost hit him on the head.

"Good aim, dunghead!" The gully dwarf picked up the brand and started walking. He didn't bother untying the rope from his waist.

"Any monsters down here?" he called. "Show yourself to Brud. No eat Brud. Taste bad, phooey." The dwarf waved the torch around. Riverwind crouched lower.

"No monsters here. Pull up now?" The rope remained slack. "Brud Stonesifter valuable fella. You want rock 'spert eaten?" A hefty chunk of paving stone whizzed down the hole. Brud skipped aside. "All very right! I look more."

Brud was no crafty tracker, but he plainly saw the broken ladder and the marks made when Catchflea and Di An had dragged the unconscious Riverwind away. He walked slowly, peering at the trail. It led him right past Riverwind.

"Valuable Brud, bait for monster. Ha," the dwarf mumbled as he snooped. "Serve very right if eaten up, then no one find rocks for masters. Ha." He stumped by Riverwind. The plainsman pulled his knife and grabbed the little man. Clamping a hand over his mouth, Riverwind then cut the rope a foot or so from the Aghar's waist. He carried the struggling gully dwarf around the rocks to his friends.

"Wake up," he said.

Catchflea rubbed his eyes. "I hope you found something to eat," he said. Brud froze a second, then redoubled his frantic wiggling. Riverwind gave him a hard squeeze and warned him to be still.

"What have you got?" Di An piped.

"A visitor. If he'll behave, I'll let him speak." Brud put his most eloquent appeal into his muddy brown eyes. "All right." Riverwind removed his hand.

"*EEEEEEEYOW!*" screamed the gully dwarf. The cave rang with his blood-chilling cry. Riverwind clamped his hand once more over Brud's mouth and ducked down behind the rocks that sheltered Catchflea and Di An. The elf girl looked disgusted.

"Treacherous worm," she said. "Pound him with a stone. That will make him quiet."

Riverwind set Brud on the ground and pushed his own face close to the dwarf's. "Now listen to me. We are very desperate criminals, and if you make one more sound to alert the goblins, I shall cut your throat." Catchflea suppressed a giggle at his young friend's fiercely ridiculous threat. Riverwind displayed his knife to Brud, then carefully lifted his hand from the little fellow's mouth.

"Great master, please don't kill Brud," he whispered.

"I won't hurt you if you behave," Riverwind said severely. "Will you answer our questions?" The gully dwarf nodded. "Where are we?"

"In cave."

"But *where*?"

"Under city."

Riverwind's grip tightened on the knife. He wouldn't really hurt the little man, but he was sorely tempted to scare him into giving straight replies. He would try once more. "What city?" he asked.

"Zak S'roth," Brud said, as if this was the most obvious thing in the world.

Xak Tsaroth! Now Riverwind knew why the place seemed familiar. His father had told him stories of the ruined city that had collapsed into the ground during the Cataclysm. Great gods! He was only about eighteen miles east of Que-Shu. But the city was supposed to be surrounded by dangerous, fever-infested swamps.

"We saw a lizard man," Catchflea said. "Who is he?"

Brud made a horrible face. "New masters. Make Aghar work hard."

"How many of them live here?"

"Too many."

Riverwind shook his head. "Where did they come from?"

"From sea. They march to city, take over, bring in goblin soldiers, make Aghar build houses, dig for rocks."

Riverwind, Catchflea, and Di An exchanged knowing looks. "What sort of rocks do they make you dig for?" asked Riverwind.

"Red rocks, brown rocks, black rocks." Di An gave a short sigh of frustration. "Brud is expert at finding rocks. Find more than anybody," he said proudly.

"What happens to the rocks?" Riverwind continued the questioning.

Brud shrugged. "Go to big house and be burned."

"Smelted," Di An said knowingly.

Riverwind peeked over the rocks toward the hole in the roof. The cut rope had been withdrawn. By now the goblins and their lizard masters would be convinced a monster had carried off poor Brud Stonesifter. What would their next step be? Send down armed warriors?

"Listen," Riverwind said. "We need food and water. If we let you go, can you arrange them for us?"

"Yes, wonderful master! I bring you good things to eat!"

"I don't trust him," Di An remarked.

Riverwind didn't either, so he said to Catchflea, "As wizard of the group, I think you ought to put a hex on our friend here, so he will obey."

"Hex?" Catchflea said vaguely. "Oh! A hex, yes. Let me see, what is my most powerful spell . . . ?" He took out his gourd and rattled the acorns over Brud's head. He waved the gourd all around the gully dwarf and uttered long, nonsensical words. Brud's eyes got wider and wider.

"Now," said Catchflea, pointing a bony finger at Brud, "if you do not return in two hours, or if you tell anyone who or where we are, your nose will grow to be five feet long, and your ears will grow as big as a warrior's shield. You understand, yes?"

Brud swallowed with an audible gulp. "Brud understand."

"Off with you then," Riverwind said. The dwarf hopped to his thick bare feet, then froze.

"Rope gone," he said. "Okay if Brud use mouse hole?"

"Mouse hole?" Catchflea repeated.

"Sure, got one." Brud leaned forward as if to go. "Brud show you?"

"By all means, yes."

"But watch your step," Di An said icily.

Brud looked her up and down and gave the elf girl a broad wink. "You pretty skinny," he said, "but I like." Di An sniffed contemptuously.

They skirted the cone of light showing through the hole. Brud led them to the far end of the cave, where the roof and floor gradually slanted down to meet each other. The plainsmen had to crouch low to save their heads. Then Di An had to crouch, as she was half a foot taller than Brud.

The gully dwarf rooted among some small loose stones, uncovering a very narrow tunnel.

"Mouse hole," he said proudly.

"The mice grow big here," Riverwind remarked.

"Not for mice. For Aghar," Brud explained. "Good for hiding. Mouse holes all over. I go now?"

"You go," said Catchflea. "But remember the hex!" Brud fingered his stub of a nose and nodded solemnly. He wriggled into the tiny opening and soon was gone.

Di An examined the aperture. "I could probably fit in there," she said.

"Why would you want to?" asked the old man.

"In case the gully doesn't return. I could go out and search for food."

"Let's give Brud a chance. He might do as we wish," Riverwind said. "If not, we'll have to slip out at night again."

Di An rubbed her sharp chin. "Goblins will be on guard above."

"I know, but it's better than starving down here."

They waited by the mouse hole for at least two hours. No one was paying much attention when a cloth-wrapped bundle finally popped out of the hole and rolled to a stop at Riverwind's feet. A second bundle dribbled out after the first, then a heavy stoneware jug. Finally, Brud emerged, head-first, grinning from ear to ear.

"Brud is back!" he declared. "Nose and ears do not grow?"

"The hex is lifted," Catchflea said, his mouth watering. With trembling fingers he untied the first bundle. Out tumbled five potatoes, still warm from their boiling. The second bundle held four more boiled potatoes. Riverwind pulled the wooden plug from the jug and sniffed.

"Wah! Whatever this is, it's gone bad!" he said.

"It's milk," Brud said. "Tall human like milk."

"Only when it's fresh!"

Di An bit gingerly into a potato. It was still mostly raw, but never having had a potato before, she didn't know. She ate it quickly, licking her fingers when she had dispatched it.

"Raw potatoes and sour milk. Is that all you brought?" asked Catchflea. Brud fingered his earlobes.

"You no like?" he said weakly.

The old soothsayer picked up a potato, brushing off some dirt. He bit it.

"Better than nothing," he mumbled through his food.

They ate all the potatoes quickly, and Catchflea commented that he wished he at least had some salt to season them with. Brud's eyes got wide, and he said, "Oh!" He dug a hand into one pocket and came out with a fat pinch of salt, well mixed with dirt and lint. He offered this to Catchflea quite seriously. The old man graciously declined.

"Did anyone notice you had come back?" Riverwind said.

"Only wife, Guma."

"What did she do?"

Brud grinned. It was not a handsome sight. "She hear monster eat me in cave, gulp. Same day I pop out mouse hole, ha! She scream loud, call me ghost."

Riverwind couldn't help but smile. "What did you do?"

"I say 'Give me fooood.' " He drew out the last word in true ghostly fashion. "Then Guma say what she always say, 'Get it yourself!' "

Catchflea cackled with laughter. Riverwind chuckled and even Di An cracked a smile.

Their merriment was short-lived. A soft and heavy thud elsewhere in the cave was followed by a spreading cloud of noxious yellow smoke. The stinking cloud oozed through the cave. "Brimstone!" Di An gasped.

"They're trying to smoke us out," Riverwind said.

"Looks like they'll succeed, yes!"

Forgetting Brud, they tried to get back to the entrance to the lower tunnel. But that part of the cave was on the other side of the hole, and the sulfur fumes were worse there. Another burlap bag, soaked in oil and blazing, was dumped into the cave. Weeping and choking, the elf girl and the plainsmen retreated to Brud's escape tunnel.

"Go, Di An!" Riverwind said. "Save yourself!"

"I won't leave you!" she said.

"We'll all choke to death," Catchflea said.

"Go, Di An. Go on!"

She protested bitterly, but Riverwind pushed her into the mouse hole. She slipped her shoulders into the narrow opening. Catchflea crouched on the floor, holding his beard over his nose and mouth. Riverwind spotted Brud.

"Doesn't the smoke hurt you?" he said, coughing between each word.

"Smell not bad to me," the gully dwarf said with a shrug.

"Will you help Di An if we don't make it, Brud?" Riverwind said.

"Skinny pretty girl. Brud look after." He boosted himself over the rim of the hole. "Farewell, criminal."

Abruptly Brud popped out onto the cave floor. Di An's tear-streaked face appeared. "Riverwind! The tunnel is large enough for you two inside! Make the entrance wider!"

They had an assortment of tools dropped by the gully dwarves in the cavern, so Riverwind and Catchflea hammered at the stone. Di An and Brud stood by. The glassy limestone splintered and sharp chips flew.

The yellow smoke was so thick now that they couldn't see across the cave. The men and Di An coughed and coughed. "Enough, enough!" Riverwind said. Di An re-entered the opening. Riverwind helped Catchflea in, and Di An dragged at the old man's arms. Riverwind followed them. The tunnel was only two feet wide, but with his shoulders bunched the young plainsman could make it.

Brud surveyed the sulfur-flooded cave. "Not smell so bad," he mused aloud. The tunnel opening he regarded with a far more critical eye. "Mouse hole ruined," he said. "Big enough for bear now."

He grabbed the lower rim of the enlarged hole, levered himself up, and wriggled through.

The mouse hole tunnel ran level for forty yards, then ended on a tight vertical shaft. Notches were chiseled in the wall, and it was easy enough for them to climb the ten yards or so to the surface.

Di An shifted a stone floor tile, and they emerged in a dark room. They lay for a while, gasping the clean air. Brud appeared and kicked the tile back over the opening.

"Where are we?" Catchflea croaked.

"Broken Jar House," Brud replied. Sure enough, the floor was littered with layer upon layer of broken pottery. "Wait, I make light."

He found a long pole standing in a corner, apparently left

for just such a purpose. Brud used the pole to poke open a shuttered window high on the wall. It was still not very bright inside the room, but enough light filtered in to reveal what a bizarre place they had stumbled into.

It was a house, tipped on its side. The surface they sat on was not a floor, but a wall of the house. Facing them was the true floor, an expanse of white tile. Many tiles had fallen, leaving dark squares in the pattern. The surface above their heads was decorated with lively frescoes showing humans rising from pallets with their hands in the air. A tall, grave figure stood at the end of the fresco, holding a slim jar.

"A doctor, or apothecary," Catchflea said. "See, he's healed the sick."

"These must have been his medicine bottles," Riverwind added. He raised a fistful of fragments. The pottery was so old it was turning to dust. The pieces crumbled in his fist.

"How did this place get this way?" Di An asked. "Why is this city an underground ruin?"

"The Cataclysm," Riverwind said solemnly. "Almost three hundred and fifty years ago, the world was rent asunder by mighty upheavals of land and sea. My father told me stories of that time. Xak Tsaroth sank into the ground."

Di An looked thoughtful. "That must have been what we in Hest knew as the Great Shattering. That was when Vartoom was cut off from the other cities of Hest," she said.

Catchflea sat upright. "*Other* cities?"

"Yes. Balowil, the City of Lead, and Arvanest, the City of Gold."

Catchflea was about to draw the elf girl into conversation about these Hestite cities when Brud shimmied up the pole to the window. "Bad to say!" he muttered.

"What is it?"

"Goblins and masters look for you." Riverwind leaped up, trying to catch the sill of the sideways window. He missed and landed with enough force to jar his aching ribs.

"Let me," said Di An. She climbed the pole as nimbly as Brud had. At the window, she pushed him aside. He kept trying to sniff behind her pointed ears.

"Stop it, worm," she said, fending him off.

"How you hear with ears like that?"

"How do you live with a face like that?" she spat.

From the window Di An could see the street. A lizard man stood at the hole. A new ladder had been lowered into the cave, and goblins were being sent down in pairs, armed with clubs. The lizard man carried a large sword. The elf girl relayed all this to her friends.

"We're in the stewpot, yes," said Catchflea.

"Life like stew," Brud observed. They waited for him to finish the analogy. Brud said nothing. He turned his back to the window. He felt he'd said it all.

The door to the Broken Jar House was on the "ceiling." Di An kicked tiles loose and climbed out on the vertical wall, with only her toes and fingertips to hold her up. Brud was rapt with admiration. Di An reached the door and pulled the handle. The corroded copper crumbled in her hand.

Di An leaned out far from the wall, one hand and both feet clinging to the narrowest of holds. With her climbing hook, she picked at the blackened hinge pin on the door. The hardened Hestite steel soon broke apart the ancient brass pin. The corner of the door sagged inward. Hooking onto the door frame, Di An swung free from the wall.

"Woo! Brud want to try!"

The elf girl ignored him. She wedged her foot against the sagging door and pushed. With a loud crack, the remaining door pin snapped. The battered wooden door fell. Di An hooked her foot on the doorjamb and vaulted out.

Brud clapped his thick, dirty hands together. The Que-Shu men applauded as well. Di An lowered the chain. Riverwind and Brud climbed out, then hauled Catchflea up with the chain.

"That fun. Do again?" said the gully dwarf hopefully. They ignored him and studied their position.

The Broken Jar House was lodged in the wall of the cavern, sixty feet above the street. The wall they were standing on slanted down, and opened on a triangular crack in the pit wall. There seemed no place to go until Brud bustled by.

"Where are you going?" Riverwind asked.

Brud pointed below and to their right. "Home to Aghar town. See wife. Hungry."

"Wait! Hold there."

Brud ignored them. He hopped from the wall of the house to a narrow ledge that ran out of the crevice. Riverwind followed, though the ledge was barely wide enough for one of his feet. Brud reached the front of the crevice and did a quick right-face. In full view of the entire city, he strolled along the ledge toward a waterfall. Riverwind could see a tunnel had been carved behind the falls. To his companions he said, "Come! Brud has shown us the way."

Di An and Catchflea worked their way around the ledge. They had to press close to the cliff face. Brud kept going.

Riverwind was halfway to the falls when they were spotted by the goblins. A shout went up. "Now we're in for it," he muttered. He tried to increase his pace.

Bolts flicked at them, bouncing off the stone wall. Brud appeared on the other side of the falls and waved. He ducked into another hole in the cliff face and vanished.

"I told you he was a worm!"

"Could we keep moving, yes? That last arrow almost parted my hair!"

A rumble from below proved to be the sound of the goblins moving a full-fledged ballista into the street. They loaded the cup with assorted stones and pulled the trigger rope. The throwing arm threshed forward, sending a shower of fist-sized rocks at the trio. One struck Di An in the back. She cried out briefly and lost her hold.

"Di An!" Riverwind shouted. Her slight body disappeared below his line of sight.

There was not time to grieve or worry. The lizard men ordered the goblins to winch down the ballista and fire again. This time Catchflea was pummeled by four or five stones. He lost his stance and plunged from sight.

Riverwind was only yards from the falls. His heart pounded, not only for his own danger, but for the fate of Di An and Catchflea. Spray was dampening his face when a large rock hit him behind the knees. His legs folded, and he dropped backward off the ledge.

I'm falling again, he thought calmly. Will this be the last time?

Chapter 18

Children of the Dragon

The lizard men were used to having their slaves, the gully dwarves, try to escape. They kept rock-throwing ballistae handy in the streets to knock the little folk off the cavern wall, should they try to leave. Since dead slaves could do little work, the lizard men had stretched large nets around the base of the walls to catch the Aghar. Now those nets caught Di An, Catchflea, and Riverwind. Goblins cut the ropes, and the whole net assembly collapsed inward, trapping the three of them.

Before they could fight or flee, each was plucked from the net by several goblins. Heavy manacles were snapped on the two men. Di An was tied with leather thongs, as her wrists were too small for the fetters. At the direction of the two brawny lizard men, the three were marched down the street toward the place they'd glimpsed earlier.

They were halted by a gated entry on the left side of the street. More armed goblins opened the gate, and the captives were driven in. Within was an entryway. A larger room was visible through the open door. The goblin soldiers pushed them to the right, to a large cell. Without a word, the three were shoved into the cell and the door closed behind them.

Catchflea sagged to the floor. All the good spirit seemed to have left him. He laid his head against the wall and closed his eyes. Riverwind strained against his fetters, but the wrought iron was nearly an inch thick. The door was no better—oak strapped with iron, four inches thick. It did indeed seem hopeless.

Di An sniffed her bonds and started chewing at them. The leather was tough, but she was able to gnaw through one strap in about half an hour.

"Good!" Riverwind said encouragingly. "Keep it up!"

"My jaw hurts," the girl complained, but she resumed chewing.

She never had a chance to finish. The door opened, revealing a lizard man wearing an officer's gold badge.

"Come! The commander would see you," he said.

A full dozen goblin guards were drawn up outside. Riverwind, Di An, and Catchflea were marched through the empty hall into another courtyard. Smells of cooking drifted in the air, torturing the hungry travelers' stomachs.

"To the right! Quick march!" roared the officer. The cadence of heavy feet increased. A large waterfall cascaded down the cliff face to their right. It flooded out the old street. The lizard men had built a wooden bridge across the swelling stream. Facing them was the blank east wall of the palace. Someone had restored the walls, but left the columned facade in ruins.

They headed for that facade. Standing among the stumps of the broken pillars was the largest, most grandly dressed lizard man they'd seen yet, undoubtedly the commander. Unlike the other, horn-beaked, lizards, the commander had a flat face, covered with small, colored scales. Also unlike them, he had no tail or wings. He wore brilliantly shiny metal armor and a sweeping blue cape. An awful air of majesty and self-confident power surrounded him.

"Shanz, are these the intruders?"

"It is they, Commander Thouriss," said the officer. "No others have turned up."

"Keep alert. Humans have the irritating habit of congregating in large numbers." The lesser officer bowed and left the prisoners facing Thouriss. The goblin guards fanned out, making a barrier between the captives and the plaza.

"Why are you here?" he said, planting his clawed hands on his hips. He was much more humanlike than the stooped, beak-nosed lizard men.

"We're lost," said Riverwind.

"Are you? Name yourselves."

The Que-Shu men told Thouriss who they were. The commander pointed at Di An. "Who is this?" he rumbled.

"A waif we adopted on our journey," said Catchflea. "An orphan. She mends our clothes and fixes our meals."

"She is not human." Di An was cringing between the two men. Thouriss pointed at her again. "Come forward, creature, that I may see you better." When Di An didn't respond, a guard prodded her with the butt of his pike.

"Who are you?" demanded Thouriss.

"Di An." It was all she could say. The commander's vast green eyes bored into hers.

"Where are you from, Deee Ahhnn?" He drew out the simple syllables, making them sound strange and potent.

The elf girl swallowed and opened her mouth, but she was so frightened no sound came out. Riverwind interjected, "Silvanesti. The girl is from Silvanesti."

Thouriss blinked his milky, membranous eyelids. "So, you have been in the east. How did you find it?"

"Uh, find it?"

"Are not the borders of Silvanesti closed to foreigners?"

"We found the girl wandering, yes," Catchflea said quickly. "It was in the New Coast region that we met."

Thouriss took a step closer to Di An. "Why did you flee Silvanesti, elf?"

She flinched at the forbidden word. Riverwind hoped her anger would overcome her fear.

"She's too frightened to speak," Riverwind said.

"Are you frightened of me, little one?" Thouriss towered almost three feet over the elf girl. He reached down and pinched the back of her dress in two fingers, lifting Di An off the ground. She began to weep. He brought her close to his serpentine face.

"Why did you run away?" he said. "Why?"

"Leave her alone!" Riverwind cried. A guard hit him with the shaft of his pike. Riverwind whirled and kicked the armored goblin in the knee. He toppled with a ringing crash. Other guards closed in. Riverwind ran up the shallow steps until he was within arm's length of Thouriss.

"Put her down!" he said.

Thouriss waved the guards away. He held the weeping girl to Riverwind, who lifted his fettered arms and took her.

"This affection your race has for others is very interesting," he said. "I do not understand it, but it is interesting. You knew I could kill you, yet you risked your life to intercede for her. Why?"

"I will not stand by and watch your bullying!" Riverwind said. The elf girl was clinging to him, her face buried in his shirt. "I care what happens to her."

Thouriss did not display any anger. Instead, he seemed intrigued by Riverwind's response. "Interesting," he said. "I must consult Krago on this."

He dispatched a guard to the closed corridor on the right. Shortly, the goblin returned with a cowled figure who clutched a large, ancient book. The cowled one walked slowly, his face bent to the written page.

"Leave your studies, Krago. I wish to ask something."

The cowl lifted, revealing blue eyes and a patch of fair hair. A surprisingly young face looked out from the hood. He closed the book with a snap and a spray of dust. Riverwind was intrigued to see a fellow human among the goblins and lizard men.

"What is it, Thouriss?" asked the young mage. His brows had lifted in surprise at the sight of the humans and elf girl, but his attention quickly returned to the lizard commander.

"What is the reason for affection between warm-blooded creatures?" asked the commander. "Why does it happen?"

Krago sighed. "We talked about this before." He shifted the heavy book in his arms. "Humans, elves, dwarves, gnomes, and kender all form attachments to others who have traits that complement their own."

The commander looked perplexed. "What traits could there be between a plainsman and an elven girl?"

Krago walked to Thouriss, his sandaled feet kicking out from under his faded clerical robes. "Reason it out, as I taught you," he said.

Riverwind listened to the exchange between the human and the reptilian commander with great interest. There seemed to be some odd bond between the two.

Thouriss's eyes widened. "Males attach to females in order to breed."

"Not likely here," Krago observed. "Consider the age difference."

"Immature warm-bloods arouse feelings of protectiveness in adults. This is the motherly instinct in females, the fatherly instinct in males." Thouriss studied Riverwind curiously, as if he could see this trait in his face. "You feel like the girl's father?"

Riverwind set Di An on her feet. He gestured to Catchflea to come forward and stand by him. The old man, with a glance at the goblin guards, did so. "We are friends and companions," Riverwind said. "Nothing, more or less."

"This is interesting!" Thouriss exclaimed. "I believe I shall study them a while."

The young cleric was already buried in his book again. "That's a military matter," he murmured. "Do as you like."

"What would a civilized person do next?" asked the commander.

"Invite us to dinner," Catchflea said quickly.

Thouriss grinned, showing needlelike fangs. "Excellent! You shall all dine with me—you too, Krago."

"But my work—"

"Oblige me!" was the sharp reply. Krago looked up and shrugged.

"At what hour?" he asked.

"The sixth." To the guards, Thouriss said, "Take them to the Court of Reception. I will send for them shortly."

The goblins flanked the trio and marched them out again. They turned right off the plaza, crossed the stream by means of a plank bridge, and entered a narrower street that paralleled the main one.

"Do you see what I see?" Riverwind said under his breath.

"I do, yes," said Catchflea. Suspended in the air in front of them was a pot—an enormous pot, hanging by a stout chain. The chain ran up and up, until it vanished in the darkness of the cavern ceiling.

"What is it?" asked Di An.

"A hoist, I believe," said Catchflea. "A way out, yes?"

"If we are lucky."

The hoist was secured some eight feet off the ground, no doubt to keep gully dwarves from meddling with it. Riverwind sized up the pot. It should hold the three of them. Now, how to reach it?

"Here you stay. Commander calls, later." The goblins took up positions around the circular courtyard. Riverwind, Catchflea, and Di An sat down under the hanging pot.

"What do you make of all this?" Riverwind asked quietly. "Who are these lizard folk?"

"Mercenaries of some sort, yes. Thouriss and Krago are different. Did you notice how Thouriss is in command, yet he asks Krago questions about the simplest things?"

"He is a bully," Di An said flatly. "A big, overgrown bully."

After a time, Shanz, the lizard officer, summoned them. A table covered by a snow-white cloth was set up amid the stumps of the broken palace columns. Heavy silver candleholders sprouted from the table, the candle flames flickering in the constant breeze off the three waterfalls. Five mismatched place settings of gold and silver were laid. Krago was already there, book open on his lap. His hood was pushed back, revealing a mane of unruly, red-blond hair. He couldn't have been more than a few years older than Riverwind.

He looked up briefly when the three approached. "Sit anywhere you like," he said, waving a hand. "But leave the head of the table for Thouriss."

Riverwind and Di An sat on one side, while Catchflea

slipped in beside the young cleric. Krago paid them no heed, but remained absorbed in his book.

Catchflea fidgeted for a time, trying to remain mannered. He glanced at the leather-bound book that so absorbed Krago, but the writing looked like Ergothic and he didn't understand it. The old man did at last pour himself a goblet of wine. It was dark, heavy, red wine, which only increased his hunger pangs.

Thouriss swept in, wrapped in a scarlet and silver cape. He flung this off dramatically.

Without tail or wings, his entire appearance and carriage was more manlike than his tall but slightly stooped officers. This was all the more eerie.

"I am late," he said superfluously. "I had to see to the start of a new task."

"What task, Commander?" Catchflea inquired politely.

"I know you were helped by a gully dwarf in your attempt to escape the city. My warriors have begun a search for the one who helped you."

Riverwind felt the blood drain from his face. "What do you intend?"

"He will be executed, of course, as an example."

Catchflea said quickly, "You may not catch him." He fervently hoped Brud had made it safely home to his wife.

"The lesson must be taught," Thouriss said. A goblin brought a bowl of steaming water. Thouriss dipped his dusty, taloned fingers in the bowl. "If we don't seize the actual dwarf, I shall take hostages and hang them instead."

Catchflea, Riverwind, and Di An exchanged horrified looks but remained silent. Thouriss finished cleaning his hands and dried them on a towel also carried by his goblin servant. He looked up at them.

Before the commander could speak, Catchflea interjected a question. "Who are you?" he asked. "You are newcomers to this land, yes?"

"Not quite. In fact, I was born here," replied Thouriss.

"Here?"

"Xak Tsaroth. Wasn't I, Krago?"

"Hmm? Yes, you were."

A pair of goblins tramped in, laden with covered trays of

food. Riverwind was quite surprised when the cover was whisked away, revealing an excellent haunch of venison, well roasted. Trays on the other end of the table held fruit and vegetables, most raw and unpeeled. Krago marked the page he was reading and shut his book. He took grapes and pears from the tray and cut the latter into neat quarters. Thouriss dragged the venison haunch in front of him and lowered his head to bite.

"Guests are served first," said Krago quietly.

Thouriss froze. He closed his wicked jaws slowly, pulled a knife from his belt, and carved the haunch. He cut slices for Riverwind, Catchflea, and Di An. Krago didn't eat meat, he explained. Then, for himself, Thouriss cut fist-sized chunks of meat and swallowed them whole, causing large bulges to appear in his neck until the meat passed out of his throat. It was both fascinating and repulsive to witness.

When the deer's leg bones were picked clean, Thouriss sat back and folded his hands across his belly. "Tell me," he said, "how is it you come to be here?"

Riverwind was ready for this. He said, "We entered a cave in the Forsaken Mountains and got lost. Trying to find our way out, we emerged in the mine below Xak Tsaroth." It wasn't a lie, even if he had left out a great deal.

Thouriss stared at him. His direct gaze discomforted Riverwind. It seemed the commander could sense that his story was not quite right.

"What is it you are mining for?" asked Catchflea quickly.

"Cinnabar," said Krago absently. "An ore of quicksilver."

"You are refining quicksilver. For what purpose?"

"We need it," Thouriss said. "That is sufficient answer."

"Quicksilver is used in the refining of gold," Di An blurted.

Krago raised an eyebrow. He said, "Do you know the working of metals?"

"Some things," the elf girl said, looking at her plate. "My people know metals." She popped a grape into her mouth.

"I have heard this. I wish you were older, that we might talk about the practices of your country," Krago said.

Di An was tiring of people mistaking her for a child. "I'm not as young as I look," she said with some vigor.

"Oh?" Thouriss said.

"I am well over two hundred years old," she said.

"Extraordinary," said the reptilian commander. "How do you explain your youthful appearance?"

"There are many like me in my country. We age, but we never grow up."

Now Krago was very alert. He leaned far over the table, to get closer to the elf girl. "Arrested development? I would like to hear more of this."

"Krago is deeply interested in such matters," interjected Thouriss. "Growth and aging are his prime areas of study."

"Ahem." Catchflea pointedly cleared his throat. "What is to become of us?"

"I haven't decided," Thouriss said. He scratched one of his metallic fingernails on his silver plate. The resulting screech set Riverwind's teeth on edge.

"We are merely travelers," Riverwind said. "We only want to go our own way."

"I will decide," Thouriss said with sudden irritation. "Do not vex me. It does not serve your cause."

"You have no right to keep us here. We are free people."

Thouriss smashed a fist on the table. A candlestick toppled and rolled off onto the ground. "I have a right to do anything I please! I command here!" Krago coughed into his water glass. Thouriss stood up in irritation. "Go back to your cell until I send for you. And when I do, you will not know if I am going to free you or have you beheaded!"

He growled an order in a harsh guttural tongue, and the guards surrounded the table. Riverwind, Catchflea, and Di An went quietly with them.

Krago rose and circled behind Thouriss. He touched a cool hand to the back of the commander's heavily muscled neck. "Your blood is racing," the cleric said soothingly. "You lost your temper for no good reason."

"I know. I know." Thouriss breathed fast through his narrow nostrils.

"The barbarian was goading you, and you did what he wanted. That is bad, Thouriss. A leader must remain cool under stress."

"I know!" Thouriss smote the tabletop again with his fist.

The thick wood cracked and a sliver pierced the tablecloth, embedding itself in his hand. He held the injured hand up, watching the greenish blood well out of the tiny wound.

"Krago," he whimpered, "take it out!"

"All right, come to my chamber."

The powerful commander trailed after the smaller, less imposing human, cradling his injured hand. "I don't feel like a leader. So many people know so much more than I do," said Thouriss.

The cleric resumed walking. "That's only natural. How old are you?"

The creature counted on his fingers. "Four, no five."

"Five months old," Krago said evenly. "Remarkable. A human at five months is still a mewling thing, unable to walk or talk. In a year, you'll be wiser and more powerful than any draconian ever created."

In Krago's study, Thouriss held still as the human plucked the splinter out with a pair of forceps. Thouriss put the wound to his lips and licked the few drops of blood away.

"Does your blood taste like mine?" he asked ingenuously.

Krago dropped the forceps in a drawer. "I don't know. I doubt it."

"Because you are human and I am not," Thouriss said. "I could kill the tall human and taste his."

"No, that would be frivolous. Besides, civilized creatures don't eat each other," said Krago.

"Why?"

"It's not polite." With a yawn, Krago reached for a thick volume on his shelf and gave it to Thouriss. "Here is a history of the Empire of Ergoth. Read this, and you'll see how civilized beings behave."

Thouriss eyed the book distastefully. "I am a warrior. I don't like to read."

"But you must try if you are to grow wiser. And soon you'll have a companion, someone to talk to about everything you learn. No longer will you be alone."

Thouriss's slit eyes widened. "Tell me her name again?"

"Lyrexis. Your mate's name will be Lyrexis."

Chapter 19

Cinnabar

"I have an idea that our captor is a child," Riverwind noted. Neither the old man nor the elf girl understood. "He has the mind and moods of a child. Krago is some kind of mentor."

"Ah!" Catchflea said. "I begin to see!"

"I don't," Di An complained.

"The reason Thouriss acts the way he does—asking questions about ordinary things, growing angry when questioned; these are the reactions of a child, yes?"

"If you say so. But what does it mean?"

Riverwind surveyed their barren cell. The torchlight from outside was fitful at best. "I'm not sure. Something strange is going on in this place. The lizard folk and their goblin soldiers are not here to build homes and grow crops. But what is their purpose?" Riverwind sat down with his back to the wall. "Catchflea, do you have your acorns?"

"Yes, the guards didn't take them."

"Consult them. See if you can discover what's brewing here."

The old man performed his ritual. He shook the gourd and dumped the nuts on the dusty stone floor. "Ha!"

Di An peered over Catchflea's shoulder. "What do you see?"

The old man's face was clouded with strain. "Darkness. Death. The acorns show death marching across the land."

Riverwind leaned forward. "Our deaths?"

"I'm not certain." The soothsayer peered closely at the acorns, touching them with one finger.

Riverwind said. "Ask about Krago and his purpose."

Round and round went the acorns in the gourd. "Ha!" Catchflea exclaimed. He perused the formation of the nuts. "I do not understand," he said, frowning. "Very strange!"

"What?"

"Here it calls him midwife. Why should it say that?"

"A midwife assists at a birth," Di An offered.

"This one shows him standing in darkness with liquid silver beads running from his cupped hands."

"Quicksilver," Di An suggested.

"And this! This is the strangest answer of all." To Riverwind it was just an acorn, lying almost vertically on its knobby cap. "A seed planted in blood. That's what I see. A seed planted in blood."

The three huddled together as the cold from the bare stone floor seeped through their clothes. No one could make much sense of Catchflea's augury. They passed a few moments, each with his own thoughts. Riverwind finally said, "We must stop them."

"How can we? They are many and strong," said Di An.

"I don't know. But if we don't, the spreading darkness and death Catchflea saw will surely be visited on our homes and families."

"It seems a certainty," the old man said, his voice pained.

"Perhaps we can enlist the Aghar in our cause . . ."

The cell door flew open without preamble. Two goblins

bulked large in the opening. "Come with us, girl," said one.

Di An clutched Riverwind's arm. "What do you want with me?"

"Master Krago wants to speak with you."

"I don't want to go!" she hissed in the plainsman's ear.

Riverwind laid his hand over hers. "Be brave," he said.

"Come, girl," one of the goblins rumbled.

Di An walked slowly to the door. The guards bore one feeble lantern. Di An cast a glance at the pale faces of her friends.

"Good-bye, giant. And you, too, old giant," she said, her voice carrying finality.

* * * * *

Di An was taken to the ruined palace, but not through the columned facade where they'd first met Thouriss. Her guards took her nearly to the base of the East Falls. There, amid the tumult and the spray, she spied a door in the palace wall, artfully painted to resemble a crack in the stone blocks. The goblins pushed her into the opening and took up positions outside.

It was close and warm inside, but Di An still shivered. She was in a dark foyer. Ahead, a warm orange light cut across the shallow corridor. She walked slowly toward the light.

The place smelled strongly of snakes. She soon saw why: the corridor was lined with a series of open-ended cells, which a small contingent of lizard men occupied. It was supper time for them. Folding leather tables groaned under the weight of deer haunches, sides of beef and pork, and whole chickens. The lizard men ate their meat raw, with much cracking of bones and tearing of pale, bloodless flesh. Di An hurried by them. A slit eye or two glanced her way, but mostly they ignored her.

The passage ended on a right turn. Water trickled down the wall, leaking in from the waterfall outside. Di An quickened her pace. Before she knew it, she was running, not knowing where she was going or why she ran. There was a new smell in the air—a familiar one. Hot metal.

The corridor abruptly ended where the way was blocked

by a massive fill of loose rock and broken stone. To the right
was a narrow door, a strip of carpet nailed over it. Di An
cautiously drew the carpet aside.

"Come in," Krago said. He was sitting in a heavy wooden
chair, books and parchments strewn around him. At his
left, a furnace gave off a steady, dull roar. A gang of gully
dwarves labored over it, feeding coal to the fire and pump-
ing large leather bellows. Other Aghar pounded pestles in a
giant mortar. Red dust clung to their faces and hands. Two
dumpy females scooped up red rocks and tossed them in the
mortar. Krago was refining cinnabar.

"Come over here," the human said. Di An approached.
The room was divided by a high bookcase, fully seven feet
tall and at least thirty feet long. The shelves were crammed
with books, scrolls, lumps of stone, beakers, vials, pots,
and retorts.

In the near corner stood a glazed stone vat. As Di An
crossed over to Krago's chair, a squat gully dwarf waddled
in front of her. The gully dwarf carried a pot brimming with
liquid silver on his head. He climbed a short ladder set beside the vat and emptied the quicksilver into it. From the
sound it made, Di An guessed the vat was almost full.

"You are extracting quicksilver," she said.

"Eh, yes, I am. Though I'm down to the last of my ore. I
need at least a hundredweight more." Krago scribbled something on a vellum page with a quill. He put down the quill.
"Come this way."

The bookcase turned at right angles, making a smaller
private area off the main room. The bookcase also enclosed
a sizable area. Di An wondered what went on behind the
wooden wall.

"Here we are. Sit." Di An perched on a folding stool.
Krago dropped onto a hard-looking frame bed. He focused
his attention on the elf girl, shutting out the sounds from the
furnace area.

"I'm very interested in this condition of yours," the cleric
began. "You really haven't aged outwardly since you were,
what, twelve? Thirteen?"

"By human terms, yes," Di An said.

"And this happens to others in your country?"

"More and more often."

"Interesting." Krago still believed Di An's homeland to be Silvanesti. "Do the wise men of your country know why this condition occurs?" he asked, leaning toward her and resting his hands on his knees.

"It is a matter of dispute," she replied. "The commonest answer is that smoke and fumes from our foundries collect in the—" She started to say "cave" and checked herself. "In the air and affect our mothers when they are with child."

"Metallic vapors poisoning the unborn," Krago mused, nodding. "This might have some bearing on my own experiments. Hmm." He searched for a pen and something to write on. "What sort of metals do your people work?" asked Krago, rummaging through his shabby robe.

"All kinds. Iron, copper, lead, silver, gold, tin."

"Not quicksilver?" He paused in his probings.

"There is little use for it. Besides, it is too dangerous to mine," she said. She thought about the gully dwarves covered in dust. "Haven't you seen the sickness in the gullies?"

"Oh, I don't pay much attention to them. Thouriss handles the workers. I merely choose the tasks they are to do."

Krago seemed mild enough, so Di An essayed a question of her own. "What are you using all the quicksilver for? Are you minting gold?"

He laughed. "Nothing so mundane! No, the liquid metal is essential for my work, that's all. But to return to you; this perpetual youth of yours, this is a valuable thing."

"I call it a curse."

Krago's brows went up. "Why?"

She looked away from him. "To remain a child by size and temperament? Never to grow? Never to know the love of a mate?" Her gaze came back to him. "I call it a curse."

"Many humans would give much to live for hundreds of years, even in the body of a child," Krago said. "So much time for research. Time to see the fruition of decades of work." His eyes were distant.

"Empty time," she said. "Empty decades."

He looked her up and down. "There are probably cures for your condition."

Her eyes widened. "Cures? Would you have such a cure?"

Krago tapped the side of his face with a finger and frowned at her in concentration. "An impurity of the blood keeps you in this state, I believe. I do have potions that can cleanse the blood." He turned and regarded the shelves that formed the walls of his sleeping quarters. Mumbling to himself, he went to a section near Di An's stool and poked about in the vials and bottles.

"There was something here—" he said. Bottles rocked and rattled as he rummaged through them. "Ah, this." He lifted a yellowed glass bottle from the rear of the shelf and brushed dust and grime from it. "Four drops of this, taken when the Silver Moon is ascendant, should clear the metallic impurity," he said. "It would be a fascinating experiment." He put the bottle back on a lower shelf and looked at Di An. "Though I fail to see why you want to grow old and die."

Di An stared at the bottle. She tried to imagine what it would be like to be an adult. So many times in her two centuries of life she had cursed her smallness, her child's body. Since meeting the plainsmen, her desire to be an adult had increased. Would Riverwind care differently for her if she were truly a woman?

A crash rose from the corner where the gully dwarves were working the furnace. The ore-scoopers had dumped a load of cinnabar over one of the pestle pounders, and the offended party was chasing the scoopers around, trying to brain them with the massive marble pestle. Despite the looks of outrage, it was an eerily silent fracas. For the gully dwarves did not utter a sound.

"How do you keep them so quiet?" Di An asked. "I thought they talked all the time."

"Thouriss had their tongues cut out, so they couldn't talk of what they see," Krago explained casually. "I must attend to them."

He left her sitting on the stool and went off to calm the gully dwarves. Di An pitied the unfortunate gully dwarves, but her attention had been captured by the yellow bottle on the shelf. She couldn't take her eyes off it. Should she take it now? She knew nothing about the moons of Krynn and their places in the sky. Would Krago actually help her?

She glanced over her shoulder. Krago was embroiled in

an argument with the Aghar. They mimed their woes to him as he urged them to get back to work. Di An slipped off the stool and snatched the bottle. She pulled the cork with her teeth and measured four drops into the palm of her hand. She licked the oily liquid off her palm and replaced the cork.

She set the bottle back in its place on the shelf. Di An's tongue was numb where the potion had touched it. The numbness spread down her throat and across her jaws. Her eyes watered. A ringing started in her ears. Medicine wasn't supposed to hurt you—merciful gods, she'd poisoned herself!

"No, no!" Krago burst out. "Put the ore in the mortar!"

The elf girl staggered to her feet. Water—she had to have water. She wandered down the length of the bookshelf, searching through tearing eyes for a life-saving drink. The books and shelf swam before her eyes. Heat seemed to roar through her. She gasped for air.

A stick of wood stuck out of the shelf, right at Di An's face level. She grasped the stick blindly to keep herself from falling. It swung down. With a clank, a section of bookcase swung inward. Oddly patterned light flooded over her. Without thinking, Di An had opened a secret door into a hidden portion of the chamber. Hoping that there was water in there, she entered. Dimly, Di An heard Krago shout behind her as she walked through the portal.

It was very bright, this place, but the heat was less intense. Di An stumbled over a rise in the floor and went down on her hands and knees. She must have remained like this for a while, for the next thing she knew, Krago was there, pulling her to her feet.

"What are you doing in here?" he was shouting at her. He peered closely at her white, strained face. "Did you take the potion?" Di An nodded dazedly. "Stupid girl! The time was not quite right. Who knows what the effect on you might be?"

The glare lessened, and Di An realized it was an effect of the potion rather than the inner room itself. She was leaning against the inside of the wooden bookcase. Stomach cramps sliced through her slight body. She gasped and bent over. Then, Krago's hand was on her shoulder.

"Drink this," he said.

She straightened and found he was holding a slim glass vial out to her. She didn't care what it was, as long as it made her feel better.

It did. It halted her pain. The details of the room leaped into clarity, and the ringing in her head stopped. Di An looked past Krago and saw that the room was filled with all sorts of strange apparatus. Magic circles were drawn on the wall; sigils and glyphs of obscure purpose covered the stone floor. A double row of alembics, pelicans, and distilling retorts lined the walls. And in the center of it all was a great vat, cast in solid glass and braced with metal straps. Now that the torment of her body had eased, she took in the contents of the strange room. She had no idea what purpose all these things could serve.

"What? What is it?" she said hoarsely.

"You might as well know," he said, folding his arms. With an exasperated sigh, Krago took the elf girl's hand. "Come and see the crowning achievement of my work."

The vat, eight feet in diameter, was filled to the rim with quicksilver. Floating half-submerged in the silver bath was a still-unformed thing. At least the details were unformed; the general shape was clear enough. Two arms, two legs, a head—the thing was red and glistening, like fresh, raw meat. A mouth split the unfeatured face. Needlelike teeth protruded from the thing's bloodless gums.

"What is it?" Di An asked, afraid to get any closer.

"My creation," Krago said. "I call her Lyrexis."

"Her?"

"Yes, she is female, make no mistake. She will be a worthy mate for Thouriss."

Thouriss's mate! Di An took a step closer to the vat. The outline of scales was visible in the translucent skin. The creature's face was flatter and more normally proportioned than a lizard man's, yet still it was not human. The cheekbones were high and wide, the skull massive but well-shaped.

Ribs showed like dark shadows under the skin. Deeper still, the double fist that was the creature's heart throbbed quickly, sending a current of blood through its tender, visible veins. Muscles lay like coiled ropes around the creature's limbs. As Di An's shadow fell across Lyrexis's face, the thing in the vat seemed to twitch and turn its sightless gaze toward her. Di An yelped and cowered back.

"It's alive! It can see me!" she gasped.

"Of course it's alive. There would be very little reason to have it here if it weren't. And it can't really see you; it's merely reacting to light and shadow, warmth or cold."

Di An backed away. "It's—it's horrible," she murmured.

"Horrible? Horrible?" Krago slipped the cowl off his head and regarded the elf girl with disdain. "Here is a feat no alchemist on the whole of Krynn ever dared attempt, and I have succeeded. I have created life. It is a triumph, you silly little girl. A complete and utter triumph!"

"But why? Why create such a thing?"

Krago gazed at the unfinished creature with pride and fascination. "It was a challenge," he said. "To create a race of beings so powerful no one could stand against them."

Di An began to look for the way out. "What about your own people? Won't your lizard folk wage war on humans, too?"

Krago was regarding the thing in the vat with admiration when a voice boomed, "Krago has no loyalty except to his art. Isn't that right, Krago?"

Thouriss filled the secret doorway in the bookshelves. Behind him, Di An could see the hulking outlines of goblin guards.

"Eh? Oh, it's you. What do you want, Thouriss?" the young cleric said distractedly.

"What is that creature doing here?" asked Thouriss, pointing at Di An.

"Oh, I called her here to discuss her aging problem. She stupidly took some of my purifying potion and wandered in here."

"So you told her about us? About Lyrexisss?" he finished the last syllable with a hiss. Thouriss strode into the room and seized Di An by the arm.

"Let me go! I don't know anything!" she cried. Struggling against his grip was like fighting the hold of a vise.

"I hardly think any harm can come of it," Krago said

dismissively.

Thouriss seemed to consider that for a moment, and then he laughed. "True. Perhaps she should know. Tell her the story, Krago. Tell her everything."

Krago couldn't resist the opportunity to boast. He summoned one of the mute gully dwarves. "Bring a stool," he said. The chair was brought, and Krago motioned Di An to it. "Sit," he told her. He made himself comfortable in a chair and began his tale.

"The draconians, what you call lizard men, are produced by the action of a magic spell on the eggs of dragons aligned with Good," Krago said. "The first to be used were eggs of brass dragons, from which the Baaz draconians were made. Next came the Kapak, or copper draconians, and the Bozak, whom you have seen here in Xak Tsaroth. They stem from bronze dragon eggs. Each race has its own peculiar strengths and weaknesses. Tails and wings, for example, are not uniform among the draconians. This makes it hard to fit them with armor, or to make cavalry soldiers out of them."

Di An knew nothing of the wars to rid Krynn of dragons, and she didn't know that dragons had become creatures of myth to most surface-dwellers. Less still did she know about draconians, but she tried to pay attention.

"But why do you do this at all?" Di An asked, confused by this new knowledge.

Thouriss said, "It is the will of Takhisis, the Queen of Darkness. She intends to build an army of draconians with which to conquer all of Krynn."

"And you do this evil thing willingly?" she said to Krago.

"Don't be impertinent," Thouriss warned. Di An shrank away from him.

"As I was saying," Krago continued blandly, "the variation in the draconians made one problem. Another was the fact that there were only so many dragon eggs available, and in order to build and maintain a standing army, the Dark Queen needs a more ready source of warriors."

"A task assigned to the ruler of Xak Tsaroth," Thouriss said. "The Great One, called Khisanth."

"A black dragon," explained Krago.

"Black dragon? Here?" Di An stood up, only to have

Thouriss's scaly hand force her back down on the stool.

"Don't worry, elf. The Great One is away, communing with our queen."

Krago's recitation was interrupted by a delegation of gully dwarves who came in with a sample of crushed ore. The young human left his place and went to the door of the secret room. He examined the ore with numbing care and pronounced it fit for smelting. When he returned to the secret room, his face was smudged with soot and the hem of his robe was black with ash.

"Where was I?" he said, dropping lightly into his chair.

"Our Queen's need for warriors," prompted Thouriss enthusiastically. He seemed to enjoy hearing the story, though no doubt he had heard it many times.

"Oh, yes. Well, Khisanth sent out agents to every corner of Ansalon, seeking a method to remedy our Queen's problem. Some of them came to Sanction, where I was under arrest for graverobbing and heretical magic. All a mistake, you understand, but very inconvenient. I had hired two Sanctionites to dig up a newly buried corpse so that I could test an alchemical preparation I'd concocted. The potion restored the corpse to animation, but not to life." He sighed, remembering. "Perhaps a bit more powdered copper or—"

"Krago," growled Thouriss impatiently.

"Mm? Yes, well, the hired men panicked, got drunk, and spilled the whole story to the city fathers. I was taken and condemned to death. I languished in prison until Khisanth's agents broke me out and whisked me back to Xak Tsaroth. Khisanth made me a proposition: unlimited resources to do any experiments I wanted, as long as I found a way to create a race of super-strong, super-intelligent draconians, who could breed like other races."

"And you accepted." Di An's voice was a whisper.

Krago blinked his blue eyes. "Obviously. It was a fateful offer that made my life's work possible. I was going to create *life!*"

He hopped up and strode to the quicksilver vat. "You see, I reasoned that there was a fundamental reason why the dragons aligned with Good were so closely linked with metals." Excitement tautened Krago's voice. He gestured to the vat. "There is a harmonic correspondence between the etheric vibrations of the higher planes of magic and the order of pure metals." Di An was baffled. Casting a look at Thouriss, she saw he could not follow the explanation either.

"That being the case," Krago continued, "it should be possible to generate dragons out of any purified metal! Do you see? Besides gold, silver, copper, bronze, and brass, you could have lead dragons, quicksilver, electrum, or any mixture!" A genuine fervor had ignited in the serious young cleric. "I chose quicksilver because it would be easy to handle. It's liquid all the time, thus eliminating the need to use dangerous molten metals. Khisanth ordered the gully dwarves and the Bozak to provide me with everything I needed. Soon, I had the quicksilver, the powdered arcana, and the celestial alignment I required. All I needed was a suitable egg."

Krago turned his back on Di An and placed his hands on the rim of the vat. "Khisanth was wary of risking a dragon egg on my first attempt, so I chose the egg of a land serpent. They grow rapidly and have many offspring. When the black moon, Nuitari, was in the ascendant, I immersed the serpent's egg in the bath of quicksilver. The powders were applied and the incantation begun. In just six weeks, Thouriss was born, fully grown, though his mind was as empty as any infant's. A completely new race, never before seen on Krynn." Here, Krago smiled. "An ophidian, as I have named this race. Thouriss's education and training as a warrior started immediately, and by the age of four months, he was more than a match for any Bozak in the city."

Thouriss hissed sharply. It was easy to see on his face the pleasure that Krago's praise brought.

"Khisanth was so pleased with Thouriss that she made him commander of all her warriors and departed to tell the Queen the news," Krago said. "I was to proceed with the second part of the grand design, the creation of a mate for Thouriss who would be the mother of this new race. Lyrexis, as I have named her, is in her fourth week of growth. By the time Khisanth returns, I hope to be able to present her with a fully developed female ophidian."

When Krago was done, Di An sat with her jaw hanging open. This human spoke so casually of the evil he was bringing down upon his own people, upon the world. He would destroy the surface world as Li El had nearly destroyed Hest.

"Nothing can stop us now," Thouriss said proudly. "Each passing day increases my wisdom and strength. When my mate is ready, I shall lead the invasion of southern Ansalon." He twined his cold, hard fingers in Di An's short hair and tugged her head upright. "The elves of Qualinost are reputed to be good fighters. I look forward to shedding their blood."

"We've finished our conversation for now, girl," Krago said amiably. "Shall I have her sent back, Thouriss?"

"Yes," Thouriss said. He had released Di An and was staring at the thing that lay in quicksilver. "The Great One will want to question her and her friends," he said. "We will pass through Que-Shu country on our way to Solace. Estimates of the barbarians' strength would be useful."

Two goblin guards took hold of Di An's arms, hoisting her off her feet. They carried her all the way back to the cell she shared with Riverwind and Catchflea. The tall plainsman was on his feet when the cell door opened. Di An rushed to him as soon as her feet touched the floor. She flung her arms around him as the cell door clanged shut.

"Are you all right?" Riverwind asked quietly.

"I saw the most terrible thing!" she said, clinging to him fiercely. "I saw it—I saw—"

Riverwind made Di An sit down, and he sat by her. Holding her ice-cold hands, he asked, "What did you see, little one?"

"The end of the world!"

Chapter 20

The Oldest Trick

Di An calmed enough to relate what she'd seen and heard. When she was done, the three of them sat in the semi-darkness, facing each other. No one spoke for a long time.

Riverwind clasped his hands tightly. "I've been idle too long. My quest has consumed my thoughts. But if Thouriss and this dragon and the Dark Queen herself mean to lay waste to my homeland and enslave my people, then there is no more sacred task than to stop them."

"How can we?" Catchflea said. "We have no weapons and we are only three against a hundred."

"How can we even escape this room?" Di An asked.

"We must get out before the dragon returns. Once it's here, we'll never get out alive," said Riverwind. He idly traced some lines in the dust with a finger. "When we do get out, I want the two of you to leave Xak Tsaroth as fast as you can. Head for Que-Shu and spread the word! If Thouriss thinks he can defeat us so easily, he's in for a sharp lesson."

"You'll not throw your life away, yes?" Catchflea said.

Riverwind laid a large hand on the old man's shoulder. "I've no intention of dying," he said firmly. "Goldmoon awaits me. That's reason enough to want to live."

Di An gave a frowning sigh. At first, Riverwind thought he'd hurt her feelings. She was hunched over, kneading her bird-thin ankles. "What's the matter?" he asked.

"I hurt," she said. "In my bones."

"Did they beat you?"

"Thouriss? No, no." She grimaced and knotted her fists in a spasm of pain. "I drank that potion, though."

"It was a foolish thing to do," Riverwind said.

"Krago gave you the antidote, yes?" Catchflea asked.

"I thought so—" Di An let out a mewling cry of pain. "Feels like my feet are being pulled off!"

Riverwind worried for the elf girl. There was no telling what effect Krago's potion might have. When he tried to help massage her ankles, she grimaced and pushed his hands aside. He stared at Di An, kneading her throbbing feet, and an idea began to form in his mind. A smile tugged at the tall warrior's lips. He began to nod. "It could work," he murmured.

He quickly outlined his idea to his companions. "If the goblins aren't used to dealing with prisoners of Di An's race, they may be taken in," he said.

"I won't have to pretend," Di An said. "It really hurts!"

Riverwind squeezed her hand in sympathy, then went to the door and crouched low beside it. Catchflea stationed himself a few feet away, in plain sight of the door. Di An crept across the cell until she was lying in direct line to the exit. "I'm ready," she whispered.

"Ready, yes." Riverwind nodded. Catchflea pounded on the door. "Help! Help, guard! The girl has fallen sick!" He pressed his ear to the door. No sound reached him. He pounded the thick wood once more. "Guard! Guard! The girl is ill! Help us!" Again, he listened. "Someone's coming!"

he hissed.

Heavy footsteps heralded the arrival of a goblin. He lifted his lantern, and a shaft of light illuminated the cell through the small window in the door.

Riverwind's body tensed. Catchflea stepped aside from the door.

"Keep quiet," rumbled the goblin and turned to go.

Catchflea exchanged a desperate look with Riverwind. Suddenly, the cell was filled with a nerve-shredding wail. Di An clutched at her stomach. "Help me!" she shrieked.

The lantern light returned. "I say, keep quiet!" rasped the goblin.

Quickly, Catchflea pressed his face to the small window. "I think she has Lemish Fever! Take her out before we are all infected. Please!" he babbled. "Your commander wants us alive! If we get the fever, we'll all die. You must take her out! Hurry!"

After several seconds' hesitation, the guard said, "You move back."

Catchflea complied with alacrity. Once more Riverwind tensed.

The bolt rattled back. The heavy door swung out. The thin beam of a hooded lantern stabbed into the cell, finding Di An writhing in genuine pain on the floor.

"Stand away," said the deep, raspy voice of a goblin. Catchflea backed up until his feet were by Di An's head. The goblin entered slowly, lantern in his left hand and a flanged mace in his right. Riverwind waited until the handle of the mace was near enough to grab. He sprang.

And the guard flashed the lantern in his face. Riverwind was blinded for a second, but closed one hand over the mace handle. The goblin swung the lantern at his head. Thus distracted, Riverwind didn't see Catchflea whip off his tattered shirt and fling it over the goblin's head.

The brass lantern banged into Riverwind's skull, but his thick hair and headband softened the blow. When it became clear he couldn't wrestle the mace away from the guard, Riverwind put his shoulder down and butted him. The goblin was a head shorter than the plainsman, but almost twice as heavy. They slammed into the wall. The guard gave a cry, muffled by Catchflea's old shirt around his head. He dropped the lantern to better grapple with Riverwind. The oil bowl spilled out and ignited. Little rivulets of flame danced across the cell, adding weird highlights to the confused scene.

Despite her pain, Di An rose and flung herself at the guard. She wrapped her arms around one meaty leg and sank her teeth into the relatively soft flesh behind his knee. The goblin growled and clawed at the girl. His ironlike nails raked her back, tearing open the copper mesh dress.

Riverwind wrenched the guard's weapon hand. The mace banged to the floor. He leaped back, seized the club, and laid the goblin out with two quick blows. The oil flames flickered and went out.

All three stood panting. "Anyone hurt?" Riverwind managed to ask.

"You mean, besides him?" Catchflea retrieved his shirt.

The goblin had a utility knife in a belt sheath. Riverwind passed this to Di An.

There was a large rip across the back of Di An's black mesh dress. The goblin had also clawed away the paint in many places, revealing bright copper. She took the knife from Riverwind and slipped it into her woven chain belt.

The foyer was empty. So was the street outside, though torches blazed along the facade of the old palace. They kept to the shadowed side of the street and worked their way toward the ruined round tower.

"Where are we going?" Catchflea whispered.

"Back into the cave," said Riverwind.

"The cave! Why?"

"Keep your voice down. Where else can we go?"

The tramp of heavy feet alerted them. Riverwind pushed Catchflea ahead of him, and together they dived for the shelter of a low, broken stone wall. Di An melted into the shadows by the guard hall. Two goblins, wrapped in green cloaks, marched past.

"How many did we hang today?" said one.

"Six," replied the other.

"It doesn't seem to bother them much," the first grunted. "They're too stupid."

They walked on. Catchflea said, "Thouriss is carrying out reprisals against the gully dwarves!"

"I heard," Riverwind said grimly.

They waved for Di An to join them. Like lightning, they flashed across the cracked and ruined road to the tumble-down tower. From there they could see the hole that led back into the caverns.

It was blocked.

The goblins had filled the hole with rubble, a very common commodity in Xak Tsaroth. Riverwind, ever a temperate man, was sorely tempted to swear blasphemies against the unjust gods. Di An wept quietly.

"There, there," Catchflea said. "We'll find another way."

"It's not just that," she sniffled. "My knees ache terribly!"

"The pain is moving up, yes," Catchflea said. He held the weeping elf girl close and stroked her short hair. To his surprise, strands came off in his hand. Catchflea discreetly let these fall to the ground and remained silent. Inside, he was very afraid for Di An. What might Krago's potion do to her?

"We'll go to the Aghar town," Riverwind decided. "Maybe there we'll find willing allies."

"Suppose they turn us over to the lizard men?" Catchflea said. "To win Thouriss's favor?"

"Gully dwarves are stupid, not cruel," Riverwind noted. "Besides, I can't think of anything better."

The two goblins had rounded the corner and were headed back toward the Court of Reception. "Let's go," Riverwind said.

They cut across the street in front of the old tower. Di An could hardly walk, much less pad silently, so Riverwind scooped her up.

It seemed to the plainsman that Di An was heavier. But, like Catchflea, he kept silent, not wishing to add to her fear. His own worry increased.

On the other side, a deep gash split the street. The stream that ran down the center of the old road splashed into the hole. Riverwind and Catchflea waded through the knee-deep water. Another street branched off directly in front of them. The blank walls of the gully dwarf settlement gave no clue as to who or what lay on the other side. Light spilled

out of the adjoining street ahead. In single file, Riverwind—
still carrying Di An—and Catchflea crept down the street,
always keeping to the shadowed side of the wall. They
halted at a corner, and Riverwind set Di An gently down.

Dropping low on the pavement, Riverwind peeked
around the corner. A small plaza opened out at the end of
the short alley, and there, lit by bundles of torches, was a
terrible sight. The goblins had erected a gallows, and a single gully dwarf still hung there. Riverwind whispered this to
his friends.

"The families must have claimed the others," Catchflea
said. "I wonder who the poor fellow is who's still there."

"Whoever he is, he doesn't deserve a fate like this," Riverwind replied. "I'm going to cut him down."

"Suppose you're seen?" Di An said.

But the plainsman was gone. He slipped around the corner and moved slowly down the street. Riverwind un-
hooked the mace from his belt and flattened himself against
the near wall. The torches threw the shadow of a lurking
goblin on the opposite wall. He was standing guard. Riverwind found a loose stone chip and tossed it into the plaza.
The guard presented his pike and growled, "Who goes
there?" When no one answered, he advanced a pace. Riverwind could have reached out and touched the wicked iron
head of the pike.

The goblin was about to return to his post when Riverwind flicked another pebble into the dark end of the square.
The guard advanced three steps this time. He never saw
Riverwind as the mace came down on his head. Riverwind
dragged the heavy creature into the alley. He donned the
goblin's cloak and helmet, and ported the pike on his shoulder. He marched out into the middle of the plaza. There
were two more goblins off to the left, but they paid no attention to one of their own.

Riverwind stepped up on the stone slab that had been set
up as the base of the gallows. The poor gully dwarf's face
was turned away, for which Riverwind was grateful. He put
his shoulder under the thick little man and cut the rope with
the pike head. Riverwind lowered the gully dwarf to the
scaffold.

It was Brud Stonesifter.

Thouriss had succeeded. Riverwind felt a lump in his throat. Along with many of his fellows, Brud had suffered and died because of them, because they had forced him to help them.

"I am sorry," Riverwind whispered.

"Huh?" said Brud.

Riverwind nearly fell over backward. "Did you speak?" he hissed, eyeing the two goblins. They were hunched over, busy in conversation. They hadn't heard.

"Uh-huh. Brud hungry. Got a rat leg I can gnaw?"

Aghar eating habits aside, Riverwind was astonished. "I saw you hanging! How can you be alive?"

"Little rope not hurt Brud. All Sluds got necks like iron. Glups, they tough, too. Bulps are sissies. They—"

"Never mind. We've got to get out of here. Where can we hide?"

"How 'bout cave?" suggested Brud, still lying on his back with his eyes closed.

"They filled the entrance with stone," Riverwind said.

"Ho, lots of ways into that cave," Brud avowed. A harsh voice intruded.

"What are you doing up there?" A draconian officer stood at the foot of the scaffold. Riverwind kept his face averted.

"Taking him down," he said in the deepest rasp he could make. "Orders."

"From whom?"

"Krago. The human wants the body to cut up."

"Huh! I always said warm-bloods were barbarians. All right. Get on." The officer turned with a flourish of white cloak and stalked away.

Riverwind stood and tucked Brud under his arm. The little miner grunted and said, "Careful, human. Brud got delicate back."

"You're supposed to be dead," Riverwind reminded him. "Be quiet."

Brud would not keep still. He prattled on about a dream he'd been having when Riverwind roused him: "—and then Highbulp, he says to my brother, 'You cannot say stew like life. Only can say life like stew.' Ho, some Highbulp. Should be Lowbulp, or Lowest of Lowbulps, or—"

"Shut up, will you? You're the most talkative corpse I've ever seen."

"Brud see talking corpse one time. Was six days dead, and birds had pecked it—"

Mercifully, Riverwind reached the alley once more, where he could set Brud on his feet. The two of them hurried along the lane. Riverwind asked Brud if any of the other Aghar had been hurt.

"Naw, hang not hurt Aghar. Like hang ham—just get better."

"Didn't the goblins or lizard men notice the other victims weren't dead?"

"Ho, uglies and scale faces not see sun rise in morning if it burn their noses. Aghar scream, cry when brother or sister go on rope. Look sad. Uglies and scale faces go away, we take down. All us look alike to them, so they not know."

Riverwind almost smiled. "Why were you still up there?" he asked.

"'Spose wife forgot me. Anyway, Brud fall asleep till you wake so rudely."

The plainsman shook his head. Crude and uncouth they might be, but no one could say the Aghar weren't a hardy breed. Imagine, falling asleep while hanging . . .

He stopped Brud with one hand. They were near the corner. Riverwind drew the cloak around him to conceal his ungoblinlike body and stepped boldly into the street. There was no sign of Catchflea or Di An. A few yards away, the North Falls pounded down the cliffside in a swirl of spray. He looked in that direction, but they were nowhere to be seen.

"Human!" called Brud. "Come look!"

On the blank wall of a large building the gully dwarf had found a smear of blood and a scattering of short, dark hair. There were nicks in the wall and pavement, nicks such as pikes or swords would make.

Thouriss had them! He had them both. Riverwind cursed his negligence.

"Where would he take them?" Riverwind demanded of Brud.

"Many bad places. Maybe old palace." The gully dwarf put his nose down to the bloodstain and sniffed loudly. "That not girl. Smell like old man."

"Can you really tell?"

"Brud sniff girl before. This not her," he answered confidently.

So Catchflea was wounded. The old man wasn't that strong and any wound would weaken him further.

The air stirred. It swirled around Riverwind and Brud, flinging dust in their eyes. The plainsman shaded his face with one hand and felt heat tingle on his skin. Through squinted eyes, Riverwind peered down the street. There was a strange light there. It flickered like firelight but was brighter than twenty torches. As his eyes adjusted to the glare, he saw that the odd light came from a ball of fire the size of his head. Tongues of flame leaped and fell, writhing around the central mass. The fireball slowly approached, weaving from side to side like a hound sniffing for a scent. Brud gave a high-pitched yelp and slid behind the plainsman.

The fireball, trailing a long tail of glowing smoke, came straight toward Riverwind's face. He could feel the heat, smell the burning. Riverwind gripped the goblin pike in two hands, ready to swat or strike the strange intruder. The glowing sphere halted just out of range.

"Riverwind," said a loud, echoing voice. "Riverwind."

"Who is it?" he shouted back.

"Greetings, barbarian! This is the voice of Thouriss. I am disappointed at the way you abused my hospitality by trying to escape. If you want to see your friends alive again, surrender yourself at the front steps of the old palace at once. Do not delay or they will die."

"How do I know they aren't already dead?" Riverwind demanded. The fireball was already moving again. It flew straight at his face. Riverwind ducked and thrust the pike at it. The fireball burst with an ear-splitting clap of thunder. Riverwind was blown off his feet—though Brud clinging to his leg didn't help his equilibrium—and landed heavily on his back. The head of the pike was vaporized, along with ten inches of the shaft. Riverwind got to his feet and kicked the useless pole aside in disgust.

Brud stood up, rubbing his rather square head. "Ow-wah! You heavy, human. Should eat less stew."

"Never mind. We've got to get to the Great Plaza right away!"

"*We*, human?" Brud said. He shook his head. "Brud go home. Have dinner."

"No, you don't." Riverwind hauled the little fellow to his feet. "I need someone to watch my back if I'm walking into a square full of lizard men and goblins. Besides, you owe me," he said.

"Brud not fighter. Let me get wife; she tougher than dog steak!"

"No, Brud, there's no time. You're quick on your feet and plenty smart." Besides, the plainsman added silently, you're all I've got. Brud's implacable expression began to soften. "With you at my back, I won't fear anything Thouriss tries to do," the plainsman coaxed.

Mention of the fearsome commander took the stiffness out of Brud's spine. He slouched and said dispiritedly, "Maybe skinny girl and old man dead. Then you and Brud walk into trap. Maybe get dead?"

Riverwind unfastened the cloak and dropped it in the street. The helmet he tossed over a pile of broken bricks. "I want you to walk behind me and keep both eyes open for treachery. Understand?" The gully dwarf nodded reluctantly. "Don't look so downcast! Think of what a great story this will be to tell your children," Riverwind said.

Brud scowled. "All children do is talk back, play loud drum music all time night and day. No 'spect for hard-working father."

Riverwind wound the rawhide thong attached to the mace handle around his knuckles. "Stand by me, Brud, and all the Aghar will respect what you are about to do." He set off toward the plaza with urgent strides.

"Huh! All Aghar pay 'spects at funeral!" he muttered. But Brud did follow on Riverwind's heels, his hanging rope still looped about his neck, its cut end trailing in the dust.

Chapter 21

The Warrior's Way

AS RIVERWIND AND BRUD ENTERED THE GREAT PLAZA, they saw that Catchflea and Di An were tied to the stumps of broken columns in the portico of the ancient building. Both were gagged. Riverwind's eyes went first to Catchflea. The old man was pale. A streak of blood was drying on his left side. Di An's face was twisted in pain. The goblins had tied her high enough on the column that her feet hung several inches above the floor. The tight ropes drove her copper metal dress into her flesh.

Thouriss stood at the head of the cracked steps, resplendent in green enameled armor mottled with black and gold to resemble a snake's skin. The ophidian commander was vain enough not to be wearing a helm, and his smooth, nearly human features contrasted sharply with the corps of goblins and draconians assembled in the plaza.

Must be the entire garrison, Riverwind thought. Perhaps a hundred armed goblins lined the curved walls that faced the plaza. At the foot of the stairs, near Thouriss, the captain, Shanz, and six more draconians stood at attention. Of Krago there was no sign. Riverwind glanced left and right. No archers on the rooftops that he could see. So far, so bad, he thought grimly.

He halted where the stream flowed into the large triangular pool that dominated the plaza. The streams from the three waterfalls that ringed Xak Tsaroth converged here. Footbridges made of stout wooden planks spanned each of the three streams, though none of these creeks was more than waist deep. Perhaps the lizard men do not enjoy getting wet, Riverwind mused. He filed this thought away as his mind raced, trying to decide on a plan.

"We're waiting, barbarian!" Thouriss boomed.

"I don't want a spear in the back," Riverwind retorted.

"I have ordered my warriors not to interfere with you."

"Warriors? These?" Riverwind waved at the silent ranks of goblins. "All they are fit for is enslaving and murdering defenseless gully dwarves."

"Bold talk coming from a warm-blood! Does the little one guard your back? Ho! Ho!" There were guffaws from the goblin soldiers. "He was dead once. Soon he will be twice dead. Come ahead and meet your own fate, barbarian!"

"Brud stay here," the gully dwarf whispered behind Riverwind. "Goblins not strike. You hear what great master say."

"Don't believe it. Thouriss would like it very much if we separated, then he could pick us off one at a time." He felt a bump as the Aghar moved even closer to him.

Riverwind advanced across the eastern footbridge. Brud stayed close to his back. At the foot of the palace steps, Riverwind paused.

"Are my friends all right?" he asked. He gripped the mace's handle so tightly that his hand went numb.

"They are well. The old one got nicked by my guards. The fool tried to stave off my warriors barehanded," Thouriss said with a sneer.

"I want to hear them speak." He put a foot up on the first

step.

Thouriss drew a gleaming two-handed sword. "Stand where you are, warm-blood." Thouriss called out, and a draconian came running to his side. "Unstop their mouths," he ordered. The lizard man unwound the gags from Di An's and Catchflea's mouths.

"Are you hurt, old man?" Riverwind called.

"Only a scratch," Catchflea replied hoarsely.

"And you, little one?"

"He means to kill you!" Di An cried.

"This is no secret," Thouriss put in genially. He motioned to the draconian, and the gags were jammed back in. Raising his sword high, he slashed an "X" in the air. "Your name will be forgotten in the ranks of the many to fall to Thouriss the Conqueror."

"Only if you plan to talk me to death," Riverwind remarked coldly.

Thouriss laughed, a very unpleasant sound, like a hot iron plunging in cold water. "You have a mace in your hand. Do you know how to use it?" he asked.

"It's not my weapon of choice."

"Shanz! Give the barbarian your blade!" The draconian clomped out of his place in the cordon. Brud cowered behind the tall plainsman, making himself as small as possible. Shanz handed Riverwind his straight sword, pommel first. Riverwind gave Shanz the mace.

"I have trained long against Shanz and the other Bozak," Thouriss said, "but I haven't yet fought a human. I am curious to discover what it's like to kill one."

"We haven't crossed blades and already you have me dead," Riverwind said. "Why should I bother to be sport for you?"

"Did I not say?" Thouriss asked with exaggerated surprise. "If you acquit yourself well, I will spare the old human and the elf girl. Does the weapon suit you, barbarian?"

"A bit heavy, but it will do," Riverwind replied. Outwardly, he seemed calm and controlled. Inside, he was seething with anger, fear, and anticipation. He had the beginnings of an idea, a way to beat the formidable commander—

His wool-gathering vanished with the first swing Thouriss made with his great sword. The two-handed blade cleaved the air toward Riverwind's skull. The plainsman backed off the steps and parried clumsily. Shanz's sword was a good deal heavier than his saber, but it looked like an actor's wooden blade compared to the monstrous weapon Thouriss wielded. Poor, terrified Brud threw himself flat on the lowest step and quivered.

The commander advanced down the palace steps two at a time. His muscles bulged and knotted beneath his scale-and-mail armor like the workings of some fantastic machine. With everyone's attention fixed on the fight, Brud leaped up and scampered up the steps of the palace. He ran right past Catchflea and vanished into the ruined interior. There was no blaming him. The old man wished he could disappear, too.

Riverwind dodged the strokes Thouriss aimed at his head.

"How am I doing?" Riverwind asked, trying not to gasp for air.

"Not badly." Thouriss brought his point up from the resting position, an underhand cut at Riverwind's chest. The plainsman met the two-hander with the flat of his borrowed blade. The impact stung his hands, but he was grateful for the added weight of the draconian sword he wielded. He turned Thouriss's attack aside. Riverwind extended his arm full-length and lunged. Thouriss made a coup parry and backed up a step. His clawed heel caught on a slab of broken marble and he stumbled. Riverwind disengaged and slashed hard across the commander's chest. The sword tip scored a bright line along Thouriss's brilliant armor. The goblins shifted their feet and muttered, but a glance from Shanz silenced them. Riverwind withdrew a pace to catch his breath. Swinging Shanz's huge sword was tiring!

"Well played," Thouriss said. "If it weren't for my armor, you'd have seen my blood."

"I noticed you wear armor, while I wear only leather," Riverwind panted.

"An even trade. The weight slows me down."

One-handed, Thouriss whirled his sword over his head.

The glittering steel seemed to leave a shining trail in the air, so fast did the commander swing it. Riverwind ducked under the spinning blade. He lunged, only to have Thouriss beat aside his attack. He lunged again, steel sliding against steel. Thouriss's serpent eyes widened as Riverwind's sword came at his throat. He stepped into the lunge, hitting the plainsman's blade with his mailed hand. The point passed over his shoulder, and the warriors closed together. Thouriss opened his mouth in a hiss of angry frustration. His two-inch fangs glistened in Riverwind's face.

The ophidian backhanded Riverwind on the jaw. He staggered back, blood running on his chin from where the mail links tore his skin.

"*Rahhh-ssss!*" Thouriss howled. "Enough play! Now you die!"

Riverwind checked his location. His back was to the plaza pool. Just where he wanted to be.

Di An moaned through her gag. She looked to Catchflea. His eyes were shut and his jaw worked as if in speech. He must be praying to his gods, she thought, and added her own silent prayers to his.

Riverwind flexed his fingers around the sharkskin grip of his borrowed sword. Thouriss was screaming at him. For all his size, Thouriss was not an experienced duelist. Riverwind was counting on that.

Thouriss charged, sword held out in front of him in both hands. Riverwind stepped forward to meet him. They traded cuts and parries—one, two, one, two—until the commander flicked his wrist and hit Riverwind in the eye with the guard of his sword. Blinded, Riverwind stumbled back. He narrowly missed a killing stroke aimed at his blind side. Water lapped at his heels. He was on the very edge of the pool.

The vision in his left eye cleared enough to see a crosswise slash coming from that side. Riverwind blocked it awkwardly. The shock of blade on blade went up his arm. He felt something hot on his arm and saw Thouriss's keen edge had just laid open the skin on his forearm. Blood welled from the cut in rich red beads. The sight of his enemy's blood restored Thouriss's good cheer.

"The wound does not trouble you, I hope?" Thouriss hissed, panting just a bit.

"It's nothing," Riverwind assured him. Blood ran down his arm, seeping into the gaps between his fingers. Riverwind's throat was raw from breathing hard, and his heart throbbed. Strangely enough, he was calmer now. Thouriss was not the perfect fighting machine he appeared to be. Not yet.

The commander wasn't going for wounds any longer. He was closing for the kill. The sunken city echoed and rang with the sound of blade meeting blade. Gully dwarves came out of their hovels and listened. Even the stolid goblin soldiers shifted restlessly as the two enemies battled before them.

Thouriss wound up for a mighty overhand slash. Riverwind was so exhausted that he could hardly bring the borrowed sword up to parry. *Now's the time.* He threw Shanz's sword point-first at Thouriss. The surprised commander altered his attack to bat away the flying weapon. When he did, Riverwind lowered his shoulder and ducked under Thouriss's sword arm. He grappled with the larger creature, wedging a leg between Thouriss's muscled knees and wrapping his arms around the commander's great torso.

Riverwind was a fine wrestler among his own people, but he had no illusions as to how long he could survive against Thouriss's brute strength. The commander howled again, this time with sardonic laughter.

"Embrace me then, warm-blood! I shall break you apart like a dead tree!" he exclaimed.

Gripping Thouriss was like hugging a statue, except this statue had a crushing grip of its own. Thouriss got a clawed hand around Riverwind's forehead and began to twist. The plainsman gasped and grunted, trying to throw his weight against the commander's tangled legs. Thouriss's hissing laugh filled his ears as his head was slowly twisted around. Somewhere deep inside, Riverwind saw the face of Goldmoon. She had learned he was dead, and though she did not weep, all the sorrow of the world was in her face. He would not let that happen to her! His eyes flew open, and he saw Di An. The elf girl's face plainly showed her own horror.

Riverwind drove his elbow into the small of the commander's back, and Thouriss pitched forward. But he retained his grip on Riverwind's waist, and so both of them plunged into the plaza pool.

The combatants sank beneath the surface.

"Riverwind!" Di An screamed. She had worked her gag off. Catchflea opened his eyes. The water in the pool was always swirling from the currents in the streams that fed it, so there was no way for him to tell where the two had gone under. The goblin soldiers broke ranks and clustered around the pool. Shanz ordered them back to their places.

Thouriss was slow to react to being submerged, but when he did, he panicked. It was as Riverwind had thought: the five-month-old commander, conceived and nurtured by evil magic, could not yet swim. Riverwind had learned to swim nearly as soon as he had learned to walk.

Thouriss let go of the plainsman and tried to kick to the surface. Riverwind wrapped an arm around the commander's legs and held him down. Thouriss thrashed and pummeled Riverwind's back with his fists. His size and power were largely negated by his fear of drowning. He broke his hold on the plainsman and again tried to go up for air. Riverwind got on his back. So strong was Thouriss, that he was able to breach the surface with all of Riverwind's weight upon him. They reared out of the water, Thouriss roaring and gasping for air. Riverwind tightened his armlock around Thouriss's neck and dragged him under again.

They sank so deep the water was violet and dark. Jagged slabs of pavement jutted up, adding to the danger. Thouriss tried to impale Riverwind on just such a slab, but the plainsman braced his feet against the stone and pushed away from it. The pressure began to affect Riverwind. His chest, his ears, his head felt as if they were in a vise and someone was cranking it tighter and tighter . . .

"They've been under a long time," Catchflea said. The old man had finally gotten his own gag off.

"Is Riverwind a good swimmer?" Di An asked tremulously.

"The finest in Que-Shu," the old man avowed, though he actually had no idea.

The draconians muttered and mumbled among themselves. The goblins shifted on their feet and kept glancing at Shanz. The draconian captain went to the edge of the pool and gazed into the water. He couldn't see either fighter. He picked up the sword he had loaned Riverwind and returned it to his sheath.

"What shall we do, sir?" one of the draconians called out.

"Keep your places!" Shanz snapped. "It was the commander's order that we not interfere!"

"Thank the gods they obey orders," Catchflea said in a low voice.

Seconds stretched into minutes. Di An wept in earnest, and Catchflea felt a lump growing in his throat as well. No one, human or reptile, could survive underwater so long.

Finally, Shanz approached. He drew his sword in such a fierce, swift fashion that Catchflea thought he was about to lose his head. Instead, the draconian cut the ropes holding him and Di An to the pillars.

"Are we free?" the soothsayer asked hopefully.

Shanz rammed his sword into its sheath. "I will take you to Master Krago. He will know what to do." A guard of four draconians surrounded Catchflea and Di An and shoved them along to Krago's private sanctum. Di An kept looking at the pool. The waters continued their giddy swirl, revealing nothing of the fate of the warriors lost beneath their surface.

* * * * *

Krago was absorbed in an ancient scroll when Shanz brought the prisoners in. "What is it?" the young cleric asked. "Why have you brought them to me?"

"Master," Shanz said, "I regret to say—I have to tell you—"

"What? Out with it."

"Commander Thouriss is—missing." Krago stood so abruptly he toppled his chair. Shanz spoke with obvious trepidation, choosing his words carefully. "He lured the tall barbarian into a duel by threatening the hostages. The barbarian fought well, until the end, when he threw away his sword and struggled hand to hand. They fell into the plaza pool and never came up."

Krago's head sagged. He stared at his toes for a long time in silence. "Khisanth will not be pleased," he said finally.

"Master Krago—" Shanz began.

"Hold a moment, Captain. Let me think." He picked up the small scroll he was reading and then put it down again. He moved around the room dazedly, his eyes small and glittering. Finally, he sat down in one of his high-backed chairs. "Leave the prisoners with me," he said blankly.

Shanz didn't like that, but orders were orders. He said, "What about Commander Thouriss?"

"Get some hooks and rope, then drag the pool," Krago said. "Find Thouriss's body. I may be able to restore it to life. If not—" The cleric shook his head. "I shall have to grow a new male in the vat."

Shanz posted four goblin guards outside Krago's door. When he was gone, Catchflea thanked the young cleric.

"You needn't bother," Krago said coldly. "I have tasks for both of you. If you cause me the slightest trouble, I'll have you hamstrung. Is that clear to you?"

It was.

The cleric sank in his chair and shook his head. "It's all too much," he groaned. "My creation destroyed, drowned like a rat!"

"You made him a warrior," Catchflea said, gathering the grieving Di An to his side. "Did you think he would live forever?"

"Thouriss was much too valuable to die in a duel," Krago replied testily. "Had he fathered sons and daughters, then I wouldn't care what happened to him."

"Is that all you can think about?" Di An asked. She rubbed her eyes to clear them. "The trouble Thouriss's death makes for your grand design?"

"Yes. Nothing else matters." Krago smoothed out the scroll on the table. "Nothing."

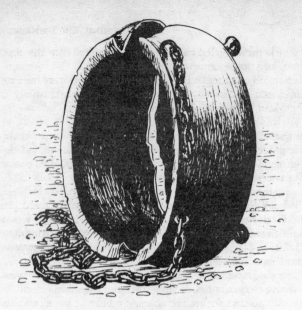

Chapter 22

From the Depths

Thouriss finally went limp in Riverwind's grasp, and he released him. The weight of Thouriss's armor took the creature down to the nether reaches of the pool.

Riverwind needed air, but he cast about for an alternative to surfacing in the center of the plaza under the eyes and arms of the goblins and their draconian masters. He found a tunnel in the eastern side of the pool, where a strong inrush of water headed. He swam into the hole and let the water carry him until he could bear it no longer. Driven by a crying need for air, Riverwind went up and surfaced in a tiny grotto. About ten inches of air space was available, so Riverwind trod water and took in deep, heady breaths of air.

The ceiling of the grotto was not natural rock. Although it was too dark for Riverwind to see, the ceiling felt like fired clay. He thought that he must be in some sort of water pipe or cistern, a remnant of the great days of Xak Tsaroth. Riverwind paddled forward in the total darkness, feeling the cracks in the thick terra cotta. The water was flowing, so there had to be a way out. He only hoped it would be big enough for him to pass through.

The bottom of the tunnel rose sharply, and he was able to get his feet under him again. Riverwind sloshed forward in a crouch. The pipe narrowed further, so he got on his hands and knees. Water lapped at his chin. He came to a fork in the pipe. He chose to go left, where a faint light seemed to shine.

On all fours, Riverwind scrambled forward toward the light. His arm wound was bleeding again, his left eye was swollen shut, and his whole body ached from the pounding Thouriss had given him. The pain didn't matter as much as getting out of this sewer and finding Di An and Catchflea.

The light was a finger-thin shaft falling down a round opening that might have been a well in ages past. A fall of rubble had partially filled the water pipe, making a small island. Riverwind tried to stand, to reach up to the light and climb out. He couldn't. The strength ebbed from his limbs, and he sank down, utterly exhausted. The blackness of unconsciousness covered him, and around him the water lapped and swirled.

*   *   *   *   *

Di An tiptoed to the end of the vat where Krago's new creation still slept. She hated the hideous thing half-sunk in its bath of quicksilver. It was growing more aware all the time; when Di An was near, it would turn its head as if looking at her. This was all the more disturbing because the monster's eyes were still unopened. Other times, Krago would come in and talk to it, telling it what a beautiful, powerful creature it was. It made Di An ill.

A day had passed since the duel. The draconians had not recovered any bodies from the pool. When the hooks continued to come up empty, Di An and Catchflea didn't know if they should be glad or sad. Riverwind must be dead; and yet, if no body were found, perhaps he had survived somehow. But he couldn't have.

Catchflea had bandaged the slight wound in his side. He was feeling stronger after the meals supplied by Krago. Di An was walking better than she had the day before. Catchflea remarked on this as she fetched jars of powder for Krago's alchemical potions.

"My ankles and legs don't hurt so much now," she admitted. "But my hips do."

Krago took the green glass jar from the elf girl without looking up from his work table. He measured a spoonful of yellowish powder, then gave the jar back to Di An.

"Are you getting taller?" he asked, his eyes narrowing as he stared at her.

She looked down at her feet as if they would tell her. "How can I be?" she asked.

"You did drink my blood purifying potion," said Krago.

"And you gave me the antidote."

"No," he said, slowly. "I gave you a philtre to soothe the stomach cramps."

Di An stared at the cleric, then turned to Catchflea. "Am I taller?" she asked.

The old soothsayer got up from his bench and drew himself up beside her. Di An's head had once crested near the bottom of his rib cage; now the crown of her head was even with his shoulders. He clasped her arms and said with a smile, "You are growing."

She could not fathom it. Her aching joints had been difficult to bear, but compared to the joy of actually growing up—being a woman—the pain was a minor annoyance. Di An begged for a mirror, so she could see for herself.

"I don't keep mirrors in my study," Krago informed her with disinterest. "Go to the vat room and try a tin tray or something."

Di An hated to go back there with the thing lying in the vat, but she could almost feel herself growing. She must see what progress she'd made. She went. On a table in the far corner of the shelf-enclosed room was a tin tray, loaded with bottles of liquids, each labeled with arcane symbols. Di An cleared them off and held the tray to her face.

The diggers of Hest owned few mirrors, so Di An had

seen her own reflection a handful of times. Now, she studied her face closely. Wasn't her chin a trifle less sharp? Was her hair a bit longer? It no longer stuck up in spiky bits but lay flatter, brushing the bottoms of her pointed ears. There was a pale blush in her skin. She touched her face lightly with three fingers. A coat of finest down had appeared on her cheek.

Behind the elf girl, Lyrexis stirred in the vat. The movement of air caused by Di An's passage and her body warmth had penetrated the creature's half-sleep. Lyrexis sat up.

Di An slipped the strap of her mesh dress off her shoulder—she'd mended the rips the goblin had made in it—and stared at her body. The changes were beginning all over. She was growing up at last. It was a bit frightening, but her pleasure far exceeded her nervousness. A wide smile brightened Di An's face.

A form crossed her line of sight, a blur in the makeshift mirror. She turned.

Lyrexis, the unfinished mate of Thouriss, had risen from her bed of quicksilver and was standing behind Di An. The bulging orbs of her eyes were still covered with pale skin. Round beads of quicksilver fell from the creature's ears and nostrils. It—she—raised a hand toward the elf girl. Di An screamed.

Krago and Catchflea rushed in. "Don't move!" Krago shouted.

"By the Great Hest, I won't!"

Krago moved up behind the semi-conscious Lyrexis. He did not touch the softly scaled flesh of his creation. Instead, he spoke to her in low, authoritative tones.

"Lyrexis, go back. Go back to your bed," he said. The creature's hand hovered not an inch from Di An's face. "Go back, Lyrexis. You shouldn't be up yet." The female ophidian swung around, hand outstretched. Krago deliberately walked into range and let the green and yellow hand touch his face.

"Go, Lyrexis. Back to your bed," he said. The round, hairless head swiveled down. Slowly, stiltedly, the creature tottered back to the vat. Krago eased it into the nourishing bath of quicksilver.

He turned angrily on Di An and curtly waved her out. Once in the study again, he exploded. "What did you do?"

"I was looking at myself in the tin tray and it sneaked up behind me!"

"Thouriss never left the vat and walked before his final awakening," Krago said. His brows knitted in thought and he folded his arms across his chest. "What does it mean?"

"Curiosity," said Catchflea. "She can sense the presence of others, yes?" Krago admitted she could. "Can she tell male from female?"

"No. At least, she has no natural knowledge of such things."

"How can she see without eyes?" Di An asked with a shudder.

"Like the serpents she was derived from, Lyrexis can sense things by their heat. You must be more hot-blooded than I or the old man." Di An flushed.

Shanz was waiting for them with a squad of goblin guards when the three of them returned to Krago's outer chambers. "What is the commotion?" Shanz grumbled.

"Lyrexis rose from her bath and walked," Krago said a trifle wearily. "The girl was startled. All is well now."

Shanz's horned nostrils flared. "Is your work undamaged?"

"Quite undamaged. The time is nigh for Lyrexis to come to life, and her reactions are becoming stronger all the time." Krago sat back and took up the scroll he'd been perusing. The powder Di An had brought him was still on the table. He set the lid on the jar and glanced at Shanz as if surprised to see him still standing there. "Is there anything else, Captain?" Krago asked briskly.

"We've found no trace of Commander Thouriss or the human. The gully dwarves report that the pool is connected with drains and tunnels that lead off to other parts of the city. I have ordered the goblins to search the old cisterns and wells for signs." Shanz hissed with frustration. "The damned gully dwarves have the whole city riddled with tunnels. It's no wonder we can't keep track of them!"

"Do what you think necessary," Krago said. "Military matters are your province, Captain."

Shanz nodded curtly and departed. When he was gone, Catchflea let out an audible sigh of relief.

Krago glanced at the old man. "He would like to see us all dead," the cleric said matter-of-factly. "Like most of his kind, he has no trust or liking for warm-blooded things."

"Why does he defer to you, then? He is afraid of something, yes?" Catchflea said.

"Our mutual patron, the black dragon, Khisanth."

"Is there actually a black dragon?" Catchflea asked.

"Most certainly," Krago replied. "Make no mistake, it is she who rules Xak Tsaroth." He looked down at the scroll spread on the table before him. Without looking up, he added, "Have you ever seen a dragon, old man?"

"Never." Catchflea shook his head.

Krago's fingers traced a line of writing on the scroll. He was silent so long that Catchflea thought their conversation was over. Suddenly, Krago looked up and locked eyes with the old soothsayer. "Khisanth will arrive soon. She will want revenge for the trouble you've caused. Your death arrives with her."

Krago returned to his study of the scroll, and Catchflea was left staring in shock at his bowed head.

Di An went to a corner of Krago's sleeping area and slipped down between two stacks of books. The pleasure of her newly discovered growth was tempered by the ever-present danger she and Catchflea lived in. Krago had saved them once, but only for his own convenience. When the dragon returned—Di An shivered at the thought—their last appeal would be gone.

Riverwind, she said silently, her lips gently forming the name. Riverwind.

*   *   *   *   *

He awoke with a start.

Riverwind was lying on an island of wet stones. It came back to him in a dizzying rush—Xak Tsaroth, Thouriss, the fight, the pool. A wall of exhaustion had fallen on him, and as he lay in the darkness it took some time for him to regain his equilibrium. His eye was swollen shut, and the cut on his arm felt stiff with dried blood. Riverwind stood and felt around the well's wall. He found what he was looking for: steps formed when the masons had set individual bricks deeper in the wall than others. He took several deep breaths and stretched his tired limbs. The brief sleep had helped some. He climbed up to where he remembered seeing daylight. The top of the well was covered with slabs of stone. Cracks between the rocks let in the dim light he recalled. Riverwind peered out. He could see the broken walls of houses around him.

His bent his neck, braced his shoulders against the blocks, and pushed. A cascade of small pebbles rolled down noisily. Undaunted, he shoved again. One slab moved sideways and the weight of the obstruction dramatically decreased. Though his arms and back were sore, he cleared the rocks away and climbed out of the well.

He'd surfaced in the ruins north and east of the great plaza. The East Falls fumed on his left. Riverwind slipped over the rubble to a low wall and saw that the pot and chain lift was resting on the pavement. A lone armed goblin guarded the pot.

The plaza area was ablaze with torches. Riverwind didn't know how long he'd been unconscious in the well, but it was obvious the goblins and draconians were still looking for their lost leader. Massed torches gave the white stones of Xak Tsaroth a bloody glow.

Riverwind. Riverwind.

He heard his name spoken, but there was no one near him. Ducking behind the wall, he wondered if his injuries were making him delirious. Yet it had sounded so real. He thought of Goldmoon. She would call him like that. Perhaps she knew he was in peril and called out to him.

Footsteps crunched through the gravel on the other side of the wall. Riverwind spied goblin feet, one pair. He lay in wait until the goblin walked past, then he sprang over the wall and grabbed the soldier from behind. The goblin was no match for his desperate strength and the large stone he wielded, and he soon had the creature laid out cold at his feet. Riverwind dragged the goblin into the ruins. He stripped off the creature's breastplate, cloak, helmet, and weapons. The apparel smelled foul. All the items were too short, but in poor light he might get by impersonating a goblin. It had worked before.

Riverwind had no idea what had happened to Catchflea or Di An. They might even be dead by now. But he had to find out, and he had one other task to take care of: seeing to the end of Krago and his hideous experiment. No inhabitant of Krynn would be safe as long as Krago could breed his race of evil ophidians.

Rather than skulk in the shadows, he marched boldly along the center of the street toward the palace. He passed several groups of guards, all of whom spoke to him in a harsh goblin dialect. Riverwind grunted and kept going.

He crossed the footbridge at the base of the East Falls and entered the ancient palace by means of the old postern door Di An had been taken to. The smell of the draconian officers' quarters was overwhelming.

"What do you want?" snarled a draconian.

Riverwind hunched his shoulders and let the helmet slide down over his nose. "Master Krago sent for me," he said gruffly.

"Well, get going," the draconian said. "Stupid goblin."

Riverwind moved on, keeping the cloak close around him. To his right were more alcovelike rooms occupied by the draconians. To his left was an empty corridor. He skirted the open door and headed down the passage.

Four goblins stood, two on each side of the door. "Master Krago sent for me," he said, keeping his face averted.

"G'wan in," said the nearest guard. Riverwind put out a hand to grasp the bronze door handle. When he did, he exposed his arm.

"Huh? What's this?" said the near goblin. He drew his sword. "You ain't one o' us!"

"Thank the gods for that!" Riverwind exclaimed. He whipped back the cloak and drew his goblin sword.

He took the chief guard's attack and turned it, thrusting his point through the goblin, below his breastplate. The guard fell backward, knocking down his comrade. Behind Riverwind, the second pair of goblins closed in. He felt a sword tip rip through his cloak. He turned sharply and harried the two guards away. The narrow corridor did not allow much room to maneuver, so the goblins' advantage of numbers was largely nullified.

"Yah-ha!" Riverwind shouted, just to rattle his foes. The goblins kept off until he found the door handle behind his back and twisted it. Riverwind slipped inside and threw the door shut.

The room was a frozen tableau. Catchflea, quill in hand, sat by Krago at the table. The young cleric's mouth was open in midword. The room was cluttered with books, papers, jars, and beakers. Riverwind didn't see Di An.

"Riverwind! You're alive!" Catchflea cried, astonished.

"So far!"

The old soothsayer hopped up, spilling the ink pot over the transcript he was making. Krago's surprise at seeing Riverwind changed to dismay at the damage done to the paper. He groaned loudly, trying to stem the flow of ink over the scroll. "Look what you've done!" he cried.

"You keep still," Riverwind warned.

He thrust his sword through the door handle and latch plate, holding the door closed. The goblins rattled and pounded on the outside. Riverwind and Catchflea pushed a table, a set of creaking shelves, and a heavy oaken chest full of chemicals against the door. As books and bottles fell from the shelves, Krago wailed, "Stop, you idiots! Those are important and valuable books. You're destroying my work!"

Riverwind withdrew the goblin sword from the door. He advanced on Krago, point held out. The young cleric stood his ground until the tip pricked his skin. He shuffled backward.

"You dare not hurt me! The dragon will wreak terrible vengeance on you if you do!" he gasped.

"You keep invoking this dragon, but I've seen no evidence of one," Riverwind said levelly. "I think it's all a pose to keep the lizard men in line and make them do what you want."

"There is a dragon, you'll see!"

"Shut up and sit down," Riverwind replied. The pounding on the door got louder and more regular. The goblins had fetched help.

"There's no room to swing a battering ram out there," the

plainsman said, "but we can't keep them out for long."

"What do we do?" asked Catchflea.

"I'm thinking." He surveyed the cleric's quarters. "Where's Di An?"

"Here."

Riverwind turned to the sound of her voice. She came from the far side of the room, rubbing her eyes as if she'd been asleep. He looked twice before he realized it really was her. The change in her was even more noticeable to him, since he hadn't watched its gradual progression. Di An had grown six inches in the short days since he'd seen her last. Her black hair now almost reached her shoulders, and her white skin had a pink tinge. Though still quite thin, she had the figure of an adult elf woman, all the more apparent in her ragged, and now short, girl's dress.

"I knew you would come back," she said. Even her voice was slightly lower.

"What's happened to you?" The young plainsman's question was punctuated by a splintering crash. The bright edge of an axe showed through a newly cut crack in the door.

"Is there another way out of here?" Riverwind demanded of Krago.

"Do you expect me to tell you?" the cleric said with a sneer.

"You will if it means your life!" Riverwind raised the crude sword to strike Krago.

"If you kill me, you will all perish. Shanz will show you no mercy."

Riverwind lowered his weapon. He grabbed Krago by the front of his robe and dragged him to his feet. The slight cleric's toes brushed the floor as Riverwind held him up.

"Tell them to back off," he said. "Back off, or I'll hack that monster you're making to bits!" Krago paled at this threat. All his work wasted—what would Khisanth do to him then?

"This is Krago!" the cleric shouted. "Get back from the door. Get back, I say!"

They heard Shanz's muffled reply, "Master Krago, are you all right?"

"For now, good Shanz. The barbarian has threatened to harm Lyrexis if you don't stop now!"

"As you wish." More muffled commands, and the axe squeaked free of the door and disappeared. "We're withdrawing," Shanz called.

"Tell them to go to the great plaza," Riverwind said. Krago repeated the order.

"Very well." Heavy footsteps tramped away.

"Show me the creature," Riverwind said.

"You will not harm her!" Krago cried, twisting in Riverwind's grip.

"Show me."

"It's almost awake," Di An said after Krago led them to the vat room. She stood apart from Riverwind and did not meet his eyes.

The vat of quicksilver churned in slow ripples as Lyrexis stiffly moved her arms and legs. In the past day, her eyes had darkened, and her lids cracked apart just enough to expose the vertical green pupils. Her scales were hardening, losing their translucency. When the humans and Di An drew near, the creature sat up and made inarticulate sounds through closed lips.

Riverwind found himself staring at Lyrexis in awe. He knew that Krago's work was evil, and yet, he had actually created life.

"This is a very crucial time!" Krago said excitedly. "When her eyes are fully open, I must perform the Spell of Awakening. It will lessen the shock of her birth and make her acknowledge me as her true, ah, parent."

Riverwind brought his mind back to the situation at hand. "We've no time for that," he said. "We're leaving, and you're our hostage."

"Ignorant lout! You don't understand! If Lyrexis awakens without the proper soothing spells, she'll run wild. There's no telling what harm she'll cause and come to!"

"Tie his hands, Catchflea. If he talks, gag him."

"He may be right, tall man. I have been reading his spells, yes? The creature has an almost human form, but it still has the mind of a serpent."

"You too, Catchflea? If the creature is going to die, let it die now before it is aware of its evil purpose."

Di An stared at Lyrexis. "I say kill it now."

"What?" asked Riverwind.

"Kill it now. Take a sword and cut off its head!"

All the agitated shouting seemed to galvanize the awakening creature. It ceased its plaintive mumbling and threw a leg over the side of the vat. Its movements were smoother now, more like those of a fully conscious being. Everyone drew back as the creature, some seven feet tall, swung to its feet.

"Lyrexis!" Krago breathed. He stepped forward to take the creature's hand. She felt the warm flesh of Krago's palm pressed to hers. She tilted her sightless head and shuddered. Her hand closed tightly over Krago's with a horrible crunching sound.

The cleric screamed. Riverwind raised his sword, but the creature jerked Krago toward her. Grabbing the cleric at the waist, she hoisted him in the air.

Riverwind said, "Old man, you and Di An get out!"

"But where? Shanz is waiting outside, yes."

"To the study!"

Krago wept and pleaded with his creation to put him down. Lyrexis's arms bowed, and she lowered him to the floor. Then, at the last second, she bent backward and launched Krago at Riverwind.

The plainsman managed to turn aside his sword, but that was about all. He went down with Krago on top of him, cracking his head on the hard stone floor. Stunned, he didn't see Lyrexis's eyelids finally split fully apart. Eyes that were startlingly yellow showed long, dagger-shaped pupils in their centers. Lyrexis surveyed the room she'd so long dwelt in. The open door beyond the bookshelves beckoned. She threw back her head and let out a hissing howl that chilled the blood of all who heard it.

"Get off me," Riverwind said, shoving Krago. The cleric groaned and painfully sat up, cradling his right hand.

"She hurt me," he said through clenched teeth. "She crushed my hand! I warned you—"

"She'll do a lot worse than that if we don't stop her," Riverwind declared. He stood up and, sword ready, prepared to cut at the creature's exposed back. Krago tangled his feet and good arm in Riverwind's legs.

"No!" he gasped. "I won't let you hurt her! I made her. She is mine to teach!"

"Let me go!" Riverwind rapped Krago on the chin with the crossguard of his stolen sword. Krago went slack, and Riverwind disentangled himself from the stunned cleric.

"Catchflea! Di An! Watch out!" he shouted as Lyrexis stormed into the study. The creature opened its mouth and screeched at the two of them. Catchflea hurled pots of powders at it, which only made it madder. Riverwind reached the door and slashed at Lyrexis. The cheap goblin steel cut the creature, but its hard scales were as tough as leather armor. Saliva glistened from her fangs, long glassy needles protruding below her upper lip. Despite his weapon, Riverwind retreated at the sight of the creature's fearsome teeth.

Lyrexis stalked him, circling the table. Riverwind kept the furniture between them, but she heaved the table out of her path and advanced on him. The plainsman cut at her, leaving long bleeding marks in the horny scales of her forearms. She ignored these hurts and came on, causing him to fall back again.

Despair crept into the warrior's heart. There seemed to be nothing he could do to stop this monster. She took his best blows as if they were insect bites.

Catchflea appeared in the door behind Lyrexis with a blazing torch. He clubbed the creature across the shoulders with it. Cuts Lyrexis could bear, but burning outraged her. She swatted the torch away, knocking Catchflea against the wall. Krago stirred, moaning. Riverwind circled around toward the old man, his blade dented and nicked from hitting the ophidian's skin.

Di An appeared in the doorway. "Shanz and his soldiers are outside again!" she cried. "They heard the noise!"

"Get back!"

Lyrexis flew at the elf girl. She crashed into Krago's study just as Shanz's goblin troops smashed their way in from the outer door. The sight of more swords infuriated the already berserk creature, and she tore into the ranks of goblins, seizing them in her long, powerful arms and biting them to death. The goblins, never the bravest of fighters, panicked and tried to flee, creating a terrible confusion.

Riverwind grabbed Krago by the collar of his robe and dragged him out. Di An was close on their heels. Catchflea limped after them. Keeping close to the wall, they stayed out of the monster's sight as it battled the yelling goblins. The goblins were ill-equipped to withstand the creature's ferocious onslaught. The last living ones fled the room, throwing away their swords and shields. Lyrexis, bleeding from dozens of minor cuts, tore out the broken door and, howling like all the fiends in the Abyss, stomped down the corridor.

Flames licked through the door of the inner chamber, fed by the ancient scrolls and weird powders. Fantastic tongues of green and violet fire lapped at the wooden book shelves.

"My work!" Krago moaned. "My books and my equipment!"

"Let it burn," Riverwind said sternly. "Only evil has come of it."

"But let us save ourselves, yes?" Catchflea said. The left side of his face was mottled with dark bruises. He checked the corridor. "It seems clear."

"Go." Catchflea scooped up a goblin shield and slipped out.

The corridor was littered with fallen goblins and their arms. Riverwind replaced his battered sword with a fresher specimen. He let go of Krago, but kept him within sword's reach. The ashen-faced cleric nursed his broken hand and stumbled ahead, muttering to himself.

Catchflea was waiting where the passage went left to the draconian officers' quarters. The rooms were a shambles. The companions didn't have long to examine the room, however; behind them, smoke and flames were beginning to fill the far end of the corridor.

They moved on through the postern and into the street. The footbridge across the stream below the East Falls was ablaze, and dead goblins were strewn around it.

"I see what happened," Riverwind said. "They set fire to the bridge to contain the monster, but it stormed over anyway."

"Which way are we going?" asked Di An.

"To the courtyard, I'm afraid. The pot lift to the surface is there."

"You'll never make it," Krago said weakly.

"You had better hope we do."

They waded through the stream, ignoring the slain soldiers floating in the water. As they gained the other side, a crack like lightning flashed from the courtyard, following by a booming roll of thunder.

"What was that?" Di An gasped.

"Shanz," Krago replied, "using one of his spells."

"Shanz can use magic?" Riverwind asked wonderingly.

"He knows two spells well. Levitation and the magical missile. That's what we just heard."

They hurried down the street, Riverwind leading with his sword flat against Krago's ribs. The sounds of fighting grew louder. The lifting pot was visible to them now, sitting on its stubby legs. As they neared the edge of the yard, the body of an armed goblin came hurtling through the air. Lyrexis stalked into view. Her tough hide bore more wounds, including a crossbow quarrel lodged in her scaly chest. She held a heavy length of timber—which looked like part of a ballista—and smashed any creature that moved into range.

Riverwind and his group crouched by the wall only a few yards from the lift. Diagonally across the courtyard, Shanz and his six draconian officers stood several steps behind a wall of shields. They wore full battle regalia, but their weapons were unbloodied. So far, none of them had closed with the rampaging creature.

Shanz waved his clawed hands. At this distance, Riverwind couldn't hear his words, but a sliver of white fire grew between his hands. He hurled the magical flame at Lyrexis. She swung her timber at it, hitting it. It exploded with a deafening crash.

"Let's go, while they're all blinded by the flash!" Riverwind said.

"No good," Krago said tersely. "The lift won't rise without gully dwarves to weigh down the counterweight."

"Where is the counterweight?"

"At the top of the lift, in the Hall of Ancestors."

Riverwind slammed the heel of his fist against the wall. "Blast!"

"Could we climb the chain?" suggested Di An.

"So many hundred feet? I could not, nor could Riverwind with his arm wound," said Catchflea.

Shanz recovered from the flare of his magic missile and spied Riverwind and company across the courtyard. He bellowed an order. The wall of shields quivered and broke apart, each shield borne by a terrified goblin. They tried to skirt Lyrexis, but she would not let them pass by unchallenged. She stormed into them, laying into them with her timber. The goblins were so demoralized that they cowered helplessly under their shields. She battered them down and slew them where they knelt.

The draconians formed a line and came at Lyrexis. The creature seemed to recognize the draconians were different from the humans and goblins, that they were cold-blooded and scaled like herself. She lowered her club and waited for them, panting. The draconians slowed and stopped a few yards from the now quiescent creature.

"Krago! Can you hear me?" Shanz called out.

The cleric looked to Riverwind. The plainsman nodded for him to answer. "I hear you, Shanz," Krago responded.

"Your offspring has slain most of the garrison. Do you hear, Krago? The goblin soldiers are defeated!"

Fire spurted from the postern gate. The plume of smoke caught Shanz's eye. "Our quarters are on fire!"

"Your schemes are ruined!" Riverwind yelled. "Stand aside and let us pass!"

"Nothing is lost but time," Shanz replied. "The Great One will be angry, but we can begin again." More loudly he said, "Let Krago go, warm-blood. Set him free and I'll allow you and your companions to go."

Di An clutched Riverwind's arm. "Don't believe him!"

"Don't worry, I don't." To Krago he muttered. "Can you raise the lift by magic?"

"Levitation? I don't know the spell," he said flatly.

Riverwind put the edge of the goblin blade to Krago's throat. "You're a free man once we get to the surface. What do you think Shanz and his dragon mistress will do to you for failing?"

Catchflea added, "They hanged gully dwarves just on the

suspicion of helping us. What will they do to you for your obvious and costly failures? It will not be pleasant, yes."

"I need an answer, warm-blood," Shanz called.

"What'll it be?" Riverwind urged Krago.

Krago looked around at the destruction of Khisanth's plans. He stared down at his ruined hand, now black and swollen. "I'll take you up," he murmured.

They stood out from the wall, Riverwind keeping his sword visible at Krago's throat. "We'll keep Master Krago a while longer," he cried. "Stand back."

Lyrexis's drooping head lifted when she heard Riverwind's voice. She hissed deep in her throat at the sight of Di An and the humans. Raising her club, she took a step toward them.

"Keep her back!" Shanz snapped. The draconians closed together, shoulder to shoulder, blocking her way. Lyrexis sidled left, then right, but her path was cut off. Frustrated, she hurled the timber at the hated warm-bloods. It sailed over Riverwind's head, smashing against the wall behind him.

They reached the lift. It was a big pot, but it would be a tight fit for all four of them. Di An scrambled in, with Catchflea close behind.

Lyrexis, with whatever instinct was instilled in her newborn mind, understood her enemies were getting away. She displayed her wicked teeth and advanced. Butting into the draconians' shields didn't discourage her. "Kill," she said distinctly. Her first words. "Enemy. Kill."

One of the draconians made a mistake. He used his sword to fend off the enraged creature. The keenly forged blade cut Lyrexis, and her reluctance to battle cold-bloods like herself vanished in an instant. She rammed her iron-nailed hand through the draconian's shield, seized him by the throat and crushed it, armor, bone, and all.

"Kill that beast," Shanz ordered.

"No!" Krago cried out.

"Get in the pot!" Riverwind demanded.

The draconians closed around Lyrexis to cut her down. Their strength and their weapons were far superior to the goblins' and they knew their business. That the newly born ophidian had not been properly prepared for her awakening made the task easier. One of Lyrexis's legs crumpled, and she fell. Draconian swords rose and fell, and the howling and hissing ended in a rattling gasp.

They were all finally in the pot, though Riverwind and Krago each had one leg dangling outside. "The spell! The spell!" Riverwind snapped. Krago turned away from his poor dead creation. He knotted his good hand into a fist and uttered the arcane words of the spell.

Shanz looked over the remains of Lyrexis and, satisfied the wild creature was dead, turned to the escaping quartet. He saw Krago with his eyes rolled back, hand clenched, mouthing the words of a spell. The stubby legs of the pot bobbled on the ground. Shanz's own magical senses tingled. He knew what Krago was doing.

"Stop!" he shouted. "Krago, I command you to stop!"

The legs lifted off the pavement.

"Stop, Krago! *Stop!*" Shanz turned a dead goblin over with his foot and picked up the soldier's crossbow. He cocked the steel bow with his bare hands and fumbled for a bolt in the goblin's belt pouch.

"Don't falter now, man," Riverwind urged.

The pot rose faster. Krago was chanting loudly now. A subtle tang filled the air around the lift, the same sort of sparkling sensation that spreads after a violent thunderstorm. The companions rose through the air, the pot rattling up against the hoisting chain. The dark roof of the cavern rushed toward them.

Shanz butted the crossbow against his shoulder and squeezed the trigger bar. The bolt flew wide, and the pot continued to rise. He quickly cocked the bow and fitted another projectile. The range was extreme, almost straight up. Shanz squinted through the brass pins that were the front sight on the bow. His finger tightened on the trigger.

"Ah!" Krago gasped suddenly, his eyelids snapping open. The sudden cessation of the spell had the intended effect. The pot wobbled and began its precipitous plunge to the floor.

"Grab the chain!" Riverwind screamed.

The three of them grabbed hold of the iron chain as the pot dropped away from them. Krago's dead body, a bolt protruding from its back, fell into the pot as the cast iron kettle plummeted to the floor, hundreds of feet below. They hung, swaying only slightly, listening to the crossbow bolts sing through the air around them.

"Is everyone here?" Riverwind hissed. His arms felt as though they were on fire.

"I'm—here," Di An whispered a few feet above him.

From Catchflea, above the elf girl, there was no sound, but his rag-covered body hugged the chain as if it were a dear friend.

"We must climb up," Riverwind said. "Move, Catchflea."

"Can't," the old man hissed. "Can't."

Riverwind couldn't spare the strength to look up. His face pressed into the cold iron, he said harshly, "If you don't move, we'll all die. Di An and I can't climb over you!"

Catchflea inched his left hand up. When it had a grip, he inched his right hand up. With his toes in the loops of the chain, he tried to take some of the strain from his thin arms. His face was deathly pale.

Di An, usually the best climber of the three, found the going tough. Her new body was much heavier than she was used to. Nothing seemed to fit just right. In silence, the three made the agonizing ascent.

As the dark shape hurtled down, Shanz and his draconians stood back. The iron kettle struck the floor with such force, it buried its bottom half in the stone and a great crack split it in two.

Shanz walked to the kettle and peered in. Krago's lifeless eyes stared up at him. The draconian leader spat. "Always thus for warm-bloods," he said to no one in particular. "Always the grand ideas which come to naught. That is why we shall prevail. With the Great Ones to lead us, our discipline will overcome all the warm-bloods and their fancy ideas."

The other draconians joined him.

"Don't just stand there," he said irritably. "Round up a hundred gully dwarves to clean up this mess and replace the pot. Do you want our mistress to see this putrid waste?" The draconians quickly dispersed, propelled by their fear of the black dragon.

Chapter 23

The Hall of Ancestors

"Not much farther! Not much farther!"

The hole at the top of the lift yawned. Sweat stung the companions' eyes and mixed with the blood on their cut hands, making their grips unsure. Catchflea disappeared into the short shaft at the top of the cavern. Di An followed, and Riverwind brought up the rear.

At the top of the shaft was a large room. Catchflea's last bit of strength went into heaving himself off the chain and onto the cold stone floor. He rolled away from the opening and lay still.

Di An and Riverwind followed suit. All three were soon laid out on the floor, wheezing and trembling.

"Why you come up that way?" asked a voice. Riverwind cracked an eyelid and saw a gang of gully dwarves watching him closely. With his black eye, wounds, and bleeding hands, he was a grim sight. His friends were no more appealing.

The bearded male that had spoken raised his bushy eyebrows. "Our job to fill one pot to raise the other," he said. "Why you climb chain?"

"We just escaped—from draconians," Riverwind managed to say.

The male shrugged and tugged at one fat earlobe. He waved to his comrades, and they bustled forward bearing water skins. Riverwind and Di An drank deeply. "Thank you," Di An said gratefully.

"Not to mention," said the young male who handled the water skin. "You pretty lady."

"What you want do about him arrow?" asked the first male, apparently the leader of the lift operators.

Riverwind sat up. "What arrow?"

"Gray beard have arrow in side." The gully dwarf pointed solemnly. "You see."

Riverwind went on hands and knees to Catchflea's side. The old man was lying on his back. The stump of a quarrel poked out of his right side. His ragged clothes were soaked with dark blood.

"You're wounded, old man!" Riverwind cried. "Why didn't you say something?"

"What could you do?" Catchflea asked weakly.

Di An knelt beside Catchflea. She tried to probe the wound with her fingers, but it was too painful for the old soothsayer.

"If we can stop the flow of blood . . . ," she said, dabbing at the edges of the wound with a piece of Catchflea's clothing. The old man caught her arm with his hand. His grasp was already cold.

"Do not trouble yourself," Catchflea said. "I am done."

"Don't say that!" she cried.

"It's true. My only regret is that I did not get to see the stars one last time." He coughed. "As the oracle said . . ."

Riverwind leaned close. "What did the oracle say?"

"You will find . . . glory. Defeat great . . . darkness. That you have done."

Riverwind looked bitter. "All I did was stay alive."

"Sleep," Catchflea said. He closed his eyes. "Sleep, yes." His hands, which had been holding Di An's and Riverwind's, slowly went slack.

Riverwind gazed down at Catchflea for a long minute. The beard, the ragged clothes, the foolish talk. Pictures raced through the plainsman's mind. He saw Catchflea telling him about the heavens when he'd been a boy, Catchflea cooking the first rabbit Riverwind had brought him many years ago, Catchflea finding their first meal on this trip, after Kyanor and his wolf pack had stolen Riverwind's sheep. He should never have brought him along. He should've made him stay in Que-Shu. He should've done so many things. Tears trickled down his cheeks.

"Catchflea was brave," Di An said softly.

Riverwind stiffened. "Catchstar. His name was Catchstar."

The plainsman continued to stare at the body of his friend. Di An, wiping away her tears, turned to the assembled gully dwarves. "Are you the leader here?" she asked the bearded one.

"Yes. Me Glip," he replied.

"What is this place, Glip?"

"This Hall of Ancestors," Glip said. He looked sadly at Catchflea. "Him dead?" At Di An's nod, he gestured at the crypts and niches that lined the corridor and said, "This burial place. You bury him here?"

"We've no time for burials. Riverwind," Di An said, touching the grieving warrior's arm. "We must go."

Riverwind inhaled deeply. "I know. I know." He brushed his tears away. Gently, he lifted the body of the old man. "I can't leave him lying here." He bore the body to one of the niches off the southern passage. He laid Catchflea down and composed his hands across his chest.

"Should I say something?" he murmured in the close darkness of the crypt.

"The gods will know him when he arrives," Di An replied.

As Riverwind and Di An returned to the top of the lift, a massive tremor ran through the temple. The dust of ages cascaded down on them. The gully dwarves scattered with yelps and squeals. Riverwind grabbed Glip by the back of his shirt as the gully dwarf ran by.

"What is it?" he demanded.

"The dragon comes!" the terrified Aghar replied. Riverwind let go. In seconds, all the gully dwarves had vanished into previously prepared nooks and "mouse holes."

The counterweight—an iron pot identical to the one that had fallen—swayed and rolled over into the hole. It bobbled upright, like a cork in the sea.

"Dragon my eye! It's Shanz! He's levitating the pot," Riverwind said. Di An took his hand and dragged him away. They ran into the south passage again, all the way to the end. The corridor continued to their right. Beautiful and intricate bas-reliefs and frescoes decorated the temple walls.

They reached a large octagonal room just as the quaking stopped. It was suddenly deathly silent and still. Di An and Riverwind froze, listening. The only sound to hear was the musical rattle of chain links paying out as the lift went down.

"Which way?" Di An whispered. To the right, more passages could be seen, but the floor had fallen in, creating a large pit that made progress difficult. On the left was a crumbling spiral staircase leading up. Up was where they wanted to go.

"Come on!" Riverwind said.

They went cautiously. The Hall of Ancestors was structurally more dubious than any other building they'd been in, in Xak Tsaroth. The stone slab steps were loose and in the half-darkness—for there were a few small brands burning here and there in wall brackets—one never knew if the next turn would lead to a quick, fatal plunge. Round and round the steps went. Riverwind's moccasins flapped around his ankles, threatening to trip him. He cast them off.

They reached the top of the huge pillar around which the steps wound and found themselves in a circular room with a high, domed ceiling. A torch burned feebly on the wall. Facing them were double doors covered with ancient gold. The patina on the yellow metal told them that the doors had probably not been disturbed since the Cataclysm.

Riverwind inserted the tip of his sword in the crack of the

doors and pushed them apart.

"Get the torch," he said in a soft voice. Di An lifted the pine knot out of its holder. Riverwind took it in his left hand and slowly walked through the doors. It was a small antechamber, empty, and in front of him was another set of identical golden doors.

"This isn't a temple, it's a maze," Riverwind said. "When do we ever get outside?" He wedged the second doors open. Cold, white light flooded over them.

Di An drew close. "What is it?"

"It must be the sanctuary," the plainsman whispered.

Before them was a high pedestal of white stone inlaid with gold. A statue carved in creamy white marble rose, in the form of a slim woman. She leaned on a tall staff that was not marble, but wood. Her long gown trailed in loose folds, as if blown by a strong breeze. Riverwind and Di An circled the statue from opposite sides. The cool light that suffused the chamber had no source, but banished the shadows from every corner of the room.

They came together again facing the statue. "Quenesti Pah," Di An said reverently. "It is the goddess."

Riverwind had never heard the name. He gazed at the youthful face, so full of compassion and quiet wisdom. "The goddess of what?" he asked, though reverently.

"The healing arts," Di An replied solemnly. "She aids those who are ill and seek relief."

"I've never heard of this Quenesti Pah," Riverwind said, never taking his eyes from the figure.

A distant clanging of metal shocked them out of their reverie. Riverwind rushed back to the antechamber and closed the first set of golden doors. He shut the second and cast about for something to bar the door with.

"Fetch me that rod," he said, meaning the staff held in the goddess's hands.

"That is a sacred staff!" Di An protested. "It belongs to the goddess!"

"I need it to block the door!" Riverwind insisted. Di An frowned, but she grasped the staff near the bottom and tugged. The carved marble fingers of the goddess held the wooden rod firmly.

"I can't free it," she said.

"Never mind! We must get out of here." The noise beyond the doors was louder. "That way!"

Di An threw open the doors facing the goddess's statue. There was another ceremonial hall beyond, and another set of double golden doors. Riverwind ran to her. A booming filled the ancient temple. Shanz and his draconians were at the first golden doors.

Riverwind fumbled with the latch on the doors. It was old and stiff. The antechamber door burst under Shanz's pounding. "Goldmoon," he said under his breath, "let all the old gods aid us who can!"

He brought the pommel of the goblin sword down smartly on the reluctant latch. It yielded with a screech, and Riverwind butted the doors apart. A brilliant hot light struck them as they rushed through the open doors of the temple.

The sun!

Di An gave a brief cry and flung an arm over her eyes. Riverwind squinted, groping for the elf girl's hand. Shouts rang in the temple chamber. Riverwind and Di An staggered down the steps of the temple, bumping blindly against the delicate, fluted columns that flanked the entrance.

Sun. *Sunlight*! It was like fire after so much time beneath the surface. But while it blinded Riverwind, it also warmed him to the core of his being and flowed like new strength into his limbs. The air was fresh and warm, free of the damp moldiness of the caverns. Even as Di An's fingers slipped from his, Riverwind relaxed his contorted eyelids and stood gladly in the blazing light as his pale face warmed.

Di An made feeble protesting sounds as she pressed her face to the ground. Riverwind quickly looked back at the temple portal. The draconians had not emerged. The ever thorough Shanz must be searching the whole building.

"Di An," the plainsman said, kneeling beside her, "are you all right?" She could make only choking gasps in reply. "What is it?"

"Too much light. Too much air!"

Her mind reeled at the sight of it. A vast openness, no roof, no walls of sturdy, comforting rock. The world was filled with air and light. Just air and light. Di An pushed the heels of her hands against her closed eyes. The darkness didn't comfort her. She knew the emptiness was there, all around her. Pain lanced through her head, and her stomach heaved. She felt as though her feet would leave the ground, as if she would fall up, not down, be swallowed, be drowned, float forever in a sea of endless, boundless, nothing . . .

She hunched herself into a tight ball and moaned. Riverwind tried to untangle her arms and legs, but she held together so firmly he only succeeded in turning her on her side. Sunlight fell across her face despite her shielding hands, and Di An let out a heartrending scream.

"No, please! The draconians will hear—"

Too late. The first armored lizard man appeared at the main door of the temple. He shouted over his shoulder to his comrades. Three more appeared.

Riverwind stepped in front of the stricken elf girl. "Here I am," he said. "Come see how a Que-Shu man defends his life!"

They knew he was dangerous, having seen him fight the mighty Thouriss, so the draconians entertained no ideas of honor and attacked in unison. Riverwind said, "Di An, run for your life!" She crept away on hands and knees. He advanced to the steps of the temple to meet his enemies.

The four lizard men attacked. Their heavier swords threatened to break the crude goblin blade Riverwind had. He traded glancing slashes with the two middle warriors, while the outside pair tried to work around him. With a skillful feint he laid open the face of one of the draconians. The creature floundered back, dazed and bleeding.

Riverwind ducked as another draconian aimed a cleaving blow at his skull. The thick steel blade gouged a chip out of one of the temple pillars. Riverwind thrust under the lizard man's high attack, skidding off his cuirass but burying his point in the draconian's shoulder. He pushed his blade in and spun forward, whirling the impaled lizard man with him. The draconian dropped his sword and sagged to his knees. Riverwind let go of the goblin blade. The draconian fell forward, driving the blade deeper under his breastplate.

The mortally wounded lizard man shuddered. He raised a wavering hand, the fingers of which were rapidly turning gray. All over the dying draconian, his dark green skin lost its color, becoming dry and hard. Riverwind gaped. The draconian changed from flesh to stone before his eyes. Even his blood, pooled on the temple floor, changed to fine gray ash.

There was no time to celebrate. The wounded warrior and his two comrades closed on the weaponless Riverwind. The plainsman dodged their straight thrusts by backing through the open doors into the temple. He prayed no more draconians were coming.

By the soft white light in the statue chamber, the scaled soldiers turned an especially vivid green. They fanned out, trying to cut Riverwind off from the side chambers and the route back to the Hall of Ancestors. Riverwind found himself backed to the base of the goddess's statue without so much as a knife. His hands slipped over the cool marble and found wood. The staff.

He swung around, keeping the enemy in sight as they drew nearer. With the intention of freeing the staff, or at least breaking off the lower half, Riverwind put all his strength into one great pull. To his surprise, the staff readily came away in his grasp.

A draconian attacked. Riverwind parried with the staff and swung the free end around, rapping the lizard man hard on the elbow. He chopped at the plainsman again, and Riverwind drove the end of the staff into the creature's left knee. It buckled, and down he went. The second draconian intervened, slashing hard at Riverwind's exposed side. He parried and parried, blocking the stout blade with a wooden staff no more than two inches thick. Thus engaged, Riverwind didn't see the crippled draconian rise on his good knee and make a desperate thrust with his blade.

The blow felt as if a hot iron had passed through the plainsman's unprotected back. Riverwind bolted away, swinging the staff like a cudgel. It connected solidly with the crippled draconian's helmet and he pitched forward, out cold.

Blood coursed down Riverwind's hip and leg. The remaining two draconians came at him from two sides. The half-blinded one made a wild swing with his sword that Riverwind knocked aside. The blade continued its wide swath until it stopped in the throat of the other draconian. He was stone before he hit the floor.

The domed chamber swam before Riverwind's eyes. He felt very cold as his life drained from the wound in his back. The last draconian, with only one good eye himself, came after him. Riverwind's staff connected with the lizard man's chin, snapping his head back. He fell and struggled for a few moments trying to get up. Riverwind found a sword and finished him off.

"Di An!" the plainsman croaked weakly. "Help me . . ." Leaning on the staff, now stained with his blood, Riverwind wobbled to the open door. Di An was nowhere in sight. There were marks in the soft, peaty soil where she had crawled away. He had to find her.

He swung a leg out to take a step, but collapsed as it crumpled under him. He retained his desperate grip on the staff. Riverwind's eyelids fluttered closed. There was no fight left in him. It was over.

Chapter 24

Sapphire Light

His life has been one of searching. Always he has wandered, over forest, hill, mountain, and plain, seeking. He needed to belong. The father he saw die in disgrace and disrepute had taught him that the gods live, even in these dark times. He believed, if only because it was his father's word. No one else listened to the old man, but Riverwind did.

He opened his eyes. "Is this death?" Riverwind said aloud. "If it is, it is a most pleasant ending to a painful life." Peace and tranquility washed over the plainsman.

He affects to be brave in the face of the unknown. How like his father he is.

Riverwind sat up. He could not see anything around him but a penetrating blue glow. "Who is speaking?" he asked.

I am the one you have sought for so long. It was in my temple that you slew the minions of Takhisis, and it is where you lie even now.

"Am I dead?" Curiously, this idea brought no fear with it.

I hold your life in the small of my hand. Your body was grievously injured, and I had to act quickly to catch your soul before it departed.

"You are . . . Quenesti Pah?"

So the folk of Silvanesti have called me. You would know me better by this symbol.

In front of Riverwind's eyes appeared a symbol in glittering steel: two teardrops joined tip to tip. The symbol worn by his beloved Goldmoon.

The plainsman sank to his knees. "Great Goddess Mishakal, forgive me!"

Forgive you for what? Your doubts? Doubt has been a plague on Krynn these centuries past. Your fear? Fear is part of being in the world of flesh and blood. It makes life quick and sweet, but also hard and deadly. There is nothing to forgive, son of Wanderer.

A white figure appeared before him. It was a woman in the prime of life, with white skin and long tresses of scarlet that tossed in a wind he could neither hear nor feel. She held the rude wooden staff Riverwind had wrenched from the statue's hands.

Stand up. Face me, Riverwind.

He did so.

I formed the staff from a single celestial sapphire, the same crystals that make up the thrones of the gods of Good. In the Age of Dreams, so many good people were hurt and maimed by the dragons of evil that I struck off this shard from my throne and sent it to Krynn, so that the priests who worshiped me could heal the sick brought to them.

The figure's lips did not move as she spoke. The wooden staff glowed brighter and brighter, until all semblance of wood was banished. *Now you see its true nature. It is the Blue Crystal Staff.*

The goddess smiled and continued. *Only one whose heart is inherently good can touch the staff and remain unharmed. It can heal, make light, dispel curses and evil com-*

pulsions, banish fear, and if welded by one in whom I have dwelt, raise the dead to life again.

"What am I to do with it, great goddess?"

Take it to your beloved. She will know what to do. My Blue Crystal Staff will fulfill your quest, and make my name known to your people once more. But it cannot long remain outside my temple, for even a fragment of celestial sapphire will decay if held too long in mortal hands. Take the staff, good Riverwind, and bear it to Goldmoon.

"I swear it, Holy One," Riverwind said. "I shall not part with your staff until I lay it in the hands of my beloved."

The white figure faded into the blue light. Riverwind felt pain in his back again, and the light intensified until he could see nothing.

"Goddess! Mishakal!" he cried. The Blue Crystal Staff fell out of the light and into his hands. A tingle ran through him, and the wound in his back healed. His swollen eye opened, clear. His cuts disappeared. For a moment, Riverwind glimpsed the hall of the gods: vast, glittering towers of crystal, the facets of which he knew were broader than the whole of Krynn. These towers were but single legs of the thrones of the gods. Their sum was beyond the comprehension of a mortal mind.

He will do well. You chose wisely, Mishakal.

Thank you, Paladine. It was his destiny to serve thus.

Send him back now.

Yes, my lord. It is done.

*   *   *   *   *

He awoke where he'd lain down to die, at the foot of the statue. Riverwind rose, unhampered by pain or bleeding. In fact, not a drop of blood spotted his ragged clothing or stained the white floor of the sacred chamber. The blue light in the temple was gone, leaving normal shadows in its place. The staff lay on the floor at the statue's base.

Riverwind picked it up. It looked like ordinary wood again. A little over five feet long, it was about an inch in diameter. He held it close to his chest as he gazed up at the image of Mishakal.

"Thank you, goddess," he said. "Thank you for my life. I will put your staff in Goldmoon's hands."

He walked out of the temple. It was night. Solinari, the silver moon, brightened the swampy lands that lay just outside the temple. This region was called the Cursed Lands, and for good reason. From Xak Tsaroth to the Forsaken Mountains, the land was a stinking miasma of black water, moss, ironwood forests, and spongy turfed "islands." Snakes, biting insects, and fever infested the Cursed Lands.

Riverwind retrieved a sword and scabbard from a dead draconian—who had now become dust—and fastened it to his belt. For a moment, he stood silently, contemplating all that had happened. The awe of what he'd seen and felt had driven all other thoughts from his mind.

Riverwind's head came up with a snap. Di An. She was lost out in the Cursed Lands somewhere, mind crumbling under the terror of the open sky. He didn't relish having to hunt for her, but she might already have fallen prey to accident, animals, marauders. Worse still, the plainsman doubted that Di An was thinking clearly. She might have blundered into a mire, or floundered in deep water while trying to wade.

Think, Riverwind. What would Di An do? There was a thirty-foot-wide well to his left. Remnants of a wall surrounded it. He saw no sign that she had gone that way.

Di An was terrified of the wide blue sky and dazzled by the sun. Yet she'd visited the surface before. Di An had said she'd only been to the upper world at night. The black sky would not have been so threatening to cavern dwellers as the cloudless vault she'd beheld upon leaving the temple. If Di An had been paralyzed during the hours of daylight, she might have recovered enough by now to creep back to the place she'd last seen Riverwind . . . here at the temple!

So sure was Riverwind that he'd made the right deduction that he called out quietly, "Di An?" More loudly. "Di An?"

A sob, then: "Here."

He turned and mounted the cracked steps again. There, slumped in a far corner of the portico, was the elf girl. She didn't move until Riverwind knelt beside her, then she flung her arms around him. Her grip was strong with fear.

273

"Are you all right?" he asked gently. She didn't answer, but kept her face pressed to his chest. "I thought you might be lost in the swamp."

"I thought you were dead!"

"No. One of the lizard men dealt me a mortal wound, but the goddess raised me up and healed all my hurts. And she gave me this." She sat back, and he brought the staff around for her to see. Di An looked puzzled so Riverwind explained what Mishakal had told him.

"The gods have favored you," she said. Di An put a hand to his cheek. Impulsively, she kissed him, but Riverwind broke away. "Don't," he said, "You know I love another."

"She is far away."

"Goldmoon is always here," he said, touching a hand to his heart.

Di An shrank from him, pulling back into the deep shadows of the temple wall. "I'm sorry. I thought, since my change, you might see me differently. Not as a child, but as a woman."

Riverwind cupped her cheek with one hand. "You are a beautiful woman, Di An. And you've been a brave companion." He found his gaze caught by her enormous dark eyes. Those eyes regarded him with frank devotion. Even as he spoke to her of the futility of her feelings for him, he found himself leaning toward her. Her hand came up and rested lightly over his on her face. Her lips were trembling. "A beautiful and true companion," he said softly.

Di An could hardly bear his nearness, his tenderness. Her heart overflowed with her love of him. "I love you, River-wind," she whispered.

Her own words broke the spell. Riverwind took his hand away and moved back. Jolted, Di An also withdrew.

"I'm sorry," he said. "You are my friend. I would lay down my life to save yours, but my heart is already given away." He finished by standing and settling the draconian sword belt around his hips. "Let's find some shelter. Tomorrow, we'll try to cross the Cursed Lands."

Di An looked away from the man's tall form, outlined in the moonlight. "Could we not cross tonight?" she asked.

"To try to find our way through that area at night would

be suicide." He offered his hand, and after a slight hesitation, Di An took it. "Tomorrow."

* * * * *

Riverwind awoke refreshed, surprisingly so for having slept on a cold stone floor. He stretched and smiled at the sunlit view showing through a window opening. He and Di An had taken refuge in a small building, somewhat secluded from the main structures around the temple. Before falling asleep, he'd worried a bit about Shanz sending more draconians after them. But the draconian leader probably thought they were miles away by now. Riverwind's vigilant hearing detected no stirrings of draconians throughout the night.

Di An was not where she had lain down during the night. When the sun had risen, she'd moved to an inside corner, buried as deeply as possible in the comforting darkness. When Riverwind went over to waken her, he found her awake, eyes wide and staring.

"Di An," he said, "are you well?"

"The light has returned," she mumbled. "The killing light."

"The sun? Yes, it returns every day," he said. Di An blinked once and didn't reply. Riverwind gave her arm a friendly squeeze and said, "I'm going down to the water to see if I can't gather up something to eat. I'm famished."

Outside, only the metallic possessions of the dead draconians remained. Even the dust from the dead creatures had blown away. Riverwind poked around until he found a long-bladed knife. He lashed the knife with a length of vine to a fairly straight ironclaw branch, making a crude spear. He caught a few fat frogs and tied them as bait in the knee-deep water, at the end of short lengths of vine. Then, he stood motionless with the sun before him, and waited. Soon the water roiled around the cut-up bait. He cast the spear into the green-black water and hauled it back. A fat, grayish fish wriggled unhappily on the knife blade. Soon, he had two more.

"Di An!" he said triumphantly, walking into their shelter. "Catfish!"

The girl from the caverns of Hest had squeezed herself into the tightest ball she could. Riverwind tried to tease her out, but she would not so much as lift her head to see what he was talking about. From helplessness he went to frustration, then anger.

"Look at me! We must leave as soon as possible. You have to overcome this fear! There isn't anything about the open air that can hurt you," he said vehemently.

He tossed the catfish on the floor by her feet. After skinning them—not an easy task with his large knife—he skewered the fillets on sticks. Over a slow, smoky fire of ironclaw twigs, Riverwind roasted the fish.

There was a soapstone font filled with rainwater in one of the ruined buildings on the north side of the temple. Using a fragment of draconian armor as a dipper, he brought cool water and a cooked fish to Di An. She would not eat. She was completely paralyzed, and didn't seem to hear Riverwind. He ate his fish and pondered the elf girl, a prisoner of her own mind. Surely this was an illness, like fever or pox.

Then he remembered: The Staff of Mishakal cured illnesses.

He didn't know exactly how to go about curing her, though. Riverwind held the staff out like a spear and touched Di An with the tip. Nothing happened. The staff remained dark, rough wood, without even the slightest glow of sapphire blue. It was no use; he just didn't know how to make it work.

"We must go to the temple," Riverwind said. He lifted Di An in his arms. She sighed and relaxed enough to lie in his grasp. "Giant," she whispered. As soon as they went outside, Di An shook and cried with fear, but Riverwind held her tightly and hurried to the temple. Inside, he knelt before the statue of the goddess.

"Great Goddess," he said, "bring your light to this girl's mind. Save her from her fear. Make her healthy once more." Nothing happened. The statue remained cold and lifeless, its delicate marble fingers curled around the empty air where once the staff had been.

Anger threatened to cloud the plainsman's mind. His hands clenched into fists, but that was no help. Going to

Di An, he scooped her up in his arms once more.

"We're going outside," he said sternly. "You have to learn that there's nothing to be afraid of. The sky is not an enemy, and there is no danger in open air."

"No!" she said, convulsing. Di An dug her fingers into his arms. "Please, no, I can't bear it!"

"You must. We must keep moving, or risk capture by Shanz."

He carried Di An out into the late morning sun. Fluffy, grayish clouds with flat bottoms sailed in the river of the sky, creating cycles of light and shade. Riverwind marched out to the sandy verge between the edge of the ancient pavement and the beginning of the ironclaw forest. Di An clung to him, face buried against his chest. Riverwind tried to disengage her. She held on with the desperation of the driven.

"Let go," he said. "Let go!" When the elf girl would not, he pried her away. Di An's eyes were wide with terror. She was dizzy, sick. She knew she would fall if he let go of her.

It tore Riverwind's heart to see her so frightened, but he knew he must be adamant. "Look at me! Look where you are! There is no danger," he said loudly.

Di An's lower lip quivered. "I can't simply tell myself to stop being afraid," she said in a barely audible voice. "It doesn't work."

"I'm going to put you down," Riverwind said. Di An sank to her knees as he set her on the ground. When he released her, she uttered a sharp cry and flung herself face down on the sandy soil. She tore at the ground with her hands, trying to dig herself a nice, safe hole.

"Stop it!" Riverwind cried. He tried to snag her wrists, but she punched him and wriggled away from his grasp. "Stop it! You're behaving like a madwoman!"

A shadow fell across the struggling figures. Riverwind paid no attention to it at first, marking it in the back of his mind as a passing cloud. But the shadow stayed over them, and he heard a steady *whuff-whuff*, which coincided with the gusts of wind that were sweeping over him.

Di An turned over on her back. She screamed and pointed a trembling finger over his shoulder. Riverwind turned, his mouth open as he continued his attempts to dissuade Di An of her fear, but all his talk evaporated. It wasn't merely the sky that the elf girl pointed at.

Poised a hundred feet above them, wings beating slowly to keep her aloft, was a dragon. The sunlight made iridescent patterns on her black scales. Her wing claws were purest white. The head at the end of her long, serpentine neck was fringed with wicked-looking horns. Khisanth, mistress of Xak Tsaroth, watched the two of them idly, as a human might watch the progress of an ant.

Riverwind was paralyzed with dragonfear. He stared at the creature above him. A monster of myth and legend. A creature he hadn't quite believed existed.

Khisanth's head tilted quizzically. Her mouth opened and a long tongue flickered out once, twice. Her horned head began to snake down toward them.

Di An gave a strangled cry and scrambled to her feet. Her fear of the dragon had overcome her terror of the outdoors. She reeled about and stumbled inside the temple.

The elf girl's actions penetrated the numbing shock that had frozen Riverwind. He forced himself to move and ran after Di An. *Seek shelter*, his brain pounded. *Seek shelter with the goddess.*

Khisanth followed his progress with her bright eyes. Idly, almost casually, she spewed a short stream of acid at the running man. Riverwind ducked into the temple just as the caustic droplets hit the front steps. The acid hissed and bubbled as it ate into the old marble.

Once inside the temple, he stood pressed against the far wall. Di An huddled on the floor at his feet. Both of them trembled and shook. Out of sight of the dragon some semblance of coherent thought returned. What were they going to do now? Khisanth had returned, and they were doomed. Riverwind knew that he could not fight a black dragon. The mere sight of the creature froze the blood in his veins.

The plainsman's despairing gaze fell on the Staff of Mishakal, which leaned against the wall. The words of the goddess sounded once more in his mind: "Only one whose heart is inherently good can touch the staff and remain unharmed." Steel would not prevail against Khisanth's acid and magic. But perhaps a simple staff, blessed by a goddess, was the answer.

Riverwind prayed to Mishakal for strength and picked up the staff. When he touched it, the staff glowed with a cold blue brilliance. He nearly dropped it in shock. He closed his eyes and tightened his grip. The goddess was with him. Her beneficent presence pervaded the staff. He could face the dragon with her help. Riverwind strode forth from the temple, holding the staff before him.

The dragon had settled on the paved stone plaza south of the temple, near the well opening. When Riverwind appeared on the steps, the dragon hissed, "What do you have there, little one?"

The staff was sky-blue sapphire. Its glow outshone the bright sun. "Keep back!" Riverwind commanded.

"I shall keep where I like," Khisanth answered idly. Her teeth were long and white. "Who are you, and why do you dare invade my realm?"

"Keep back, I say!"

"I've no patience for bandying words with humans. That's a pretty blue stick. Give it to me and I'll give you your life."

"Very generous to give me what I already have," the plainsman said shakily.

"You live only as long as I allow," the dragon snapped, her calm thinning. She uncoiled a foreleg, her foot-long talons sinking into the marble paving as if it were pudding. "Lay down the staff and run for your life, puny mortal."

Riverwind grasped the crystal staff with both hands. "No," he replied.

The dragon's mouth flew open, and poisonous, acid steam bellowed forth. Riverwind shut his eyes and clutched the staff. He had no time to move. Khisanth poured forth a cloud dense enough to dissolve a troop of cavalry. Riverwind braced himself for disaster.

But he was astonished when the deadly fog flowed around and did not touch him. The plainsman swallowed hard. His knees were weak. The staff—the goddess—had saved his life once more. The artifact's glow had increased, burning into his brain. Riverwind advanced, holding the Staff of Mishakal out like a two-handed sword.

"What are you doing?" hissed the dragon. "Stand where you are!"

"I thought you wanted the staff," he said evenly. "I'm bringing it to you."

"Foolish mortal," the dragon sneered. "Do you believe that you can defeat me with that?" In spite of her words, Khisanth backed a step, her powerful legs bunched to spring, her wings unfurled. She was enormous. "I will take you apart bone by bone, you and all you care for!" Khisanth threatened malignly.

Riverwind continued his advance, his faith in the staff as unwavering as its blue glow. Khisanth said one word in the language of magic, and the bright light of the sun vanished. A blackness shrouded Riverwind. The dragon had cast a spell of darkness.

Though the blackness was very disorienting, Riverwind's grip on the Staff of Mishakal was a steely one. He thrust it forward and the end connected with Khisanth's leg. A bright spark lanced out and crackled with a thunderous sound against the black scales. Riverwind felt the shock tingle through his body. Khisanth laughed out loud.

"You think that silly stick could hurt me?" the dragon cried. "I'll not waste any more time on you, mortal filth. But I shall remember you!" Riverwind held his breath. He heard the dragon's claws scraping the edge of the well wall and then heard the sounds of her descent, growing fainter.

The darkness lifted, and Riverwind staggered in the suddenly bright day. He had to lean on the staff as his body began to shake with long-suppressed terror. Still, he marveled that the staff had saved him and diverted the dragon from Di An.

The blue crystal staff lost its aura and assumed its guise of wood. Riverwind braced it on his shoulder and ran for the temple. Once the dragon reached Xak Tsaroth, Shanz would tell her the whole story, and then her wrath would go far beyond mere pique. With sheer cliffs behind him and a vast swamp before him, Riverwind worried if there was any place in the world he could go to escape Khisanth's fury.

Chapter 25

Death On Black Wings

Di An still lay on the temple floor, staring upward with wide, white eyes. Riverwind spoke to her gently.

"It's all right," he said. "The dragon is gone for now."

"I found nothing in the tunnel, master."

Riverwind started. "What? What did you say?"

"The tunnel is empty, Mors. What shall I do now?" Di An asked. She turned her face toward him. No fear showed, only an unnatural calmness and a strange light in her eyes.

Riverwind's puzzlement fell away. Di An's mind was broken. Too much fear had sent her away to a more familiar and safer time and place, when she was a lowly scout for Mors.

"Can you walk?" he asked.

"Yes. May I carry my lord's spear?"

"No," Riverwind said. "Follow me. The dragon could return at any time."

They left the temple and crossed the plaza by the well. The trees ended on the water, and Riverwind told Di An to climb upon his back. She complied meekly. He waded into the black water, flies and mosquitoes buzzing around his face. He went in up to his chin, then the bottom rose and he was able to walk onto a bare, dry island. The Cursed Lands seemed to stretch out around them forever, an endless vista of dark green foliage, black stagnant water, and dry sandy spits rising from quiet lagoons. Behind the companions, the temple of Mishakal was lost in the trees.

Riverwind set Di An down, and they rapidly crossed the island and came to another band of open water. He carried the befuddled elf girl through that one, too, though he slipped halfway across and both of their heads went under. He struggled against her dead weight, for Di An was so removed from reality that she didn't even fight to keep her head above water. Wheezing and spitting the foul water of the swamp, the plainsman managed to get their heads above water. Riverwind staggered ashore on another barren island only a dozen yards wide and collapsed.

"The cave is very damp," Di An said, her hair hanging in dripping ringlets. "We'd better avoid this route in the future."

The sun had nearly set. Its ruddy glow spread over the dull swamp, giving it an almost golden tinge. To the east, the high dome of the temple of Mishakal just barely showed above the treetops.

"We can't go on the way we have," Riverwind said, almost to himself. "Plunging straight into these mires. One of these times we'll go so deep we'll never get out."

"I wish I had a slice of bread," Di An commented. "And a nice red apple."

"So do I." Riverwind rubbed his face briskly with his hands. "We've got to push on. Though the swamp seems endless, I believe we ought to be able to reach the mountains by morning."

"The copper deposits in this cave are very rich."

The plainsman took Di An's hand and gave it a gentle

squeeze. She looked at him and smiled. "You are a very kind master, Mors."

Suddenly, the staff, which had been lying across Riverwind's knees, began to glow. Riverwind jumped up, holding it out like a blazing torch. "On your feet," he said, staring at the staff. "Something's happening!"

Even at the distance of almost a mile, Riverwind could feel the leading edge of the dragonfear projected by Khisanth. The dragon was coming. He jerked Di An to her feet and started down the sloping sand to the water's edge.

A black shape rose in the twilight sky above the ruined city. Even in her muddled state, Di An felt the dragonfear. She gasped with apprehension and pulled her hand free of Riverwind's—not to run away from him, but to run ahead of him.

They splashed into the dirty water. Scum clung to their legs, browning the elf girl's pale white skin. Riverwind wouldn't look back to see if the dragon was coming. The staff was glowing brighter, like a beacon in the half-light. As they slogged through the shallow mire, a gust of wind swept over them as Khisanth's wings disturbed the air.

The Blue Crystal Staff went dark as suddenly as it had begun to glow. The dragon circled around for an attack.

"No!" Riverwind shouted, shaking the inert wooden rod. "Don't leave! What did I do wrong?"

Khisanth extended her long, snaky neck. Her mouth gaped as she drew in air. "Meddling vermin!" she roared. A steaming mist of acid gushed from the dragon's throat. It settled over the swamp like a lethal fog. Riverwind saw the yellowish cloud descending, but the Staff of Mishakal was useless wood in his grip.

"Get down!" he said to the weeping Di An.

"Help me, Mors!" she pleaded fearfully. Riverwind grabbed her arms and threw her down in the brackish water. He followed close behind.

It was dark and unpleasantly warm in that muddy soup. He held Di An close and stayed under for as long as he could hold his breath. Then, he raised his head cautiously. The poisonous acid was drifting away on the wind, but the iron-claw trees on a nearby high point showed signs of withering.

Their hard, shiny leaves shriveled, turned black, and dropped like dead birds into the water.

Khisanth was flapping hard to regain height. Dragging Di An along by the wrist, Riverwind splashed into shallower water, toward a bed of marsh reeds. The dragon was banking left, circling around for another attack.

Working fast, Riverwind lopped off two stalks and snapped the flowering heads off the reeds. He pushed Di An down into the soft, muddy clot of roots. "Put this end in your mouth," he explained hurriedly. "Breathe through it. And don't move until I tell you, all right?"

Riverwind made sure she had the reed in her mouth. He eased her down into the black gruel of mud, then lay down beside her and submerged himself. Warm mud trickled in his ears. Reed roots poked him in the sides and back. Riverwind lay very still, listening, listening—

He distinctly heard the *whoosh* as the dragon passed over. Khisanth screeched, "Where are you, worms? You cannot hide from me!"

The dragon flew back and forth over the swamp, crying maledictions and spewing acid on anything that moved. An hour passed. Then two. The creatures of the swamp returned to their habits even as Riverwind and Di An lay embedded in their home. Slithery things slipped over and around him; crawling things with many legs marched up and down his motionless body. He wanted to yell, to scrape the itchy, filthy mud from his skin, but he knew that Khisanth was waiting, watching, circling, ready to tear them both to pieces.

The dragon eventually ceased its frustrated crying and kept watch silently, tempting her prey to reveal themselves. But Riverwind's resolve never weakened. He waited for what seemed like half the night before raising himself to the surface. Foul water ran off his face. He opened his eyes. A glistening green face was only inches from his.

He puckered his lips, blew hard, and the frog hopped away. The two bright moons of Krynn were up, their combined light casting a pinkish aura over the swamp. The sky was clear of clouds and the dragon. Riverwind sat up. Gobs of gray mud slid off his chest. He reached over and roused

Di An. She was slow to respond. He shook her. Di An sat up, mudbugs scurrying off her shoulders and neck. "Hello, Father," she said. "I'm hungry."

"I know. I'm hungry, too." He turned his head slowly, listening and looking. "I think the dragon has gone." Riverwind stood. Di An gave a mild exclamation. "What is it?" he asked.

"You have warts."

"Warts? What?" Riverwind ran a hand down the back of one leg and felt soft lumps on his skin. He twisted around to see.

"Filthy leeches!" he cried. Nearly a dozen spotted the backs of his legs. Di An rose. She hadn't a one. Apparently Hestite blood didn't appeal to them.

"My eye for a crock of salt!" he groaned. "Or a heated brand!"

"Shall I make a fire, Father?" the elf girl asked.

"No!" Riverwind said sharply. "The dragon might see it." Shivering with disgust, Riverwind used his sword to scrape the nasty creatures off. When he was done, his legs were streaked with blood. He looked as if he'd been in a fearsome battle.

"We've got to get out of this swamp," he said. "We'll be better off in the highlands even if the dragon does continue to hunt us." Di An's answer was dreamy and nonsensical.

With the stars to guide him, Riverwind chose a path that led due west. It took them through the black heart of the Cursed Lands, Fever Lake. They tramped all night in slimy water up to Riverwind's thighs. He remembered the leeches and shook with revulsion. Di An hummed a repetitive tune.

"Do you have to do that?" he asked through chattering teeth. She paid him no heed, and he turned on her in a quick blaze of fury. "Be quiet!"

Di An stared blankly at him, unmindful of the flies and gnats that crawled across her face.

Riverwind passed a hand across his forehead. The heat of his dry brow was evident. "I've got the fever," he said. "And no wonder. Lying in the mud all night, and those damned bloodsuckers—" Di An aroused such pity in him that his anger went away as quickly as it had arisen. "I'm sorry I shouted," Riverwind said. A chill swept over him. "It's—ahh—not your fault."

"You are kind." She pushed a strand of mud-caked hair behind her high-pointed ear. "Mors, are you certain this is the right tunnel?"

Riverwind looked west across the flat, marshy plain and sighed. "It's the only tunnel we've got," he said. He hooked his arm in hers. "Come. Let's not waste the darkness."

* * * * *

Shanz and his remaining draconian soldiers stood on a dry spit of sand not far from the temple of Mishakal. Hulking large above them was the upright form of Khisanth.

"They have entered Fever Lake," Shanz said. His reptilian eyes could pierce the dark of night and follow Riverwind and Di An by the heat of their trail. From where he stood now, he could see their path twisting dimly away.

"No warm-blood has ever crossed the lake and lived," the dragon said smugly.

"What is your bidding, Great One?" Shanz asked.

Khisanth's massive foreclaw rested lightly on the draconian's bare head. She petted Shanz as a woman would stroke a cat. "We have much work to do here. In a few days, go out and recover that staff. I cannot allow so powerful a talisman to fall into human hands."

"It shall be done, Great One."

"Excellent. Then I shall see to the enlargement of your garrison. Prepare for the arrival of more troops."

Shanz asked, "The end of Krago's plan does not distress you?"

"Not overly much, little Shanz. Like all humans, Krago imagined he could seize hold of the elemental forces with his soft, bare hands. Only the race of dragons can achieve such things." Khisanth opened her wings prior to leaping into flight. "Our armies will conquer Krynn without help from humans," she said.

"They will be fodder for our swords!" Shanz declared.

"As I expect." Khisanth sprang into the air, made one lazy circle, and flew back to Xak Tsaroth. Shanz and his officers

remained a few moments. The captain stared out at the
darkness and watched the faint traces of scarlet dim and disappear into the sickly miasma rising out of Fever Lake.

*　*　*　*　*

The sun struck their backs when it first cleared the horizon. A gray mist rose from the shallow waters of the lake.
Frogs and water bugs ceased their night songs with the coming of the light, so an eerie silence fell over the swamp.

Riverwind ached from head to toe from the poisoning of
his blood by the fever. Chills and shakes came upon him in
great surges, often so strong that he had to stop walking.
His eyes burned, and his throat was raw. He did not have
the strength or concentration to hunt, fish, or even gather
wild grasses to eat.

The fever had come to Di An, too. Her teeth rattled when
the chills racked her slim body, and when the fever burned
her face, Di An's breath came in short, hard gasps.
Throughout it all she remained in her lost dream of home,
the familiar caverns of Hest.

Still they slogged forward. There was no place to rest except in the stinking boggy water. Riverwind couldn't believe
the dragon would forget and let them go, if only because she
wouldn't want word of her presence in Xak Tsaroth to
spread. It was this idea that drove him on. That and the
Staff of Mishakal, which he never let leave his fevered grip.

"I return in triumph," he whispered. "I have fulfilled Arrowthorn's impossible quest." Riverwind smiled over chattering teeth. "All of Que-Shu will watch as I hand the Staff
of Mishakal to my beloved. She will hold it proudly aloft.
She will know how to use it. The villagers will cheer, and
Arrowthorn will have to agree to our joining. Our joining,
Goldmoon. Our joining . . ."

Riverwind moved doggedly through the swamp, the
imagined cheers of his people still ringing in his ears.

The sun burned away the mist, and in the distance the
plainsman saw something that cheered his heart enor-
mously. Rising like blue shadows from the marshy plain
were the mountains. They were not forsaken to him, but a

glorious sight.

"Do you see?" he said excitedly to Di An. "The mountains! Beautiful, wonderful mountains! Clear, cold streams, game, fish."

"Slice of bread . . . a pear . . . a peach . . . ," Di An murmured. "'Neath the golden waterfall. Strange. I feel strange."

"It's the fever," he said.

Di An laid a hand on her breast. "Why am I like this?" She looked down at her mud-spattered legs. "Those are not my legs!" she said, her voice rising. "What has happened to me?"

Riverwind extended a trembling hand. "You grew up, remember? Krago gave you a potion."

Her face contorted. "You—you're trying to trick me. You're not Mors! I'm not in my body! What have you done to me?"

"Stop it! Listen to me. You are Di An, and I am Riverwind. We've escaped from Xak Tsaroth and the underground world."

"Lies—evil magic. You work for Li El! You are an illusion of the queen!"

Di An turned and started to run from Riverwind. He leaped and caught her, wrapping her in his arms. She struggled and raved that Li El was destroying her mind.

"Listen to me! Listen to me!" Riverwind kept repeating. Di An's response was to sink her teeth into his hand. That broke his fever-weakened composure. He struck her crisply on the jaw, and she sagged in his arms. The elf girl was featherlight, but holding her and the staff was a burden. Still, Riverwind dragged himself and his charges toward the promise of the distant blue mountains.

The marsh became more shallow. Small hummocks of dry land rose above the smooth water. Rather than a cause for joy, these dry hills proved a great challenge; Riverwind had to climb up and over them, or lengthen his journey further by going around them. Finally, with the edge of Fever Lake in sight, his legs failed him. He collapsed on a moss-covered, low hummock, Di An beside him and the Staff of Mishakal between. Riverwind did not lose consciousness.

He simply lay face down in the moss, breathing in quick, shallow gasps and burning with fever.

Great Goddess, I've failed you, he thought. This is as far as I can go.

Are you so certain? asked the sweet voice of Mishakal. Riverwind tried vainly to rise, but couldn't. *You have reservoirs of strength you haven't tapped yet*, she said.

He could feel the fever heat pouring from his face and his heart laboring in his chest. "I don't think I have any strength left," he said into the moss. "Please, merciful Mishakal, heal me. Show me how to use your staff."

Heal you? But what of the girl next to you? She is ill, also.

"Can't you heal us both?"

I choose not to.

Riverwind's dry mouth finally stopped his tongue, but the goddess heard his unspoken "why?"

Virtue is won by struggle, not by ease. Nothing is learned when a task is made easy to do, or a problem is solved without difficulty. The gods require that mortals suffer, fight, and die for virtue, in order to prove and preserve the worth of these ideals. Only evil promises expedience.

Riverwind wasn't sure he understood. If the goddess's words were true, why did she bother speaking to him now?

Because you have a task greater than your own life. To restore belief in the gods by bringing forth my staff; that is a labor of glory.

"Should I be the one you heal?" he whispered through swollen lips.

I will heal you or the girl. Decide, and lay the staff across whoever you chose.

Riverwind heaved himself up on his hands and looked into the sky. "You condemn one of us to death, the other to perpetual madness! Where is the justice in that?" he demanded.

The voice of Mishakal was gone.

On the ground beside Riverwind lay her staff. As he watched, the dull wood began to shimmer. A glow, palest blue at first, suffused the staff. The radiance grew brighter, its color deeper, and the staff was once more a thing of sapphire crystal. Riverwind reached out for it.

And quickly withdrew his hand. Who was more valuable? he wondered. He had a divine mission, to bring the staff to Goldmoon. But Di An had a mission, too. Her people were waiting for news of the surface world. She could be the one to bring it to them. Mors would be angry—but if she could offer to lead the Hestites up to the blue sky, he certainly would forgive her. If Di An died, it might be years before the Hestites got the help they needed. The poor food and sickly air would only increase the diggers' suffering, and no one would ever know of it.

No one but the gods.

Riverwind raged against Mishakal. She had done this deliberately! She posed him this question and left him to decide: life or death, divine will or human compassion. How could he choose?

Di An murmured under her breath, almost awake. He left his anger for a moment and studied the elf girl—no, she was a girl no longer. Di An lay there, caked with mud and dried scum; her copper mesh dress hung in tatters, the black color long since scuffed off most of the red metal links. Here was a person two hundred years old, who had lived longer as a child and slave than he had lived as a free man. Di An loved him, or thought she did. Could he dismiss her feelings as the whim of a child? What would she do if the choice were hers? He knew the answer to that. He knew he couldn't put his own needs before hers.

Riverwind turned her grimy, slightly sunburned face to him. A new bruise was showing on her jaw where he'd hit her. It stabbed him to his heart. Brushing the dried dirt from her lips, Riverwind bent down and kissed Di An lightly. He raised the glowing staff of blue crystal and laid it across her body. Just as he did, her eyes fluttered open.

"Riverwind," she said clearly, staring directly at him.

In a single, silent, blinding flash, the elf woman and the sacred sapphire staff vanished.

Chapter 26

"Whom the gods favor is a hero born"

—Astinus, *The Iconochronous*

Gone!

Riverwind groped in the dirt where Di An and the staff had been. This was no figment of his sickness-strained mind. The woman and rod were gone. He rocked back on his haunches and stared blankly at the spot. He had made the wrong choice. The Blue Crystal Staff was lost, his quest had failed. Pain welled up in his heart and exploded. His anguished scream reverberated across Fever Lake. Animal sounds ceased, and all was quiet.

Riverwind fell face down on the ground. Tears welled up

in his eyes. He had chosen wrong. He had failed Mishakal.
He had failed Goldmoon. Catchflea had died for nothing.
He pressed his face into the dirt, feeling it scrape his cheeks.
How could he go home? How could he face Goldmoon
again without the staff? She was lost to him forever.

The plainsman lay quiet for a long time, a great despair
consuming him.

Finally, he got slowly to his feet and looked toward the
Forsaken Mountains. The shaft leading down to Hest was
there; he would throw himself down it. Riverwind's bowed
back straightened a bit with this decision. The magic in the
shaft was gone; he would die in the fall. Then no one would
know his shame.

*   *   *   *   *

Mors, master of the realm of Hest, sat unmoving in a hard
stone chair, listening to the chosen representatives of the
diggers and warriors argue over how to distribute the meager harvest of wheat. They had been disputing for a long
time, and Mors was rapidly losing what little patience he
had. The crop was the smallest in Hest's history, and word
had come that the fruit trees were dying as well. Without
magic, there was no way to preserve them. There would be
hunger in Vartoom before long.

Mors resolved to quell the petty bickering by force if need
be, but even as he prepared to shout for order, a strange
thing happened. He saw a glimmer of light. It stunned him,
for he had lived in total blackness since the day Karn had
blinded him. The light was only a gleam, a firefly flash of
blue, but still he saw it and it shocked him.

Mors stood. A digger representative called a question to
him. The blind warrior did not hear him. Gradually the hall
fell silent. Mors remained standing, motionless. The twinkle
of light still glimmered before his sightless eyes.

"Muster fifty soldiers in the street," he said evenly.
"Lightly clad, with spears only."

"My lord," said an elder digger, "what is it?"

"Something is happening," Mors replied. "I can see it." For
the first time in many years, he strode out of a room without

staff or elf to guide him. The assembly stirred with curiosity. What was afoot?

Mors followed the light out to the street. Somehow he knew where it was—he could feel it as well as see it. Though his surroundings were as invisible to him as ever, by following the flickering light he avoided all obstacles. He simply knew where to put his feet. The light beckoned him on. The tramp of soldiers' feet told him that his escort had arrived.

"Who is in command?" Mors asked.

"I, my lord, Prem," said the elf officer.

"Do you know the great temple of our ancestors?"

"The haunted temple?" asked Prem.

"The same. We will go there at once, but only I will enter. Is that clear?"

"Certainly, my lord. What is going on?"

"I don't know yet," Mors replied firmly. "I fear—" He did not finish. How could he say it? How could he tell them his fear that the blue glimmer was caused by Li El. *Dead* Li El.

Mors led them across the ruined fields. The flickering glow grew stronger and steadier. The soldiers jangled along in close formation. Mors was consumed by curiosity and dread. A hundred days had passed since the deaths of Li El and Vvelz. No magic had occurred in Hest since then. Both brother and sister had been burned on funeral pyres. Nothing of them remained. And now this . . .

After two hours' quick march, the warriors scrambled up the broken rocky path to the temple. As they gained the plateau where the temple stood, they stopped dead in their tracks. Mors heard their footsteps cease. He sharply demanded a reason.

Prem said, "There's a light in the temple, my lord!"

"You see it, too!"

"We all do."

"Form a line!" Mors barked. "I'm going inside. I don't want anything to get out, understand?" The warriors formed a half-circle facing the vast entrance to the abandoned temple. They watched in awe as Mors advanced up the worn steps into the field of azure light.

A feeling of gentle beneficence wrapped around Mors like a blanket. Part of him was aware this was a magical effect, perhaps not real, but it was such a profound feeling that he lost most of his apprehension. The blue glow intensified until his eyes began to burn. A groan escaped his lips, and he lifted his hands to his face. He saw the rough, thickened tips of his fingers. His groan of pain changed to a strangled cry of astonishment. He dropped his hands and staggered back against a massive, fluted column.

Mors could see. Before him was the floor of the temple, littered with broken columns and other debris. He saw all of it with startling clarity. He really could see.

The light still called him forward. He walked among the lordly columns until he came upon the source of the brilliant blue light.

Floating a foot off the rutted floor was the upright figure of an elf woman, eyes closed, arms tight against her sides. She was clad in the black shift of a Hestite digger, but the copper cloth was torn and the black paint chipped and scratched. A few inches in front of the woman, hovering vertically, was a magnificent staff of sapphire. The blue light emanated from it.

Mors went down on one knee. "Who—who are you?" he whispered.

Listen, said a fluting voice inside his head. *Hear me*.

Tears formed in his newly cleared eyes. Mors asked again, "Who are you?"

I am the one your ancestors knew as Quenesti Pah.

Mors inhaled sharply. "The goddess?"

This woman of your race I return to you. She has striven mightily in the cause of good. To save her from madness and death, I have brought her back home.

"Who is she, divinity?" Mors asked.

Her name is Di An.

"My little eyes! An Di—" He started to rise, but the goddess spoke one final time to him, and the strength of her voice drove him back to his knees.

Let this place become sacred again. Keep my laws, and the bounty of health and healing shall be yours. This woman shall be my priestess, and through her I will make myself known to all your people.

Mors bowed his head. "It shall be done," he vowed.

"Thank you, divinity, for restoring my sight." But the goddess was gone.

The blue aura vanished next, leaving Di An standing on the floor. Finally, the sapphire staff disappeared, too. Di An wavered like a sleepwalker. Mors moved quickly to her side and braced her up.

Her eyes opened slowly. "Mors? Is that you?" she asked weakly.

"It is. You have changed, little digger."

"I've grown up. Are you . . . angry that I went away?"

"I was, but no longer."

Di An thought that it was strange to feel Mors's arm around her waist. Strange, but good. She asked, "Did you hear the words of the goddess, too? Did you see her sacred staff?" When Mors nodded, she added, "I dwelled in the realm of the gods. For how long, I don't know. Riverwind and I were trying to escape from the dragon, and there were men like lizards—"

"Dragon!" Mors exclaimed. "Men like lizards? Are you sure your head is clear?"

Di An fixed him with a startling stare. Her formerly dark eyes were now a brilliant blue, the same color as the staff of Quenesti Pah. "My head is quite clear, Mors." She thought of poor Catchflea, dead at the hands of the draconians. She saw Riverwind burning with fever—was he safe? "And my heart is quite heavy."

Mors and Di An went out to the waiting warriors. He could hardly believe this cool, ethereal woman was the barren child who had led him around during his darkest days.

"I shall always try to lead you well," Di An said in a confidential tone. Mors blinked. She'd read his thoughts. "After all, I would not be here now if I hadn't followed you—even as I led you."

Mors presented Di An to the warriors, and they saluted her by raising their spears high. That done, Mors was at a loss. He asked Di An what she wanted to do.

She looked out over the smoky, poisoned cavern. She thought of all the barren children laboring in the fields and mines. Though she could now remember the surface world without fear, she knew she belonged in Hest, with her own people. As her bright gaze took in the hazy vista, Di An said, "I want to heal this place. And, perhaps, heal myself."

* * * * *

Somehow Riverwind managed to make it to the base of the mountains. One foot after the other, he plodded through a day and a night and a day. His decision to throw himself down the shaft drove him. Though other methods of death threatened him—hunger and thirst among them—he was obsessed with the notion that he must die in the shaft. Somehow that would be right.

Riverwind felt baked hard from the fever heat inside him, so the discovery of a spring of sweet water in a cleft of the rocks was as great a gift as he ever thought to receive.

His thirst slaked, the hunger that tightened his belly into a knot returned. Riverwind had no bow and hardly expected to take any game with his bare hands. He found some pine nuts growing in clusters around some of the taller boulders. He ate hundreds of the tiny, thready seeds. That helped a little, but he couldn't live on them. As night fell again, he lay atop a gently rounded boulder, the peaks of the mountains looming over him. He would never make it up the mountainside in his weakened condition. He would fail in his resolve to die in the shaft. I can't even carry that quest through, he thought bitterly.

The stars came out. He saw the broken scales of Hiddukel, the bison head of Kiri-Jolith, the black hood of Morgion. Beside Morgion, just peeking over the tops of the mountains, was the constellation Mishakal. Like the steel amulet he'd given Goldmoon, the stars of Mishakal formed two joined circles. "The Endless Chase," his father had called it. If you traced the loop with your finger, you never reached the end.

"What does it mean?" the boy Riverwind had asked.

"It means, no matter where you wander, the goddess is always with you," his father had replied.

Always with you—like the face of Goldmoon, which was never long out of his thoughts. Riverwind closed his eyes and conjured up her image. The silver-golden hair, the flashing eyes, the soft, red lips. . . . The sight caused tears to trickle from under his closed eyelids. She was so beautiful. His quest having failed, she would marry another. Arrowthorn would insist. He had never approved of Riverwind anyway.

The idea of Goldmoon as another man's wife sent a surge of anger through Riverwind. Despair had not completely consumed him. He would never permit Arrowthorn to marry her to another! He would steal her away first—

His eyes snapped open. How stupid! How selfish! He'd forgotten his other vital task, to warn everyone of the draconians and their plans for conquest. That alone should be reason enough to return to Que-Shu. And his courting quest was not a failure. While he lived, the quest would go on. And if it took ten years or a hundred, Goldmoon would wait for him. He knew how strong her spirit and her will were. She would never be forced into marriage.

Riverwind got up from the boulder and started climbing. Every mountain begins the same way, he thought grimly. From the bottom, going up. And that's the way, ill or hearty, he had to take them.

It was a nightmare climb. The plainsman's legs shivered in the cooling mountain air, and more than a few times they failed, buckling and throwing him to the ground. When that happened, Riverwind clawed his way along with his fingers. Never mind that blood flowed from his torn nails. Never mind the blurring of his sight by the still-raging fever. He had to continue his journey.

He reached a small plateau and rolled over on his back to catch his breath. It streamed out, a thin white vapor in the night air. Only a moment to rest, just a short moment.

The Blue Crystal Staff materialized in the air above him. He moaned, thinking it was a feverish delusion, but when Riverwind put out a hand to grasp the floating staff, his fingers closed around smooth, hard sapphire. The staff had returned. It was cold and bright in his hand. The magic aura subsided, and Riverwind felt the rough, dark wood.

"Thank you, Mishakal," he said. "Thank you!" The mountain rang with his cry.

He wondered what had happened to Di An, where she

was. The goddess must have helped her. She must have. He said a silent prayer for the elf woman.

Riverwind resumed his climb. He leaned heavily on the five-foot-long rod, and it supported him on the long ascent.

In the days that followed, Riverwind's fortunes waxed and waned. In the high, narrow valleys of the Forsaken Mountains, he found wild berries and roots to eat, but no game he could catch bare-handed. The swamp fever would fade for an hour, or a day, only to strike him again, reducing the plainsman to a huddled, shivering wreck. During these periods, Riverwind wandered aimlessly off his chosen path, sometimes three or four leagues in the wrong direction. His mind grew dull with the heat and pain. He cut his hands and feet, stumbling over sharp stones. He wandered for three days, delirious, only to be brought to his senses by a sudden downpour of ice-cold rain. It was then that he discovered how lost he was. The peaks around him were unfamiliar, and the forest unlike any he'd entered before.

While Riverwind stood in the cold rain, marshaling his thoughts, he heard a young man's voice say, "What do you want, vagabond?"

He turned and saw he had stumbled into the open near a camp. Two stout wagons were set axle to axle, a canvas tent spread out before them. A fire burned fitfully under the sodden tarp. Standing between Riverwind and the camp was a young man in a dripping cape and rain-soaked hat. He held a slim-bladed sword. The point faced Riverwind.

"I said, what do you want?" repeated the young man. From beneath his hat, yellow-hair gleamed.

"I'm lost," Riverwind said.

"Well, wandering thieves aren't welcome here!"

"There's no need for threats," Riverwind said. His teeth chattered as the cold of the rain seemed to penetrate to his bones. "I'm not a brigand."

"How do I know that?" asked the blond fellow. "You're a big fellow and you carry a stout stick."

"Look, could I warm myself by your fire? I am chilled through and through."

"No! Be off!" He stamped his foot for emphasis, but only succeeded in splashing mud on his own boots.

Riverwind considered trying to disarm the youngster, but before he could act on the notion, his temporary sense of balance fled, and the next thing he knew, he was lying in the mud on his back. The blond boy was joined by another figure in a hooded cape.

"Who's that? What did you do to him?" asked the hooded one. The voice sounded like a girl's.

"I did nothing," replied the boy. "He's only some beggar."

"He has the bearing of a warrior," the girl observed. "But he looks quite ill."

"We can't take in every starving robber who passes."

"Well, we certainly can't leave him out here in the rain!" the girl declared. Riverwind wanted to applaud her good manners, but he was too weak to even make a sound.

The girl tried to lift him by an arm, but wasn't strong enough. The boy watched for a moment, then joined in. The two of them half-carried, half-dragged Riverwind to the wagons. With much straining and complaining, they hoisted him into one wagon.

The canvas flap fell, and the boy removed his hat. He had a high forehead and lots of freckles. His gray eyes were bloodshot. The girl slipped back her hood. She had a pleasant, plump face, a button nose, and curly black hair.

"Hand me a cloth, Darmon," said the girl. The boy plucked a rag from the bow frame of the roof and gave it to her. She blotted Riverwind's face and neck, wrung out the rag, and dried his hands and arms.

"Thank you," the plainsman managed to say.

"What's your name?" asked the girl gently.

"Riverwind."

The boy, Darmon, snorted. "A barbarian name!" he declared. The girl shushed him.

"Don't take him too seriously," she advised the young plainsman. "Darmon likes to think he has noble blood, and that allows him to look down on other people."

"I do have noble blood, Lona! My uncle is Lord Bedric of—"

"So you've told me. And told me." The girl wrung her cloth again. "My name is Arlona. Lona for short. What happened to you, Riverwind, that put you in such a state?"

He blinked his burning eyes and marshaled his thoughts. "I'm trying to get home," he said. "To Que-Shu. My beloved is there, waiting for me. I have to give this staff to Goldmoon." It lay beside him on the pallet of blankets.

"That thing?" Darmon said, pointing at the staff with one toe. "What's so special about that old stick?"

"The Staff of Mishakal. It fulfills my quest," Riverwind said feverishly.

The boy rolled his eyes and shook his head, muttering, "Barbarians."

Lona made some hot soup, and while it simmered she told Riverwind how she and Darmon came to be out here in the middle of nowhere.

"Darmon and I are the last survivors of Quidnin's Royal Theatre Company," Lona said, stirring the broth. "We'd been on the road from the New Ports for Solace when Master Quidnin had a falling out with the wagon leader over the best route to take. Quidnin won out, unfortunately, and we went east." The dark-haired girl stared into the pot. "It seems we should have gone west. We ended up in the mountains. The drovers were furious with Quidnin for getting us lost. There was a terrible argument, and the drovers abandoned us. Quidnin was still certain that we couldn't be too far off. He sent scouts one by one to search for help, for food, for water. None of the scouts ever came back. Of the eleven people in the theatre company when we set out from the New Ports, only Darmon and I remain."

"Actors?" Riverwind said. He sipped the mug of weak but hot broth Lona had given him, and felt better. He reached out and fingered the end of the blade Darmon had presented to him in the rain. It bent easily under his thumb. The sword was a prop, made of tin.

"Hey!" Darmon protested. "You'll ruin it! Stop!" He shifted to the other side of the wagon, out of Riverwind's reach. The plainsman chuckled at the realization that he'd been threatened by a boy with a toy sword.

"How did you come to be out here?" Lona asked, watching him intently with bright brown eyes.

"I've traveled from Xak Tsaroth," Riverwind said. "I found this staff there. Before that—" He frowned. "The details are hazy. There was a girl . . . a girl with dark hair."

Lona pressed a cool hand to his cheek. "You have a high fever," she said. "It's no wonder your head is addled."

Riverwind drank more broth. "How long have you been out here alone?" he asked.

"The last of the adults, a fellow named Varabo, rode off on the last cart horse, promising to return in a day if he didn't meet up with assistance," Lona said. "That was a week past, and we've been waiting here in the middle of nowhere ever since."

"I told Varabo I should be the one to go," Darmon said. "I knew he'd never find the way out."

"Let me get my strength back, and I'll guide you out of the mountains," Riverwind said.

"You!" Darmon sneered. "I thought you were lost, too."

"The fever has dulled my senses," replied the plainsman. He was developing a dislike for the arrogant boy. "Once my head clears, I can show you exactly how to get to Solace, if that's where you want to go."

"Hmm, I suppose you'll want to share our food."

Lona slapped Darmon lightly on the leg. "He's welcome to anything we have," she insisted. Lona frowned at Riverwind's decayed leather clothing. "I can stitch up some of Quidnin's clothes for you, I think. You're taller, but at least they'll cover you."

"Thank you."

"Lona's the company seamstress. She enjoys sewing and all," Darmon sniffed.

With warmth in his belly and a dry blanket over him, Riverwind fell asleep. He dreamed of Goldmoon. She waited for him, arms outstretched. Suddenly, her face changed and she had short, dark hair. This woman he didn't recognize, though her name seemed just out of reach.

Gray clouds torn to shreds by a fresh wind scudded across the mountain sky. Riverwind scratched under his new, uncomfortable clothes. Lona had mended a linen shirt and tight-fitting breeches for him. She rummaged through a dozen pairs of shoes before she found some wooden-soled half-boots that fit Riverwind's feet. This eclectic ensemble was not to his taste—the shirt had faded red stripes, and the pants were much too tight—but it was better than wandering around three-quarters naked, like some savage.

Riverwind had a long argument with Darmon when he told the boy they would have to abandon the wagons. All their theatrical gear was in them, Darmon protested. But who will pull the wagons? Riverwind reminded him. In the end, sullen and silent, Darmon packed what items he wanted in a wooden carrying case and joined Riverwind and Lona on foot.

They followed the narrow wagon track down the slope of the mountain. The great forest spread out around them. Riverwind had to pause frequently to rest. During these respites he noticed how a few of the leaves on some trees were beginning to acquire their fall colors. He saw clumps of yellow starflowers, which he knew bloomed only at the end of the summer season. Finally, at a rest break, he remarked on how strange it seemed that summer was nearly over.

"Why is that strange?" asked Darmon.

Riverwind stared at the young man. "It was late summer when I left Que-Shu," Riverwind said. "I feel I've been traveling for a long time and yet it is still the end of summer."

"Perhaps you mix up the seasons?" Darmon said. "Haven't you been paying attention?"

"Be civil!" Lona chided.

"In truth, I think I was in a place that had no seasons." Riverwind rubbed his temples with his long fingers. "I don't know how that can be so," he said.

"It will all come back to you when you are well," Lona said. She reached in a bag and brought out a handful of dried apple slices. She gave a few to Darmon and Riverwind. Riverwind nibbled absently on the fruit. He tried hard to remember. Bits and pieces floated through his mind—a murderous thing flying through the air with black wings, a kind and loving blue light—it made no sense, and it made his head hurt. He gave up for a while.

Gapped as his memory was, some things were quite clear. He knew exactly where they were: an arm of the Forsaken Mountains thrust south and east into the forest. There was a high pass into the southern range of mountains that led directly to the high plateau. The Sageway East ran along the northern edge of the plateau, and once on it, Que-Shu was an easy two days' march away. That memory was also clear—his home was Que-Shu, and there Goldmoon awaited him.

He explained the route to Darmon and Lona, and they agreed to go that way. As they walked, Lona told Riverwind how she and Darmon came to be with the Royal Theatre Company.

"We're orphans, Darmon and I," she began. "My mother worked as a seamstress and cook for the company. She died a year ago of the flux, and I inherited her duties."

"I'm sorry," Riverwind said sincerely.

"Oh, she had a better life than most, and she didn't suffer much in the end. But, Darmon, he ran away from home to be an actor." She arched her dark eyebrows and assumed a lofty air.

"My aristocratic family didn't approve of a son acting in plays," Darmon said. He turned his face into the crosswind and let the air stir his loose blond hair. "They didn't understand I was born to be an artist."

What rot, Riverwind thought. He said, "What will the two of you do when you reach Solace?"

"If the stars are with us, we should find Quidnin or some of the company there," Lona said.

"And if you don't?"

"We'll start our own company," Darmon said firmly.

Riverwind did not voice his own belief that all the actors were dead—starved or murdered—in the vast loneliness of the mountains. Kind Arlona and arrogant Darmon would most likely have nothing waiting for them in Solace. Nothing but a dead end.

Riverwind had a bad attack of the chills that night, in spite of the jar of hot water Lona gave him to hold against his chest. His teeth chattered so loudly he asked Darmon to whittle a white wood twig for him to bite down on. When sleep finally claimed him, he dreamed again. This time the images were more muddled than before.

He stood in a black space. Something flew overhead, a black, winged creature that had haunted his sleep the night before. Out of the dark, a woman's voice called his name.

Her voice was familiar. She walked out of the darkness toward him. Her hair was long and golden, and her beautiful face was sad. As she passed by him, Riverwind saw tears on her smooth cheeks. She moved on, still calling his name, until the darkness had once more swallowed her.

With a low cry, Riverwind came awake. He lay shivering and clutching the jar to his chest. Who was she? he wondered. Who was that woman? He should know. She was very important. The questions pounded his brain until, finally, sleep washed over him.

They reached the pass before noon of the next day. A few hours' climb up the steep path, and the trio stood on the high plateau. A remnant of the Cataclysm, the plateau had been formed when a great splash of rock and mud filled in a valley in the mountains. Among the Que-Shu it was said that if you dug into the brown soil of the plateau, you would find houses, animals . . . and people, all buried exactly where they stood at the time of the Cataclysm.

As it was, the plateau was a pleasant, grassy interval in the rugged, stony ocean of peaks. Bighorn sheep and mountain goats ran in herds on the plateau, and Riverwind fervently wished to hunt them. But, alas, he had no bow, nor even a decent javelin to hurl.

Darmon was quiet as they stood on the plateau. He seemed intimidated by the presence of the taller, older man, though Riverwind was probably no more than a handful of years his senior. Darmon kept as far away from the plainsman as was convenient. Leaning on his wooden staff, Riverwind sat down on a large rock to rest. Lona settled on the ground near him and searched through her bag for a midday snack. Darmon remained standing, several yards away, surveying the way they had come.

"Raisins?" Lona offered Riverwind a handful of the fruit.

He laid the staff on the ground by his left foot and took the proffered fruit. Lona began to eat her own handful slowly. "You certainly don't let that staff out of your sight," the young woman said.

Riverwind looked down at the homely staff. "It is very important."

"It's only a stick of wood," Darmon said, moving in to get

a share of raisins.

"Darmon," Lona chided. "It's important to Riverwind."

The boy shook his head and went back to his study of their position.

"Why is it important?" Lona asked.

Riverwind picked up the wooden rod. He ran his hands over it and frowned. "It's not just wood," he said softly. "It's really . . ." The effort of concentration made his head hurt. He gripped the staff so tightly his knuckles whitened. "I don't know. I can't remember. Have I never told you?"

Lona shook her head sadly. "No, Riverwind. You haven't mentioned it at all. I thought you'd carved it yourself."

"No. No, I didn't," Riverwind leaned his face against the wood. "At least, I don't think I did. I think I'm supposed to give it to someone."

"Who?" asked Darmon and popped his last raisin in his mouth.

"I can't remember." The words were barely audible.

"Well, don't fret over it," Lona said cheerily. "I'm sure everything will be clear again once you're well." She hoisted her gear and said, "We should be moving now."

She and Darmon were quickly ready, but Riverwind sat on his rock, staring at the staff.

"Come on, barbarian," Darmon said. "We're ready to go."

Riverwind finally sighed deeply and stood, shouldering his pack. The staff swung out and swept past Darmon. He jumped back quickly.

"Watch it!" he cried. "Keep that dirty stick off my clothes."

Riverwind apologized and took a firmer grip on the staff.

"It's only a piece of wood, Darmon," Lona said. "It won't bite you."

The three of them moved on across the plateau. Riverwind's face showed his anxiety. His memory was so dark. There were so many gaps. But he was on his way home. No matter what else was unclear, that was certain. He was on the road home.

When they camped that night, Lona made hot broth for him again. She boiled what looked like an ox-bone in some water and added a sprinkling of powder from a tiny drawstring bag that she wore around her neck. Riverwind asked her what was in the bag.

"Spice," she said. "Our poor soup bone is practically glass smooth from boiling, so the broth needs something extra to flavor it." Riverwind peered at the old bone and nodded. The broth was still nearly tasteless.

That night—the third since meeting the two young people—Riverwind had no troubling dreams. The indistinct face of the woman with golden hair floated in and out of his mind, but there was no pain attached to this. He awoke rested and refreshed, and felt stronger than he had in days. He breathed in the warm air and touched the staff lying on the ground.

He would take it to Que-Shu. Once it was there, someone would surely know what to do with it. He worried a bit over the gaps in his memory, but he felt so much better physically that he was certain his memory would return, too.

That morning, Lona brought him his broth. Riverwind stared at the nearly clear liquid in the mug. It was really quite bad, but he didn't want to hurt Lona's feeling. After all, she was sharing what little they had. So, when neither of the others was looking, Riverwind poured the broth out on the ground. He would try to find some game for them today. This would help ease the strain on their meager food supply.

Later that morning, the Sageway appeared in the distance. Riverwind felt great relief. His memory of directions was still sound.

"Does the road run all the way to Solace?" Darmon asked as they took in the vista of the ancient road, green grass sprouting between its bricks.

"Yes, though it branches at different points," Riverwind noted.

"Do many travelers use it?" asked Lona.

"Many do, though there isn't much trade going west and east. Most traders ply the routes north and south, from Qualinesti up to Solace and across the sea to Solamnia."

Darmon shouldered the strap he'd tacked to his case and said, "Let's go, I'm eager to get to Solace."

Riverwind caught his toe on a hummock of grass. He stumbled and threw out his arms to keep his balance. The staff, in his right hand, swung out and hit Lona on the shoulder. With a low cry, she leaped sideways.

"Are you all right?" Darmon asked, coming quickly to her side.

Riverwind apologized. "It was an accident, Lona. I hope I didn't hurt you."

Lona took her hand from her left shoulder and smiled thinly. "I'm fine. Do you think that silly stick could hurt me?" She picked up her knapsack with her right hand, but she held her left arm rather stiffly.

Riverwind stood unmoving. Lona's words echoed in his mind. *Do you think that silly stick could hurt me?*

He felt very strange. He'd heard those words before. Someone had said them to him not so very long ago. Who? *Do you think that silly stick could hurt me?*

Lona still hadn't moved, and Darmon was fussing over her shoulder. "No, it couldn't have hurt you," Riverwind said, frowning. "It barely touched you." He stared at the young woman for so long that she shifted uncomfortably and glanced at Darmon. He put a hand to his forehead. "I've heard those words before," Riverwind muttered. He strained to remember, the throbbing in his head growing worse.

"What words?" Darmon asked. When no answer was forthcoming, the boy rolled his eyes. "Ignorant barbarian."

Riverwind's head came up, and he stared at Darmon. "What did you say?" he asked. Darmon glanced at Arlona. Riverwind pointed the staff at the boy.

"What're you doing?" he snapped. "Get that filthy stick away from me. What's wrong with you?"

"It's only a silly stick," Riverwind said. He turned to Lona. "The two of you are acting very strangely." *Do you think that silly stick could hurt me?* "There is something wrong here."

Lona pulled Darmon back a few steps. She smiled at Riverwind. "Nonsense. You're only imagining things," she said. "There's nothing wrong with us."

"Who are you? Who are you really?" Riverwind demanded. Though he had sensed something odd about the two, he really had no clear idea just what the matter was. He quickly found out.

Before Riverwind's astonished eyes, the two young people began to change. Darmon's hair flew away on the wind like dandelion seed, and his freckled skin seemed to melt in strips. Riverwind cried out in horror. Darmon's gray eyes became yellow slits, and his green, scaly body elongated, a pair of wings rising and flexing behind him. His beaked face opened in a wide, hissing grin. Riverwind saw him in his true form and a name he'd forgotten popped into his mind.

"Shanz," Riverwind croaked, his voice hoarse with shock. "You're Shanz."

"And me, little man? Do you remember me?" The voice was not Lona's. She was no more. Her dull peasant clothes were a mere heap of rags on the ground. In her place, coiled tightly and wings furled, was a black dragon.

"Khisanth." Riverwind breathed the name. She had said those familiar words to him back in Xak Tsaroth when he'd first faced her with the staff. "I remember." Riverwind backed up several steps, holding the Staff of Mishakal—for he knew that that's what it was—before him.

"I commend you, Shanz," said the dragon. "You said the human might survive the Cursed Lands, and you were right."

"The warrior who bested Thouriss was not likely to succumb to mud and fever," Shanz replied. "And your illusions, mistress, were an excellent touch." His sword was out. Riverwind looked quickly from dragon to draconian to see who would move against him first.

"Why did you play this game with me?" the plainsman asked bitterly. "Why pretend to be Darmon and Arlona? You found me; you could have killed me any time."

"I still can," rumbled the dragon. "When it suits me. But—" She lowered her horned head, canting it sideways in a darkly thoughtful gesture. "I wanted to retrieve the staff you carry. It contains much power, power that I want for myself. If you had died in the swamp, it might've fallen into other hands."

"It's useless to you," Riverwind declared. He had his eye on something on the ground. Among the rough clothing was the small drawstring bag with the "spice" in it. "You may want this staff, but neither you nor Shanz can touch it. You need me to carry it for you. That's why you were giving me the 'spice.' You wanted to destroy my memory, and then my will."

"Nonsense! I can take that little twig any time I wish," said Khisanth.

Riverwind poked at the dragon's face. A blue spark arced from the staff's tip to the beast's cheek. Khisanth hissed loudly and jerked her head back.

"Nothing evil can bear the touch of this staff," Riverwind told her coldly.

Khisanth opened her mouth in a terrifying snarl. Razor-sharp fangs and acid saliva were only a few feet from Riverwind. He gripped the staff with both hands.

The draconian brought his sword down. Riverwind blocked it with the staff. Holding Mishakal's sacred rod like a quarterstaff, he took all of Shanz's attacks and delivered a few of his own. The advantage Riverwind had was he didn't have to strike Shanz hard; merely touching him delivered a violent shock. Armor didn't protect him.

Within a minute of the battle's start, Riverwind planted the end of the staff hard into Shanz's pointed chin. The draconian's jawbone shattered, and the full magical force of Mishakal's staff coursed through his frame like lightning. Shanz uttered a protracted groan and fell to the ground. His body twitched and then was still.

Khisanth froze. Instead of attacking Riverwind immediately, she moved to Shanz's body. Her head snaked down, and she sniffed at the corpse, her eyes never leaving the plainsman's face. Her expression was hideous. No more illusions and trickery, she decided. It's time to kill this impudent mortal.

Riverwind took a step backward. Without warning, the dragon's head shot up, and her chest expanded as she inhaled deeply. She was preparing to breathe acid mist all over Riverwind. The plainsman dove into the pile of old clothes and found the drawstring bag of spice. He tore the top open and flung the contents, a yellowish powder, into the dragon's face, then scrambled madly away. Khisanth was still inhaling, and most of the powder was drawn into her nose.

The dragon shook her head from side to side, lungs filled with the alchemical powder. With a rasping roar, Khisanth blew the dust out in a cloud mixed with her own acid breath. Riverwind felt the edge of the stinging mist, tasted its metallic bite on his lips. He shut his eyes tightly and ran. The ground shook as the black dragon crashed to the ground and began to roll in the grass. She tore the sod and howled in a voice like thunder. Riverwind ran blindly, stumbling frequently, but he didn't stop until he felt the paving of the Sageway under his feet. Only then did he look back. A column of dirt and dust rose high in the air, marking the spot where Khisanth was thrashing in rage and pain.

* * * * *

Goldmoon, daughter of Arrowthorn, sat in the chieftain's chair, her head perched on a clenched fist. Though she was bored to death, outwardly she maintained an air of intelligent interest. Two Que-Shu men stood before her, in front of the chieftain's home, disputing the ownership of a cow, and were just as loud about their respective rights now as when the trial had begun, over an hour ago.

A disturbance arose on the other side of the empty village arena. Goldmoon raised her head when she heard the shouts and saw the dust churned up from the dry path by many Que-Shu feet. "Be silent a moment," she said to the quarreling men. The two reluctantly ceased their disputation. The noise grew louder, and the outer fringe of a large crowd began to spill around the edges of the sunken arena.

Goldmoon stood. Her attendants likewise rose. She said, "Fetch my father." Two brawny men nodded and entered the chieftain's house. They returned shortly carrying a litter in which the bent form of Arrowthorn sat. Fate had dealt the chieftain a bitter blow. Ten months after he'd sent Riverwind on his Courting Quest, a mysterious illness had laid the chieftain low, leaving him unable to walk or talk intelligibly. His eyes told the true story, though; the mind of Arrowthorn still dwelled within the ruined body, a helpless prisoner of his own flesh.

The crowd flowed into the arena, down the stone seat-steps and up the other side. Children pranced among the adults with growing excitement. Goldmoon strained to see around the Temple of the Ancestors, which blocked her view. It would not do for chieftain's daughter to wade into the crowd like a common person. She had to remain cool and detached, though she ached with curiosity.

The Que-Shu folk thinned at what was the center of the disturbance. A lone figure walked slowly in the eye of this human tempest; a tall figure, head above the crowd, who leaned on a dark wooden staff as he walked.

A single tear stung Goldmoon's eye. It could not be— after so long!

The tall man skirted the arena, choosing a course near the village hall. The afternoon sun broke over that building, throwing a cloak of shadow over him.

Arrowthorn made a low, gurgling sound. Goldmoon reached over to his litter and grasped his hand.

The murmur of the crowd resolved into a steady chant. There was no doubt any longer, for what the Que-Shu people repeated over and over was a name: Riverwind.

Goldmoon couldn't bear it any longer. She slipped free of her father's feeble grasp and moved. But she moved slowly and with the dignity of her position. The people parted, making a path for her directly to Riverwind. He was between the village hall and the Temple of the Ancestors when he saw her, and stopped. Goldmoon halted, too. He was thin, and sunburn painted his face. Riverwind lifted a hand in greeting.

"Goldmoon," he said hoarsely. "I remember."

She spoke his name, then, to her horror, he collapsed. The crowd closed in on the fallen man, but Goldmoon cried, "Get back!"

She hurried to his side, ignoring her spotless white hem trailing in the dirt. Goldmoon fell on her knees and turned Riverwind's face to the sky.

"My beloved," he said.

"Yes, yes, I'm here," she replied softly. To the assembled crowd, she said, "Fetch a healer! He is roasting with fever!"

Goldmoon stroked his blistered face. "My love," she whispered, "I prayed to all the true gods you would return safely to me. They have answered my prayers." Riverwind slowly brought the staff up to her face. "What is it?" she asked.

"Proof. This is the Staff of Mishakal. Our quest is over." She tried to take the staff, but his fingers were locked on it. Not until the healer had come and administered a soothing herbal potion did Riverwind's hand relax enough for her to pry the staff away.

At Goldmoon's command, strong men lifted Riverwind. She ordered him to be taken to the chieftain's house. The men looked at each other wonderingly, but they obeyed. Goldmoon had been chieftain in all but name since her father's illness, and she had led her people well.

She strode ahead of the litter that held the young plainsman. The crowd parted respectfully. When she reached the spot where she'd left her father, she saw Loreman was there. He was one of the few who resisted her rule. The scheming old man was speaking into Arrowthorn's ear, and he stiffened when he saw Goldmoon staring at him.

"Take my father and Riverwind inside. Healer, attend to the son of Wanderer." The litter bearers, their burdens, and the healer went into the house. Loreman cleared his throat, halting Goldmoon before she could follow.

"What?" she asked coldly.

"Riverwind has returned. Does he admit defeat in his quest?" said Loreman.

"Not at all. He has triumphed."

"Where then is the proof of the old, dead gods?"

She thrust the staff out at him. "Here! Riverwind brings this, the sacred staff of the goddess Mishakal."

Loreman smiled. "An impressive piece of wood," he said sarcastically.

"I will speak with Riverwind and learn more," Goldmoon said. "You need not concern yourself."

"Heresy always concerns me."

"Enough! I am needed within." She swept past Loreman, attempting to hide her loathing.

She went to Riverwind's side. A screen of hides had been hung around his bed for privacy. Goldmoon slipped in and dismissed the healer. When they were alone, she kissed him.

His face was wet.

"Are those your tears or mine?" she said, sniffing.

"Ours," he said, his voice like a sigh.

"Loreman asked if you had failed in your quest. I said you hadn't. How can we prove it, beloved?"

Riverwind coughed raggedly. Goldmoon lit a stick of curative incense by his bed. The aromatic smoke drifted over the room. There was something about the smoke that struck a chord in him, a place he'd seen, a person he'd known. Goldmoon looked down at him tenderly. He put a hardened hand to her soft cheek. "The staff is a sliver from the throne of the goddess," he explained. "Made of sapphire. It is disguised as wood, but will show its true nature when needed. The goddess herself gave it to me. She said I was to give it to you."

Goldmoon's eyes widened and she gasped. "To me? Why? What shall I do with it?"

"Heal the sick. Repel evil. Perhaps even raise the dead."

Goldmoon regarded the crude wooden stave with awe. So much power—could she wield it justly?

Even as the thought crossed her mind, the handworn wood began to glow. In a heartbeat, the rod lying across Goldmoon's lap became a fiercely glowing scepter. The chieftain's daughter felt the presence of the goddess, knew the rightness of her holding the crystal staff. Riverwind grasped the staff also, and the sky-blue aura passed up his arm to envelop him.

"I don't remember much of what happened to me," Riverwind said. "There was great hardship and an evil place where death rode on black wings. I know that people died, good people, like the old soothsayer, Catchstar. There was a girl—a woman, I think—who saved my life. It's all so blurred and confused." He looked into her eyes. "But throughout my trials, the one truth I held firm was you. Your love always broke through the veils cast around me. It saved more than my life. It saved my soul."

Goldmoon couldn't speak through her tears, but her hand on Riverwind's face was soft and warm.

The divine glow penetrated and healed Riverwind's fever-plagued body. When it finally dimmed and receded, he lifted his arms and embraced the woman he loved.